Nothing but Trouble

Nothing but Trouble

Bettye Griffin

Dafina Books

KENSINGTON PUBLISHING CORP.

DAFINA BOOKS are published by

Kensington Publishing Corp.
850 Third Avenue
New York, NY 10022

All Kensington titles, imprints, and distributed lines are available at special quantity discounts for bulk purchases for sales promotion, premiums, fund-raising, educational or institutional use.

Dafina Books and the Dafina logo Reg. U.S. Pat. & TM Off.

ISBN 0-7394-6438-8

Printed in the United States of America

For B.E.U.

Acknowledgments

Family first: Bernard Underwood, Mrs. Eva M. Griffin, Timothy
Underwood, Katrina Underwood, Aaron Underwood.
Kimberly Rowe-Van Allen, who reads works in progress and
offers invaluable input.
Elaine English, agent extraordinaire.
The Book Clubs: Sistah Girl Book Club of Orange Park, Florida;
Man in the Middle Book Club, Jacksonville, Florida;
Sisters United Book Club, Jacksonville, Florida.

Jeffrey Shannon of Anderson Merchandisers.
To anyone I might have forgotten, please understand that the
folks in New York needed this, like, yesterday, so any oversights
are a result of haste.

Chapter 1

When Dana awoke that fateful summer day in mid-June, it seemed like just another Saturday. The glittering sunlight and blue skies held no clues that, after today, her life would never be the same.

It was a busier weekend than most because of Father's Day on Sunday. She and Kenny were holding their annual cookout and swim party. Dana always made a big fuss for Father's Day. She and Kenny had one child, a daughter they named Brittany. They had wanted more children, but after suffering a harrowing miscarriage, she had been lucky to have Brittany the following year. She never did get pregnant again.

Dana had another reason for making a big fuss for Father's Day. Circumstances had robbed her of her own father at age seventeen. For years afterward she hated the third Sunday in June. Then when Brittany was born, everything changed, and now it was her favorite holiday—even more so than Christmas, which she regarded as a lot of work.

Dana checked her watch nervously. She had barely left Brittany and her friend Vanessa, but this was the first time she had allowed Brittany to shop in the mall unescorted by an adult. Brittany's request to shop for Kenny's Father's Day gift with Vanessa horrified her. Everyone knew malls ranked second only to schools as favorite haunts for predators. Brittany pointed out that she was almost twelve, and Dana knew the time had come to loosen the strings just a bit. Before the girls even got out of the car, she instructed them to stick together and not talk to any strangers, and to keep their tiny shoulder bags draped diagonally across their torsos and zipped up at all times. She watched with a bit of sadness as her daughter and her friend headed off to the food court, where they would have lunch before heading for the men's accessories department at JCPenney.

Dana walked with quick steps toward Ruby Tuesday, where she would meet her own friends, Norell and Cécile, for lunch. She had left her cell phone with Brittany and had keyed in Norell's cell number in case Brittany needed an adult.

She didn't expect to see the habitually late Cécile waiting, but Dana spotted Norell outside the restaurant, smoking a cigarette. She was easy to spot: taller than average, with hair that fell past her shoulders in an appealing honey blond, courtesy of a skilled colorist.

Norell Bellamy looked better than ever. Thirty-six years old and six months into her first marriage, she was one of those fortunate women who could eat anything she wanted, as much as she wanted, without gaining weight. On the other hand, their mutual friend Cécile, who was only thirty-three, had married Michael Rivers on Valentine's Day, just four months ago, and already showed signs of weight gain.

"Don't you know those things will kill you?" Dana said good-naturedly as she approached her friend.

Norell blew out a cloud of smoke. "Gotta die of something," she said philosophically.

Dana looked at the Dillard's shopping bag between Norell's knees. "I see you've done some shopping."

"I picked up some new lingerie. Vic wanted to wait six months before trying, and it's been six months."

Dana smiled. "I guess I know what you'll be doing tonight."

"Oh, Dana, I can't wait to have my baby. You and Cécile are lucky to have had your kids young. They'll be finished with college and out of the house, and y'all will still be in your forties. If I have a baby next year, I'll be almost sixty by the time it graduates from college. And Vic! He'll probably be dead."

"Norell!"

"I'm just trying to be realistic. He's forty-nine now. All right, maybe he won't be dead, but he'll be in his seventies. No wonder he's not too thrilled about starting over."

"He isn't? You didn't tell me that."

"I shouldn't say he's not thrilled; that's not really true," Norell clarified. "He just wanted us to wait a bit."

Dana suspected Norell was holding back something, but she dismissed it as none of her business. As the oldest of the three and the one with the most serene life, for years she had been unofficial den mother to both Norell and Cécile. She listened to their problems and offered advice, but it was only natural for their new husbands to step into the role of best friend and confidant.

It delighted her that both her best friends had settled down. The party tomorrow would be their first summer get-together with their families. Cécile had three daughters from her first marriage, and her husband Michael brought two sons and a daughter to their blended family. Norell didn't yet have children of her own, but was step-mother to Vic's two teenage daughters. All of them were coming over. She expected it to be the first of many such family events. Norell and Cécile were like sisters to her.

Dana had lost her own sister, Gail, over twenty years ago, when, on a rain-slicked road, their car slid into the path of an oncoming vehicle, killing both Gail and their mother. In one of those un-explainable twists of fate, Dana emerged from the backseat with only a few cuts and bruises and a sprained knee.

"Look, here's Cécile," Norell said.

Dana waved at her approaching friend. Cécile wore a a paisley print sleeveless dress that nicely hid the additional poundage she carried on her five-foot-three-inch frame. "I hope you guys weren't waiting too long," she said after they exchanged greetings.

"Nah. I just had a cigarette so I wouldn't be stricken by nicotine withdrawal," Norell said with a smile.

They entered the restaurant and placed their orders. When the waiter placed a large burger platter in front of Cécile, Dana, who'd ordered a salad with roast chicken strips, put her hand on her heart and feigned shock. "Ooh, the calories, but it smells delicious, especially those onion rings."

"Have one," Cécile offered. "I know I've got no business eating like this. I can't believe how much weight I've gained. This is going to be my last fried food for the week."

"A new week starts tomorrow, Cécile," Norell pointed out with an amused smile.

"I mean until next Friday. I'm doing portion control, too."

"So, how was the soccer game?" Dana asked.

Cécile immediately launched into a description of her stepson's goals and passes. Dana thought it commendable how her friend had so easily slipped into the mother role for her stepchildren, whose own mother had died in a car crash with a man she was rumored to be having an affair with. But Cécile's devotion bordered on the obsessive; she talked about her extended family to the point of being loquacious. Dana found it tiresome, but for Norell, who so desperately wanted to be a mother herself, it had to be torturous.

Dana nodded at appropriate intervals while Cécile droned on and on, relaxing when she finally wound down. But then Cécile began to volunteer information about how each of her other family members would be spending the day. Dana felt Norell's foot nudge her shin as Cécile rattled on and on, pausing only momentarily to take another bite of her burger. Dana and Norell exchanged glances, Dana biting gently on her lower lip to keep from laughing when Norell held up a hand where only Dana could see it and moved her fingers to simulate an ever-moving mouth.

"So how's work?" Dana asked as Cécile dipped a handful of French fries in ketchup and popped them into her mouth.

"Oh, it's all right. Same old stuff that breaks your heart. Drug addicts old enough to be collecting Social Security, forty-year-olds dying of cancer, children with genetic disorders—"

"That's why I volunteered to do clinic work," Norell said. "I didn't want all that depressing stuff. But even with that, sometimes I think I'm turning into a typical bored suburban housewife, with nothing to do but buy clothes, putter in the garden, and go to the hairdresser or the spa. I've been seriously thinking about going back to the office just to give me interaction with people."

Dana made a face. "I love working at home. I'd *never* want to go back to the office. Not that it's an option, since I've got my own clients now."

"I think you're lucky, Norell," Cécile added.

"And with six kids, I can only dream of having that much free time."

"I'm starting to feel isolated," Norell explained. "So much of my day is solitary. You two don't have that problem. Besides, Kenny and Michael get home a lot earlier than Vic does."

"I think you should try to hold off a bit, Norell," Dana suggested. "Trust me, once that baby comes you won't have to worry about not having enough to do."

"Baby?" Cécile's mouth dropped open. "Norell, are you—"

"Not yet. But we're going to start trying."

Cécile nodded, then resumed eating. She amazed Dana by not only cleaning her plate and draining her malt glass, but also ordering apple pie à la mode for dessert and devouring that as well. She even picked up a piece of fallen golden brown piecrust from her plate. Dana half expected her to pick up the plate and lick the trails of melted ice cream.

"Tell me, Cécile, are you going to go home and eat dinner after such a humongous lunch?" Norell asked.

Dana was wondering the same thing. She didn't ask because she couldn't think of a way to phrase it tactfully. She wasn't as bold as Norell.

"Of course not. This is my last meal until breakfast tomorrow. I'm not even cooking tonight. Michael's going to order pizza. I'll probably log on and do some work, make a few bucks. We could always use it for the house."

"You guys going to take the big remodeling plunge?" Norell asked.

"As soon as things get a little quiet."

"Oh." The one syllable dripped with doubt, but Dana knew exactly how Norell felt. With six active children ranging from three to thirteen, the Rivers household would always have a certain degree of chaos. Perhaps Michael wanted to make sure their blending of families would be a lasting one before undertaking the expense of adding on. They'd only been married four months, but from the beginning Cécile kept saying they planned to enlarge the house, and it sounded less convincing each time. Dana wished she would just stop talking about it.

"I guess you're like the old woman who lived in a shoe," Norell remarked.

"I'm sure my shoe, as you call it, will soon be made into a boot," Cécile said testily.

Dana held her breath, waiting for Norell to make an equally salty reply. This had happened before. Their friendship dated back eight years, meeting as coworkers at the Precise Transcription Service. One by one, they left the office, Norell and Cécile to participate in the work-from-home program, and Dana to launch her own service. They met regularly for lunch, but with all the friction between Norell and Cécile lately, these outings weren't as much fun as they used to be. Dana knew Norell was more than a little jealous of Cécile's status as a mother, and Cécile knew it, too.

The silence that followed threatened to become awkward until Norell spoke. "What time did you want us to come over tomorrow, Dana?"

"Oh, about three should be good."

"You need help with anything?" Cécile offered.

"No, thanks. Kenny and I are going to the store tonight while Brittany spends the night at Vanessa's." Dana signaled for their checks. She didn't regret the end of their lunch. When Norell and Cécile had these little flare-ups it made her feel like peanut butter, stuck to jelly on one side and to bread on the other. She wished Norell wouldn't bait Cécile like she did.

It pleased Dana to find Brittany and Vanessa sitting on a bench outside the restaurant waiting for her. She hugged her friends goodbye. Norell went off in a cloud of Chanel, while Cécile left behind the unmistakable scent of onion rings.

After dropping off the girls at Vanessa's, Dana headed home. She frowned as she tasted the onions that still lingered on her breath. They had tasted fine in her salad at lunch, but now that her meal was over, she didn't like the aftertaste. She never carried mints, but as soon as she got home she'd rinse with mouthwash.

As she drove, Dana wondered how her father would be spending Father's Day. She hadn't done anything to mark the day for him, not even gotten him a card. All the ones she'd seen were so syrupy, full of loving Helen Steiner Rice emotions she didn't feel. In the end she always settled for an awkward minute-long phone call, and would undoubtedly do the same tomorrow. She had good reason for her hostility, but perhaps she should try harder. He was getting old, and he was the only survivor of the family she'd been born into. In her heart she knew she'd carry guilt with her the rest of her life if anything happened to him with them still on the outs.

"Hi!" Dana called out as she entered her home. She knew Kenny was home; his Eclipse was in the driveway.

He didn't answer. She stopped in the hall bath and splashed her mouth with mint-flavored mouthwash, then went upstairs to their bedroom. Kenny often took naps on Saturday afternoons.

She half expected to see him stretched out across their bed, but he wasn't there, so she went back downstairs. It was hot out; perhaps he'd gone for a quick swim. She could change and join him. They had the whole house to themselves, now that Brittany was gone until tomorrow. Maybe they'd even go skinny-dipping if they stayed up late enough . . . and their neighbors retired early.

She stood at the glass door and looked outside. He wasn't on the patio, nor was he in the pool. Could he be tinkering around in the garage? Since it was detached, that would explain why he hadn't heard her calling out to him.

The two-story garage—a vacant bedroom with an adjoining bath occupied its second floor—sat just a few yards to the right of the patio. They always parked in the driveway, preferring to use the climate-controlled garage as a combined storage and exercise room. Kenny had even installed a television and hooked up cable so they could watch as they lifted weights or walked on the treadmill.

The knob of the side door turned easily under Dana's palm. She immediately heard the television and sighed with relief. It had been a trifle spooky, calling out and looking for Kenny with no response. He lay on his exercise bench, lifting weights.

"There you are. Didn't you hear me—" She broke off as she realized something was wrong. The barbell had teetered to one side, one end of it lying across his throat at an angle that would make it difficult, if not impossible, for him to breathe. She moved closer and noticed the limp way his arms were hanging and the ashen gray of his face and neck. Her hand flew to her mouth, and a strangled cry rose in her throat.

"Kenny!" She ran to him and lifted the barbell off, using both hands, breathing hard with the effort. There was a tube-shaped indentation at the base of his neck, and no sign of breathing. His face had lost its color, looking eerily like an actor with too-light foundation. "Kenny," she whispered, her voice breaking as she felt frantically for a pulse and felt nothing.

She ran into the house, grabbed the phone, and dialed 911. "Please send someone right away! I think my husband's . . . Oh God, I think he's dead!"

Chapter 2

Eight Months Later

Dana rushed into the offices of Drs. McCormick and Hausmann, psychiatrists, three minutes before their office closed at six P.M. She was later than usual in delivering their dictated patient notes, but as long as she got there before they went home for the day, technically no one could accuse her of being tardy. She did have a good excuse; a quick oil change and tire rotation this morning had turned into a complete brake job.

Still, she apologized profusely to the office manager. This was her favorite client, and she definitely didn't want to tick them off. They tended to use the same wording in their assessments, and since they had so many repeat patients, all she had to do was cut and paste older dictations into new ones and edit them as she listened. She found it sad that so many people with mental-health problems didn't seem to be getting any better, but it also represented an easy way for her to make money in a situation where she desperately needed it.

She'd been up since 5:00 A.M., and with the exception of a forty-minute catnap, had been in motion all day. Her largest client, a family practice, had just added a new doctor, their third. The physicians and the nurse practitioner each saw up to fifteen patients a day, and between her two clients she had almost more work than she could handle. In spite of this, she now contracted additional work from another local service. And since her checking account balance got lower and lower each month, it still wasn't enough.

Unfortunately for her, the only life insurance Kenny had was the coverage that came through his work, a paltry $25,000. Because the medical examiner determined he had suffered a spasm while lifting weights, the policy paid double for death by accident, and she had received $50,000, but Dana had a mortgage payment, a car payment, utilities, health insurance, and food, which of course were just the basics. Plenty of extras figured into her budget as well, like Brittany's weekly piano lessons and dance lessons, and cable TV. She'd had the premium channels turned off, and she hadn't been to the manicurist or hairdresser in months, but she didn't see how else she could economize. Part of her wanted to ask Cécile, who bragged that she fed her entire family of eight on less than a hundred dollars a week, for tips, but that would mean admitting she was in trouble. Dana had spent her entire adult life putting on a brave face, to the point where it had become ingrained in her.

Nor did she confide in Brittany. Instead, she told her daughter they had nothing to worry about, but in truth she was beginning to get frightened. Kenny's funeral costs had been high, largely because of the expense of shipping his body to his native Bahamas for burial, which she knew he would have wanted. She was going through the remainder of the insurance proceeds rapidly, spending as though Kenny were still bringing home a paycheck twice a month, which of course he wasn't. After eight months, it was clear she didn't have much time before the rest of the money was gone.

Dana's memories of what happened after she found Kenny that afternoon were fuzzy at best, even after all these months. As she placed hysterical phone calls, she remembered taking a moment to be grateful that Brittany wasn't at home to see him lying there. First she called 911 and then Norell, who hadn't gotten home from the mall yet, and finally Cécile, who sped right over, arriving just after the paramedics, and holding Dana upright when light-headedness made her begin to sway. She did remember the paramedics theorizing that Kenny had suffered a spasm while lifting the seventy-five-pound weight and essentially dropped it, the bar crushing his airway. She thought she heard one of them say to another, "Prime example of why you should never work out alone."

Her friends had proved invaluable during that time. Norell and Vic went with her to make the funeral and burial arrangements; and Cécile, in spite of her obligations to her own large family, was always close at hand, making sure Brittany ate and offering consolation, a hug, a few words of encouragement, or merely a shoulder to cry on.

Norell and Cécile had put aside their personal squabbles and petty jealousies and pulled together to help her. As a result, the women's three-way friendship of nearly a decade had strengthened.

Neighbors and parents of Brittany's friends dropped off roast chickens, potato salads, and casseroles, which helped tremendously, especially after Kenny's parents arrived with Niles, their eldest son, whose multiple sclerosis confined him to a wheelchair.

To Dana's surprise, her own father, Raymond Britt, had come to the funeral, driving up from Miami with his second wife. She rarely saw him, and whenever she did the air was thick with tension. Perhaps he felt guilty for his words and actions after the family life they knew abruptly ended at an intersection in a mass of shattered glass and twisted steel. Her jaw tightened as she remembered. Her father *should* feel guilty.

Overcome by grief, she'd looked to him for comfort and tried to offer him the same, but he barely acknowledged her. When family and close friends gathered at the house after her mother and Gail's joint service, Dana overheard a friend telling him that at least he still had Dana, that he hadn't lost his entire family. To her shock, her father tearfully confessed that he could cope a lot better "if I'd lost the one and still had the other two."

His friend looked taken aback, and Dana had gasped. When her father turned around and saw her standing there he'd rushed to her and apologized, but she could tell his regret lay not in the way he felt, but in that she'd heard him say it.

The next day he sent her to live with his sister, who lived several miles away, under the guise of seeing that she received meals and care while he coped with his grief. Dana didn't know at the time that she'd never live in her father's house again. A stay intended for only a week or two had stretched into over a year, until she left for college. Her Aunt Joan and her family welcomed her and included her in all their activities, but the pain of her father's abandonment prevented her from appreciating the love they showed her until years later.

She'd met Kenny her junior year and married him right after she graduated, intending to live happily ever after the rest of their lives. Neither of them could know that 'till death do us part' would come after just fifteen years.

After Kenny's service, Dana spent a few awkward moments talking to her father. As she accepted his condolences, she tried not to think about those unhappy months at Aunt Joan's, but now that she'd suffered another loss, a comparison was inevitable. But she couldn't imagine sending Brittany to live with an aunt while she struggled to accept Kenny's death. Brittany didn't even *have* an aunt. Gail had been Dana's only sibling, and Niles was Kenny's.

In Brittany, Dana saw a reason to keep going. Brittany was a comfort to her, just as she had wanted to be a comfort to her father so many years ago. Every time she looked at Brittany she saw a reason to make a future. In contrast, her father had viewed her as a living being who should have been a ghost.

Dana stared sightlessly at the red traffic light in front of her, only alerted of its change to green by the impatient honking of the driver behind her. She promptly shifted her foot to the gas, but her thoughts stayed on the same subject even as her Camry moved forward. It was so unfair, the way death had touched her again, robbing her so suddenly of someone she loved and cutting his life short. Had it not been for the crash her mother would now be in her mid-sixties and still vital, and Gail would only be in her early forties. Even Aunt Joan had passed away much too young some time ago, a victim of cancer. And Kenny, the one who'd most recently joined all of them . . .

She felt moisture pooling in her eyes and blinked it away. Instead, she looked at the Ziploc bag on the seat beside her, bulging with microcassette tapes to be transcribed.

She had no time for tears; she had work to do.

One of the first things Dana did after Kenny's accident was put his Eclipse and his weights up for sale. They both sold quickly, but still, every time she pulled into her driveway after six P.M. a tiny part of her psyche that ignored reality expected to see his car there. Then it hit her all over again that he wouldn't ever be coming home, and that was when the misgivings started: *If only I had gotten home earlier. Kenny wouldn't have been alone. I could have gotten that weight off him before he suffocated.* It had become part of her daily routine.

She pulled up in front of the detached garage. She and Kenny were thrilled when they found this house nine years before. She used to feel pride at the sight of her well-tended home, built in a community purposely designed to look like a throwback to an earlier era, when houses were built close to the sidewalk, with wide front porches and separate garages. Now she felt a combination of rage and exhaustion. Kenny had died in the garage, and even though she knew it wasn't rational, she hated the sight of the structure. But it took energy to sustain anger, energy she needed to reserve for the hours of work still in front of her.

Dana found Brittany in the kitchen, wearing oven mitts on both hands as she removed a meat loaf from the oven. "The timer just went off, Mom."

"Good. I don't know about you, but I'm hungry."

"Did you get to the office before they closed?"

"Yes. Traffic wasn't bad. Everything's fine," she said in the bright tone she always used when she talked to her daughter. It sounded less than authentic these days, even to her own ears.

"You look tired, Mom."

"I had a lot of work to do today, but tomorrow my load will be lighter. It's Wednesday, and they either close early or don't come in at all."

"You want me to make the mashed potatoes?"

"Sure. Put in a little extra milk, will you?"

"Okay, but it'll have to be evaporated milk. I opened a can to use for the meat loaf because we didn't have any real milk."

"We've got milk. I just bought some last night."

"I didn't see it, Mom."

Dana opened the refrigerator portion of the side-by-side. She fully expected to see the plastic gallon container tucked in the wide shelf inside the door rather than on the glass shelves in front, the only place Brittany had probably looked. Kids could be so lazy sometimes.

But there was no container. Dana frowned, and her eyes widened when she realized there could be only one solution as to the whereabouts of the milk. "I'll be right back." She slammed the refrigerator shut and ran toward the back door. Outside, she raised the trunk of her Camry, and there was the jug of milk, nestled in a corner so it wouldn't fall over. Damn it! She thought she'd brought everything inside last night.

She wrapped her fingers around the handle. It was warm, and certainly the contents were spoiled after being in the hot trunk all day. She carried it inside.

"Don't drink this; it's sour," she said to Brittany. "It's been in the trunk since last night."

Brittany made a face. "Then why are you putting it back in the fridge?"

Because I can't afford to waste a whole gallon of milk. "I'm going to let it get cold. Tomorrow I'll open it, pour out a little bit, and then bring it back to the store and tell them it tasted funny. They'll give me another gallon. I know it's sneaky, but we have to economize, Britt." Work on her car's brakes had been costly, just another example of how hard it was to make it on her own. Suddenly she felt like crying.

"Like turning off HBO and Showtime?"

"Yes. We can't afford that right now."

"But what about Daddy's life insurance, all that money you got?"

Dana chose her words carefully. She didn't want to come out and say that Kenny, whom Brittany idolized, had been grossly underinsured, setting the stage for their current predicament. He wasn't yet forty and had been in excellent health, but because he was worried about the multiple sclerosis that so cruelly attacked his older brother, he thought it more prudent to invest in expensive disability insurance. Purchasing additional life insurance to raise his coverage to at least a quarter million had been on his to-do list, but unfortunately for Dana and Brittany, his fatal accident occurred before he got around to it.

When the first premium for the disability insurance came in after his funeral, Dana had angrily scrawled "deceased" over it in large red letters and sent it back. She pictured the underwriters at the insurance company being relieved at not having to ante up the value of a hefty double-indemnity life insurance policy, which only made her more furious. Death was the ultimate disability, yet she had little to show for it.

After dinner Dana ran water and dishwashing liquid in the sink. She rarely used the dishwasher these days; it cost too much to run. She hummed along as Brittany pounded out the theme from *Titanic* on the piano. Actually, she sounded pretty good, playing the familiar melody smoothly and in tempo. She and Brittany always joked that if Brittany wanted to enter the Miss America pageant, she could play the piano for her talent, but none of that classical stuff most contestants played. Adding a few arpeggios here and there was all she needed to be ready for competition.

Dana sighed. Too bad *she* couldn't play the piano. She could get a job playing at a hotel or hospital lobby somewhere. She had to think of a way to come up with more money.

As she washed out a glass she heard a crunching sound, then felt a sudden stinging in her left hand. She winced in pain and raised her hand to investigate.

A red cloud filled the dishwater, and her hand was covered with blood.

Chapter 3

Cécile reached into the bag of gummi bears she kept by her computer and shoved a handful into her mouth. She took a moment to savor the taste she loved, then took another stab at deciphering the dictation coming through her headphones. She depressed the foot pedal again and listened, then shook her head in disgust. The grammar used by the female resident whose dictation she was presently transcribing, whom she could tell from her inflection was a sister, was incredibly bad. She found it inconceivable that anyone could complete four years of college, four years of medical school, and an internship, and still sound like she was fresh out of the 'hood. No wonder she was working at a community hospital. At least the ones for whom English was a second language had an excuse for not being able to structure a sentence.

Cécile knew she'd been fortunate in that respect. If she'd learned French first, she doubted she would be in this line of work, where excellent written English skills were a must. But her parents, Claude and Catherine Mehu, who emigrated from their native Haiti as a young married couple, felt their six children would need skill in the language of their adopted country. Thus, they spoke French only privately, using English in the presence of Cécile and her siblings. As a result, the Mehu children had always formed their thoughts in English. At Claude and Catherine's insistence, all their offspring took French in school, but to their disappointment only their youngest daughter, Micheline, had actually become fluent.

It had been a little difficult growing up where all the other kids on the block spouted French like they were in downtown Port Au

Prince. The kids used to tease the Mehu children for their lack of knowledge. But now that they were grown Cécile wondered how many of them grossed a thousand dollars a week, not bad wages for someone who worked from home, in pajamas if she so wished.

Still, she understood the importance of fitting in. When Michael's sons vetoed brown-bagging their lunches, she didn't object. If the boys' middle school classmates all bought lunch in the cafeteria, she readily understood their wanting to do the same, even though they often asked her to make lunch for them on the weekends. They liked the creative lunches Cécile created, low in fat and high in protein so the children wouldn't nod off during their afternoon science lessons. The girls loved eating bagels smeared with peanut butter and topped with sliced bananas, or kabobs of low fat turkey, low fat cheese, cherry tomatoes that went *splat* in their mouths, and pineapple chunks.

Cécile transmitted the troublesome dictation and mentally planned her dinner menu as she waited for the sound files of the next job to load. She frowned when the phone rang. She adhered to a strict schedule and disliked interruptions. Working at home required supreme discipline; there were a hundred distractions just steps away.

But then again, maybe it was Michael calling to say hello. She smiled at the thought of her husband as she reached for the receiver. "Hello."

"Cécile, it's Dana."

The urgency in Dana's voice alarmed her, and she inadvertently leaned forward in her chair, the same as she'd do if they were talking in person. "Dana, what's wrong?"

"I had to go to the emergency room last night. I cut my hand on a glass I was washing. It just broke apart in my hand. It wasn't a cheap glass, but the way it cracked you'd think it was a jelly jar."

"Oh, no! Are you all right?"

"Physically, yes. They stitched me up and updated my tetanus shot. But it was a deep cut, Cécile. They had to stitch it in layers. The doctor instructed me not to type for the next four weeks, or I'd risk opening up the cut again."

"Four weeks? My God, Dana, can you afford to do that?"

"No, but I have no choice. If I pop my stitches it'll turn into *eight* weeks." She sighed. "I'm in trouble, Cécile. I can't make it financially without Kenny."

Cécile didn't know what to say. For months Dana had resisted making any comments about her situation, other than that she and Brittany were getting along fine. Cécile didn't believe her, but hearing her admit the truth after so long came as a shock. Finally she settled for, "I'm so sorry, Dana. You never let on—"

"I know. I was afraid to face it myself, but the bottom line is, I won't be able to support this lifestyle much longer without Kenny." She chuckled. "Lifestyle. You'd think I was a millionaire or something."

"Dana, you live in a nice house with a pool, and you drive a nice car. Believe it or not, that's a lifestyle."

"Maybe. It just doesn't seem like it. But I thought about what I could do all last night after I got back from the ER. I came up with three possibilities to raise money, and I'd like to do all three."

"What are they?"

"I stopped scowling at my garage long enough to realize that the room above it can be rented out. Even though the renter won't have access to my house, since it's just a few feet away I'd only consider renting to a female. Maybe a college student or something."

"That's a good idea. It has a kitchenette, doesn't it?"

"Yes and no. Kenny put in a small countertop and sink with a dual cabinet below it, but we never did get around to getting the appliances. I guess I can pick up a minifridge, and microwaves are cheap now. Like they say, you've got to spend money to make money. But I should be able to get at least four hundred a month for it, maybe four twenty-five. You don't know of anyone who might be interested, do you?"

"No. Maybe you can post a notice at UNF. But four or five hundred a month might be steep for a college kid. A lot of them share apartments with fully equipped kitchens for the same money per person, or even less."

Dana thought about this for a moment. "But here they'll have more privacy."

"I hope you can find someone." Cécile didn't quite succeed at keeping the doubt out of her voice.

"Anyway, that's my first idea," Dana said. "As for the second, last night I decided that paying for health insurance is killing me. I'm putting out seven hundred dollars a month for medical and dental coverage. If I worked as an employee I'd probably pay less than half that amount. So I'm going to apply to some of the large services that have people transcribing at home."

"It's good that you'll be able to save money, but can you do that and still run your service? That's like working two full-time jobs."

"No, I can't work full-time for someone else and continue with my own clients, so the only way I can make it work is to ditch my existing service and set up something larger." Dana hoped she sounded strong and confident. She'd lain awake most of the night thinking about it, but this was the first time she'd spoken the words aloud. "I need to become a corporation with at least five top-producing MTs"—she used the acronym for medical transcriptionist—"on my payroll, with me getting a piece of every line they produce. Some people have gotten rich that way, and I think I can do reasonably well."

"That sounds wonderful," Cécile said, "but I think it might be easier said than done."

"Yeah. That's what I thought, too. But when I called Patricia Fairfield of Transcription Express this morning to ask if she could take over my clients for the next four weeks, she mentioned that she's going to be retiring, and she asked if I'd be interested in taking over her clients when I heal."

"Dana, that sounds like a good omen if I ever heard one."

"I honestly believe it's a sign from above that this is the right thing for me to do. Pat's been established for years, and she said she bills thirteen to fifteen thousand every month."

"Pretty respectable numbers for an operation run out of a spare room of your house," Cécile conceded.

"And I have the potential to increase that. Pat's already referred me to a sports-medicine clinic that approached her about transcribing their notes," Dana continued. "I meet with them tomorrow afternoon. If I can land this account, that'll be a good start. I understand it's huge."

"That's wonderful, Dana!" Cécile hadn't heard this much excitement in her friend's voice since before Kenny died last June.

"And that's why I'm calling. I want to know if you're interested in joining me as a partner."

"A partner! Uh, I don't know. What exactly is involved?"

Dana's reply came fast. "Money."

"I don't have much of that," Cécile promptly replied.

"Neither do I, but I want to get a loan. I need to do it now, while I still have good bank balances, so they won't ask me to put up the equity in my house."

"How much do you figure we'll need?" Cécile asked cautiously.

"Twenty-five thousand, at a minimum. But since I already spoke to Norell and she's interested, I suppose we could get by with twenty-four. It's easier to divide by three."

"Eight thousand dollars apiece. That's still a lot of money, Dana. I'm just a working stiff with maybe a hundred bucks hidden in my underwear drawer."

Dana didn't point out that she was sure Cécile and Michael had a bank account. "I know, but we're going to need it. We'll have to get set up so we can get voice files off the Internet, and that will probably involve hiring a computer consultant at sixty or seventy dollars an hour."

They spent the next few minutes discussing technical issues. "Cécile, I'm not just going after local work," Dana explained. "I want to run regular ads in medical publications to give us exposure to physicians all over the country."

"Sounds expensive."

"Absolutely. We'll also need a Web site. And I don't know how much Pat will want for her client list. It'll add up pretty quickly. Plus we'll need operating capital for payroll and stuff. I know from experience that clients don't always issue checks as soon as they receive your invoice. That's why I've been doing work for Pat, to provide me with some ready cash while I'm waiting for my clients to ante up."

Cécile's shoulders slumped. "It sounds like a fabulous opportunity, Dana, but I'm afraid I wouldn't be very good at running a business. I just don't have the personality to be a supervisor. What would I have to offer?"

"Mainly your eight thousand dollars, but your transcription skills, too, Cécile. And since you're certified, you'd be great at telling our ICs which word forms the AAMT approves of."

"Independent contractors? Not employees?"

"ICs, absolutely. That way we won't have to worry about payroll taxes, vacations, health insurance, and all that."

"What about our salaries?"

"We'll each draw an hourly rate for administrative work and a line rate for transcription. I'd like to issue paychecks weekly. That'll cost us more than paying every two weeks or twice a month, but it'll make us more appealing than our competition so we can get the best people out there."

"Will we get the same line rate as the people contracting from us?

How are we supposed to make any money?" Cécile sounded incredulous.

"Through the profits. As a partner, you'll receive a third of the profits, to be paid annually. Of course, I don't know how long it'll take for us to recoup our initial investment, but most businesses don't turn profits right away. That's why we have to have money in reserve."

"Do you really feel we'll have enough work from the jump to keep the three of us plus a staff busy?"

"If we get the sports medicine clinic, absolutely. Remember, you and I will be only part-time. Norell is prepared to quit Precise to work full-time for the new company."

"It sounds great, Dana. I'd like to be part of it, but I can't make a decision about anything requiring that much money without talking to Michael first."

"I understand. Let me know, will you?"

"Of course. It might be a few days. I'll call you as soon as I know myself."

After Cécile hung up she found she was so excited about the possibility of going into business that she couldn't concentrate on her work. She logged off, and since she didn't believe in wasting time sitting around doing nothing, she pulled out the vacuum and plugged it in. As she ran it back and forth over the carpet, she thought about Dana, who had clearly been under great strain. She'd never been one to confide her business, and Cécile didn't want to pry, but there'd been clear signs of trouble. Dana's clothes hung on her now; she'd dropped about twenty pounds, probably from stress. Her normally glowing dark skin had grown dull and sometimes even erupted in raised bumps, and her face reflected the hard look of someone who wasn't getting enough sleep. She never wore makeup anymore, not even lipstick, and she hadn't touched up her perm in months. But just now she had sounded really excited and lively for the first time since Kenny died.

Cécile felt proud of Dana for taking action the way she had. She was sure she'd do well. Cécile couldn't imagine running her own transcription service, even a one-woman operation. It just wasn't her nature to negotiate rates and chase down payments. But she did know how it felt to be driven by desperation.

Three years ago, when she learned that Louis Belarge, her first husband and father of her daughters, had fathered a son with another woman, she immediately made arrangements to take the girls and leave. Louis had laughed at her, saying she wouldn't last two weeks on her own, but she'd fooled his cheating ass.

It hadn't been easy. She'd rented a large one-bedroom apartment and told the management that her husband had custody of their children so they wouldn't force her to spend more for a second bedroom. She set up the bedroom for the girls and slept on the couch. Precise Transcription had just instituted a work-at-home program, and she bought a computer and signed up.

It took time getting the kids to understand that Mommy was off limits while she was working unless it was really important, especially with her working out in the open, in a corner of the dining area. And sometimes, despite all of her best efforts, the bills for the computer, the new furniture, payments on her car, and other household expenses were too much, and they had to subsist on chicken, ground beef, and peanut-butter-and-jelly sandwiches, usually in the days immediately preceding payday. It was true her life was a lot more tranquil now that she'd remarried, but the memory of that scary time would be with her forever, and she decided it would never happen again.

Determined to increase her paycheck, she'd set about creating an extensive library of shorthand—some people called them macros—that reduced the number of keystrokes she used and ultimately made her Precise Transcription's biggest producer, putting out ten thousand lines a week. Her paycheck increased dramatically and had stayed elevated ever since.

Even with a total of six kids between them, she and Michael managed just fine, in large part due to the low mortgage payment on Michael's house, which she and her girls had moved into after their marriage. The house, in an old, established neighborhood near the St. Johns River, had been comfortable when it was just Michael, Jonathan, Damon, and Monet; but now that the family had expanded it was awfully tight. Nothing had changed for the boys, but nine-year-old Monet now shared her bedroom with three stepsisters, and with two bunk beds and two dressers crammed in there, they literally couldn't turn around without bumping into something.

The biggest problem was lack of closets. Cécile had to store their less-used clothing in storage boxes in the detached garage. Running out there every five minutes to get this or that had gotten old real fast.

The master suite wasn't much better. Only slightly larger than the other two bedrooms, it barely had space for their queen-size bed, chest, and highboy. The television had to go on top of her double-wide dresser because there was no place to put a TV stand, and the room's lone closet was inadequate. Fortunately, since she had been working at home, her wardrobe consisted largely of T-shirts and sweatpants. She supposed people today had larger wardrobes than they did back when this house was built, sometime between the two world wars. The room's only advantage was the attached full bath that the previous owners had added on.

Other than the small bedrooms, the house wasn't bad. It had an alcove that gave her both a place to work and a place to sew. The spacious kitchen had been modernized by the previous owners, as had the hall bath, and they had a full dining room and decent-sized yard. But those attributes couldn't make up for the lack of space in the bedrooms.

Cécile had treaded rather delicately regarding the topic of the house being too small, and although Michael initially showed enthusiasm about the idea of remodeling, that was as far as it had gotten. They'd been married over a year now, and it was still something he was "gonna" do.

She knew the reason for his reluctance. Each month he wrote a check for an amount less than what most people paid to rent a one-bedroom apartment. Michael Rivers was as close to the man of her dreams as she was going to get, but he did have a tendency to be a little tight with a dollar sometimes. The matter of household expenses had to be considered with such a large family, but sometimes she felt she couldn't get through another day living like this. She wanted to go outside, throw her arms up, look heavenward, and scream, "Give me space!"

Maybe she was being unreasonable, but it wasn't like they couldn't afford to pay two or three times as much as they were now. They had the income to do it, and surely that income would increase if she went into business with Dana and Norell.

She put away the vacuum and went to the phone. It was time to approach Michael about Dana's proposition.

"I'm full," Michael said, pressing his palms against his stomach, which had gotten a little rounder since they married. "Those stuffed peppers were good, Cécile."

His sentiments were echoed by the others.

"The secret is Norell's fresh green peppers."

"Seems to me that she gives away her whole vegetable garden," Michael remarked.

"No, that's not really true, but she does grow too much for just her and Vic to eat." She glanced at the wall clock. "Time for the news," she announced. Her work was done for the night. The kids were responsible for clearing the table and cleaning the kitchen.

Cécile sat down to watch the news with Michael, a bag of gummi bears resting on her lap. That Brian Williams was awfully cute. She'd switched to NBC the moment Tom Brokaw retired.

Cécile rolled her eyes when the phone began to ring. Talk about lousy timing. She grabbed the kitchen extension. Probably one of those pushy eighth-grade girls calling Jonathan. She blew out her breath in annoyance. They wouldn't even let the boy do his homework in peace, and when he started high school in the fall, it would only get worse.

But it was her mother, calling from West Palm Beach. "Mama, is everything all right?" Cécile asked anxiously. Her mother, always conscious of long-distance rates, always called on weekends or in the morning before 8:00 A.M., not at 6:45 on a Wednesday night. Her mother clearly was not calling merely to say hello; something was up.

"Everything's okay," Catherine replied. "I just wanted to let you know . . . Well, you know Michie lost her job. The lawyers she worked for had to lay off a coupla people."

"Yes, you told me a couple of weeks ago. She got a nice severance package, though, didn't she?"

"Well, not all in one piece. They go'n' keep payin' her for eight weeks. She'll get a check every other Friday, jus' like she was still workin'. Plus she'll get her vacation."

"I don't understand, Mama. What's the problem?"

"There ain't one, well, not really. Michie said she was gonna call you, but in case she forgot to, I wanted to make sure you knew she's comin' up that way. I guess she did forget."

"Michie's coming *here*? To Jacksonville? Why?"

"She got a job interview Tuesday. She checked the want ads in the Jacksonville papers on her computer. She's gonna drive up the day before."

"How long will she be here?"

"She's movin' there. She put all her stuff in storage and gave up her apartment. She says she wants a change of scene."

Cécile thought of her overcrowded house and instantly became alarmed. "She's not planning on staying here, is she?" That would be a difficult situation. She and Michael had no room for a houseguest, and it would be just like her sister to show up unannounced, expecting room and board. They were sisters, but they had never been friends.

"No, baby. She got a hotel room. But she'll be by to see you. She gave her job your address to mail her checks to. Now listen, Cécile," Catherine said. "I know you and Michie don' always see eye to eye, but I hope you two can start gettin' along better. You're our only girls and you both grown; you should be close. Maybe livin' inna same city'll help."

Cécile didn't answer. She and her younger sister didn't get along because somewhere along the line Micheline had gotten the idea that the world was supposed to grovel at her feet. It was a pretty lofty attitude for someone from their humble beginnings—their father worked as a landscaper, and their mother did office and house cleaning—but what Micheline wanted, Micheline usually got, and that annoyed Cécile.

It was true that her little sister had done well. She had gotten her education with a combination of a partial scholarship, funds she raised by working part-time, and from a student loan. She now had a promising career as a paralegal and talked about going on to law school. She also had an active social life, including a half-dozen admirers vying for her affections. She zipped around town in a sporty new VW Bug convertible.

On the other hand, when Cécile was Micheline's age, she had been struggling to cope with a marriage that was already faltering, complicated by the existence of one small child and a nagging fear that she might be pregnant again, which turned out to be correct. She resented Micheline's carefree existence, feeling she could use a little responsibility in her life instead of gallivanting around between the mall and the manicurist to get ready for her dates. But the fact that Micheline could just pack up and come to a new town because she was bored suggested she was irresponsible as ever.

"Cécile? Are you listenin'?"

She blinked, abruptly halting her negative thoughts toward her sister. "Yes, Mama. I'll make a special effort to get along with Michie. I promise."

"Everything all right?" Michael asked when she joined him in the living room.

"No, not really. My sister's moving to Jacksonville. She'll be here Friday."

"You mean I'll finally get to meet the famous Micheline?"

"Whoop-de-doo," she replied flatly.

He put an arm around her. "I know your sister isn't one of your favorite people, but this might be good for both of you. You two can have lunch together, like you do with Dana and Norell, and maybe in the process start to get along better."

"I promised Mama I'd try. She's worried about Michie coming to a city where I'm the only one she knows. But it's not that I dislike her. I guess I'm just content to not see her very often."

"Well, you can always use being a business owner as an excuse."

She looked at him sharply. "Are you sure, Michael?"

"Of course there's some risk involved, but I think the three of you will do very well. I predict you'll recoup our investment in less than a year."

"Oh, Michael, thank you!" She threw her arms around his neck, her palms tightly grasping the back of his head and neck to keep him close. He gently pushed her away, but his quick glance at the doorway told her it was out of concern that one of the children might walk in on them.

Cécile felt almost giddy as she clumsily moved away from him, nearly losing her balance in the process. Damn it, she had to lose those thirty pounds. The future looked too bright to be clouded by the health problems from dragging around extra weight. She and Dana and Norell were going to be successful and make a lot of money. She'd keep her current job and put every penny their new venture brought in toward having the house remodeled. Once that was done, everything would be perfect and she could deal with anything.

Even Micheline.

Chapter 4

Norell applied full makeup and slipped into one of her numerous lounging outfits, this one a sea blue gauzy creation with a V-neck blouse and matching wide-legged pants. She tried several looks with her just-below-the-shoulder tresses, a flattering reddish-gold color courtesy of a skilled beautician, before deciding that an upsweep worked best. It made the most of her impressive bustline. It was important that she look especially good tonight. She needed Vic's support now more than ever.

She surveyed herself in the full-length oval standing mirror in her bedroom. She had to admit she looked pretty doggone good for thirty-seven. Hell, if it weren't for that space between her front teeth she'd be flawless, at least on the outside.

Sometimes Norell could hardly believe the changes that had occurred in her life. Less than two years before she'd been struggling to pay her bills, two steps ahead of collection, and now she presided over a spacious villa near the Intracoastal Waterway, with nothing much to worry about other than looking good for her husband when he came home from work.

Keeping the house clean didn't take much effort. They had a maid service come in every other week, and since neither she nor Vic were particularly messy people, it usually stayed neat between visits. She transcribed part time in the afternoons, between one-thirty and five-thirty. Norell didn't really have to work, but it gave her something to do. Between her work, her gardening, and her domestic responsibilities, Norell managed to stay busy. Having no financial burdens was a marvelous a state of affairs, but an emptiness gnawed at her incessantly—and it became strongest whenever she got close to the beautifully decorated bedroom Vic kept for his two teenage daughters.

Norell had been told by her gynecologist years before that she would have a difficult time conceiving because her uterus was extremely tilted. She hadn't worried too much about it at the time; she'd only been twenty-one, and back then having children was a plan for the distant future. Later, while working night and day to pay her bills, she hadn't even had time to date, and she chalked up the idea of having a family of her own as simply not meant for her. She even mentioned that she would probably not be having children to an examiner at the women's center where she went for her health care, and the woman promptly suggested that she consider a hysterectomy. It would prevent the possibility of reproductive organ malignancy developing in the future, she said. It made sense, because of Norell's family history—both her parents had succumbed to cancer at relatively young ages—but it had also been a turning point, for at that precise moment Norell realized she wasn't ready to give up hope.

After she married Vic she was glad she hadn't. It looked like all her dreams were going to come true, even though it was a tad late. But as the months went by and her period showed up every four weeks just like the full moon, Norell found herself growing more and more anxious. The words she'd heard so many years ago came back. But she was no longer twenty-one, with her entire adulthood still in front of her; she was thirty-seven and thinking about things like retirement savings and how to avoid osteoporosis.

Vic arrived home a shade before seven-thirty. He usually left the house in the morning a few minutes before nine, arriving at his bail bonds office in time to receive the anxious friends and family of prisoners whose bail amounts had been set at the nine A.M. court session. Commuting later than most people helped him get back and forth without encountering the considerable traffic on the roads leading to and from the Beaches area.

He came up behind her in the kitchen, wrapped his arms around her waist, and planted a loud, wet kiss on the side of her neck.

"That you, honey?" she asked innocently.

"Better be. What're you making?"

"Steak. It's marinated; that's why it smells so good. The potatoes are in the microwave, and the salad is in the fridge." She turned around and slipped her arms around his neck. As she kissed his mouth, Vic grabbed her buttocks, pulling her into his groin.

"Mmm . . . I see you brought me a little something," she said, wiggling her hips into his erection. "When do I get it?"

Vic chuckled deep in his throat. "Not now; I gotta eat first."

Norell had a spark in her step as she lit the candles on the table. Vic Bellamy might be fifty years old, but he was a fabulous lover who could leave her exhausted and drenched in sweat. Her reproductive equipment might not work properly, but there was nothing wrong with the part of her that reached sexual gratification.

"I had a doctor's appointment today," she remarked as they ate. She had decorated the table with inexpensive fresh flowers, black-eyed Susans and violets, from Wal-Mart. She hesitated lighting candles, fearing that would be overkill, before going ahead with it.

"Oh? Anything wrong?"

"No. I went to see an infertility specialist. I told you about it." The fact that he'd forgotten couldn't be taken as a good sign, but Norell wasn't surprised. Vic already had three children and didn't seem too eager to start a second family, even though before they got married he said they could start trying after six months. She sensed he experienced secret relief as each subsequent month proved no baby was on the way.

"Oh yeah, I remember now. So what'd he say?"

"He wants to do some tests. He thinks it's something more than just a tilted uterus, and he wants to determine if there's any damage to my tubes. While I was there he told me about different options we can consider. He also wants you to come in."

"Me? What for?"

"To test your, uh, little squiggies."

Vic put down his wineglass. "There's nothing wrong with my sperm count, Norell. I have three children, remember?"

"Yes, a twenty-six-year-old son, and two teenage daughters. He wants to test you because it's been so long since you fathered a child. Even though he says he's pretty sure the problem is all with me," she added quickly.

"Yeah, well if he's so sure, let him treat you and leave me out of it."

Norell chose her words carefully on what was a delicate topic. She knew the ability to make babies was as important, if not more important, to a man as the ability to conceive and carry was to women, and to have that ability questioned was like questioning his manhood. "It's purely a precautionary measure, Vic. It would be a waste of time to treat me if it turns out there's something wrong with you. It's unlikely, but not impossible."

"So what am I supposed to do, go down to his office and jack off in a cup?"

"I wish you wouldn't be so crass about it. This is important to me, Vic. Why don't you think about it for a while?" *But don't take too long,* she silently implored. While the physician pointed out that thirty-seven was much better than thirty-eight, which in turn was much better than thirty-nine, he had stressed that time was not on her side.

She decided the topic had been discussed sufficiently for one evening. "How was work today?" she asked to change the subject.

After dinner, Norell relaxed in the living room with a book while Vic watched TV. A jangling phone suddenly broke into the relative quiet. She put a hand on the receiver and waited, as was her habit, for it to ring two complete times before picking it up. "Hello."

"Norell, it's Dana."

"Hi! What's up?"

"I called so you can wish me luck. I'm going to the bank tomorrow. Brittany's friend's father is branch manager at the same bank where we, where I have my mortgage, so I figured I'd start with him, see if he can influence the loan officer in my favor." Dana paused. "But there's something else I need to talk to you about."

"What's that?" The commercial that had been playing ended, and Norell caught sight of Vic gesturing at her to keep quiet so he could watch the program. "Hold on, Dana, I'm going to switch phones."

When she was settled in the master bedroom she resumed the conversation. "Sorry about that. Vic's really into some documentary about Alcatraz prison. It's the bail bondsman in him, I guess. What's on your mind?"

"I want to know if you'll be Brittany's guardian in case anything happens to me."

Norell's mouth dropped open. "Dana! I thought you were going to ask me to go with you to the bank for moral support or something. This is serious."

"Yes, it is. If anything happens to me, Brittany will have no one. I guess I shouldn't write off Kenny's parents, but they live in a different country, they're older, and they've had their hearts broken by the fates of their two sons. Brittany would be a lot happier here in Jacksonville, and of course Cécile already has a huge family."

"I'd be happy to take care of her, Dana."

"Norell, not so fast. Think about it. Talk to Vic. I'd also like you to be the executrix of my estate. I'm putting in a clause saying that Brittany won't have full control over whatever money there is until she's thirty, so if I die before that, you'd have to make the determination about what she should get and when. I don't want her selling the house and blowing the proceeds on silly things like clothes and cars."

Norell found Dana's planning impressive. She reasoned it was all part of being a responsible parent. Hopefully one day she, too, would have a child to look out for. "You're really getting your house in order, aren't you? Setting up a business, looking for a renter, and now Brittany's guardianship."

"You'd be surprised at what comes to mind when you've been forbidden to put any stress on your right hand. I wish I'd thought of trying to rent that room last year instead of wishing the building didn't exist."

"Any luck yet finding a tenant?"

"No, but the semester is just about over. I might have to wait until the kids come back in August, unless I can find someone who's taking summer classes." Dana yawned. "Excuse me."

"Sounds like you'd better get a good night's sleep. You've got a big day tomorrow."

"I can't go to bed. I'm getting ready to mow the lawn. Well, Brittany has to help me push the mower because of my hand."

"But Dana, it's after eight o'clock. It'll be dark soon."

"That's the best time, when the sun's gone in and it's still light. It's much cooler."

Once again Norell found herself at a loss for words. Before Dana cut her hand she had literally worked from sunup to sundown. Even now she spent most of her time assembling a business plan, struggling to peck at the keyboard with only her left hand.

Norell suddenly felt guilty for the easy life that allowed her to work just part-time, and fill the rest of the days with light housework, books, old movies on the classic movie channel, and gardening. After dinner each night she relaxed with her husband until it was time to go to bed, while poor Dana was outside pushing a lawn mower. Suddenly embarrassed, she changed the subject. "Did you want me to sign something to make your wishes official? Not that anything is going to happen to you, Dana."

Dana chuckled. "Thanks for your optimism. Sometimes I feel like I won't last another five minutes. And yes, it does need to be official. I've got a software program that helps complete simple legal documents. I'll get the form printed out, and we can bring it to the bank and have our signatures notarized. But I mean it when I say think about it, Norell. Vic, too."

"Vic won't mind. He's okay with older kids, like his daughters. It's babies he objects to." A note of bitterness crept into Norell's voice.

"Uh, do you want to talk about it?"

"No," Norell said quickly. Dana had enough problems. She didn't need to be burdened with someone else's. "Just a temporary roadblock. We'll get past it."

Chapter 5

Dana ran a comb through her short hair. She'd had it touched up and cut at a beauty school for seventeen dollars, and they hadn't done a half bad job.

She had dressed casually in a pale yellow pantsuit and paisley print short-sleeved blouse, her completed loan application and business plan tucked into a pocket of her butterscotch-colored leather portfolio.

Funny how kids could remind adults of the facts. Brittany's friend Vanessa was the one who gave her the idea to come here in the first place. Dana had been at the dining-room table poring over the figures Pat Fairfield provided her, as well as her own financial picture, trying to assemble it all into something impressive, when Vanessa, who was spending the night with Brittany, asked what she was doing.

"I'm trying to expand the business I run," Dana told her. "But it isn't easy. Expansion takes money."

"If you need money you should call my Popi. He runs a bank."

Dana remembered then that Vanessa's father, Gil, managed a branch of the bank where she kept her money. She'd forgotten all about that. She'd rarely seen Gil since he and Vanessa's mother Irene separated over a year ago and he rented out an apartment at the beach.

When she reached the bank, Dana gave her name to the receptionist, then sat on a striped sofa and waited. She'd barely had time to read an interesting-looking recipe for a beef stirfry in one of the reception area magazines when the receptionist said, "Mrs. Covington, Mr. Albacete will see you now. It's the last office on the right."

"Thank you." Dana turned and carefully tore out the page with the recipe on it, then folded it and tucked it into her portfolio. She mentally defended her defacing of the bank's magazine by reasoning that it was an old publication and she could no longer buy it.

"Gil, thanks so much for seeing me," she said as she entered a large office with impressive dark wood furnishings. Sunlight from two windows behind his desk kept the room from appearing too somber.

He rose. "How are you, Dana?"

"I'm good, thanks." She held out her hand, which he took, but he quickly moved in to give her a quick, impersonal hug. She breathed in his cologne and momentarily closed her eyes. There was nothing better than a man who smelled as good as he looked, and Gil Albacete, in his navy suit; snazzy blue, rust, and white tie; and matching silk hankie, looked damn good. She wondered what had gone wrong between him and Irene. They'd made such a handsome couple, he with his sexy green eyes and sandy brown hair, and she with her olive complexion and thick, curly dark hair. She knew their marriage was in trouble from comments Brittany made after spending time with Vanessa: "Mom, Mr. Albacete was out real late last night," or "Mom, Mr. and Mrs. Albacete had a big argument before she brought me home."

"Have a seat," he said, gesturing toward the two armless chairs facing his desk.

She complied, placing her purse at her side and her portfolio in her lap. "I know I should have gone directly to a loan officer, but I thought it wouldn't hurt if I saw you first."

He leaned back in his high-backed leather chair, his green eyes fixated on her. "Why don't you tell me what it is you're trying to accomplish?"

God, he was handsome. She'd never seen him dressed for work. But that was the last thing she needed to be thinking about. She'd better snap out of it. "I have an opportunity to purchase an existing medical-transcription service, and I've already lined up a new client who wants us to handle their transcriptions effective May first. I have two partners, and we're each putting in eight thousand dollars. But both my partners can write checks for that amount. I can't."

"You have a savings account here, don't you?"

"Yes. We moved all our banking here when we got the mortgage for the house we—I live in now. But I don't want to touch my savings. It's bad enough that I haven't been able to add a penny to it since Kenny's accident." After ten months she still referred to Kenny's tragic demise as his "accident." "I've put something together with estimates of anticipated billing for the new client, plus copies of invoices from the existing service." She pulled the report from her portfolio and passed it to him.

Gil perused the report, the only sound in the room soft music from the local jazz station on the radio. For Dana, the song seemed to go on eternally.

"I'm going to need some time to go over this," he finally said. "But eight thousand dollars isn't a large amount of money, especially for a depositor who has respectable savings and a mortgage with us. If you wanted to buy a car you'd need more money than that. The issue is, of course, the risk. A car can be taken back in the case of default. But a business without expensive assets is something else."

Dana leaned forward anxiously. "How long do you suppose it will take for an answer? We have a lot to do if we're to go live May first."

"Give me until close of business tomorrow. But while I have you here I need some more information from you."

"I have my completed application here."

"That's a start."

At his request Dana gave him her Social Security and account numbers. The fingers of her right hand nervously drummed the fabric-covered arm of her chair.

Gil looked up and smiled. "Try not to be nervous, Dana. I'm sure it'll all work out."

Dana wished she had a hundred dollars for each time someone had said that to her in the last month. The cut to her hand required her to use her nest egg for an entire month's expenses, which made her financial situation even more perilous. "I have to do this, Gil. Kenny was the main wage earner between us, and I won't be able to sustain a two-income lifestyle on one income indefinitely. I have maybe until the end of the year." She stopped and took a deep breath, aware of the urgency in her voice. "I don't want to sound undignified," she said calmly, "but it's important you understand just how imperative this is. We plan to use subcontractors to do the transcription. One of my partners will work for the company full time, and two of us will devote part-time hours to transcription because we still need to work full-time." She looked at him pleadingly. "I'm doing everything I can to maintain Brittany's quality of life, or at least keep the changes to a minimum."

"How is Brittany, Dana?" he asked gently.

She smiled, knowing he was trying to get her mind off of her troubles. Funny. The last ten months hadn't brought many changes for her friends, other than the fact that they got along a lot better these days. Norell was still trying to get pregnant, and Cécile, although she'd managed to lose a little weight, was still trying to get Michael to spring for a larger house. On the other hand, Gil and Irene had gone from being separated to being divorced. "She's twelve, and is blossoming into a lovely young woman. As is Vanessa," she added.

Now it was Gil's turn to grin. He turned the brass frame photograph on his desk around, allowing Dana to see his daughter beaming for the camera, her chin resting on her hand in an obvious photographer-suggested pose. "She is, isn't she?"

Dana reached for her purse and slung it over her shoulder. "If you don't need anything else, Gil, I guess I'll be going." She stood, and so did he, coming from around his desk to walk her to his office door. He stood only about five-nine, but he'd been blessed with everything else. Besides, not being a six footer certainly hadn't prevented Tom Cruise from being the object of many a woman's fantasy.

"I'll run your credit, take a thorough look at your expected billables, and make my recommendation to the loan officer," he said. "And I promise to have an answer for you by tomorrow, so try not to toss and turn tonight."

"I won't." She held out her hand, and he grasped it and shook it firmly, his other hand on her shoulder.

Dana anticipated lying awake long into the night, worrying about the outcome of her loan application, but she was so emotionally worn out that she fell asleep within minutes.

The next day, she was in the car, delivering reports and returning tapes to her clients, when her cell phone rang. Dana regularly forwarded her office line to her cell so she wouldn't miss any potential calls from Brittany's school or from her clients. "Dana Covington," she said in greeting.

"Good news, Dana," a man's voice greeted cheerfully. "Your loan's been approved."

"Gil?"

"Yes. Sorry, I should have identified myself."

She laughed. "No, you did it fine. You told me the main thing I wanted to hear first. When can I pick up the check?"

"Tomorrow, any time after twelve noon."

"I wasn't expecting to hear from you until this afternoon."

"I always say it'll take longer than I expect it to. That way I'm always making people happy."

"You've certainly made *me* happy. Thank you so much, Gil."

"You don't have to thank me. If you didn't qualify, I couldn't have helped you. It's true that the savings account you opened after Kenny died has a declining balance, but your checking account is stable, and your credit was fine."

"I'm so happy," she said in a choked voice. "Where do I go tomorrow, the loan department?"

"Yes. They'll have the papers all drawn up."

"All right. And Gil, thanks again."

Dana wiggled her toes in her closed shoes. The world suddenly looked so much prettier. The sky seemed bluer, the clouds looked fluffier, and the grass looked as green as emeralds. She wanted to share her good news, and she was close to Cécile's house. She'd just take a minute to tell Cécile they were officially in business.

Dana pulled up along the curb in front of the Rivers home, just behind a tomato-red Volkswagen bug with its top down. It looked like Cécile had company, certainly out of character for her. Anyone who knew Cécile knew how much she disliked interruptions during her working hours. She applied supreme discipline to her work, but it paid off in the form of an enviably high paycheck every two weeks.

Dana had gotten within a few yards of the front door when it opened and Cécile emerged with a slim, fair-skinned woman.

"Dana!" Cécile exclaimed. "What a nice surprise."

"I'm sorry to interrupt, but I was in the neighborhood and wanted to share my good news."

"This must be the day for good news," the other woman said as Cécile squealed with anticipation. "I was just offered the job I interviewed for last week." She held out her hand. "I'm Micheline Mehu, Cécile's sister."

"I'm Dana." She shook the French-manicured hand and glanced at

Cécile's sister in admiration. Everything about Micheline was polished: Her makeup, her crisp, white long-sleeved blouse, her starched jeans. "I didn't notice the resemblance at first, but now I do," she said. Micheline stood two or three inches taller than Cécile's five feet, three inches, and her slim build reminded Dana of how Cécile looked in those early days at Precise. Micheline had different coloring—fair skin compared to her sister's rich honey complexion, and tawny gold hair that looked natural but probably wasn't, in contrast to Cécile's black tresses—but they shared the same prominent cheekbones and the same button nose. "Are you living in Jacksonville now?"

"I will as soon as I find a place."

Dana drew in her breath. Could it be possible that she could be approved for a bank loan and rent out her vacant room on the same day? "I don't know exactly what you're in the market for, but if you'd like to save some rent money I've got a nice, cozy room available. It's above my garage. It's generally described as in-law quarters, except that most elderly people have difficulty climbing stairs. Did Cécile tell you about it?" She glanced at her friend, who shook her head slightly, an unreadable expression on her face.

"No, she sure didn't. But I wouldn't mind renting a room for a month or two while I really get to know the city and decide where I want to live."

Dana pulled a business card out of her purse. "You can reach me at this number. I'll be there later this afternoon. You can come see it then if you'd like."

"Great! I'll call you. Bye, Sis."

"Bye, Micheline. And congratulations." Cécile took Dana's arm. "Come on in and have lunch with me."

"Are you sure?"

"I was just about to have a salad with roast chicken strips, and there's plenty."

Dana sat at the kitchen table while Cécile assembled the salads. "I suppose you're wondering why I didn't tell you about my sister," Cécile remarked as she laid banana pepper slices on beds of lettuce, cucumber, tomatoes, and sliced olives.

"Yes, I was curious. You know how desperate I am to rent that room."

Cécile sighed. "I thought about it, Dana, but in all honesty I don't believe Micheline would be your ideal tenant. When she lived in West Palm Beach she frequently paid her rent late because she went on clothes-buying sprees or last-minute vacations. I know you'll be counting on that rent money every month."

"Yes, but those were nameless, faceless landlords. Besides, I'm a friend of yours, so surely she wouldn't want to make you look bad."

Cécile removed the roast chicken slices from the microwave and divided them between the two salads. "I wouldn't count on that," she said as she carried the plates to the table and set one down in front of Dana. "And I'd hate to be caught in the middle. I wouldn't want you to hold it against me, Dana."

"I don't think it'll be a problem. Besides, she said it would only be for a few months."

"I know my sister, Dana. She's trouble. But just remember, I tried to warn you."

Chapter 6

Norell put down her magazine in disgust. In an article about the influx of babies being born to celebrities, a popular actor's wife had been quoted as saying, "A child is the most wonderful thing that can happen to a parent." Considering that children were what gave parents their status in the first place, it was a rather silly statement. Clearly the new mother was overjoyed, and in her happiness probably hadn't realized how inane her comment sounded, but Norell didn't see why the editor didn't catch it and change "parent" to "person," which was surely the original intent. Maybe it was a little dishonest, but surely the interviewer could have prompted the woman into correcting herself so she wouldn't look like such a waterhead when the article was published. She wondered if the interviewer had left it that way on purpose.

Norell knew she had no cause to get all worked up about such a minute detail, but she recognized that it came from her own frustration. It had been a whole week, and Vic hadn't said anything about going to see the doctor. She had proceeded with her own workup, and she was feeling reasonably confident that the problem rested with her, based on the preliminary findings of a blocked fallopian tube and a uterus so tilted it was practically lying on its side. What disturbed her was Vic's lack of interest in a subject of utmost importance to her. It was just fine for her to see to the needs of his daughters when they came for their twice-monthly weekend visits, but not for him to help her conceive offspring of her own, and Norell thought that stank.

She went ahead and scheduled surgery to have her fallopian tubes unblocked. She'd already alerted Dana and Cécile, assuring them that it wasn't a major procedure and would only require two weeks of recuperation. She waited to inform Vic, since his daughters were coming for the weekend and she didn't want them to come into a tense atmosphere, just in case he took it badly.

Instead she made a special effort to be nice to the girls. Jessica was fifteen and Amber thirteen, both sweet kids. At first they'd been wary and viewed her as a threat when she and Vic were just dating, but they accepted her eventually and sometimes even asked for her advice. Both were old enough to remember when their parents lived harmoniously under the same roof, and Norell had heard it said that children of divorced parents always held out hopes of a reconciliation, no matter how long ago or how bitter the divorce. Vic also had a son from an early relationship before he was married, who lived in Orlando near his mother.

On Sunday evening Norell declined to go along when Vic brought the girls home. He would undoubtedly go inside for a few minutes and talk with his ex-wife, Phyllis. Norell had met her predecessor once, shortly after she and Vic exchanged vows in a local wedding chapel. He said his children's mother deserved to be acquainted with their new stepmother, and she agreed he had a point. The key word was "acquainted." No one expected them to be best buddies. At the time Phyllis had been divorced from Vic for four years. Brown skinned and pretty, with dimples and what was generally referred to as "good bones," she also carried about eighty extra pounds on her short frame. Norell instinctively knew a direct link existed between Phyllis's weight problem and her status as a divorced woman. When Norell delicately asked Vic what had gone wrong in his marriage, he mumbled something about them having grown apart and her just not turning him on anymore. Subtlety had never been one of Vic's strong points; he'd practically come out and said she had gotten fat as a pig.

Fortunately, weight had never been a problem for Norell. In the fifteen months she and Vic had been married, she had retained her figure to the pound. She went to the gym daily and took a half-hour step aerobics class, then, after resting a bit, spent another ten minutes on the moving stepper without missing a beat. Not turning Vic on wasn't a problem; he could hardly keep his hands off her. Actually, other than Vic's indifference to her current plight, she had no complaints about her marriage or her life. She lived a good life, yes, but she was still a very important step short of living happily ever after, the way she'd always dreamed of.

She finished the sandwich she'd made from last night's roast chicken and rinsed her plate in the sink. Then she refilled her glass, this time with filtered water instead of Sprite, and strolled back to the office in front of the house.

The ringing phone startled the quiet of the house. Norell picked up the receiver and heard Dana joyously announce, "It's official! I've got a tenant!"

Norell was immediately caught up in Dana's happiness. "Dana, that's wonderful! Who?"

"Cécile's sister, Micheline. She's moved up here from West Palm. She just got a job, and she's moving in Saturday. It won't be long-term—she says eventually she'll want to rent an apartment—but at least I can count on her for the next month. I offered her a discount if she paid for the entire month up front, and she took it. She gave me four hundred and fifty dollars."

"But Saturday isn't the beginning of the month, Dana."

"For rent purposes we agreed that a month would be thirty days from the day she moves in."

"Wow. First the loan, now the tenant. It looks like things are really falling into place for you." Happy as she was for Dana, Norell couldn't help feeling a little left out. Dana had a renter for her spare room, and Cécile's sister, whom Norell had not met, had a new job. When would *her* luck change, damn it?

Dana continued in the bubbly manner that should have been infectious but couldn't penetrate Norell's blues. "I'm just thrilled. I was hoping you and Cécile could come over Friday and discuss our plan of action."

"Sure."

"Good. I know it's time for you to get back to work, and I've got to pick up my loan check and sign the papers. I'll be in touch."

Dana turned up the volume of the Marilyn Scott CD and sang along as she drove to the bank. Everything was truly going to be all right now. Cutting her hand had seemed like a kiss of death at the time, but being unable to work had forced her to formulate a plan and take action instead of standing by idly, watching her world disintegrate.

A white Eclipse passed her in the opposite direction, reminding Dana that she had three angels looking out for her: Her mother, her sister, and now Kenny.

"I'm here to pick up my loan check," Dana informed the receptionist, realizing too late that Gil hadn't told her who to ask for. "I guess I need to see someone in the loan department."

"What's your name, Miss?"

"Dana Covington."

"Oh, yes. Mr. Albacete asked to see you when you came in. Just a moment, please." The receptionist discreetly got Gil on the line and nodded in affirmation. "You can go right back. Do you remember where his office is?"

"Yes, I do. Thank you."

Gil looked up when she tapped on his open office door. He broke into a broad grin. "Congratulations, Miss Business Owner."

"Oh, thank you. I appreciate everything you've done for me, Gil." By now he had risen and walked around his desk to meet her, and she shook his hand. "In addition to making a recommendation to the loan officer, I've got a hunch you rushed it through."

"May first will be here before you know it," he said with a smile.

Dana glanced at his desk. "Am I signing the papers here in your office?"

"No. Actually, you'll sign the papers and get the check from the loan department upstairs. I asked reception to send you to me to see if you would allow me to take you for a celebration lunch." His stomach growled a perfect punctuation. "Excuse me," he said sheepishly. "It is about that time, you know."

"Yes, I know. And I'd love to have lunch. Of course, I don't know how long it'll take me to sign the papers upstairs. The loan officer assigned to my paperwork might have gone out to lunch himself."

"That won't be a problem. The officers always sign the papers ahead of time. If yours is at lunch, another will explain them to you and tell you where to sign. When dealing with small loans like yours, we can be a little less rigid." He guided her the few steps to the door. "When you're done, just let the receptionist know, and I'll be right out."

They went to Copeland's, where they ordered po'boy sandwiches, shrimp for Dana and catfish for Gil.

"So you're calling yourselves CDN Transcription," he remarked. "Let me guess—the initials of you and your partners?"

"Yes. We started with DNC, in the order of which we came aboard. But we decided it sounded too much like a gynecological procedure, so we played around until we found something that sounded nicer."

"Have you taken steps to formally organize?"

"Oh, yes. We've got a business license, a logo, business cards, invoice forms, stationery, and a bank account." Dana gasped. That last part just slipped out.

"Ah-hah! And you didn't open your business account with us." Gil nodded knowingly.

She shrugged. "Actually, one of my partners found a bank that offers very favorable terms to small businesses like ours." Then she giggled. "Your bank already has just about every cent I have in the world. You don't have to have it all, do you?"

"No, I guess not. It's the businessman in me. It sounds like CDN is going to have impressive receivables, and naturally I'd like them to be deposited at my bank."

"I guess I should have come to you first," Dana said apologetically.

"No big deal. Are you planning to incorporate?"

"Yes, the paperwork has been initiated. We've also registered our company name with the State of Florida, so we're good for the time being."

"It sounds like you ladies really have it together." He smiled at her across the table. "How's your sandwich?"

"Oh, it's wonderful. I almost feel like I'm in New Orleans."

"New Orleans is one of my favorite cities. I wouldn't want to live there, not even before the hurricane, but I try to get there at least every other year. Incidentally, I was going to ask if you would consider letting Brittany come with Vanessa and me this summer. Vanessa will enjoy it much better if she has a friend along her own age."

"Oh, I don't know," Dana said. "The French Quarter can be a little racy for kids their age, don't you think?"

"Absolutely," he agreed. "Which is why I never stay too close to Bourbon Street. But I promise you I'd get a suite in a good-quality hotel, someplace where they'd be perfectly safe if I chose to go out on my own for a few hours. And I'm driving, so there would be no plane fare involved," he added.

Dana wiped her mouth with a corner of the napkin. "In that case, I guess it'll be okay."

He leaned in a little closer, suggesting he was about to say something from the heart. "You know, Dana, Vanessa really gets a lot of comfort from her girlfriends since Irene and I broke up, and of course Brittany is her closest friend."

"I can probably say the same about Vanessa since Kenny's accident. I think they're both very fortunate to have each other to help them through their respective hard times."

"I agree." Gil pushed his plate toward the edge of the table. "Hey, how about sharing an order of bananas Foster?"

Dana enjoyed the dessert. She rarely imbibed and couldn't identify which liquor flavored the sauce, but she liked it, whatever it was. When the waiter placed a single bill near Gil's end of the table she reached for her wallet. "I'll pay half."

"Put your wallet away. I invited you, remember?"

The outside parking lot was full, and they had parked near but not next to each other. Standing behind her cream-colored Camry, Dana fished through her purse for her keys. "That was fun, Gil. Thanks to you, I really feel like the sky's the limit, that anything's possible." She held out her hand, and he took it, but instead of shaking it, he moved in for a friendly hug that somehow seemed much more appropriate. Dana allowed herself to close her eyes for just a few seconds while inhaling the pleasing blend of his cologne and his male scent. For a fleeting moment, she wished she had put on a little bit of fragrance herself. She knew she didn't smell unpleasant, but it would have been nice to give off something a little more tantalizing than Lever soap.

Not that it mattered, of course. Gil Albacete was just a friend.

Chapter 7

Cécile rolled her eyes at her computer screen. CDN had begun the process of recruiting transcription contractors, and she wasn't impressed with what she saw. If these applicants represented the quality of workers available, they'd never find good help.

She stuffed some gummi bears in her mouth, then impulsively picked up the phone and dialed Norell. The strain in their friendship last year had healed with Dana's tragedy as they joined forces to help their friend. Had they still been bickering, becoming business partners would have been out of the question.

Still, Cécile tried not to bring up her family around Norell, whom she knew was going through a difficult time with fertility problems. Cécile felt Norell would make a great mother and hoped it would happen for her. Concentrating on CDN was probably just what she needed to take her mind off of her anxiety about not conceiving. Sometimes that's all it took. She'd probably be pregnant in no time.

"Hey," she said when Norell answered the phone. "Are you having any better luck than I am?"

"Either these people are just out of school or they don't believe in proofreading," Norell replied. "Neither one is a trait we want."

"Do you suppose Dana made the test too hard, using all those sound-alike words?"

"I don't think so. We want to make sure they can think, if not when they type, then at least when they read it over. I've looked at a dozen tests and only have two that are perfect, although a couple were borderline."

"I'm about the same. We'll have to discuss this at Dana's tomorrow."

"Speaking of which," Norell said, "since we've been having our staff meetings at Dana's, and since that's where we'll meet with new hires for orientation, how do you feel about compensating her a little extra for providing CDN's headquarters? We both know she can use all the help she can get."

"I think that's a great idea, Norell. We can refer to it as rent, so she won't feel like we're treating her like a charity case. She's very proud, you know."

"I know."

Cécile had rejected yet another applicant when she heard shouting from the girls' room. Wearily she pushed back from her desk. Michael and the boys had gone to the Y to play basketball. Until now she'd managed to get a reasonable amount of work done.

She rapped on the open door of the small, crowded bedroom. "All right, what's the problem?"

"Mama, Monet won't move her clothes out of my drawer," Gaby said. Seven years old and the middle of Cécile's three girls, she would never get lost in a shuffle. From the time she formed her first words, Gaby had always spoken out.

"That's right, Mama," Josie, the oldest at ten, quickly added.

"But it's not fair. I need more drawer space. Their stuff is taking up the whole closet," Monet said in a pleading voice.

Cécile quickly sensed a potential blowup. Monet's cross-armed stance suggested she wouldn't be backing down. Cécile guessed she was maybe two remarks away from reminding the others that this had been *her* room before they all moved in with her. She had to prevent that from happening and forming a rift that would take months to heal.

"Listen to me, girls," she said. "I know you guys are squeezed in like ten pounds of baloney in a nine-pound bag, but until we can do something about it, you do have to share this room."

"When are you and Michael going to get us a bigger house?" Josie asked.

"When the time is right," Cécile said in a firm tone that cautioned against further questioning. "Now, this is what I want you to do." She did a quick inspection of each drawer of the lone double dresser. "There's a lot of junk in here. Tomorrow I'll get each one of you a big plastic drawer. You can each have one to put all this stuff in. That'll free up a lot of room." She turned at the flash of headlights through the partially open blinds. A red VW bug pulled up along the curb.

"Mama, it's Auntie Michie," Gaby said excitedly.

"Wait a second." But all four girls had already taken off for the front door. She called after them sternly. "Josette Belarge, don't you dare open that door until I get there!" In a series of smooth movements, Cécile turned the hanging bar to close the blinds, then pulled the lined curtains together so that the strong Florida morning sunlight wouldn't wake the children prematurely.

They all stood waiting for her when she stepped into the living room.

"Mama, can we open the door now?" Gaby asked.

"We can see it's Auntie Michie through the window," Josie added.

"All right, go ahead." Cécile stood back while Micheline greeted all four girls with hugs and lifted the youngest, Eleith. Cécile was glad she didn't leave Monet out. Her stepdaughter's round face beamed as her new auntie pinched her cheek and told her how pretty she was. But then again, if there was one thing Micheline knew how to do, it was to be charming.

Micheline walked over to Cécile, still carrying four-year-old Eleith, who gazed at her aunt with awe. "Hi, Sis!" she said, pressing her cheek against Cécile's and kissing the air.

"Hey. What brings you over this way?"

"I had dinner with some people at that Cuban restaurant near here. It turned out to be a bust, so I made an excuse and got out of there. I figured I'd stop in and say hello before I went back to my hotel."

"You all ready to move?"

"All set. I'm flying to West Palm tomorrow afternoon. I've got a van reserved to drive back. Daddy's going to help me load a few things. I'll be back in Jacksonville early Saturday afternoon. Do you think Michael and the boys can help me get my stuff up the stairs at Dana's? It'll only take about half an hour."

"I'm sure they can." Cécile looked at her sister thoughtfully. "Michie . . . I hope you're going to be a responsible tenant. Dana is counting on it."

Micheline bent and put Eleith down. Josie, Monet, and Gaby hovered nearby. "Hey kids, why don't you go back to what you were doing, and I'll be in to see you in a minute, okay?" She waited a moment while the children departed, then turned back to Cécile. "Don't worry," she said coldly. "I'm not going to embarrass you."

"I'm not so much worried about being embarrassed as I am about Dana's finances getting messed up because Jones New York is having a sale."

Micheline met Cécile's cool stare. "I told Mama not to tell you about that."

"She was worried you'd be evicted."

"That was a long time ago. I'm expecting a large bonus very soon. I can go on a shopping spree and still pay my rent."

Something about the smug way Micheline raised her chin made Cécile suspicious about the origin of the bonus she bragged about. It came to her suddenly. "That was a lie about being laid off, wasn't it?"

"No, it wasn't. I did get laid off. I just worked out a more favorable separation package than your average ex-employee."

"I can just imagine," Cécile remarked, her voice dry as hay.

Micheline's smile faded. She spun around gracefully and walked off in the direction of the girls' room.

Cécile decided to go back to work. She was engrossed in another applicant's test when she heard approaching footsteps behind her.

"There you are," Micheline said cheerily. She glanced around at the work area and the family photos on the wall. "Isn't this cute."

Cécile could tell she didn't mean it and was just being facetious. Her jaw grew rigid. Only her promise to her mother and the nearby presence of her children made her keep her temper in check.

"Mama does her sewing here," Josie volunteered.

"And her tran . . . transcription, too," Monet added.

"Getting ready to go?" Cécile asked, hoping her bright tone covered how badly she wanted Micheline to leave.

"Yeah, time to head on back to the hotel."

"Auntie Michie, you never stay long when you come to see us," Gaby sulked.

"That's because I've got a lot going on. You guys know I love you. Besides, you're going to see me again on Saturday."

"I'll walk you out," Cécile offered.

But Micheline had picked up a framed photo. "Oh, how lovely!" she exclaimed.

Cécile smiled warmly at the studio portrait of Michael with his jacket-and-tie-clad sons, Jonathan and Damon, as well as Monet, wearing a beige flowered dress with a big lace collar. "That's the picture Michael had taken the day we met at the studio. Here's the one the girls and I had done that day." She handed Micheline the heavy ceramic frame containing one of the poses she had taken with Josie, Gaby, and Eleith, in the maroon velvet dresses she had just gotten out of layaway.

"Oh Cécile, you looked so different!"

Cécile stopped smiling. She knew Micheline meant she looked much better in the photograph, which was nearly three years old. She'd still been slim, her hair was freshly cut, and she wore lipstick and blush. Hearing Micheline's innocent exclamation bruised Cécile's ego, but there wasn't a damn thing she could say, because her sister was right. She'd let herself go, going months between haircuts and messing up her diet with those addictive gummi bears.

She became uncomfortably aware of the difference between her appearance and her sister's. Micheline's side-parted hair had been styled in a shoulder-length blunt cut that looked like it required little maintenance, her eyebrows had been professionally waxed, her nails were perfect ovals painted in a French manicure, and she wore carefully applied blush and rose-colored lipstick. The ring fingers of both her hands were adorned with rings, and she wore a delicate-looking gold-banded watch on her right wrist and a series of gold bangles on her left.

Cécile, on the other hand, wore her "work uniform" of T-shirt and sweatpants, which only made her more conscious of the twenty-five extra pounds she still carried. She wore simple gold ball earrings, the kind babies and very little girls wore when their ears were first pierced, and she had a plain Timex with a brown leather band. The only good thing that could be said about her nails was that no dirt lodged under them. She wore her curly jet-black hair short, but the flattering style she'd originally had it cut in had long since grown out into a shapeless mass. Seeing Micheline made her realize how badly she needed to get to the salon for a cut.

"I think that's so sweet that you two met when waiting to have your pictures taken," Micheline went on, not noticing Cécile's lack of reaction to her previous remark.

"Yes," Cécile said, brightening at the memory. "I had just left Louis maybe three months before. I wanted to get a portrait done of the girls and me while they were still small and so adorable, so I bought all of us those beautiful velvet dresses. The photographer was on schedule, so Michael and I didn't really get a chance to talk, other than telling each other how nice we looked. Michael told me afterward that he asked the receptionist to schedule him to see his kids' proofs at the same time I was coming in to see mine. He got there early so he'd be sure to see me. That was when we started to talk, and one thing led to another."

"It just goes to show, you can meet the man of your dreams anywhere."

Cécile looked at Micheline curiously. Had she imagined it, or had she caught a note of wistfulness in her sister's voice? She was closer to thirty than twenty. Had she begun to have urges to settle down?

Micheline carefully placed the photographs back on the top of Cécile's desk. "You've got a nice family, Sis."

Together they walked toward the front door. "I'm sure you'll have the same once you settle down," Cécile said. She felt generous, now that she sensed she had something Micheline wanted. That definitely beat out the dumpy feeling she'd had just minutes before.

"I'm sure I will, too. But I'm only twenty-seven. I've got plenty of time yet to get married. No man is going to saddle me with a bunch of kids. When it's time there'll be one child, so I can regain my figure right away with no hassle. No starvation diets or ruthless exercise regimens to get back into shape after the second, thank you."

"That's a myth, Michie. Every woman is different. Some women bounce right back into shape even if they have five or six, while others struggle to lose the weight they've gained after having just one. Look at me. I was fine with all three of mine. I didn't gain weight until after I married Michael."

"Well, that's in the future. I'm not ready for a husband and child yet."

"When will you be ready?"

Micheline smiled confidently. "The day I meet someone who will take care of me in style. And I've got a feeling I'll find him right here in Jacksonville."

Cécile returned her sister's smile. She wished Micheline's Mr. Right lots of luck, whoever he was.

Chapter 8

Norell went into the hospital on Wednesday. Vic brought her in, and she had a vague recollection of him watching her with concern etched on his face when she was wheeled out of the OR after a thorough exploration of her reproductive system.

Afterward her abdomen felt like someone had dropped a twenty-pound weight on it. She also had the added stress of having Vic hovering over her like an anxious old lady. "Why don't you go to work, honey?" she suggested. I'm so sleepy . . . There's no point in you sitting here listening to me snore. Even Doctor Patel won't be back with the results until the morning. I'm too tired to talk to him now anyway. Go on, Vic. I promise I'll be right here when you come back." She started to chuckle at her little joke, but the action caused movement in her abdominal area, and her face quickly contorted with pain.

Still, she managed to convince Vic that she was all right. He kissed her cheek and promised to be back by six. Norell closed her eyes and was asleep within minutes. She dreamed she was being wheeled into the delivery room, and later, that she was holding an infant. Her infant.

Her doctor showed up early the morning after her surgery. Even as he asked her how she felt, Norell could tell the news wasn't good. Dr. Patel—she always joked that name must be Hindi for "Smith" because it was so common—wasn't smiling.

"I'm sore as hell," she replied. "So," she continued in the brightest tone her discomfort and fear would allow, "what'd you see down there?"

"There was no evidence of the blockage we saw on the scan," Dr. Patel said. "You might have had a spasm at the time we did the testing. But I did see extensive scarring on your fallopian tubes, which I'm afraid will make conception highly unlikely." He paused to let his words sink in.

"Oh." Norell closed her eyes for a moment. "I guess the doctor who did my D&C six years ago scarred up my tubes. That has to be it. I've never had any infections or any other surgical procedures." She named her former gynecologist. "I'm sure you know him, or know of him. I thought he looked a little old to still be practicing. He's probably working to support a gambling problem. Or maybe he drinks."

Dr. Patel nervously chewed on his lower lip.

"Yes, yes, I know. You don't want to speak out against one of your colleagues," she said. "And it's not like I can prove he messed me up, anyway, not after all this time."

"I know it's disappointing, Norell, but it's not the end. There's always ZIFT."

He talked a little more about ZIFT, a variation of the in vitro fertilization process, where one of her newly fertilized eggs was inserted into fallopian tubes with the hope that it would follow nature's course and travel on its own to her uterus. She nodded. "Yes. I'll talk to my husband about it. I guess we'll go from there."

When the doctor left she lay still, the tears rolling down her cheeks.

Norell relayed Dr. Patel's news to Vic when he came in shortly afterward. He immediately sat on the edge of the bed and pulled her close. "I'm so sorry, baby," he said. "But don't throw in the towel just yet. There's still a chance. I'll let them test me, and if everything checks out we'll try that procedure the doctor suggested."

She shut her eyes tightly. What an immeasurable comfort to know at last that he was in her corner. For a while there it looked like she was in this on her own. But a couple of things niggled at her relentlessly, and she couldn't keep them to herself anymore. "Are you sure you want to do this, Vic?" she asked, pulling away so she could see his reaction. "You're not just saying it because you know how disappointed I am?"

"I'm sure. I know I haven't been very supportive. I was just being selfish. I know we talked about having kids before we got married, but when you didn't get pregnant I began to get used to the idea of having you all to myself, and I liked it. I'm sorry, Norell."

She sighed. "I'm glad you saw the light. But I'll be honest with you, I'm not sure if I want to go on with it myself."

Vic's surprise appeared genuine. "You're not? Why?"

"Because I'd so hoped I'd be able to get pregnant the natural way. But your showing no interest in my problem hurt almost as much as not getting pregnant month after month. You never said anything about getting tested until just now, although you've known about it for weeks."

Vic placed a hand on her thigh. "I'm sorry I hurt you, Norell."

"I know."

He looked at her thoughtfully. "You've got something else on your mind. Tell me."

"I'm thinking about how you've already invested in CDN for me. And I'm wondering what the price tag will be for this new thing Doctor Patel wants to try. I know we're comfortable, Vic, but it's an awful lot of output." She sighed. "I'd like to meet with Doctor Patel and find out more about both the chance of success and the cost. We probably should determine what we're going to do before you even go in for an exam. I'd hate for you to jack off in a cup if you don't have to," she said with a wan smile.

"Whatever you want, baby."

She lay her head back, her hand in Vic's. "Then that's what we'll do. In the meantime I've got CDN to keep me busy, so at least I won't be thinking about babies all the time. Not that that's an issue right now; this pain takes precedence over everything." She smiled weakly, then pressed the button of her analgesia dispenser and gave herself another dose of Demerol.

Norell went home the next day. She spent the next week mostly resting, with only minimal activity. Dana and Cécile came over to cheer her up and discuss a little business. The news was exciting. Dana had met with Patricia Fairfield about purchasing five of her clients to transfer to CDN on the fifteenth of the month. They discussed Pat's asking price and agreed to it. "Of course, this is contingent on the clients agreeing to have their accounts transferred," Dana cautioned. "They'll be paying the same amount they were before, but sometimes people are funny. I'll be prepared to meet with all the office managers next week to assure them about how qualified we are."

"How about the quality of the accounts?" Norell asked. "A lot of the girls are complaining that their pay has gone down because some of the dictators are so difficult to understand and require more time." At-home transcriptionists were traditionally paid on a production basis for work they actually completed, so they couldn't do their laundry or their grocery shopping while on the payroll. "How do we know Pat isn't giving us her worst accounts?"

"I'm familiar with the five we're buying now, and they aren't bad," Dana said. "A couple of English-as-a-second-language docs, a couple of mumble-mouthed Americans, but we'll have the people we got from Pat continue to work on them. They'd prefer to work on familiar accounts rather than something new."

"I think it's good that we're waiting an additional two weeks to start with Pat's clients," Cécile said. "It gives us time to take care of any bugs in the sports-medicine clinic and in Dana's clients. Besides, you never know. After Dana's hand and Norell's surgery, it might be my turn to have to go to the ER or into the hospital!"

The next weeks were filled with hiring staff, meeting with their computer consultant, and training. During that time Dana's hand completely healed, and Norell, too, was given medical clearance to return to work. Somehow it all got done, and CDN Transcription went live on May first, as planned.

To celebrate, Dana, Cécile, and Norell went out to dinner. Norell suggested they go to a restaurant in San Marco that had become popular with the African-American corporate crowd.

Dana hadn't known of this fact, and she looked around curiously at the patrons who had arrived while they were eating. "There's a lot of us here, aren't there?" she remarked. "You generally don't see that in this part of town. Is something special going on?"

"Oh, I think they have a deejay or something," Norell said innocently.

Dana's eyes narrowed suspiciously. "Oh? This social atmosphere wouldn't have anything to do with why you chose this particular restaurant, would it?"

"I'm not interested in dancing," Norell said, suddenly sounding weak. "I just had surgery three weeks ago, remember?"

Dana didn't point out that Norell had since gotten the green light from her physician to proceed with her normal activities.

"The food is awfully good here," Cécile said, her words a bit mumbled because she spoke through a mouthful of Mediterranean salad. "This is such a huge salad. I'll probably want to take a nap after I finish."

Dana was accustomed to Cécile's lustful eating habits, but she wondered if Cécile noticed that she looked heavier these days, like she'd gained back the fifteen pounds or so she'd lost and then some. Probably all those gummi bears she downed. "Are you all right, Cécile?" she asked, concern in her voice. "I've called you a couple of times in the last week or so, and you've been sleeping. What you said the other week about going to the hospital was supposed to be a joke. You haven't taken on too much, have you?"

"Oh, I'm all right. I just need to stop eating so much, that's all."

"Maybe you're pregnant," Norell said, laughing. They all remembered Cécile going in for a tubal ligation after she gave birth to her youngest, Eleith.

Dana and Cécile joined in laughing at the joke, and while Dana was glad to see Norell laughing about a pregnancy after receiving bad news about her own chances for conception, she still suspected her friends had an ulterior motive in selecting this particular restaurant on this particular night. She knew what it was, too. Norell and Cécile wanted her to meet a man.

"Listen, girls," she said. "I think it's sweet of you to think about me the way you do, like insisting that our company pay me two hundred dollars a month for providing an office headquarters and meeting space, but this is too much. I'm not interested in dating. I've got too much on my plate already." During the last few weeks spent preparing to launch CDN, Dana had begun working full-time as an at-home MT for a large nationwide service, through which she would receive health benefits. The cost of medical and dental insurance through her new employer would be less than half of the check she wrote each month for private insurance for herself and Brittany. She'd taken the final step in her financial plan. She felt rather proud of her accomplishments, or at least she did when she wasn't tired from her demanding schedule.

"We're not trying to get you to date, Dana," Norell said. "That would be awfully frivolous of us. It's not like we don't have problems of our own, is it, Cécile?"

"Absolutely."

Dana didn't doubt it, but she decided to let the matter drop. She agreed with Cécile; the food here was tasty. She cut off a piece of crab-stuffed flounder and raised it to her mouth.

They were almost finished eating when Cécile exclaimed, "Look, there's my sister! Yoo-hoo, Michie!"

Micheline turned at the sound of her name, her hair bouncing with the movement of her head. She immediately headed toward their table. "Hi, Sis," she said, bending gracefully to kiss the air near her sister's cheek. "Hello, Dana," she said after she straightened, then smiled at Norell.

"I'm Norell. It's nice to meet you. I've heard about you from both Cécile and Dana."

"Nice to meet you, too. Are you here for Wild Wednesday?"

All three women laughed. "No, we're just having dinner," Cécile answered. "Our company officially began today. The doctors are dictating, the MTs are transcribing, and everything is working fine. We felt we deserved a reward, so here we are. We're just about finished, but why don't you join us?"

Micheline pulled out the fourth chair at the table and sat down. "I don't get it," she said. "If your company is up and running, why aren't you girls at home typing?"

Norell's attempt at a chuckle came out sounding more like a grunt. "Our contractors do the transcribing," she replied dryly. "As the owners, we do mostly proofreading and QA. The idea is to have a staff do most of the everyday work."

"And for us to get paid," Cécile added. "Dana and I only work part time for CDN, even though we're full partners."

"Oh, I see," Micheline said flippantly. Anyone could tell she didn't really care. "Hey, I hope you guys plan to stick around a bit after dinner. You've got a great table, close to the action."

Norell spoke up before Dana could reply. "I guess it won't hurt to see what goes on. Maybe for an hour or so."

"I have to pick up Brittany," Dana protested.

"She's fine at my house, and she's certainly no trouble for Michael," Cécile said. "With six kids, what's one more?"

"But it's a school night."

"It's seven o'clock, Dana. Nobody's talking about staying out all night."

Micheline looked on with amusement. "So what's it going to be?"

"Oh, all right," Dana said. "I'll stay an hour." Anything to get that smirk off Micheline's face. She'd had little contact with her tenant, but she'd just seen a side of her she didn't particularly care for.

Dana quickly caught on to the idea of Wild Wednesday. Its name suggested a rowdy crowd in loose-fitting jeans and gym shoes, but these were mature folks, well dressed. Everywhere she looked there were men wearing silk ties, crisply starched shirts, gold tie clips, and glossy wing tips, even occasional cuff links; and for women, traditional suits, smart separates, tasteful jewelry, and pumps. Slacks on females were nonexistent. Dana suspected that patrons dressed this way even if they had professions requiring uniforms, like police officers or nurses. It might have been years since she'd been single, but some things never changed. She imagined that among the first words of conversation between new acquaintances were, "What do you do?"

The music played at a comfortably loud volume. Slowly the dance floor filled. Much of the crowd gathered around the rectangular bar or in the booths lining the wall behind it. The waitress removed their dinner plates and glasses and took their drink orders: wine for Dana and Cécile, a sea breeze for Norell. Micheline ordered something Dana had never heard of, a green-apple martini.

Eventually all the women were asked to dance, but Cécile declined. "I'll watch your purses if you want to leave them," she offered.

"Are you all right?" Dana asked.

"Yes, I just don't feel like dancing." Cécile added a smile for reassurance, but a terrible suspicion had just occurred to her. She'd just eaten a typically oversized restaurant salad, but she was still hungry. She always seemed to be hungry lately, and if she wasn't hungry she was sleepy. If that wasn't enough, Micheline had leaned over and quietly asked if she'd been gaining weight, giving her thigh a pat.

Cécile knew by the snug fit of her clothes that she'd picked up the pounds she'd struggled so hard to lose over the last year. She'd had a hard time finding something to wear tonight that wasn't too tight. She settled on a dress she'd made herself a few years back, a butterscotch-and-black-striped coatdress with a white collar. It was roomy enough to not squeeze her, and its vertical stripes made her look both thinner and taller.

Cécile had dismissed her weight gain as a temporary phase that would pass, but when Michie slapped her heavy thigh and made that comment, somehow it all came together. Never feeling full, no matter how much she ate, the weight gain, the fatigue.

She was pregnant. There could be no other explanation. Just her luck to be the one in two hundred and fifty women for whom tubal ligations ultimately failed. Periods had never been a gauge for her; she'd continued them throughout her pregnancies with Josie, Gaby, and Eleith. When she discussed it with her mother, Catherine said the same had been true for her.

Just thinking about it made Cécile feel ill. Her house was already so overcrowded. Where would they put another baby?

Dana left the ladies' room feeling refreshed and confident, courtesy of a paper towel to wipe the perspiration from her face, a fresh coat of lipstick, and a quick comb-through of her hair. Now she was very glad she'd stayed. She hadn't had this much fun in years.

She'd gotten midway past the bar on her way back to the table when a hand suddenly clamped her midarm. She froze in her tracks at the unexpected action, then sought out the face that went with the arm. She could tell from the large size of the hand as well as the firm grip that it belonged to a male.

"I startled you; I'm sorry."

Something struck her as familiar about the dark-skinned man speaking, but Dana couldn't remember where they had met.

"You're Mrs. Covington, aren't you?" he asked.

His reference to her as Mrs. Covington set off immediate recognition in Dana's mind, probably because there were so few people who called her that. Some type of professional association. Then it came to her. "You're . . ." she bit her lower lip when she realized she couldn't remember his name, finally settling for, "You're the one who bought my husband's car."

He laughed at her attempt to conceal her lapse in memory. "Sean Sizemore."

"Of course, now I remember. How are you? And how's the car?" Remembering the rather forceful way he had grabbed her arm, she hoped he wasn't going to tell her it didn't run right. Damn it, she probably shouldn't have asked.

But Sean merely grinned and said, "It's running great. It's nice to see you. I don't think I've ever seen you here before."

"Spoken like a true regular."

"Well, it's not like I've got a bar stool named after me or any-thing." They laughed. "Actually, I've been in pretty regularly since my wife and I separated two months ago," he added.

"Oh, I'm sorry to hear that." Dana was no marriage counselor, but if anyone were to ask her for advice, she would recommend imagining that their partner had died, rather than still around and just getting on their reserve nerves. If any love remained, that should help both parties recover it in a hurry. But she could hardly say that to Sean. He was merely making a statement, and she had no call to make like Dr. Phil.

"Thanks, but actually it'd been coming for a long time. By the time I bought your car I knew it was just a matter of time."

She nodded. No doubt he'd bought the two-seater Eclipse in an-ticipation of the single life. "I guess that's just how it goes some-times."

"Can I get you a drink, Dana?"

She was caught off guard, both by his offer and by his sudden use of her first name, although there really was no need for him to con-tinue to address her formally. "Oh . . . no, thanks. I have one at the table."

"You're not leaving anytime soon, are you?"

"Probably within an hour. I'm enjoying myself, but I don't want my daughter up past her bedtime." She laughed. "It was good to see you again, Sean."

"You'll see me again before you leave." He reached out and gave her hand a squeeze, just for a second. Dana smiled a farewell and moved on.

She couldn't remember the last time she felt so free and un-encumbered. The music was wonderful—classics from the late seven-ties and early eighties intermixed with recent cuts. Norell and Cécile hadn't had such a bad idea after all. Hell, she might just come back next week and do it again.

Norell gasped as the music blended into a new song. She gestured to her partner. "I'm worn out," she said, although she felt certain he couldn't hear her words over the music.

He took her elbow and guided her off of the dance floor. "How about you and me talking over a drink?" he asked.

She held up her left hand and pointed to her prominent engage-ment and wedding rings. "Sorry. I'm just doing a little dancing, that's all." Norell enjoyed the disappointment on her partner's face. It did her ego good to know she could still turn heads. This man was tall, good looking, and young, probably a good six or seven years her junior.

Heaven knew she deserved some comfort after receiving the bad news that her dream of being a mother probably would not come true. She and Vic had met with Dr. Patel, and she didn't like the low odds he gave them of successfully conceiving a baby, especially when paired with the high cost. She'd heard horror stories of people who began expensive fertility treatments which weren't covered by health insurance, confident that they would be successful on the first try, only to find themselves facing financial ruin after going through attempt after attempt. She likened it to a gambler at a slot machine, thinking the next pull of the lever would be the big payoff. Vic made good money, but his income fluctuated. An entire week could go by with him posting only a thousand-dollar bond. Other weeks he could earn twenty thousand or more. He'd already done so much for her; she simply couldn't ask for more. Norell knew enough about life to know that everyone didn't get a happy ending. And aside from not having a baby, her life wasn't bad at all.

She'd met Vic after the worst time of her life, shortly after her mother died from an inoperable brain tumor. Watching her mother's deterioration was like déjà vu for Norell. Just nine years before, her father had been diagnosed with pancreatic cancer. Like her mother years later, he waited until his discomfort became unbearable before consulting a physician, but by then the disease was advanced. Diagnosed just before the Fourth of July, he died the day after Labor Day. His grieving family found a small amount of solace in the relative brevity of his discomfort.

Unfortunately, her mother was not as lucky. The disease ravaged her for nearly a year, spreading through her body. It was a cruel and lingering death, with Gloria Jamison unable to swallow food in her last days. Norell took comfort from her mother's meeting death at home in her own bed, tended to by home-hospice personnel, rather than at a hospital. By this time her brother Eric had joined the service and was on a ship somewhere in the Mediterranean. He flew in for the funeral, but soon she was on her own once more.

Norell had begun working from home when her mother was diagnosed so she could care for her, and she returned to work in the office after her mother's death. Months of being confined to home had left her hungry for the rapport of colleagues. This time around, however, her coworkers did not include her two closest allies, for Dana had left Precise to launch her own transcription service and Cécile had joined the work-at-home program because she'd left her cheating husband and couldn't afford day care for her three daughters.

Norell also needed to have her medical insurance reinstated, which would occur after sixty days. Later, she would joke that her appendix apparently didn't know she still had four weeks to go. The bill was delivered within five days of her arrival home. The cost of a forty-eight-hour hospital stay came to seventy-three hundred dollars, a large chunk of which was the surgeon's fee. That wasn't bad pay, considering it took maybe twenty minutes to remove an appendix.

Norell managed to keep her hospital account out of collections, but times were tough. She'd foolishly gone on a spending spree when the reality of being alone in the world set in, and in the process had spent nearly all of her share of her mother's meager estate, money that could have otherwise gone toward her hospital bill.

That was her station in life when she met and fell in love with Vic. He paid the balance of her hospital bill right after they were married. Suddenly she had no worries, and everything to look forward to. Or so she thought.

Norell's shoulders stiffened. Dealing with her huge disappointment always made her tense. But she knew how to relax.

She gestured for the waitress and ordered another sea breeze.

Dana danced with Sean twice over the next forty-five minutes, and when she and her friends prepared to leave he offered to see them to their cars, starting with Norell, who walked rather slowly.

"Do you think she'll be all right?" he asked as Norell plopped into the driver's seat.

"Oh, sure. She's just walking slow because of her high heels," Dana said. "Her feet must be killing her after all that dancing."

When they reached her Camry she got behind the wheel and rolled down the window to say good-bye when Sean suddenly leaned over and said, "Let's have dinner Saturday."

Chapter 9

Dana undressed and slipped into a V-neck nylon-and-lace nightgown, then lay across her bed, deep in thought.

Kenny had been dead, and she alone, for nearly a year. She was a healthy woman in the earliest years of middle age. Surely it was natural for her to start thinking about men. Everything reminded her of sex. Even one of her clients, a man notorious for getting on the phone with no idea of what he would say, sounded like he was in the throes of something quite exciting with all those "Uh . . . uh . . . uh" grunting noises he made while groping for his next words. And just last week she'd made a telling error, typing "orgasm" in a patient's lab results when the doctor actually said "organism." A Freudian slip if she'd ever heard one.

She felt comfortable with her wish to have a man in her life, but she worried about everyone else's reaction. How Brittany would feel, what her neighbors would say if they saw a strange man coming to her house, and even—and this was *really* dumb—how Kenny would react if he were alive, like she'd really be considering dating some man if her husband was with her. But he wasn't, of course, and she'd spent nearly a year trying to support Brittany alone and felt she deserved a little attention. It wasn't like she was looking for some man to worship her, but a little appreciation of her attributes would be nice.

She decided she needed to talk it out with someone. Cécile was home, of course—Dana had dropped her off when she picked up Brittany—but she was probably busy making sure her brood was prepared for the next day and that they got to bed. Besides, from the way Cécile had yawned all the way home, she would probably make a beeline for her own bed after taking care of her family. Better to confide in Norell.

Dana glanced at her watch. She should probably wait a few more minutes to give Norell time to get home.

From the way Norell answered the phone, stretching a simple "Hello" into three syllables, Dana could tell she had a buzz.

"Someone's feeling no pain," she said knowingly.

"I just got in," Norell said. "It took longer than usual because I stayed at thirty miles an hour all the way. Just trying to be cautious. It would have been terribly ironic if Vic had to bail his own wife out of jail."

Dana suddenly felt ashamed for not paying closer attention to her friend's condition. Sean had implied Norell might be impaired when they left the restaurant, but she'd honestly thought Norell's halting, uneven steps were nothing more than a case of three-inch heels on tired feet. Her friend didn't drink excessively any more, not since she'd married Vic. "Norell, how many sea breezes did you have?"

"Just three. Technically, four. The last one was a double."

"Well, the next time we go out to celebrate I'm driving you home. I had no idea you'd had that much."

"Oh, I'm all right. I won't even have a headache tomorrow. I'm about to go in and jump Vic's bones."

A twinge of envy immediately snaked its way through Dana's gut. "Thanks for sharing," she said in a droll tone. "But do you have just a few minutes to give me some advice?"

"Sure. What's up?"

Dana told Norell about Sean and his invitation. She needed the encouragement she knew Norell would give her.

"Wait a minute. This guy bought Kenny's car?"

"Yes. That's how I met him."

"And he's still driving it, I presume."

Dana shrugged. "I guess."

"Doesn't that make you uncomfortable, the thought of riding alongside a strange man in the same car that you rode in alongside your husband?"

"Oh. I hadn't thought of that. It'll be a little weird, I guess, but that's no reason not to go out with him. A lot of people drive white Eclipses."

"It's not just *a* white Eclipse, Dana, it's *the* white Eclipse. The one that used to be parked in your driveway. The one Kenny drove."

Dana found herself regretting having made this call. "I don't think it's that big a deal, Norell."

"If that's what you think. But you have to consider Brittany's feelings."

"She won't see it," Dana said quickly.

"She'll stay at her friend's house?"

"No, I think this is the weekend Vanessa spends with her father. I'll have to get my neighbor's daughter to babysit. I'll send them to a show or something."

"How will they get there?" Norell asked. "That girl isn't old enough to drive, is she?"

Dana's shoulders slumped. Norell was firing off questions like the police grilling a murder suspect, and even though it was getting on her nerves, she knew Norell had her best interests at heart. And wasn't that why she'd called in the first place, to get Norell's take on the situation? She forced herself to listen, but she couldn't help recalling the good old days when Norell or Cécile would be the ones listening to the advice *she* gave.

"Even if the babysitter is old enough to drive," Norell continued, "her parents probably won't allow her to drive Brittany anywhere. It's too big a responsibility for a kid her age. If anything should happen while she has Brittany in the car it'll set the stage for suits and countersuits."

"Tina is sixteen, but I suppose you're right. Her duties as babysitter shouldn't involve anything else but staying with Brittany here in the house." She sighed. "And since I can't arrange for an off-premises babysitter, I'll have to call Sean and cancel."

"Wait a minute. Don't be so damn drastic. Brittany can spend the night here with us. Vic's daughters are coming this weekend. They're a little older than Brittany, but they'll get along fine. It's not like they've never met."

"Are you sure, Norell?"

"What's one more kid around to do my bidding, peel me a grape, and paint my toenails?" She giggled. "Seriously, though, I think going out with this guy will be good for you, Dana. Although I certainly wish he drove a different vehicle—"

"So you said," Dana interrupted. She had to admit she didn't like thinking about Sean driving Kenny's old car.

"And I'm certainly surprised by this development, Miss I'm-Not-Ready-to-Date-Right-Now," Norell concluded. "What did Cécile say?"

"I didn't mention it to her. I don't think Cécile is feeling well these days. She must have yawned five times in the ten minutes it took to get to her house."

"She's been doing a lot of extra work for CDN, just like you and me. But she's got more to do at home than we do, like cooking for eight people every night. She's probably just tired. Now that the preliminary work is done and we're rolling, she'll be fine."

"I hope so." Dana didn't believe Norell's attempt at reassurance. Norell had never shown much respect for Cécile's culinary efforts, saying that all she did was throw a double portion of meat or poultry into two casserole dishes, add some vegetables and some liquid, stick it in the oven for an hour and call it dinner. Norell, who ate a diet heavy with beef and rich sauces, sardonically likened Cécile's well-balanced, low-fat meals to eating in a household where someone had recently suffered a stroke. When Dana praised the paella Cécile served last year when she and Michael hosted dinner for them and their spouses, Norell remained unimpressed, pointing out that this, too, was essentially a one-dish meal.

Norell simply didn't share her worry about Cécile.

The moment Dana's car was out of sight of her home, Cécile got behind the wheel of her Windstar and drove to Kmart, the nearest store still open where she could purchase a pregnancy test kit. In her heart she already knew what the result would be, but having proof would make it real.

She returned to a quiet house. The girls were all in bed. The boys, whose middle-school classes didn't begin until after nine, quietly watched television in their room, and Michael was engrossed in an episode of *CSI,* so she had plenty of time to think in the privacy of the master bathroom.

It occurred to her that something good might come out of all of this. Michael had resisted getting a larger house for so long, but once he learned about the new baby, he'd be forced to take action. Even he would have to concede that a family of nine could not continue living like this. Not only would she get to have a baby with the man she loved, but she'd get a new house out of it as well.

After she got out of the shower and dried herself off, she retrieved the test kit from the vanity cabinet beneath the sink. As she expected, the window of the stick had turned pink.

She emerged from the bathroom just as Michael was pulling off his clothes. At thirty-nine, he hardly had a movie-star body—Cécile could definitely pinch more than an inch from his middle—but he looked good to her nonetheless. Knowing that he'd gotten a little flabby made her feel more comfortable about her own weight gain.

"You ready to turn in?" he asked.

"I have to tell you something first."

His eyes widened curiously. "True-confession time, huh?"

Cécile sat cross legged on the bed, her satiny nightgown covering her legs. "I'm sure you've noticed I've put on some weight lately."

"That's no big deal. You don't hear me complaining, do you? You look good to me, Cécile."

"Thanks. I'm glad you feel that way, because if anything I'll be gaining more weight before I lose any."

Michael frowned. "I don't get it. You planning an eating binge or something?"

"No. I'm pregnant."

"You *can't* be pregnant, not after getting your tubes tied."

"They don't always take, at least not permanently. I'm afraid mine didn't."

His eyes narrowed. "So you're serious. We're going to have another baby."

"Yes, Michael, it's true. I know seven kids is a lot . . ."

"People are going to think we're trying to populate the world."

Cécile tensed at the sarcasm in his voice. He seemed annoyed at the prospect of another child. She hadn't counted on that reaction. She'd thought he'd be as happy as she was.

Maybe he needed some time to realize what a blessing a new baby was. After all, her own first reaction just a few hours ago had been dread and worry.

"Michael," she began, "I know it won't be easy, raising so many children, but we do live pretty comfortably. And if it's a girl, she can wear all of Eleith's clothes. We should be able to manage just fine. Of course, we'll have to get a larger house."

"I was waiting for that," he said coldly. "What'd you do, Cécile, jiggle your tubes loose to force my hand?"

Shocked, she drew in her breath. "What a terrible thing to say! Of course I didn't get pregnant deliberately. This was purely an accident of nature. And I don't understand why you're so dead set against getting a bigger house. The girls are cramped something terrible. If we had four bedrooms, Josie and Monet could share one, and Gaby and

Eleith could share the other. The baby can stay with Gaby and Eleith."

"Why not just get a house with five bedrooms? That way the baby can have its own damn room. Just tell me this, Cécile. Where's all this money coming from? Have you seen the prices of homes lately? Are you forgetting that we just spent eight grand so you could go into business? Who knows how long it'll be until you see any returns?"

She jerked, startled by his about-face regarding CDN. How convenient for him to suddenly forget how sure he'd been that they would recoup their investment within a year. "Come on, Michael. We should be able to get a good price for this place. It's appreciated well beyond what you paid for it. There should be enough equity in it to make a tidy profit."

"Sure, there'll be a profit. But not enough to make up the difference in the mortgage payment over thirty years."

God, he was cheap. "So what do we do? Just stay here? All nine of us?"

"See if you can find a place big enough for one-fifty. I won't go higher." Michael laid back and pulled the covers over him, his back to her, making the silent statement that he was through.

Cécile reached for the remote control and snapped off the television, then laid down and punched her pillows. How the hell was she supposed to find a reasonably large four-bedroom house for less than one hundred and fifty thousand dollars? Five or ten years ago she could have, but not now. Michael had set an impossible goal, and he was prepared to stay right here when she couldn't satisfy his wishes. Tears sprang to her eyes. It wasn't fair. All Michael saw was a well-organized home. He didn't realize how hard she had to work to make it so. She'd done her job too well.

She had another reason to be upset. His accusation about her pregnancy really stung. She knew that plenty of women deliberately stopped birth control, thinking a baby could salvage failing marriages or hold on to a man who was about to bolt, but she wasn't one of them. She couldn't help it if she got pregnant so easily. The only baby she'd actually been happy about initially was her eldest, Josie. After her relationship with Louis began to deteriorate, she'd been disappointed to learn she was carrying Gaby, and devastated later when she got pregnant with Eleith.

But she loved them all, just as she'd love this new baby.

Chapter 10

Dana wrapped up her workweek Friday afternoon, then looked in her closet to see what she might be able to wear for her date tomorrow with Sean. She knew they were going to dinner, but she wished she knew where. She didn't want to dress for someplace nice, like the Hilltop or River City Brewing, if they were going to a more casual setting, like The Outback or Clark's Fish Camp.

She ultimately decided on an ankle-grazing maroon paisley skirt. She could pair it with a casual top, and flats or low-heeled mules, and be dressed appropriately for any restaurant.

After dinner she spent a few hours in her office proofreading reports for CDN. There was enough work on the system for her to transcribe if she wanted to, but she felt too jumpy and nervous to attempt it. As she read she used extra care, not wanting any errors to slip by. She could hear Brittany talking and laughing on the phone. Her daughter sounded so happy. Dana wondered how her news would affect Brittany's mood. She hadn't told her yet about her date, and she intended to put it off as long as she could.

She turned at the sound of Brittany's knock. "Hi!" she said, swiveling her chair so that it faced the doorway.

"Hi, Mom. Can I go skating tomorrow?"

"Where and who with?"

"At the rink in Mandarin with Nikki and Shanequa. Shanequa's mother is gonna pick us up and bring us back."

"In the afternoon?"

Brittany made a face. "With all those little kids? Nah. They have a teen session from eight to midnight. But Shanequa's mother is going to pick us up at ten-thirty. She says that's late enough for us to be out."

"I agree with her. Technically, you're not even teenagers yet."

"I can go, then?"

"Uh, no."

"Why not, Mom?"

Dana had been dreading this moment. She'd hoped to put it off until tomorrow afternoon. "Because I've arranged for you to stay over at Norell's tomorrow night. I made some plans to go out, and you can't stay at home alone."

"But why can't you get Tina to stay here? That way I can still go skating, and if you're not here yet when I get home she'll be here."

"Because Tina's mother won't want her to stay here alone at night. She's a babysitter, not a housesitter."

"Okay, so I won't go skating. I'll just stay home with Tina. It'll be better than going out to Miss Norell's. What would I do there?"

"No, Brittany."

"Why not?"

Dana sighed. "Because . . . Brittany . . . I don't want you to be shocked or anything, but . . . I'm going on a date tomorrow night." She studied her daughter's expression carefully, anxious to see her first reaction, which she knew would be the honest one, no matter what Brittany said afterward.

"A date?" Brittany asked. "With a man?"

"Um, yeah." Dana's tone was tentative. "That's why you'll have to go to Norell's tomorrow. I think it would be best if I keep you away from my social life."

Brittany's face puckered. "But you just went out Wednesday. Are you gonna be going out all the time now, sending me off to Miss Cécile's and Miss Norell's so I won't be in the way?"

Dana's heart wrenched. "No, honey," she said gently. She reached for Brittany's hand and squeezed it. "Please don't feel like you're in the way. You're never, ever in the way. No one means more to me than you. This week has been very social for me, but it's not going to be a regular thing, I promise. I'm a little old to be hanging out every night." She looked at her daughter, whose eyes had the sad look of a wounded puppy. "Britt? Your thoughts?"

"Since you want to know how I feel, does that mean you won't go if I say I don't want you to?"

"No, it doesn't," Dana replied, realizing too late how sharp she sounded. In a gentler tone she added, "Look, Britt, I know this is strange and new and a little scary. It is to me, too. But we have to face the fact that Daddy's gone. He's not coming back. I miss him terribly, but there has to be more to my life than work. I've worked very hard these last months, and now that things are a little easier I'd like to relax a little and have some fun. I'm not getting any younger, you know."

"I want you to have fun, Mom," Brittany said, and Dana waited for the "but" she knew would follow.

"I just don't want you to bring home a new daddy for me," Brittany concluded.

Dana's mouth fell open, but nothing came out. She had known Brittany had something else to say, but her statement was the absolute last thing she'd expected to hear. "I think you're putting the cart before the horse," she replied dryly. "You can rest assured that I'm only going out to dinner, not to the chapel."

Sean arrived promptly. A suddenly shy Dana greeted him and took her keys and purse. She double latched the door, and when she turned she almost stopped breathing at the first sight of Kenny's old white Eclipse sitting in the driveway, like Kenny had come home after being away for close to a year.

It's Sean's car now, she told herself repeatedly as she walked toward it on leaden legs.

If Sean noticed her nervousness he didn't comment on it. He seated her inside, and she closed her eyes briefly while he walked around to the other side, opening them as he got in the driver's seat. *It's just initial shock. I'm all right now.*

Sean drove to Interstate 95 and headed south. "There's a good German restaurant in Saint Augustine," he said. "I learned to like German food while I was in the army. Of course, if you don't care for German cuisine there's plenty of other places. Seafood, Italian, steak. . . ."

"I've never had German food, but I like trying new things, so that's fine." Now that she was inside the car she found it much easier to forget its history, and she actually felt relaxed.

Sean had the radio set to an easy-listening station, and he amazed Dana by knowing all the words to Don McLean's seventies pop classic *American Pie*. "I've always loved that song," he said after the last chorus.

"Not one of my favorites," Dana responded a little dubiously. She only tuned in to that particular station when she couldn't find anything else to listen to. Rock music could be just as insulting to her ears as rap, but at least this station didn't play anything that sounded like an acid trip. Among her favorites were that Steve Miller song about the space cowboy known as *The Joker* and Fleetwood Mac's *Dreams*. Both tunes had sentimental roots; she and her sister Gail used to sing them when they were young. While she felt it was sweet of Sean to share his taste in music with her, she didn't feel like telling him about Gail and her tragic fate. "But you sang it very nicely," she added, wanting to be polite.

"Thanks. I listen to this station a lot, or the jazz station, which is more likely to be playing something by Luther than real jazz. Today's music is garbage. Occasionally they'll play something from back in the day on the R&B station, but I don't like listening to all those remakes of songs that were done better the first time out."

"I'm with you on that one. If I had any talent for songwriting I'd make a fortune. Scriptwriting, too, for that matter, since no one seems to be able to come up with anything original there, either."

At the restaurant Sean suggested she try Jaeger schnitzel, which she enjoyed. They had dinner to a background of live accordion music. Dana chuckled when two young girls, apparently sisters, got on the floor and danced the Macarena. She recognized the steps but never would have recognized the theme music; to Dana everything the man played on that accordion sounded like *The Third Man Theme*.

They began with impersonal topics of conversation, but eventually turned to their marriages. Dana admitted that Kenny's shortage of insurance protection had led to some hard times for her, but, wanting to end on an upbeat note, added that she'd taken steps to improve her lot and things were much better now. Sean confided that he and his wife's constant arguments led to his moving out. "It's very difficult to blend when one party has kids," he remarked, "and she has two sons, neither of whom are crazy about me."

What'd you do, slug one of 'em? She suppressed a smile at her private thought. "I guess it can be. Two of my friends recently married men with kids, and fortunately everything seems to be working out for both of them. And who knows, the two of you might still be able to work it out." She wanted to keep things light, to let him know it was okay for him to still be married, that she wasn't expecting anything from him.

Sean shrugged. "We'll see." Then he said, "Come on, let's dance."
"You're kidding. To *this?*"
"Sure. We can do a two-step."
Laughing, Dana got to her feet.

They listened to the oldies station again on the way home, singing along with people like Martha and the Vandellas and Paul Revere and the Raiders, old songs Dana didn't even realize she knew the words to. At her door Sean placed his hands firmly on her shoulders, pulled her to him, and kissed her oh-so-briefly, teasing her with his tongue and leaving her breathless . . . and more aware than ever of what she was missing. "Good night, Dana," he said. "We'll do it again soon, huh?"

"I'd like that. Good night, Sean."

Chapter 11

Once upstairs in her bedroom, Dana dialed Norell's number. Brittany had brightened up when she learned that Vic's daughters would be at Norell's, but Dana wanted to check on her and make sure all was well.

One of Vic's daughters answered; Dana didn't know which one. "Hi, this is Dana," she said. "Is Brittany around?"

"Oh, hi, Miss Dana. This is Amber. I'll get her for you."

Brittany's voice came over the line within seconds. "Hi, Mom!"

"Hi, sweetie. I just wanted to let you know I'm home and ask if you're having a good time."

"You're home kind of early. Didn't you have a nice time?"

Dana found Brittany's concern for her touching. "Yes, actually I did. But it doesn't take that long to have dinner, even with driving down to Saint Augustine and back. What about you? What are you doing?"

"I went to the movies with Jessica and Amber. We ate at Panera Bread while we were out. Now we're just watching TV."

"Are you having fun?"

"Oh, yeah. Did you want to talk to Miss Norell?"

Dana could hear laughter in the background. She guessed that Brittany was anxious to get back to the girls and therefore wanted to pass her off to Norell. She didn't mind. Brittany's happiness counted more than anything else. "Sure."

She waited for a long minute or two before Norell picked up. "Hi!"

"Hi. I hope I'm not calling at a bad time," Dana said.

"I've got a few minutes. We're entertaining Rodney and Karen."

"Oh." Dana knew Norell didn't care for the company of the woman who remained a good friend of Vic's first wife. "We can always talk in the morning."

"No, I'm dying to hear all about it. I told them I might be a few minutes. They know your daughter is here. They probably assume you're just calling to check on her."

"She seems to be enjoying herself."

"Yes, she likes being with the girls. But back to you and Sean."

Dana chuckled. She moved into a reclining position in the center of her bed, bent one knee and rested her other ankle on it. "Okay. We went down to Saint Augustine and had German food."

"German food! Like bratwurst and sauerkraut?"

"Actually, Jaeger schnitzel and spaetzel. Apparently Sean did a hitch in the Army and spent some time over there. It was good, but kind of heavy. I'll bet there's a ton of overweight people over there.

"Anyway," Dana continued, "There was this man there playing the accordion. The music was terrible—think Lawrence Welk—but we danced, and it was kinda nice, actually."

"Did he kiss you?"

Just thinking about it made Dana flash her teeth. Norell couldn't see her, of course, but she picked up on the silence.

"Ooh!" she squealed. "Tell me about it."

"It was just a kiss, Norell. Brief and to the point. And I enjoyed every second." She added softly, "It's been a long time for me."

"I take it that means you'll be seeing him again."

"He made me feel good, Norell. So feminine. Being with him made me realize that Kenny had gotten lazy about things he always used to do for me, like put me in the car or hold my hand."

"So are you telling me that when Vic and I have been married for fifteen years, he won't treat me quite the same as he does now?"

"I don't think it's deliberate," Dana said hastily. "I think men just get comfortable with their wives and unconsciously get a little lazy."

"I'm glad you had a good time, honey."

"Thanks. I know you are. Norell, this may sound ridiculous, but I've already decided I'm going to sleep with him."

"That doesn't sound ridiculous to me. But I was single a lot longer than you were. Sometimes one date is all it takes to know. And sometimes I didn't wait until the second date to do it."

"Well, I don't know about that, but I do need some sexual release. After that he can go back to his wife for all I care."

"Hold up," Norell said abruptly. "His wife? He's *married*?"

"They're separated. Apparently some friction between him and his wife's kids. Unless there's more to it than that, it shouldn't be too hard to patch up. But in the meantime I'll take him if she doesn't want him." Dana paused, conscious of the silence on the other end of the line. "I take it you don't approve."

Norell didn't speak right away. "Why don't we talk tomorrow?" she finally suggested.

Dana had a sudden flashback of her mother ominously saying "Just wait till your father gets home" after she'd broken something or misbehaved as a child. "All right. Thanks for listening, Norell. I'll be out tomorrow to pick up Brittany."

Norell slowly replaced the receiver. Married! Bad enough that Sean drove the car that had once belonged to Kenny, but he had a wife to boot. Dana must truly be desperate to be willing to overlook so much. The whole thing made her feel a little queasy. She slowly returned to the living room to join the others.

Then again, maybe her queasiness came from vodka. She'd been quietly refilling her glass all night. It was the only way she could cope with Karen Weathers.

Norell always found these evenings difficult. Vic's friend Rodney was all right, but Karen, his wife, was a good friend of Phyllis's, and Norell could tell she resented Vic's divorcing Phyllis and then marrying someone a dozen years younger. Karen often steered the conversation to events that had occurred years before, effectively shutting Norell out.

As ticked off as Norell got at Karen's maneuvers whenever they were thrown together, tonight it was worse. Children were the main topic of conversation. Rodney and Karen had three sons, two of whom still lived at home. Norell gathered from the conversation that they were having difficulty motivating the youngest one, who at fifteen was flunking math and barely passing English and history. She sat quietly, smoking cigarette after cigarette and sipping drink after drink, as Vic recounted the difficulty he had had with his own son, who had lived with him during high school and college, and how he'd handled it.

"Kids," Karen said with a sigh. Then she flashed a sly grin, showing incisors that were too long and gave her the appearance of being part canine. "So," she said, for once including Norell in the conversation, "do you two plan on shopping for diapers anytime soon?"

"No," Norell replied tightly. Karen's sweet expression hadn't fooled her. She knew the innocent-sounding query masked a malicious intent. Vic must have confided in Rodney her fertility woes, who in turn shared them with Karen. The scenario infuriated her. Just wait till she got Vic alone.

"I'm too old to have a kid in diapers," Vic said easily. "People would think I'm the grandfather."

Norell, determined not to let Karen's deviousness get the better of her, calmly leaned back in her chair and took another swig.

At the end of the evening Norell felt mellow enough to bid the Weatherses good night with genuine warmth. She enjoyed Karen's frown as she hugged Rodney and kissed his cheek in farewell. *What is she, scared that maybe I'll try to steal her man, even if he's Vic's best buddy?*

Norell slipped into a sheer, ice blue chemise-style nightgown with dark blue satin piping. She brushed her side-parted tawny locks out becomingly around her shoulders. Impulsively she began taking large pinches of various areas of her body. Her stomach, which got most of her attention in workouts, was firm and flat. But she frowned when she noted soft spots on her upper arms. It was time to work on that area. She still remembered her eleventh grade English teacher, Mrs. McNulty, whose inside upper arms shook like Jell-O whenever she wrote on the blackboard. Norell vowed to begin working on her arms next week. Right now there was another exercise she had in mind.

Norell, on her knees, clutched the brass love knot headboard tightly. She straddled Vic's head and rotated her pelvis from front to back. She could stay here and let him lick her all night long. Well, maybe not *all* night. Her knees felt like they'd give out any minute, and wouldn't that be something? "Woman Collapses and Suffocates Husband During Oral Sex," the headline would read.

Only her pending climax kept her from laughing out loud.

"I want you to do something for me," Vic said after they laid on their respective sides of the bed, trying to cool off and catch their breath.

"I'm not getting up, Vic. Whatever it is you want, you'll have to get it yourself."

"No, I don't want something to drink. I did something I shouldn't have done, and I don't want you to be angry with me."

"What'd you do?" Norell asked, although she knew what he was about to confess.

"I mentioned our situation to Rodney. I told him to keep it between us, but the minute Karen asked if we planned to have kids, I knew he'd told her about it. I'm sorry, Norell. Rodney's been my buddy since high school. If I can't talk to him, who can I talk to?"

"Vic, why you always tell me somethin' tha's gonna make me mad right after we have sex?" Her words came out slightly slurred.

He chuckled. "I'm no fool. I'm hoping you'll be feeling too good to want to fight."

She squeezed his hand. "I do'n wanna fight, either. I jus' wanna go to sleep. G'night." She closed her eyes, and within minutes was fast asleep, like she'd just received an anesthetic.

Vic covered his sleeping wife. He wasn't surprised to see how quickly she had knocked out. When he straightened out the wet bar after Rodney and Karen left, he'd been shocked to see that Norell had put away a third of a bottle of Smirnoff. She hadn't said ten words the rest of the night after her terse response to Karen's question about their plans for children; she'd merely relaxed in her chair and appeared to be enjoying the conversation and background music, her eyes becoming heavy lidded. He'd caught the mischievous glint in Karen's eye when she'd asked if they planned to start a family, and expected Norell to give him grief for telling Karen about her problem the minute they were alone, even if it had actually been Rodney he'd confided in. Now he knew she was mellow because she'd been quietly getting sloshed, and it wasn't the first time. Just a few nights ago she'd come home blitzed after she'd been out with her girlfriends.

Vic didn't know how to handle the situation. Surely Norell's reason for hitting the bottle like this was her unhappiness about being unable to conceive. Back when they were dating, she confided in him that she'd found herself depending on alcohol to help ease the pain of her mother's death and the financial problems she experienced after her emergency appendectomy. As they grew closer, her drinking slowed to a drip, but once again she found herself in a painful situation. If something didn't give, his wife would become a lush. He'd hoped that going into business with Dana and Cécile would keep her busy enough to forget about having a baby, but while CDN Transcription was a priority for her, he knew she still hurt.

Vic also felt more than a little guilty because he really hadn't wanted another child. They'd talked about having kids before they got married, and he said yes only because he knew it was what she wanted. One of the reasons Norell had been so attractive to him was that she'd already been told it would be difficult for her to conceive. Vic liked the idea of a younger—but not too young—still-shapely wife who was completely unencumbered and who would make him and his two younger children the center of her universe. He barely had in-laws, since Norell's brother was on a ship somewhere halfway across the world and lived on a base in San Diego when he was in port.

The perfect situation Vic pounced on now faced a major threat, for if Norell continued to drink like this, she would only ruin her health and her looks. He didn't stay with Phyllis when she'd let herself go, and they had been married for a long time. He wouldn't be staying with Norell, either, if she started getting all puffy from drinking too much, but damned if he wouldn't do everything possible to prevent that from happening. Maybe he'd gingerly broach the subject of her going into therapy to cope with the depression that made her crave alcohol.

In a way it was almost too bad, though. When she was drunk she fucked like the Energizer bunny, even though afterward she was dead to the world.

Chapter 12

"This is nice, isn't it, us just being girls together on a Sunday afternoon?" Cécile said, beaming at Micheline across their table at Chili's.

"Yes, it is," Micheline agreed. "I'm glad you could get away. How's business, anyway?"

"Of course, it's only been a week, but so far, it's going really well. I think we're going to do fine."

"Somehow I thought you'd have to be chained to your computer, typing away. Are your friends minding the store?"

Cécile felt a twinge of annoyance that Micheline, despite having been firmly told by Norell that the partners weren't mere typists, continued to make condescending remarks about their line of work. She pushed her irritation away, thinking of her promise to her mother to get along with her sister. "Actually, Norell's covering the help desk. For problems, we have instant messaging set up that whoever's on duty checks constantly," she explained. "Dana takes calls on her office line only in case of an emergency. She's the only one of us who has a separate phone line installed in her office, but it wouldn't be fair for her to have to take calls day and night. Some of our contractors prefer to work at two and three in the morning."

"No, I agree that Dana can't have her phone ringing at that hour." Micheline said. "She really seems very nice. I hope she's making it all right without her husband."

"Oh, she'll be fine," Cécile said. She felt it would be disloyal to discuss Dana's financial problems with her sister. If she knew

Micheline, she'd find a way to take advantage of the situation, so the less she knew, the better. "Are you all settled?"

"Yeah. But I'll be glad to find an apartment. I'm not much for living in tiny spaces. I don't know how you—" Micheline quickly broke off. She hadn't meant to say she didn't know how Cécile stood it, but unfortunately she'd said enough so that her intent was pretty clear.

She decided to just keep talking. No point in apologizing. After all, she hadn't completed the statement, even if Cécile probably knew what she'd been about to say. "I've been looking at apartments and have even seen a few I like."

"Oh? Whereabouts?"

Micheline took a moment to be grateful that Cécile had let her blunder pass. "All over town. One's in Riverside, one's in the Southeast, around Tinseltown, and one's at the Beaches."

"The Beaches is nice. That's where Norell lives."

Micheline was glad Cécile mentioned Norell. She'd been curious ever since meeting Norell the other night at Wild Wednesday. Dana and Cecile had both dressed nicely for the occasion, but Micheline recognized that the turquoise suit, alligator pumps of the same color, matching shoulder bag, and jewelry Norell wore were expensive. Micheline expected all of Cécile's friends to be struggling housewives. Norell didn't fit the profile, and she would love to know the story behind it.

"Does she?" she said now. "I'll bet it's nice."

"Oh, it's real nice. She just got married a little over a year ago—"

"First time?"

"Yes. Her husband's about a dozen years older than she is, and he's pretty well off. They have a beautiful house. It's not all that close to the water, but it's real nice just the same. Jewel-tiled floors, dream kitchen, a patio with pool between the two downstairs bedrooms. . . ."

Micheline nodded. So Norell had a well-off, older husband. That explained why she could dress so nicely. Hell, she'd marry somebody who was forty in a heartbeat, if it meant she could dress like Norell did, and if he could satisfy her sexually. If a time came when he couldn't keep up with the program she'd divorce his ass . . . and get a nice settlement, of course.

Cécile leaned forward and spoke in a low voice. "Micheline, can you keep a secret?"

"Sure."

Cécile leaned back. "I'm pregnant."

Micheline's response came quickly. "You're kidding."

"No. I had my tubes tied, but apparently it failed. That happens sometimes, you know, even after the first year."

"Can you sue your doctor?"

"No. I signed a form accepting that possibility. I haven't had time to schedule an appointment with my doctor yet to tell him."

"That's nice and all, Sis, but where are you going to put it?"

She sighed. "Michael has been talking about remodeling ever since before we got married. We need it desperately. You've seen how cramped the girls are. I told him that with a new baby coming we should just buy a bigger house."

"That makes sense."

"He's mad at me."

"Why, for heaven's sake?"

"Because he feels I got pregnant on purpose to force him to make a move."

"That's silly!"

"I know. But he's annoyed at the money we'll have to put out each month on a bigger house. He's lived in his house for eleven years. The mortgage payment is four hundred and sixty-nine dollars."

"Wow. That *is* hard to give up. I'll have to pay about seven hundred for a decent apartment."

"It might not happen. He says he won't spend more than one-fifty on a new house."

Micheline shrugged. "I'm no real estate pro, Sis, but in today's market, wouldn't that buy a house about the same size as the one you've got now?"

"That's exactly right. So what's the point? At least with the house we've got now we know all its little idiosyncrasies—you know, which floorboards creak and which faucet handle is a little hard to turn."

"Adding on will be cheaper than buying a new house."

"It'll also be a structural and a living nightmare," Cécile declared. "I hate houses that have rooms added on. You can always tell because the two parts never match." She smiled sheepishly at the irony of confiding in her sister, something she never expected to do. "Thanks, Michie. I just felt like I had to share that with somebody. I hate putting my problems on Dana, and I'd like to put off telling Norell I'm pregnant as long as I can."

Micheline immediately perked up. "Oh? Why's that?"

"Because she's having trouble trying to get pregnant. She even had some surgery done on her reproductive system, but they told her she probably won't ever have a baby."

"Oh, how sad. How does her husband feel about that?"

"He's worried about how *she* feels. This is a second marriage for him, and he already has a couple of kids, so it's not a great tragedy for him personally."

It had pleased Micheline to hear that Norell, with her fancy wardrobe, her diamonds and sapphires, and her beautiful beach house, had fertility problems. In her opinion, no one should lead a charmed life, unless it was her. Look at Dana. She had a nice house, too, in a pretty neighborhood, and drove a nice cream-colored, fully equipped Camry, but Micheline sensed she had financial problems because she'd been a little too eager to get Micheline to rent her spare room. Cécile hadn't volunteered any information, probably out of loyalty.

Micheline decided not to press the issue, although as with Norell, she would have loved to know the background history. You never knew when information might come in handy.

"So, how was your weekend?" Cécile asked. "Any hot dates?"

"Oh, I went out on Friday night with a nice guy. I met him at Wild Wednesday."

"Ah, you just met him. Tell me about him, Michie."

She shrugged. "He's just an ordinary fellow. I think we can have some fun together." Now it was her turn to lean forward eagerly. "So tell me, when do you start house hunting?"

"We're going out this afternoon. What about you? What're your plans for the rest of the day?"

"I'm getting together with one of my old friends. You remember Yolanda L'Esperance from Riviera Beach?"

"Just vaguely. It's been so long. Is she here in Jacksonville now?"

"Yes. She's married, and she just had a baby." Micheline sat back in her chair, happy to have successfully changed the subject.

For the less said about her Friday-night date, the better.

Chapter 13

Cécile's breath caught in her throat. "Michael, look!" She pointed with a stubby fingernail to the figure on the information sheet of the model house they'd just looked at.

He squinted. "Are you kidding? This house is three hundred and twenty-five thousand dollars? For what?"

"And that's just the base price. I'm sure that doesn't include any bells and whistles they've got in the model."

Michael put down the paper. "Come on, let's get out of here. We can forget about new construction. It's gone through the roof."

They got back into their car and continued driving to their original destination, an open house nearby. Cécile wrote off the unscheduled stop-off as a mistake. To her disappointment, even the open house proved to be futile, for the house being sold—although relatively new with four bedrooms, two baths, and an asking price within their range—turned out to be too small. The master suite was fine, but the three smaller bedrooms weren't large enough to house two children apiece, plus a third in one of them when the baby was older.

Cécile felt terribly disappointed. They'd just begun looking, but from what she'd seen in the paper and in those free "House for Sale" booklets, residential real estate had gotten awfully expensive. She'd always felt Michael had been exaggerating the expense because of his frugal nature, but now she knew better. Would they really be able to manage? Michael's Expedition was fairly new, but the van she drove was seven years old and wouldn't last forever. What if it had to be replaced while they still had two or three years' worth of hefty payments on the Expedition? A much larger mortgage plus two car payments . . . Would they have to cut out all the extras, send out for pizza instead of having family dinners at Bennigan's or Motogo Japanese restaurant, where the chefs prepared their meal right there at the table? What about their family membership at the Y, and the girls' soccer league? Those extras all cost money, money they wouldn't have if their mortgage payment suddenly quadrupled. Maybe they should skip the new house and remodel the one they had. A new master suite and bath would solve the problem, but where would they put it? Their yard was already relatively small, and adding on an upstairs would be major construction.

Michael broke into her thoughts. "Don't get all gloomy on me, Cécile. This is the first time we've looked, and you're acting like you want to give up. You didn't expect to find something today, did you?"

"Now you're making me feel silly," she protested. "Of course I didn't expect to find the perfect house today. But what we did see isn't very encouraging."

"We already knew that. I tell you, this kid is going to send us to the poorhouse."

"Yeah," she said dully, not wanting to admit just how unprepared she'd been . . . and too hurt to respond to his hurtful remark about the baby. "We already knew."

At first Micheline didn't recognize the strange feeling that stemmed from the base of her throat and ran into her chest. Then she realized it was envy. No wonder she hadn't been able to define it. Micheline rarely felt envious of anyone. She was accustomed to others feeling that way about her, but she couldn't help it as she watched her old friend Yolanda L'Esperance proudly show off her new baby. Yolanda had married Robert Isaacs, a Jacksonville dentist. Before the baby she'd worked as a bookkeeper for a restaurant, but she had given up her job. "We want to have at least one more child, and I probably won't go back to work until my youngest is in school," she told Micheline.

Micheline and Yolanda had grown up in the same neighborhood in Riviera Beach, largely populated by domestic and blue collar workers who performed services in nearby superwealthy Palm Beach. They'd gone through school together, but now Yolanda had a handsome, successful husband, a beautiful baby boy, and a lovely home. All Micheline had was a nice car, a stunning wardrobe, a few pieces of good jewelry, and a few dollars in the bank. She essentially lived in one room, even if it was just temporary while she decided what part of town to settle in.

Romantically, she didn't even have any real prospects. The man she'd given her phone number to at Wild Wednesday had made no secret of the fact that he was presently separated from his wife. Micheline knew that meant he wasn't getting sex regularly and felt horny. That was all right, for she felt the same way. She was prepared to accept him at face value and have some fun. But what he didn't know yet was that he'd have to spend some money on her before she gave anything up.

Her lips formed into a slight smile. He'd made a move on her as they left the comedy club they'd gone to, which just happened to be located inside a hotel. She gave him points for style, if not for speed.

Looking around at Yolanda's comfortable surroundings made Micheline realize she wasn't getting any younger. She really needed to start looking for a husband. The idea of being married had always appealed to her, especially if she could swing a setup like this. No way would she be like Cécile, working her butt off typing all day while living in a two-by-four house and taking care of all those damn kids, half of whom weren't even hers.

"You know, Michie," Yolanda was saying, "Rob has a colleague who just broke up with his girlfriend. I'd love to introduce the two of you. I think you'd like each other, and he's a real catch."

Micheline's envy evaporated. No longer was Yolanda a braggart, rubbing her face in her domestic bliss and semiswank lifestyle, but a friend who wanted her to meet a successful man, too. Sight unseen, Micheline resolved to make Rob's dentist friend forget all about his former girlfriend, provided he was as good a catch as Yolanda said he was, and provided they were sexually compatible.

No, that wasn't right. She'd wait until she had him hooked before she slept with him. If she handled it carefully, she could get her sexual gratification with the man she was seeing now—she had a date with him tonight—while giving the dentist a line that she was a good Catholic girl who didn't believe in premarital sex. In her heart Micheline knew she could trust Yolanda's judgment. If Yolanda said he was good looking, he was sure to be just that.

Micheline had moved ahead to thinking about children's names when Yolanda said, "I'll call Rob to see when we can get this set up."

"Wonderful," Micheline said.

Feeling hopeful about the future beat feeling jealous any day.

Chapter 14

"Well, I must say," Dana said, "this is a very nice surprise."

Irene Albacete, sitting across from Dana in the booth, nodded in agreement. "I'm beginning my Mother's Day feeling like a queen."

Next to them, their respective daughters beamed. "It was my idea," they said in unison, then looked at each other indignantly.

"It's perfectly reasonable for it to have occurred to both of you at the same time," Irene said reassuringly. She held up her menu. "Mmmm. The ham and eggs looks very tasty. What are you having, Dana?"

"Order anything you want, Mom," Brittany said confidently. "Money is no object."

"Well, if you're sure. . . ."

"An-y-thing you want," Brittany repeated.

Dana suppressed a smile. She remembered the air mail envelope that came last week addressed to Brittany from the Covingtons in Nassau. It must have contained cash so Brittany could do something special in honor of Mother's Day. Dana knew her in-laws really couldn't afford the expenditure—they put everything they could into an annuity for Niles for his care after they were gone—but they wanted her first Mother's Day without Kenny to be a happy one.

She didn't know how much they'd sent, but she guessed they'd been generous. Perkins was one of the nicer restaurants in its category, definitely a cut above Denny's or Shoney's. In addition to Brittany's insisting that she order whatever she want from the menu, she had also awakened Dana with a colorful bouquet of spring flowers and presented her with a lovely sterling silver amethyst pendant, a reference to Dana's February birthday.

"Well," Dana said, perusing the menu, "since money's no object and I'm starving, I think I'll go with the big breakfast, the one with a little bit of everything." She stole a glance over at Brittany, wanting to make sure it was all right.

But Brittany showed no distress. "I'm getting the blueberry pancakes."

"And I want the Belgian waffles with strawberries," Vanessa added.

Irene flagged down a waitress. Ten minutes later their food was delivered. "My goodness, Dana, that's a lot of food!" Irene exclaimed. "Are you really going to finish all that?"

Dana cast a satisfied look at the three large pancakes, scrambled eggs, home-fried potatoes, and bacon. "Oh, I'll finish it, all right. But I won't eat anything else all day."

"I'll skip lunch, but I'll have dinner," Irene said.

"My Popi is taking my Mama out to dinner," Vanessa announced happily.

"Oh, how nice," Dana said, careful not to let the wistfulness she felt creep into her voice. Kenny used to take her out for Mother's Day. They used to celebrate the night before, when the restaurants were less crowded. This year, this meal would be the high point of her weekend. Although she'd had lunch with Sean on Thursday, he'd told her he would be unable to see her this weekend because he would be spending the afternoon with his mother. Absently she wondered if he planned on seeing his estranged wife as well.

Irene looked a little embarrassed at Vanessa's outburst. Because of her fair complexion, the color of milk with a few chocolate drops, it was easy to tell she was blushing. Between her happiness and Vanessa's, Dana wondered if perhaps a reconciliation was in the works between Irene and Gil, whom she hadn't seen since their lunch together.

She couldn't understand why that prospect made her feel sad.

Norell awoke in a sour mood. In honor of Mother's Day, one of the cable networks was showing a feature of *Imitation of Life*, *Stella Dallas*, *Mildred Pierce*, and *Madame X*, all classic stories of maternal sacrifice. That programming executive was going to have half the country dabbing at their eyes.

She absolutely hated Mother's Day. Not only did it remind her of how much she missed her own mother, but it reminded her of her own longing for a child, a longing she now knew would never be fulfilled.

She shuffled languidly to the front door when the doorbell sounded, her colorful caftan billowing behind her as she walked, not caring that the soles of her slippers were scratching her gleaming tile-edged hardwood floors. Vic had invited a few friends over to watch the NBA semifinals. Somebody must be arriving early. Vic had gone to pick up some Chinese food and hadn't returned yet, and she had the set tuned in to *Imitation of Life*. She used to enjoy the glossy Ross Hunter production with its Jean Louis outfits, but now she felt that Lana Turner delivered her lines with all the genuineness of cubic zirconia.

"Who is it?" Norell asked through the closed door.

"Da-na."

"And Cé-ci-el," said a second voice in the same singsong manner.

Norell's mouth dropped open. She quickly reached to unlatch the door and flung it open.

"We thought you could stand some company this afternoon," Dana explained as they entered the house.

"But it's Mother's Day!"

"That's the point," Cécile said.

"But you've got your own families. What are you doing out here with me?" The mere thought of Dana and Cécile wanting to spend Mother's Day with her made her get all choked up, and her voice broke.

"Now, we're not having any of that," Dana admonished.

"Michael's watching the kids so I could enjoy the afternoon," Cécile added. "They're busy making dinner for me."

Norell smiled at her two best friends through vision blurred by tears. "You two are the best." She held out her arms, and they moved in for a group hug.

They'd just sat in the living room when Vic returned. "Hi, girls," Vic greeted cheerfully as he passed through on his way to the kitchen, a white plastic bag hanging from each hand.

"Hi, Vic."

Norell noted that he didn't seem surprised to see Dana and Cécile. She walked over to assist him with unloading the bags.

"Vic, you bought enough food for an army," Norell commented as she lifted carton after carton from the bags. "Who's coming, anyway?"

"Just Rodney and Gregory. And, of course, Dana and Cécile."

"You did know they were coming!" she exclaimed.

"We didn't think it was such a hot idea to just show up unannounced in case you really weren't in the mood," Cécile said. "Vic said it would be fine for us to surprise you."

Norell gave Vic's arm an affectionate squeeze. "It was a good surprise. Thank you." The doorbell rang just as she finished talking.

"I'll get it," Vic said.

"I'll get the plates and stuff," Dana offered, rising.

"There's paper plates in the pantry," Norell called out.

At the door Vic greeted Rodney, then called out to someone who was apparently just pulling up. They all came inside together.

Norell soon saw there were five more guests, not three. Rodney had brought two of his sons along. Good thing Vic bought plenty of food.

She greeted her guests. Cécile already knew Rodney, and Norell introduced her to Gregory Weston. Gregory was a bounty hunter whose services Vic used to track down his clients who skipped bail. It didn't happen often—Vic didn't post bail for clients unless their family members or very good friends gave him the impression that they would move heaven and earth to get the incarcerated individual out of jail. He often said that if Grandma was reluctant to put up her house for the imprisoned, it was probably because she knew he or she wasn't any good, so why should *he* risk it?

Dana emerged from the kitchen and set the plates and plastic utensils on the table. "Okay, guys, I think we should hit this before it gets cold."

"Ladies first," Vic said.

"No, you men fix your plates first," Norell said, "so we can sit at the table and talk while y'all watch the game."

Dana greeted Rodney and said hello to his sons. Then she introduced herself to the man she hadn't met before. At maybe six-three and in the three-hundred-pound range, he looked like a linebacker, an overweight one. His large size probably preve doing much running without getting short of breath.

"Ah, so *you're* Dana. It's nice to meet you."

"You've heard of me?"

Gregory looked embarrassed. "Ah . . . Norell talk quently. I understand you and she are real good fi business partners as well."

"Yes, we are." Instantly Dana knew Norell was trying to fix her up with this bear of a man to get her away from Sean. It annoyed her, but she couldn't take it out on Gregory. He seemed nice enough, even though he gave her the impression that he'd like to gobble her up like a turkey dinner. She was searching for a pleasant parting comment so she could make a graceful exit when Vic joined them.

"I see you two have met," Vic said, putting an arm around each of them like he was proud of them or something. "This is my main man, Dana. No one can hide from him."

"Hide? Why would anyone want to hide from you, Gregory?" Dana asked.

"Because I'm a bounty hunter."

"Bounty hunter?" Dana repeated. "That makes me think of the Wild West. Do they still exist?"

"People jump bail every day," Gregory replied with a smile. "But instead of horses I use airplanes and cars."

"He's the best in the Southeast," Vic said.

Cécile and Dana moved the food cartons off to one end of the table while Norell fixed beverages for the men. Then they fixed their own plates and settled in to eat.

"Dana, did you meet Gregory?" Norell asked.

"Yes, I did." A sixth sense urged her to glance over at the area near the Bellamy's wide-screen television. Sure enough, Gregory Weston's gaze was affixed to her. But instead of being embarrassed at having been caught, his smile merely broadened. Dana simply flashed a quick, insincere smile—the kind she used for posed photographs—and turned away.

"So what'd you think?" Norell pressed.

"I didn't." She calmly helped herself to another helping of rice.

Cécile jumped into the breach. "Well, guys, it's official. Michael and I have begun house hunting. We went out last weekend and again yesterday." She deliberately left out the parts about Michael still being cool toward her because of the coming baby, and that the prospects for finding a large enough house they could afford looked dismal.

"That's wonderful, Cécile!" Dana exclaimed, glad to have the conversation on a matter other than Gregory Weston. "I knew Michael would come around sooner or later."

"Well, that's good news," Norell said. "It's miraculous how all of you can live in the house you have now without falling over each other's feet."

Dana's eyes grew wide. How could Norell say such a thing?

Cécile glared at her. "Well, Norell, if you had six kids this house would seem small, too."

Norell's lower lip quivered, and Cécile covered her mouth with her hand, like she'd realized too late that her reference to children must have cut like a sharp blade. "I'm sorry, Norell," she said. "I didn't mean to be so thoughtless, but you weren't exactly considerate yourself."

"I know. I apologize. I guess I'm a little jealous of you because you can have a baby just like that, and I can't."

"I'm sorry, Norell. I wish I had the answer, but I don't."

Norell sighed. "I know." She turned to Dana. "So where is Brittany this afternoon? Did you leave her home alone?"

Dana took a moment to let out the breath she'd been holding. The exchange between Norell and Cécile had the potential to get really nasty, but now it looked like it would be all right, thank God. Sometimes she could just strangle Norell. That girl really needed to learn to control that mouth of hers. "No. I made a deal with her best friend's mother. She's watching Brittany this afternoon, and when she goes out with her ex-husband tonight, Vanessa will stay with me." Now she realized why she had that sinking feeling when she heard about Irene's dinner with Gil. Irene had a second chance with her husband, while hers was gone forever.

As mothers of best friends, she and Irene had known each other for six years, but Irene had always been close mouthed, almost haughty in her bearing. When she and Irene made arrangements to watch each other's children, she'd volunteered her plans to spend the afternoon with a friend whose difficulty conceiving would make the day difficult, but Irene mentioned nothing about her plans to dine with Gil. If Vanessa hadn't blurted out Irene's plans at breakfast she still wouldn't know about it.

Cécile relaxed in her chair. The unpleasant moment had passed, but she dreaded having to tell Norell she was pregnant again. She'd have to put it off as long as she could.

After they finished eating they cleared the table, amid the cheers of the fellows gathered around the television. "Let's go upstairs and watch *Mildred Pierce*," Norell suggested.

"Hey, you don't want to watch the game with us?" Vic asked, sounding playfully insulted.

"Vic, you know basketball bores me."

"At least it's not always the Bulls, the Bulls, the Bulls, like it was when Jordan was playing," Rodney said.

Gregory laughed. "Yeah, back in the day, everybody pretty much knew the outcome. I know there were times I was hoping somebody would drop a barbell on his head."

No one said a word, and all eyes other than Gregory's and Rodney's sons' turned to Dana, who found her spine had suddenly gone unnaturally stiff.

"Come on, girls. Let's go see Joan Crawford in her shoulder pads," Norell said hastily. Then a player on one of the teams made a stunning three-point shot, and admiring shouts broke the awkward moment. As Dana passed on her way to the stairs she noticed Vic lean over and whisper something to Gregory, who winced and hung his head.

The movie had already begun when they tuned in. Because the game went into overtime, it was in its closing seconds when Dana, Cécile, and Norell came downstairs after the film ended. When Dana said good-bye to Gregory, who conveniently stood in the dining room isolated from the others, he reached out and grasped her forearm. "Dana, I said something very insensitive before. I didn't know about your husband. I'm really sorry."

"There was no way you could know; I realize that. But thanks. I appreciate your concern." She smiled at him and slipped away.

She sincerely meant what she said. Anyone could make a gaffe if they didn't know all the facts. It actually worked out to her advantage, for she'd been sure that Gregory would have asked her out otherwise. He seemed nice enough, and he certainly was different from anyone she'd known, both in his size and in his profession, but she simply didn't find him attractive, and that was that.

"It looks like Gregory's sweet on you," Cécile said to Dana on the drive home.

"He'll get over it, I'm sure."

"Did I tell you about the guy I met last week at Wild Wednesday?"

"No! What are *you* doing meeting a guy?"

"I was sitting alone while you all were dancing. He obviously thought I was available. He was fine with a capital F. Dark skinned with big brown eyes and a great build. Anyway, he said to me, 'Hi there, I'm Casanova.'"

"Casanova!"

"My thoughts exactly, which is why I said, 'Sure you are, and I'm Madame Pompadour.' From the stunned look on his face I realized he was telling the truth. But there was no way for me to take the words back."

Dana sighed. "Is there a point to this story, Cécile? Besides the fact that parents should give more thought to the names they choose for their kids?"

"Of course. Try not to hold Gregory's remark against him. How could he possibly have known Kenny died lifting weights?"

"What he said has nothing to do with it. He apologized to me when we were leaving. I think Vic tipped him off. But he's not my type. Besides, I'm already seeing Sean."

"Who's got a wife tucked away, and a car that used to belong to Kenny."

Dana sighed. "Not you, too, Cécile. Norell has already made it clear that she's against it, too."

"You're vulnerable, Dana. You know it, and I'm sure he knows it, too."

"I'm not going to get attached to Sean, Cécile."

"So you say. But the whole thing gives me the creeps. Hey, you want some gummi bears?" She put her hand in the bag on the console.

"God, no. Because of you I'm all gummied out. I can't even eat jelly beans anymore." Dana watched as Cécile scooped up a handful of the candy. She hoped Cécile saw her dentist regularly. Those things could be murder on a person's teeth, and Cécile downed them as if they were one of the four basic food groups.

"And speaking of giving me the creeps, I'm glad Norell's leaning against having in vitro," Cécile said after she swallowed.

"And why's that?"

"If you ask me, it's carrying science too far. I think if you can't have a baby the natural way, you should just adopt or forget about it."

"Easy for you to say, Cécile, you've got kids."

"Yes, bless their pain-in-the-butt hearts. But if I didn't, I wouldn't even consider having any artificial process."

"Again, that's easy for you to say. Try to imagine how you'd feel if you and Michael decided you wanted a child together and you couldn't because you'd had your tubes tied. Would you want to have it reversed? And what if you still didn't get pregnant? You might sing a different tune then."

Cécile paused. "It's a moot point, Dana. My tubes untied by themselves. I'm pregnant now."

Dana drew in her breath. "You're pregnant? Even after a tubal ligation? Oh, I get it! That's why you're looking for a new place."

"I can't very well have my baby sleep on the roof, can I?"

"How far along are you?"

"The doctor says two months, so we're looking at mid-December. I didn't want to say anything because I don't know how Norell's going to take it. Promise you won't tell her."

"I promise. No way am I getting in the middle of that." Dana feared that the relationship between Cécile and Norell was about to get a lot worse. Friendship alone had great value, but now they had a lot more at stake. She hoped CDN could survive the storms that were sure to come.

Chapter 15

Dana waved good-bye to Sean as he drove off. At her request he had turned off his headlights as they approached the house, and she watched as he flicked them back on. Brittany, inside with the babysitter, hadn't yet seen his car, and if Dana had her way she would never know about it. She still felt uncomfortable in it herself—she couldn't stop thinking of it as Kenny's—and even if she told Brittany it was just a coincidence that Sean had a car just like her daddy's, it was bound to be upsetting for her.

Actually, when Dana was inside the car she didn't think about it. Seats, center arm rest, and instrument panel notwithstanding, a car was a car. Only when she approached it from the outside did memories come back, and with them that queasy feeling. Sean, for his part, dealt with the sticky situation by not mentioning it at all.

Still, they were progressing nicely. They'd met for lunch on Wednesday. Tonight at the movies he'd taken her hand during the inevitable bedroom scene, a scene she found incredibly erotic in spite of knowing that every detail had been carefully orchestrated by a multiperson movie crew, right down to each bead of sweat on the actors' faces. Good Lord, she'd gotten to the point where even staged sex got her motor running, and she had the uncomfortable feeling that Sean somehow knew she hadn't had an experience since Kenny died. It was all she could do to keep from moaning aloud when he stroked her sensitive palm with the pad of his thumb.

When he pulled up almost—but not quite—in front of the house he kissed her good night, briefly, but with such intensity Dana found herself thinking about it off and on all day. "You know, you could get to be a habit for me," he'd whispered just before planting a last quick peck on her lips.

Inside, Dana found Brittany and Tina, the babysitter, watching Brittany's *Titanic* tape. The ship was making its final descent into the North Atlantic, a scene Brittany had seen at least a dozen times before. Dana paid Tina and walked her to her home a few doors down. When she returned home, Brittany had changed into her pajamas. "Good night, Mom," she said, giving Dana a hug and kiss before disappearing into her bedroom.

In the privacy of her bedroom, Dana removed her clothing, intending to slip on a night shirt and go to bed. She'd put in a full day and planned to get up early in the morning to work for CDN. But when she caught a glimpse of her reflection in the mirror over her dresser, she impulsively walked over to it. Then, wanting a better view, she went to the full-length mirror on the back of the bathroom door. She'd never given much thought to her physique, but no one other than Kenny had known her body since she was twenty years old. Well, nineteen years had passed since then. It was time to take a good, hard look at herself.

She tried to be critical as she studied her reflection, but in truth, she saw little to find fault with. Her skin was reasonably smooth, although it didn't have that glow like the models in *Essence* or *Black Elegance*, but at least it had no more traces of the mild acne of her younger years. She was maybe ten pounds heavier than she'd been fifteen years ago, not enough to be of any real significance. Her stomach was reasonably flat, if a little soft; and her boobs were still upright, even if they tended to roll toward her armpits when she lay down, but hell, she was pushing forty. If her boobs stuck in the air like two oranges at this stage of the game, that would only mean they weren't real.

She turned around. Good, her butt didn't sag. Impetuously she spread her arms and said, "Ta-daaaaaaaah," like she had just jumped out of a birthday cake at a men's party.

Her smile turned to a frown when she saw the thick stubble of hair on her armpits. She lowered one arm and with her fingers explored the growth under the other. Not having a man in her life meant she could cut back on the less-noticeable aspects of grooming, at least until she started wearing shorts and sleeveless tops or went swimming. All right, so she'd already gone swimming this season, but in her own pool. Brittany and her friends didn't care about the stubble on her legs. But she had to get rid of this excess hair before offering herself to Sean, including shaping up that jungle between her legs.

She still had time. She'd explained to him weeks ago that she could only go out with him on one weekend night because she wouldn't leave Brittany more than that. He understood. They would probably have lunch together at least once next week, but there would be no actual date before next weekend.

Dana didn't particularly care for going out on Friday nights. Combined with work, it made for too long a day. Last weekend when she mentioned her preference for Saturday night to Sean, he said Friday would work better for him. He didn't elaborate, and when he suggested they go out on Friday again this week she couldn't help wondering what his Saturday-night plans were.

One thing for sure: Sean's actions tonight had made it clear that the time for mere hand-holding was over.

Dana met Sean for lunch on Wednesday, and it pleased her when he invited her to dinner on Saturday for a change. She recognized the name of the restaurant right away and knew it sat inside a downtown hotel. "That'll work well," she said casually. "Saturday is always much better for me than Friday." She hoped this would begin a new trend for them. At last he'd finally gotten the message.

She hadn't bought herself anything new in months—just because her financial picture looked more promising these days didn't mean she could afford to indulge herself—but she detoured to the mall on her way home and bought some new underwear. Thursday she slathered her legs with baby oil and ran the razor up and down all the surfaces until they felt like satin. Friday she treated herself to a professional pedicure. The soles of her feet felt as smooth as cognac going down her throat. No wonder Norell swore by them.

By Saturday she had only one decision to make: What to wear. Dana didn't want to ask Norell or Cécile because they'd both been so vocal about their disapproval of the affair. She decided to ask the fashionable Micheline, but when she didn't see Micheline's Bug in the driveway she scribbled a note on a yellow Post-It and left it on her door.

With everything under control, Dana sat down and did some transcription for CDN. She checked her watch anxiously. Five o'-clock, and no Micheline. If she didn't return soon, Dana would be on her own, and she desperately wanted a second opinion. She really didn't have anyone else she could ask. Her babysitter's family had gone off to Orlando for the weekend. Her neighbors, Judy and Peter Sidney, were home, but Dana had noticed a definite chill in Judy since Kenny's accident. The way Judy's hand visibly tightened around Peter's arm whenever Dana waved hello told her Judy believed she planned to make a play for her husband. Dana didn't understand Judy's change in attitude. She had done nothing to make her neighbor believe that widowhood had turned her into a predator. Some women were just funny that way, she supposed.

As Dana was finishing her work, the doorbell rang. She hoped it would be Micheline, but since it was the front door, in her heart she knew it was more likely to be Vanessa Albacete. Brittany was set to attend a sleepover tonight at Vanessa's. Irene had promised Vanessa a new CD and was bringing her to Coconuts to get it, and their plan included stopping on their way there to pick up Brittany. Now that Brittany's guests had arrived, naturally she was nowhere in sight. She probably couldn't hear the bell over the loud music she played behind her closed bedroom door.

Through the sheer panels covering the narrow-paned windows that flanked the front door, Dana recognized the profile of Irene Albacete. She opened the door. "Hi, there! Come on in."

They came inside, and Dana said to Vanessa, "I think Brittany's in her room. Why don't you go on up?" Vanessa promptly disappeared, and Dana involuntarily winced at the loud clunking sound the preteen's platform shoes made on her bare living room floor and the stairs.

Irene laughed. "She's still at that awkward age. Fortunately, our place has wall-to-wall."

"Oh, I'm sorry." Dana was embarrassed that Irene had noticed her displeased expression. "Can I get you something to drink?"

"Ice water will be fine."

They went to the kitchen, and Dana had just reached for a glass when she heard knocking on the back door. This had to be Micheline.

"Never a dull moment," Dana said to Irene with a smile. "Please sit down, and I'll be right back. You're sure you won't have a glass of wine instead?"

"Water's fine, thanks." Irene glanced at her watch. "I should tell the girls to hurry. We need to get that CD and be home before the rest of the girls arrive."

"Do you think you can stay five more minutes?" Dana asked. She felt she might as well get the opinions of two women. As Irene nodded, Dana rushed to the back door, where Micheline stood.

"You wanted to see me?" she said, a strange expression on her face. It reminded Dana of a child who knew she had done wrong and was about to be reprimanded by a parent. How odd, she thought.

"Yes. Can you come in for a minute? I've got company."

"Sure."

Back in the kitchen, Dana introduced Micheline to Irene, then poured filtered water from the refrigerator dispenser for both women, who sat at the small round table in a corner nook. She sat with them, her palms resting on her thighs. "I'm glad both of you are here at the same time. This way I can get two opinions."

"Opinions about what?" Irene asked.

"Well, I've got a date tonight. It's kind of a special date, and I wasn't sure what to wear."

Micheline took a long swig of water. When she put it down the apprehensive expression was gone, replaced by a wide grin. "Ah, a special date! Do you know where you're going? That's the first piece of information you need to be able to dress appropriately."

"We're going to have dinner at Juliette's downtown."

"You have to forgive me, Dana; I'm not familiar with that," Micheline said apologetically.

"That's right, you haven't been in town very long, have you?"

"Juliette's is one of Jacksonville's nicer restaurants," Irene said. "My husband and I went there a few times for special occasions."

Irene's use of the term "husband" versus the correct "ex-husband" sent an immediate red flag to Dana's brain. Had her dinner with Gil on Mother's Day gone well? Irene, as usual, hadn't volunteered any information when she came to pick up Vanessa afterward. Or maybe Irene, a devout Catholic, just didn't like admitting her divorceé status. Not that Dana ever expected to learn her motives. In all the years she and Irene had known each other, they never once advanced beyond small talk.

"It's inside the Omni Hotel," Irene added.

"Ooohhh," Micheline added, her knowing glance lingering on Dana.

The way Micheline stretched out a single-syllable word into three syllables, paired with Irene's not-quite-suppressed sly smile, made Dana wonder if it was better not to seek their advice. She silently cursed Irene for pointing out the restaurant's location, as well as herself for saying it was a special date. She might as well have written her planned activity for the evening across her forehead with lipstick.

"I'm presuming you've narrowed down the possibilities to a few. I'd be happy to give you my opinion," Irene offered.

"Actually, I have. Can you bear with me while I run upstairs and get them?"

"Does Brittany know about your date?"

Dana drew in her breath. Irene had a good point. Brittany didn't know she had plans for the evening. "On second thought, maybe it would be better if you guys came upstairs with me."

Micheline drained the rest of her water. "Sure."

Dana led the way up the two-part staircase to the master bedroom. On her bed lay two outfits, one a peach suit with above-the-knee pleated suit paired with a draped white blouse, the other a green-and-black sleeveless cocktail dress, tea length, with a jaunty sash at the side and matching green shawl.

"They're both lovely," Irene began, "but I think I would go with the suit. I like that blouse with it. It looks soft and feminine, not businesslike."

"I've got beige mules to wear with it," Dana said.

"Definitely better than pumps. You'll fit right in, whether your date wears a suit or a sports coat."

"I agree," Micheline said. "Besides, if you two get a hotel room, you'll be less conspicuous in the morning in the suit than you would be in that dress."

"Whoa. Who said anything about getting a room?" Dana said.

"Well, you did say it was a special date."

"Yes, but not special *that* way." Dana hoped she sounded convincing, but judging by the skeptical look on Micheline's face, Dana half expected to see her waiting by the window to see what time she came home.

Chapter 16

Dana closed her eyes. Her breath escaped from her lips in low moans that escalated as her climax intensified. She had almost forgotten how just plain good sex could be.

Sean rolled off her onto his back, and Dana sneaked a peek at the shriveled, liquid-filled condom on his now-limp penis. It had been years since she'd seen one.

"Umph, umph, umph," Sean said as he slowly raised to a sitting position. "You can give me a heart attack."

"Oh, no, not the first time out. The third, maybe."

"The third? Sounds like you've got real serious plans for me tonight."

Dana feigned hurt feelings. "Aren't you interested?"

He removed the used prophylactic, tossed it into the trash, and quickly turned to take her in his arms, nuzzling hungrily on her neck. "You know I am. Did I make you happy?"

She snuggled comfortably in his embrace. "Extremely."

"Good. We'll wait a few minutes, give me a chance to catch my breath, and then I'll give you some more, uh, happiness." He chuckled. "Can we take our time, or do you have to be home by a certain hour?"

"No. Brittany is spending the night with a friend."

His moved his large hand up and down her body. "Great. So we've got the whole night."

Norell shifted uncomfortably in her chair. This new dermatology account—the first CDN had garnered through its advertising—made her fidgety. Visit after visit about teenagers with acne, adults with rosacea, and youngsters with diseases like impetigo and scabies had her wanting to scratch herself all over, and for hours afterward she felt imaginary beings crawling up her skin.

Transcribing consecutive similar cases made Norell miss the days of multispecialty hospital work, but she couldn't argue with success. CDN was doing great. This week alone they'd had two more inquiries from medical practices. She and Dana were scheduled to meet with representatives from both of them next week.

For some reason Norell felt especially energized this evening. She worked until ten-thirty P.M., which coupled with her work earlier in the day, was enough to complete all the dictation for that client. The work wasn't due back until Tuesday. The client would be pleased, and so would Dana and Cécile. Several of their contractors had left the CDN roster altogether, while others had cut down on their hours. CDN paid competitive rates and more frequently than their competitors, but some of the women cited the need for health benefits due to marital breakups or spousal layoffs. Others had forgotten to pay their quarterly self-employment taxes, were now in hot water with the IRS, and had decided to work as employees so taxes would automatically be deducted from their earnings. It had been difficult to find qualified replacements, and the workload for the three partners had gotten heavier, particularly for her, since Dana and Cécile both had other jobs.

They've got families, too.

Norell pushed that thought out of her head. How long, she wondered, would it be before this terrible longing for a child of her own went away? Would she still hurt like this a year from now? In five years? Ten?

As she straightened up her desk she wondered what Dana was doing right about now. Dana had said Sean would pick her up for dinner at seven-thirty, three hours ago. They'd certainly had plenty of time to eat by now. Dana had named the restaurant where they would be dining, and Norell knew it was conveniently located in the lobby of a downtown hotel. Dana seemed especially excited about tonight, and since she'd been dating Sean for weeks it could only be for one reason. Norell fervently hoped Dana would sleep with him once or twice and then drop him, but she was afraid that once Dana had a sample she wouldn't want to let go. She feared her friend would be hurt in the end.

"Hey Norell, it's after ten. How long you gonna be?" Vic called from downstairs.

"I'm just finishing up," she called back. She sighed quietly. Vic hadn't bothered to disguise an annoyed tone. He clearly resented the time she devoted to CDN. Norell didn't understand what the big deal was. She'd asked if he wanted to go out, maybe bowling or something, since Jessica and Amber were here this weekend. He said no, suggesting they stay in and order pizza and rent a movie. The girls picked some sci-fi movie, a genre Norell hated. After eating her pizza, she'd excused herself and gone up to her office. She could hear Vic and the girls reacting to the film. Obviously they were having a good time, but she simply couldn't get interested in the movie, and Lord knew she had plenty of work to do.

She descended the stairs. "How was the movie?" she asked cheerfully.

"It was good. How was work?"

"Fulfilling."

"Oh Norell, you work too hard," Jessica said.

"Working hard is a given when you run a business. Look how hard your father works." She wished she could tell them how Vic had jumped through hoops just a few days ago to obtain a fifty-thousand-dollar cash bond for a client who'd been busted for operating a meth lab. It was rare for Vic to land what he considered a dream client, the type who kept hundreds of thousands in the bank as a general rule so that he could always pay ten percent of quarter- and half-million-dollar bonds. Vic ran around like crazy that day and didn't even get home until he'd gotten his client released at 10:00 P.M., and he fell into bed and was snoring within minutes. But let her try to operate a business of her own, and she got accused of neglecting him. She knew what he would say if she brought up his drug-dealing client: "I made fifty grand that day, Norell. You won't make that much in a year, at least not your first year." So she just kept quiet.

"Norell, you gonna clean up in here?" Vic asked.

She glanced around at the drinking glasses dripping onto coasters on the coffee table, the greasy plates holding remnants of half-eaten pizza crusts, and the dining room table, with its pizza boxes, no doubt with big grease stains on the bottoms. "No," she calmly replied. "I think we can entrust that to Jessica and Amber."

"Oh, maaaaan," Amber moaned.

"Don't forget to wipe the table good," Norell said, unfazed. "Good night."

* * *

Norell, brushing her hair in front of her vanity, looked up as Vic entered their bedroom and closed the door behind him. "Norell, what's wrong with you?"

"Nothing's wrong with me," she said, calmly moving the brush to the hair growing from the nape of her neck. "I just don't like being treated like I'm the maid."

"I've never treated you like a maid."

"You waited for me to come downstairs so you could ask me to clean up the mess you and the girls made. What would you call it?" When Vic hesitated she rushed on. "When they're home with their mother, I'm not around to clean up after them."

"All four of us ate, Norell."

"Yes, all of us did. But I think it's very inconsiderate of you to ask me to clean up, especially when you know I'd been working."

He took a few steps toward her, having recovered from being caught off guard moments before. "Before you started this company you wouldn't have been upstairs working. You would have been sitting in the room with us, even if you were just reading a book."

Norell lowered the brush and stared at him incredulously. "Is *that* what all this is about? You think I'm spending too much time working? Vic, that's not fair. You know CDN is short handed. If we don't deliver the work on time we have to adjust the billing for being late. Having your own business means long hours. You, of all people, should know that. And I didn't go into this venture so it could fail." Her eyes searched his face anxiously. The last thing she wanted was for CDN to come between them.

"Vic?" she prompted.

"Yeah. You coming to bed?"

Two hours later Norell lay on her back, staring at the rapid circling of the ceiling fan. Vic lay beside her, stretched out on his stomach in the large king-size bed, his snores and the gentle whirring of the fan the only sounds in the room. The sex had been exciting and fulfilling as ever, but the moment it was over the tension returned, hanging between them like a steel curtain.

Norell felt Vic was behaving like a petulant child. He, more than anyone, knew her fears. Hadn't he said that CDN would be good therapy for her? First he wanted her to go into business, then the moment it became a little inconvenient for him, he pouted.

At last her eyelids became heavy. *One thing is for sure*, she thought as sleep overtook her, *I'm in business to stay. Vic better get used to it.*

Chapter 17

Dana found her reintroduction to sex after a yearlong absence thrilling. Over the next week she and Sean met as often as they could. Sean, who had moved in with his mother after his marital breakup, rented a room in a motel on Phillips Highway—the old U.S. 1—Tuesday after work, which allowed Dana to get home to Brittany by seven-thirty. While Dana enjoyed the illicit nature of their rendezvous, she didn't care for the shabby surroundings. When she hesitantly shared her feelings with him, he suggested, "What about your place?"

"Of course not! My daughter is there!"

"I'm talking about when she's in school. I can take a longer lunch hour."

Dana thought about it and decided it was better to be with Sean in her own bed than at that awful motel, where the sheets were clean but the carpet was so filthy she didn't even want to walk barefoot on it.

Sean came over on Thursday for an hour of bliss. "Can you get away on Saturday?" he asked. "Let's go out for some dinner, and then get a room. Someplace nice."

Dana immediately brightened. There'd been just one blight on her rapturous mood, something she tried not to think about but found herself lingering on in spite of her best efforts. Sean's suggestion made her think that maybe she'd just imagined it after all. "I should be able to get away, but not for the whole night. The latest my babysitter works is midnight."

* * *

Dana and Sean kissed in his Eclipse still parked in front of her house like two teenagers who didn't want the evening to come to an end. But it was ten minutes to twelve, and she had to get Tina home by midnight or else risk losing her babysitting services.

"I had a wonderful time," she said shyly. They'd had a quick, informal dinner at The Loop in San Marco, then gotten a room at the Radisson Riverwalk.

"Me, too. What're you doing tomorrow?"

"Maybe going to the beach." Actually, Dana had definite plans to bring Brittany and Cécile's three older girls to the beach, but Sean didn't have to know that.

"Good idea. It's supposed to go up to ninety-four degrees tomorrow. Which beach do you go to?"

"Jax."

"All right. I'll catch up with you sometime before the day is over."

Dana went stiff. That sounded awfully final. Wasn't he going to walk her to the door?

She hesitated a moment before realizing Sean wasn't making any move to get out of the car. She considered saying something playful to remind him of his manners, but couldn't come up with anything that didn't sound like a rebuke. Still, it bothered her. She'd noticed little changes in his behavior ever since last Saturday, the first time they slept together. Did he feel that since they'd been intimate those little courtesies were no longer necessary?

"Good night," she said, opening the door.

She could hear the car's motor running in the stillness of the night. At least he didn't drive off the minute she got out. At her door she turned and waved before going inside. Only then did he put on the car's lights and pull away from the curb.

She wondered if he was going back to the hotel. She didn't remember him turning in his key. It was still early. He probably had something like eleven hours before he had to be out, so it probably did make sense for him to get his money's worth.

Dana rested the heavy Igloo cooler on the sand. It held a dozen cans of soda. "All right," she said to the four children, who had thrown down the items they were assigned to carry and were already stripping to their swimsuits. "I want everybody to put on some sunscreen before going in the water. No one goes out past chest level. You guys are used to swimming in the pool. The beach is different because of the waves; you can't really swim here. Keep an eye on where you are. The currents will push you down the beach. Just remember the lifeguard should be straight ahead. And, most important, I want you to stay together. Brittany and Josie, you two are the oldest. Watch out for Monet and Gaby, okay?"

"All right, Miss Dana," Josie Belarge said easily.

"Would you look out for Vanessa, Mommy?" Brittany asked.

Dana glanced around at the dense crowd. "Yes, but there's still an awful lot of people out here. I don't know how you expect to find her."

"She said this is the part of the beach where her father always takes them."

Dana, not sharing her daughter's optimism, merely shrugged. In an instant all four of the kids were running toward the water, leaving her alone. She set up her beach chair and its matching umbrella, then straightened up the old, faded quilt that lay on the sand. She even folded the towels the kids had thrown down so carelessly.

Next she fiddled with the portable radio, changing it from the hip-hop station Brittany always listened to to something easier on her ears. Then she had nothing else left to do, and she knew she could no longer put off what she dreaded.

The swimsuit Dana wore beneath her T-shirt and shorts was a far cry from the skimpy bikinis she had worn at eighteen or twenty—the sarong skirt and modestly scooped front and back necklines covered her as much as a tank top and shorts would. The simple act of undressing in public made her uncomfortable. She knew it was silly, but she imagined that the eyes of everyone in the vicinity were glued to her.

She pulled off her shorts with one quick yank, managing to simultaneously lower herself into her low-slung beach chair without losing her balance. The shirt came off after she sat back down. Dana put on her sunglasses, and in the act of reaching for her sunblock she glanced around to see if anyone was watching her. No one seemed particularly interested. Now she felt silly for being so self-conscious.

Dana enjoyed coming to the beach, a twenty-five-minute drive from her home. She didn't come very often only because she had a pool. Still, nothing compared to the salty smell of the ocean and the soothing sound of the surf rushing in. So what if the car was so full of sand by the time they got home that it had to be vacuumed, in spite of everyone rinsing with the hose at the beach exit? And so what if they had to do a thorough rinse with the pool hose once they got home to keep the ever-present white dirt from making its way into the house?

She applied sunblock and put on her straw hat for added protection, then popped open a can of no-name lemon-lime soda—Brittany called it "fake Sprite"—and opened the paperback she was reading. She had plenty of time to get in the water with the kids. For now she was going to chill.

It pleased her to notice several admiring glances thrown her way as she sat and read her book and sipped her soda, her knees raised and her ankles crossed in ladylike fashion. She rested a hand over her calf and absently stroked the unfamiliar smoothness of her leg. She felt so attractive, so feminine, a simple feeling she hadn't experienced in months. The transitory glances from strangers were only a small contributor to her gratification. Most of it came from the way Sean made her feel last night. Just thinking about it made her toes curl and sent a little shiver through her upper body.

She wondered what he was doing right now. He'd said he would call her, and the female in her hoped he called before she arrived home. She didn't want to give him the impression that she never left the house. Then again, she'd mentioned the possibility of going to the beach, so she might not hear from him until this evening, when he could be fairly certain she'd be home.

She leaned back to get an unobstructed view of the shoreline. She rather liked Neptune Beach, a little further north. Although crowded, it didn't have the wall-to-wall people found at Jax Beach, nor did it have the loud music and sometimes raucous behavior found at its neighbor to the south, which had more bars in its vicinity. She'd probably come to this section from now on.

It was easy to keep an eye on the children. All four girls wore bathing caps, which made them stand out among the swimmers. Brittany never objected to wearing the cap when she swam at home, but she usually balked at wearing it in public, insisting that no one wore bathing caps anymore. Fortunately, Cécile was just as adamant about protecting her daughters' hair from the elements as Dana was about Brittany's, and seeing that the Belarge sisters and Monet Rivers wore caps kept Brittany from whining.

The four girls were far from the only black females on the beach wearing bathing caps, and in Dana's opinion the Olympic-style caps they wore were far more becoming than the old-fashioned type with chin straps the others wore. Long hair was the trend nowadays, which was probably why Brittany, unlike Dana at that age, had never asked to cut her hair. It reached to her shoulder blades, and she usually wore it in a ponytail. The caps fit snugly on the sides, but there was enough room in the back to accommodate all but the longest and thickest heads of hair.

After an hour and a half in the water, the children returned, their appetites whetted by the salt air. Sandwiches, potato chips, pickles, and cookies were consumed, and sodas were gulped down, followed by an hour's worth of sand sculpting. When they went back into the water, Dana went with them.

She loved the surf, but not as much as the youngsters. "I'm going to dry off," she told them after about forty-five minutes.

Back in her chair, she peeled off her bathing cap and combed the flatness out of her hair. She could feel the sand inside her suit where it had landed after standing up against repeated waves, and she suddenly wished she could take a shower right here and now. She'd give the kids another half hour, and then that would be it. She couldn't stand feeling the scratchy sand all over herself, and didn't know how the kids dealt with it. She likened it to toddlers running around happily with a load in their diapers, but of course it had been many years since any of them were toddlers.

She indulged in some people-watching instead of returning to her book. There were plenty of size-four bikini-clad blond types lying on blankets soaking up sun, some on their stomachs with their tops untied to avoid those pesky tan lines. The over-thirty-five set was generally, like Dana, more covered up, at least the females. Men, on the other hand, didn't seem to care if the world saw their beer bellies hanging awkwardly over the front of their trunks.

Then there was the woman who was with a large group, including several children. Perhaps she didn't have a bathing suit, or maybe it had become too small, since the sister was plump. At any rate, she was swimming in a pair of dark shorts and a white heavy cotton T-shirt, which in its wet state stuck to her firm breasts like a second skin. It wasn't as bad as those lightweight fabric shirts, where every bump of the areolae were outlined, but it nevertheless left little to the imagination. The woman didn't seem to care about her revealing silhouette as she frolicked in the surf. Dana rolled her eyes, thinking that it truly did take all kinds of people to make a world.

The black couple a few yards to the right was a stark contrast to the wet T-shirt. They looked like they belonged in an ad for cigarettes or beer. The woman was light skinned with a short brown ponytail, wearing an orange maillot cut dangerously low in the back. Dana couldn't see the man too well; he seemed to delight in going underwater and pulling the woman down on top of himself. He wore goggles—not a bad idea, considering how salty the water was.

When Dana tired of looking at the other beachgoers she knew it was time to go home. She stood up and tried to catch the kids' attention by waving to them, but their backs were to her. She walked down toward them, her feet and ankles getting wet as the tide rushed in. "It's time to go," she called when she had their attention.

She waited for them to come out of the water, then brought up the rear. As she turned she saw the couple from down the beach, who had been pushed by the tide closer to where she stood. The man removed his goggles, letting them dangle around his neck from a rubber strap.

Good Lord, it was Sean!

Dana turned her head quickly. He hadn't seen her, and she didn't want him to. Less than twelve hours ago they had been wrapped in each other's arms, and now he was with another woman? Was this his wife? Someone else? What was going on with him, anyway?

She rushed back to the blanket, careful to keep her back to the ocean. "All right, let's pack up and get out of here. Everybody, get your stuff and carry the same things you brought in." She watched impatiently as the girls began shaking out the towels. "Don't worry about getting all the sand out; just take them. We'll shake them when we get home. That's why I brought all those garbage bags, so we can just stuff them in and put them in the trunk. Let's go."

Dana sneaked one last glance at Sean and his companion. They were leaving the water, and he was carrying her in a sickening display of affection. Because of the way the woman had her arms around his neck and her face turned, Dana could only see a partial profile. Her jaw set in a hard line. No wonder he had asked her which beach she went to. He had this outing planned and didn't want to run into her.

"Oh, look, there's Vanessa!" Brittany exclaimed. She immediately began running to her friend.

No way was Dana going to stick around for an embarrassing confrontation with Sean. "We're leaving, Brittany. You can say hello, and then come on. I'll expect you over by the hose in two minutes,"

Dana called after her. Then she turned to Cécile's daughters. "Come on girls, let's go."

One by one, Dana sprayed her three charges with the hose the city provided, rinsing them thoroughly, then turned it on herself, pulling her swimsuit out with one hand to get the sand off her skin.

She turned around. No sign of Brittany, and it had been nearly ten minutes. Doggone it, she'd told Brittany to make it quick. She'd come to this beach in the first place because Brittany wanted to catch up with Vanessa.

No, that wasn't fair. She couldn't blame this on Brittany. She should be grateful, for if she'd gone to Jax Beach like she'd planned, she never would have known of Sean's duplicity. Last night he'd made love to her, and this afternoon he was with another woman.

"Josie," she said, "I want you all to stay right here with our stuff. I'm going to get Brittany. Don't move, all right?"

"All right, Miss Dana."

Dana took off in search of Brittany. Her footsteps felt clumsy because of the soft sand. She spotted Brittany and started heading in that direction when she noticed the woman in the orange maillot sitting up and leaning forward. Sean lay behind her and was rubbing something—probably sunscreen—into the skin of her back. She couldn't bring herself to keep moving and stopped where she stood, wanting to get a better look at Sean's companion.

The woman shifted position, leaning back with her arms outstretched behind her. She looked up and met Dana's gaze, then gasped in shock.

Dana, too, sucked in her breath when she recognized her tenant, Micheline Mehu. Her tawny hair looked darker in its wet state.

Sean, aware of something amiss, sat up to see what had upset Micheline. His eyes grew wide with almost comical speed.

Dana moved in until she stood directly opposite them. "Hello, Sean, Micheline," she said calmly. "Sean, when you asked me which beach I went to when you brought me home last night, I didn't realize you had an ulterior motive. But it just so happens that my daughter asked me to come to this beach so she could meet up with her friend." She forced a smile. "Surprise, surprise.

"You'll excuse me now. I have to get my daughter because we're leaving. Oh, and by the way, Micheline," she added sweetly, "your lease isn't being renewed. Bye-bye now."

She walked off, savoring their shocked expressions.

Chapter 18

Dana found Brittany a few yards down the beach from Sean. "Brittany Covington. Didn't I tell you to just say hello and come on? We're waiting for you!"

"Hello, Miss Dana," Vanessa said politely but reservedly, clearly cowed by Dana's annoyance.

Dana immediately warmed up. "Hello, Vanessa."

"But Mom," Brittany said, "Vanessa and her daddy are leaving, too. Mr. Gil is rinsing his shoes out in the water, see?"

Dana turned to see Gil approaching, a black sandal dripping water in each hand. He wore a powder blue undershirt and dark blue trunks. The skin exposed by his barely-there shirt hinted at an impressive physique that hadn't been as noticeable in his suits and ties.

She waved to him, and he raised his chin in acknowledgment.

"We've been out here three hours, and I can't stand this sand anymore," he said when he reached them. "I told Vanessa that if she wants to swim more she can do it at the pool at the apartment."

"I know what you mean. We're leaving as well." She glanced over at the beach entrance. "I have my friend's three daughters with me, and I'm afraid I've left them alone too long. We really have to go, Brittany."

"Why don't you all come over and swim a while?" Gil suggested. "I'll even feed you. I've got a huge package of hamburger meat."

"Oh Mom, can we?" Brittany asked, jumping up and down in her eagerness.

Dana hesitated a moment. "Right now, you and I need to get to Josie, Monet, and Gaby." To Gil she said, "How about we wait for you there and talk about it then?"

"Yes, you'd better make sure your friend's kids are okay. We'll be along in a minute."

Dana dove into the pool at Gil Albacete's apartment complex, hoping she wouldn't land flat on her belly. Being around Gil made her conscious of every move she made. He was movie-star hand-some.

"Mom!" Brittany called out. "You forgot your bathing cap."

Dana intentionally hadn't put it on. She'd decided it would be worth washing and rolling her hair tonight if it meant looking good in front of Gil. Surely Irene, with her thick curly hair, had never worn a swim cap, and neither did Vanessa, whose long hair had nat-ural waves in it and didn't need straightening.

The girls were already in the shallow end of the pool. Dana swam toward them in what she hoped were graceful strokes.

"Look, here comes my papa," Vanessa shouted just as Dana reached the shallow end.

She shifted onto her back in time to see a shirtless Gil dive in from the side of the deep end. Stiff insurance premiums in Northeast Florida had effectively eliminated the presence of diving boards from all public and residential-complex pools. Dana would have loved to see Gil do a perfect jackknife from a board. She had no doubts he could do it. A man who looked as good as he did could do anything.

The group spent about an hour in the water. Surprisingly for such a hot day, only a few other people ventured into the water. Most of the tenants present were there strictly to work on their tans.

Dana, Gil, and the children hooked up with a foursome of adoles-cent boys who had a ball, and they all played a version of water vol-leyball.

"Popi, I'm hungry," Vanessa said after nearly an hour.

"All right, I guess I'll start dinner."

"I'll help you, Gil," Dana said quickly. She felt a bit guilty be-cause there were so many in her party. Dana felt Gil's offer was sin-cere, but she nevertheless felt that the least she could do was help out.

"Come on, girls," she called. "You can't stay in the water unsu-pervised." The apartment pool, like those in all apartments and con-dos throughout Jacksonville, did not have a lifeguard on duty. She hung back as the girls made their way to the stairs at the shallow end and climbed out one by one.

Once inside Gil's town house, Dana first excused herself and went to the powder room, where she placed a white terry turban on her head to keep it hidden as it dried into what she knew would be a frizzy mess. Upon joining Gil in the kitchen, she insisted on helping with the food preparation.

"You really don't have to," he replied. "I'm very handy in the kitchen."

I'll just bet you are, and in the bedroom, too. Funny. She hadn't thought about Gil in weeks, ever since she'd started seeing Sean. But all of a sudden Sean was out of her life, and here was Gil, looking as luscious as ever.

She knew nothing would ever come of it—for all she knew Gil was back with Irene, at least unofficially—but her fascination with him bolstered her spirit. It proved that Sean hadn't done any permanent damage to her psyche. Norell and Cécile had been right in predicting he would hurt her. He had, but she knew her heart would heal.

Micheline got home before Dana did. She and Sean hadn't exactly rushed—after Dana busted them they'd simply shrugged and gone back to lounging in the sun. She hadn't even bothered to point out to Sean that he'd lied to her and was still seeing Dana. She'd known all along, but she really didn't care, and Sean knew it.

Now she wondered if Dana was stalling coming home because she dreaded facing her. The thought of having such power made her feel heady. Hell, this was Dana's house. *She* certainly wouldn't let a tenant make her avoid her own home. If that had been her, she would have gone straight home and asked the renter when she would be vacating.

Micheline decided that she needed to contact Cécile and give her a carefully edited version of what happened. After all, Dana was her friend, and she'd probably go crying to Cécile about what a monster her sister was. She might be over there spilling her guts already.

Nah. Micheline decided that Dana would be too hurt to confide in anyone right now. She'd want to wait a day or two, run it over in her mind, try to figure out what she'd done wrong. Of course, she'd done nothing wrong. Sean was a typical man with typical lack of willpower when it came to women. That's what she'd counted on.

She'd go see Cécile tomorrow, call from work and suggest they meet for lunch. Cécile would be so surprised.

And when they met she'd get the *real* surprise.

One thing for sure, Micheline thought. She'd better hurry up and find a new place to live. Dana had all but told her to get out. She'd contact the manager of those apartments she'd really liked and arrange to move in as soon as possible. No big deal. She'd already decided to move there anyway. She wanted to have a Plan B in place for living arrangements, since she'd been playing with fire over the last few weeks and never knew when a burn might occur.

Micheline could still see Sean's shocked expression that night they met when she gave him her address. "That might be a little awkward," he'd said. "I . . . used to date the woman who owns that house."

"Dana?" she'd said, feigning surprise.

"Yes. I met her when she put her husband's car up for sale after he died. I wouldn't want to run into her. It would be embarrassing for both of us."

"I understand, Sean, but if you want to take me out, you have to pick me up."

They compromised in that Sean did come to pick her up, but he parked in front of the house next door. Micheline noticed he never turned on his headlights until they had driven past Dana's house.

Micheline knew Sean had lied when he indicated his affair with Dana was in the past. And she knew that Dana's special date at the Omni Hotel had been with Sean. It was probably the first sex she'd had since her husband died a year before. No wonder she'd been so excited.

Micheline had kept tabs on Sean that night at Wild Wednesday. She'd seen him talking to Dana, and she was outside having a cigarette when Sean escorted Dana, Cécile, and a whipped-looking Norell to their cars. He didn't approach Micheline until he returned, spending an hour or so with her and making a date for that Friday night before she left. She'd figured out that he'd chosen that night because he'd already reserved Saturday for Dana.

Micheline hadn't liked being relegated to second-best night of the week. After that first date she'd insisted they go out on Saturday. But she moved their next date to Friday when Yolanda held a dinner party Saturday evening and introduced her to Errol Trent, her husband's friend who was also a dentist. When Dana asked for advice on what to wear to her special date, Micheline knew Sean had taken advantage of her absence and reserved a room to spend with Dana at the Omni. She'd say that much for him, he was a resourceful son-of-a-gun.

She hummed a few bars of a favorite tune. Everything would work out fine. She'd get settled in her apartment and have no dating restrictions whatsoever. Originally she preferred the Beaches area, but recent hurricane activity made her decide against living too close to the ocean. She settled for a one-bedroom loft in a brand-new complex in the southeast section of town. Besides the loft bedroom, her apartment came equipped with a stacked washer and dryer. She could be at the beach in twenty minutes, the airport in twenty-five, and downtown to work in fifteen. Micheline didn't relish moving her furniture from a storage unit into an apartment. She didn't want to ask Errol to help her; they'd just met, and it was way too soon to start asking for favors. She could probably get Sean to help her. After all, it was his fault that she had to move. And it would be one more opportunity to rub Dana's nose in their affair.

Not that she disliked Dana. She just found it annoying that Sean had talked to her first. They'd sat together at the same table for a good half hour—she'd spotted him looking her way and waited expectantly for him to make his move on her, but he picked Dana first. Then after Dana left he came to her like she was some kind of afterthought. How dare he?

Who was Dana, anyway? Just one of Cécile's dull housewife friends. Cécile talked about her friends all the time, but the only one that looked like she was the least bit interesting was Norell, and now Micheline knew that even she wasn't anything special. What kind of pathetic woman couldn't get pregnant?

The faint sound of a motor prompted Micheline to take a discreet look out her window. She saw the moonroof of Dana's Camry closing. So she had finally come home.

Micheline glanced at her watch. She'd wait ten minutes, then go over and tell Dana she'd be moving out.

When Dana heard the knock on the backdoor she knew it was Micheline. Her neck and shoulders immediately tensed. She wasn't interested in hearing any apologies. All she wanted to know was when Micheline planned to move out. The girl had made a fool of her. The way she reacted when she saw Dana proved it. If Micheline hadn't known about Sean she would have smiled and said a friendly hello, not given her that guilty look like the kid caught with her hand in the proverbial cookie jar.

Now she knew how Sean had been spending those Saturday

nights he said wouldn't work for him, asking instead to see her on Friday except for the last two weeks, when he'd gotten her into bed. Now Dana wished she'd listened to Cécile. Micheline Mehu was bad news, nothing but trouble.

Cécile sat at her kitchen table, staring open mouthed at her sister. "Are you sure you're talking about the same man? The same Sean who drives a white Eclipse?"

"Yes," Micheline replied, sounding distressed. "Can you believe the gall? He knew I lived on Dana's property, but he asked me out anyway."

"Are you sure you didn't know he was dating Dana, Michie?"

Micheline bristled. "Of course I didn't know. Like I told you, he said he *used* to date her but it was all over. Why would you even ask me if I knew, Cécile?"

"Oh, maybe just to prove to yourself that you're the cutest thing around. Sometimes people build up their egos by tearing other people's egos down. Or maybe you're annoyed at me for asking you not to do anything that would hurt my friend."

"Listen, I'm just trying to give you a heads-up, keep you informed about what's happening. And I wanted you to hear it from me. Heaven only knows what Dana will tell you."

The moment Micheline was gone, leaving another broken heart behind her, Cécile picked up her cordless and dialed Dana's number. "I'm so sorry," she said without preamble when Dana answered.

Dana made a lame attempt at a chuckle. "I gather you talked to Micheline."

"Yes, she came over to have lunch with me." Cecile paused. "I don't know what else to say, Dana. I'm so embarrassed by my sister's behavior. She says Sean told her you and he had had an affair that was in the past."

"Hmph. That would explain why she looked so shocked to see me at the beach. I thought that meant she knew Sean was dating me, too. Maybe I was too harsh on her, Cécile. I told her she had to get out."

"Don't worry about it. She's all prepared to go."

"I guess Sean's the real bad guy here. Not only did he lie to Micheline, but he actually tried to get away with dating two women who are practically roommates. How much nerve does that take?"

"Yeah, that's true," Cecile admitted.

"And something else. I feel foolish telling you this, Cécile, but I noticed a change in Sean's attitude since we started having sex."

"Changed how?"

"He wasn't as attentive or considerate as he was before. He used to open the passenger door of the car for me first, for example. The last couple of times we went out, he got in the driver's seat and then popped the door lock for me. I tried to tell myself that the timing was just coincidental, but it wasn't."

"Have you heard from him?"

"No, and I don't expect to. It's over. I've got to accept that I've been cast aside in favor of a woman fifteen years younger than me."

"You're exaggerating, Dana. Micheline is twenty-seven."

"And I'm thirty-nine, so she's only a dozen years younger. I know you're trying, Cécile, but it doesn't make it any easier to take." Dana sighed. "But Sean is out of my life and Micheline soon will be. I'll get over it. And I'll remember that you tried to warn me."

It surprised Dana that she coped with Sean's betrayal so well. Knowing that Micheline planned to leave next week helped, and so had confiding in Cécile about Sean's change in attitude. Thank God Cécile hadn't said, "I told you so." Maybe Norell wouldn't say it, either, but Norell's personality wasn't as considerate as Cécile's. Besides, unlike Cécile, Norell had no need to feel embarrassed about the whole thing. Micheline wasn't *her* sister.

"Cécile, can you do me a favor?" she asked. "Can we keep this between us? I'd prefer Norell didn't know about it. I don't feel like her getting all in my face and saying I should have listened to her and never gone out with Sean in the first place. I know you didn't like the idea either, but you were never as vocal about it as she was."

"This is *your* business, Dana. It's not my place to tell Norell anything."

"Thanks, hon."

Dana felt much better when she hung up. She hadn't told Cécile about the other person who helped her through this unpleasant episode, although unknowingly. Laughing and talking with Gil Albacete had the effect of a hot toddy on a cold. It made her feel all warm and tingly inside, made her want to stretch out like a cat, then curl up.

Preferably with someone.

Chapter 19

Vic Bellamy walked expectantly into the kitchen after parking his car and entering the house through the garage. He found it spotless . . . and empty. He frowned. This was the third time this week he had come home to find Norell buried in work. Shit. He thought her having decided against pursuing the procedure her doctor recommended was a good thing, but she had jumped into work like it was a lifeline, not even giving herself sufficient time to recuperate from her surgery, at least in his opinion. Now the needs of CDN rated first on her list of priorities. Vic was not happy about being number two.

He went to her office and tapped on the open door.

"Oh, hi, honey. I was hoping I'd be all done by the time you got home."

"I left a little earlier today."

He did a quick scan of the room and noticed her straightening up, like it was the end of her workday. That was an improvement, at least, over previous days, when she returned to her office the minute the dishwasher began to hum.

"I was just about to leave to pick up the large steak and cheese calzone I ordered from Paesano's."

"Sounds good. I'll be in the living room, watching the news."

Norell found herself short of breath when Vic left the room. She could always sense when he was displeased with her long hours—his movements would become stiff, his body language cold. Instead of easy conversation, long silences often stretched between them, or he gave one-word answers to her questions. And at night, he would keep his distance from her in bed. She'd have to be crazy not to realize something was amiss.

Because she didn't want the problem to escalate into something major, she had rushed to get a certain amount of work completed by the time he came home. She'd done it, but there had been no time to cook or to shop. It was nine-thirty when she sat down to work in her office, after a leisurely breakfast with Vic and doing her housework. It hardly seemed possible, but the time now was ten past seven. Nearly ten hours was plenty long enough for a workday, though this day was actually shorter than most of the ones she'd had lately.

It was probably her own fault they were so busy. She had been in the dentist's office, waiting to have her six-month cleaning and checkup, when she noticed a man in the waiting area dictating into a hand-held recorder. She immediately handed him one of her business cards and introduced herself. It turned out he was a mortgage banker preparing a special report, one that his secretary would not be able to handle because of her other duties. Norell had accepted the job, even though the transcription wasn't medical related. She'd delivered the reports to him this morning. They turned out to be longer than she thought—thirty-two typed pages, all of which had to be proofread. On top of that, there had been all of the CDN backlog to take care of. But the broker was pleased with her work and said he would have more by the end of the week.

Norell decided that she couldn't handle the extra workload—CDN was too backlogged—but Jessica, Vic's older daughter, could do it. She was a good typist with excellent English skills, and she'd expressed interest in working as an MT part time while she studied nursing in college. Of course, this particular assignment was associated with the real-estate business rather than patient care, but it would be good transcription experience and easier to do because the dictator used everyday language. Norell had already spoken to Jessica about helping out, and the teen was looking forward to making a few dollars.

Jessica would have to come to the house to use the transcribing unit and computer, and also to have Norell readily available for any questions, but Norell didn't mind, even if the girls weren't scheduled to spend the weekend this week. Amber would probably be bored by it all and would stay home with Phyllis. And once Jessica finished her work she'd go home as well. In the meantime, Norell could relax with Vic while her stepdaughter worked. Maybe she and Vic could re-capture some of what they'd lost these last months.

Michael and Cécile got out of the Expedition. He headed for the rear of the vehicle, where he had placed the girls' overnight bags. Cécile hugged her daughters good-bye.

"So what does your daddy have planned for you guys this week-end?" she asked.

"We're going to that big water park in Georgia!" Gaby ex-claimed, clearly excited about the prospect.

"Well, that sounds like a lot of fun. You guys be good, all right?"

Michael handed Josie, Gaby, and Eleith their overnight bags and hugged them good-bye, then leaned against the car while Cécile walked them to Louis's door. She and Louis were civil, but spoke as little as possible. When her first husband opened the door she merely said hello, then said she would be back for them at six P.M. on Sunday unless he had any objections.

"That'll be fine," he said. "Say good-bye to Mommy, girls."

The trio waved to her, and she blew them a kiss, then returned to Michael, who seated her in the truck, which involved a high step up.

"Everything okay?" he asked when he had gotten behind the wheel.

"Louis doesn't upset me anymore, Michael. He hasn't for a long time now."

"I know he hasn't. But your personality has changed a little over the past few weeks. Must be hormones."

She sighed. "I've been pregnant enough times to breeze through it. I think it's more like being overworked. Much as I love the girls, I'm kind of glad to be getting a break. There's so much to do, what with the household matters, work, CDN—"

"And house hunting," he added.

"Yes, that too." She chuckled weakly.

"Well, there's a lot of real-estate ads in the Saturday paper. The kids will be okay at home alone for a few hours. What say we pick up a newspaper, go over the real-estate ads over some breakfast, and then do some looking?"

Cécile looked at him in surprise. He'd been so negative about house hunting after that first time, expressing over and over again how the coming baby was going to ruin them financially, that she'd been going out alone weekend afternoons. She found herself alternating between enjoying the peaceful time without listening to Michael grouse and resenting his taking the kids bowling or to the movies while she ran herself ragged trying to find a comfortable, affordable place for them to live. She wondered if this was his method of punishing her for getting pregnant, and for the first time ever she felt her marriage might be in danger. But now renewed enthusiasm flowed through her veins. "Sure," she said.

Cécile and Michael walked from the driveway to their front door hand in hand. "I'm going to lie down," she said dejectedly when he unlocked the door. This session of house hunting had been no more fruitful than their previous searches, amounting to hours that could have been spent doing something more productive.

He nuzzled her neck. "Go ahead," he said when he straightened up. "I guess I'll take the kids to rent some videos to keep them busy, and then I'll join you. But don't be so discouraged, Cécile. We'll find a house eventually. I don't understand why you're in such a tearing hurry. It won't be the end of the world if we live here until after the baby comes. He or she will sleep in the room with us anyway the first few months."

At least he hadn't said anything negative. "Michael, we'll be tripping all over the crib. We barely have room for our bedroom furniture." After a moment's hesitation, Cécile decided to share her true fear with him. "Besides, if we don't get a house now, I'm afraid we never will. I have terrible visions of seven kids running around the house, with the baby's bed pushed against a wall in the alcove where I do my work."

"We'll find a larger house, Cécile. In the meantime, let's be glad that we're still getting a financial break." He patted her shoulder. "Go on in and lie down. I'll take care of the kids."

She looked around the small bedroom before closing her eyes. She couldn't imagine putting a baby crib in here. How would she manage to get out of bed with it sandwiched between the bed and the wall?

In spite of the day's disappointment, she recognized the silver lining. At last Michael seemed to have accepted the idea of having another child. The angry scowl she'd seen so often since she'd told him had disappeared.

She moved into the center of the bed, lying with one hand resting on her swelling abdomen. In case she did drift off, she wanted to be aware when Michael laid down with her, and if she was in the middle of the bed, he was sure to tell her to move over. It would take him at least thirty minutes to go to the video store and come back, and in that time she could get a rejuvenating catnap. She saw an opportunity she wasn't about to pass up.

Monet and the boys would be occupied with their movie rentals for at least three hours, and the darkening skies above suggested an afternoon storm. A few hours behind closed doors with Michael on a rainy Saturday afternoon would be a real treat. She couldn't think of a more ideal way to at least begin to heal what had been the first real threat to their marriage.

"Errol," Micheline said, her voice holding a warning.

"Hmm?"

"I think we need to slow down."

"Oh, come on Michie, you can't get me all hot and bothered and then say no."

She wrenched out of his grasp. "Errol, believe me, it's getting to me too, but I know that I shouldn't . . . and I won't."

"Come on, Michie, you aren't going to tell me you're a virgin, are you?"

"No, I can't tell you that. But the time that I was intimate with someone, it didn't have a happy ending. He said he loved me, but he didn't."

That got to Errol. He immediately stiffened, his body language as well as his facial expression, and she feared she'd made a serious misstep in trying to get him to say he loved her this soon.

"Well, I'm not saying that I love you. I can't say that. But you know I'm crazy about you, and I'm crazy *for* you. Micheline, you've been around long enough to know that sex and love are often two different things."

"Yes, but I want both," she said stubbornly. "If that makes me a weirdo, then so be it."

For a few moments the silence hung heavily in the air between them. Then Errol softened. "C'mere, you," he said, holding out his arms. They shared a brief, almost impersonal hug.

"All right, I'm gone," he said against her hair, although she had done no prodding. He leaned in forward for one last quick kiss.

Micheline closed the door behind him, a satisfied smile on her face. Her friend Yolanda's instincts had been right on. She and Errol hit it off from the beginning. They'd gone to dinner the following Saturday. If Sean thought it odd that she'd been unavailable two Saturday nights in a row, he hadn't mentioned it. Instead he suggested Sunday brunch at River City Brewing, a downtown spot overlooking the St. Johns River. Then they went back to her place for a quick roll in the hay before heading out to the beach, where they'd had that embarrassing run-in with Dana. The very next day she had gone to the apartment rental office, where she'd arranged to move into her apartment before the first of the month on a prorated rent basis. Sean had helped her move.

She loved her new apartment. The complex was brand new, so new that her apartment had had no prior occupants. After she and Sean had the furniture in, she pushed it all to the center of the respective rooms and painted her bedroom a relaxing sea green and her living room a rich apricot. It meant not getting her security deposit back, for she knew that when it came time to leave here she wasn't about to paint it all white again. But Micheline felt it was worth the two hundred fifty dollars she would lose if it meant not having to look at hospital-white walls. In her living room that would have looked particularly awful, since she had white furniture.

In just two weeks she had managed to make a sparsely furnished apartment both comfortable and homey. She wanted Errol to know she had good homemaking skills.

She turned on the television with the remote control, then stretched out on the sofa, her hands clasped behind her head. Perfect. One of the networks was airing *Pretty Woman*, one of her favorite movies. Wow. Imagine meeting someone who looked like Richard Gere had in his prime—these days he looked like any other old fellow in his fifties—who had all the money in the world, and have him fall in love with you. She raised her hands over her head in a stretch of her entire body. That wasn't likely to happen to her. Not that she had anything to complain about. Errol Trent represented a catch that no woman in her right mind would throw back.

Life was good.

Chapter 20

Brittany left for a three-day stay in New Orleans with Gil and Vanessa the week after school let out. "Mom, it's fun here," Brittany said when she called from their hotel. "There are people juggling and making like statues in the street, and some people wear crazy outfits. We saw one man dressed in a purple coat trimmed with white-and-black fur, and these thick-soled white boots."

"And a huge Afro, too, I'll bet."

"How did you know?"

"Just a hunch." The man Brittany saw obviously enjoyed dressing in the seventies style. "Tell me about your hotel."

"Vanessa and me—I mean Vanessa and I—have our own room and bathroom upstairs. Mr. Gil's room is downstairs. We have our own bathroom up here, too."

"Have you eaten?"

"Did we! Mr. Gil brought us to a deli where the sandwiches are as long as my whole arm. Tomorrow he's going to bring us to see a real live plantation outside of the city."

"You'll probably learn a lot about our people's history. Is Mr. Albacete there? I'd like to talk to him for a minute."

"Sure, Mom. I'll call you tomorrow."

Dana heard the thumping sound as Brittany descended the stairs to Gil's quarters. A moment later Gil's cheerful voice touched her ear. "Hi, Dana."

"Hi! I hear the girls are having a good time."

"Yeah, we walked across the French Quarter and ate at Johnny Po'Boys. They got a kick out of some of the sights."

"I'm sure they did. Brittany described someone who sounded like a pimp." She couldn't keep the concern out of her voice.

"Yeah, well, you find all kinds of folks in the Quarter. You've been here; you know that. But don't worry, Dana. I gave them the lecture about not laughing or staring at people, and no one will approach them with me around. We're in a nice hotel."

"Yes, I know." Dana had visited the hotel's Web site when Gil gave her the name of the place he chose.

"I'm going to go over to Harrah's and hit the blackjack table in about an hour, but I'll be back before dark. The girls have plenty to eat. They could only eat half of their po'boys at lunch, so they brought the other half back with them. They picked up some dessert at Johnny's as well, and of course they couldn't eat it, so they doggie bagged that as well."

"Do you really think they'll be okay there by themselves?"

"Of course, Dana. If I didn't, I'd never leave them. Vanessa will call my cell phone if she needs me for anything. Stop worrying, will you?" he said good-naturedly.

"It's just that Brittany is all I have left, Gil. If anything happened to her I couldn't bear it."

For a moment silence filled the air. "I hope I didn't sound insensitive," Gil said, "but I hope you understand that I love my daughter as much as you love yours."

Dana felt about a big as a pin. "Now I feel stupid."

"That wasn't my intention, Dana."

"I know."

"Tell you what. I'll call you when I get back to the room. Will that make you feel better?"

"Yes, it will."

"All right then. You'll hear from me in a few hours."

"Oh, I'm so happy to see you!" Dana exclaimed, pulling Brittany into a tight embrace. "I missed you so much!"

"Gee, Mom, I was only gone for three days. What are you going to do when I go to Nassau?" Brittany traditionally spent a month with her grandparents and uncle.

"I'll be all right." Dana tore herself away, not wanting Brittany to feel smothered. She waved to Vanessa, who sat in the front seat of Gil's Murano, and then turned to Gil, who had gotten out from behind the driver's seat and retrieved Brittany's small suitcase from the trunk. "Back safe and sound," he said pleasantly. Then, speaking to Vanessa, he said, "You can stay there. I'm just going to carry this in, and I'll be right out." He fell into step beside Dana.

"Safe and sound, thanks to you, Gil," she said. "You're right, I shouldn't have worried. Next time I'll know better."

"Maybe next time you'll come along."

They smiled at each other, and suddenly Dana felt something other than a friendly bond between two single parents. Gil was looking at her in a way he never had before. She knew that look, the look a man gives a woman he's interested in.

Her tongue suddenly expanded in her mouth, making it hard to talk. "Well, maybe," she managed to say.

Gil put Brittany's bag down. "I'd better get Vanessa home. I'm sure her mother is anxious."

"Thanks again for bringing Brittany along, Gil."

"Sure. I'll be talking to you, okay?"

"Okay." She shut the door the moment he stepped outside. Her heart was beating fast enough to power a jet. Had she imagined it, or had Gil Albacete just flirted with her? And what had he meant by saying he would be talking to her?

She'd already had a relationship with an inappropriate man that ended badly. She didn't want to do it again. Fantasizing about Gil as a man both desirable and unattainable was one thing. Acting on her fantasy by getting involved with him was something else. Of course, the possibility always existed that she'd just imagined the way he looked at her. She hoped so.

Because if she hadn't, she could very easily find herself in the middle of a situation she didn't have the faintest idea how to handle.

Chapter 21

The new workweek began on a high point. Through CDN's ad on the Internet, Norell had found two new transcriptionists who would be working full-time. One lived in South Carolina, the other in Texas. Norell spent the morning on a conference call training them on the software and the formatting of the accounts they would be working on.

By Thursday Norell found herself wishing it was Saturday; she was exhausted. Even with two new people their workload remained heavy, and there were other distractions. Paying the household bills had always been Norell's responsibility, but being so busy, she could barely keep up with getting dinner on the table. She'd bought a pair of shoes on sale at Dillard's last month and had forgotten to mail in her check. Because the bill was due today, she had to drive over to the mall or be slapped with a late fee that would be more than the cost of her purchase.

While she was there, she thought maybe she could pick up a little something for Dana. This wasn't a good time for her friend, who faced the dual blow of the first anniversary of Kenny's accident and Father's Day.

Then there was that mysterious business with Sean. She didn't know what was going on with that. Dana announced without elaboration, and in a tone that suggested she didn't wish to discuss the matter further, that she would no longer be seeing him. Norell had asked Cécile about it, and she hadn't known anything either. Maybe he'd reconciled with his wife or something. At any rate, Norell agreed with Cécile's statement that whatever happened, Dana was better off without him.

Under these circumstances Norell felt Dana warranted some special attention, no matter how busy she was. Still, these errands were taking time away from her already busy schedule. Vic wouldn't be happy with how late she would have to work tonight. She'd make it up to him by suggesting they meet downtown for dinner tomorrow. Since it was Friday, she would have the entire weekend to get the work completed before it came due on Monday.

She turned into the mall entrance, continuing to drive until she was near her destination. The mall had just opened for business a half hour ago and wasn't crowded. She started to pull into a space right past the ones reserved for persons with disabilities when she noticed a small white sign at the foot of the space. Norell squinted—she didn't know if it was her imagination, but her vision didn't seem as sharp as it used to be. Probably all those hours in front of the computer screen. Maybe this was a special space for the Employee of the Month or something.

To her amazement, when she focused on the sign, it read "PARK-ING FOR EXPECTANT MOTHERS." She sucked her teeth and drove on. That was the stupidest thing she'd seen in a long time. Parking for expectant mothers! Why not parking for tall people, or for short people, fat people, skinny people, good-looking people, ugly people? It seemed to Norell that plenty of other people could use a parking space this close to the mall entrance. Elderly people, for example. Plenty of senior citizens had difficulty walking, but not necessarily to the extent where they qualified for handicapped parking. My goodness, if every old person in Florida needed a handicapped parking spot, there wouldn't be anything left for the rest of the population. And what about the woman struggling with several small children, particularly if one was an infant? Surely she would benefit from having a space close to the entrance. It would reduce the amount of time needed to escort children through traffic, since drivers often seemed to think they were on a highway instead of in a parking lot.

She was tempted to park there any damn way, but in the end drove a few spaces down to an empty spot. Why this ridiculous admiration of women who were mothers? It almost bordered on worship. It was a club of which she'd never be a member. She'd have to get used to it.

The sight of someone actually using a pay phone triggered the thought that her phone bill was due. She'd have to pay it online as soon as she got home. Each month it got harder and harder to keep up with her household while satisfying the demands of her business. She was going to have to take some time away from CDN to get her bills in order, maybe arrange to have them paid by automatic bank draft. Vic would have a fit if the phone or lights got cut off because she'd forgotten to pay the bill.

She glanced at her watch. She still had to go to OfficeMax and pick up a new toner for her printer; she had to print out the payroll checks and statements today. She'd really have to hustle if she planned to surprise Vic with dinner. He'd been so grumpy lately; she tried to make an extra effort to please him. She planned to make his favorite, linguine with white clam sauce, tonight.

She was back at home, rewarding herself with a cigarette after installing the toner while the paychecks printed, when Dana called. "Can you help me with the sports-medicine clinic, Norell? I can't do this all by myself, and Cécile's not working today because of the funeral." Cécile's aunt had died a few days before in South Florida, so she, her daughters, and her sister Micheline had driven down to attend the services.

"Yes, I just finished the payroll. I'm going to start transcribing in a little bit and work well into the evening. Don't worry, we'll get it done." Norell hated transcribing for that account—she found all those sprained wrists and ankles and torn ligaments boring—but she had a financial stake in keeping the client happy, so she'd force herself. She supposed hearing about muscle and joint pains for a few hours was better than working with her absolute least favorite, obstetrics.

"How's Cécile doing?" she asked. "That's no picnic, driving all the way down to West Palm and then back again."

"At least she has her sister with her to help with the driving." After the incident with Sean, Dana didn't like mentioning Micheline by name. "I told her to take it easy. She wouldn't want to bring on a miscarriage."

"Miscarriage? Cécile's *pregnant*?"

Dana didn't answer right away, and Norell had a feeling she was lamenting having let what obviously had been a secret slip out. "How can that be?" she pressed. "She had a tubal ligation, remember?"

"Norell, how many times have you transcribed the doctor saying that the patients were informed of the odds of failure?"

"Yes, but I've never heard of it actually happening. Wait a minute. They also say there's a possibility of an ectopic—"

"She had a test. The fetus is in the uterus, where it belongs."

Norell recognized the hard edge in Dana's voice. "I know what you're thinking, Dana. You think I'm such a monster, and maybe I am. But I went through so much and have nothing to show for it, and she's got a house full of kids. She gets everything while I have nothing."

"Norell, there's no excuse for wishing a tubal pregnancy on Cécile. Besides, you're exaggerating. You have a husband who loves you, a beautiful home, money in the bank, and you're healthy."

"Cécile's got all those things you mentioned, except the beautiful home, and since she said they're looking, she'll soon have that too. And she has much more." Norell took a deep breath. *Everyone doesn't get a happy ending*, she reminded herself. "I don't really wish anything bad for Cécile or her baby, and I know it's not up to her to decide who gets what out of life, but with her having so many babies you'd think I'd be able to have just one."

"In an ideal world, you would be."

A few tears of frustration had escaped from Norell's eyes as she talked, but suddenly she remembered that sign at the mall parking lot. She pictured Cécile pulling her van into that space and getting out, and suddenly Norell began crying openly in great sobs that left her gasping for air. "I'm sorry," she said when she caught her breath.

"Norell, I wish there was something I could do."

"It's all right. It's just such a shock. I'll get over it." Her tears subsided, and she chuckled, or tried to. It came out sounding more like a sniffle. "I can hear Cécile going on and on now. I swear, that girl talks about her kids more than Kathie Lee Gifford used to when she was on TV."

"Are you sure you're going to be all right? I feel terrible, spilling it like that. I promised Cécile I wouldn't say anything. Maybe she won't be too upset with me, since I know she dreaded telling you. You've been very brave, doing so much for CDN and everything, but I can imagine how devastating this whole experience has been for you."

"It's hard trying to get used to. Sometimes I can go to the mall, like I did this morning, and look right through all those toddlers in strollers or those adorable display windows at Baby Gap, and then other times it gets me down, like it did when we used to go on Saturday afternoons. Even back then I had a feeling I might have a problem conceiving, because of what my doctor told me years ago."

On the other end of the line Dana nodded. Before Kenny's accident she and Norell used to hit the mall just about every weekend, walking up and down the shop-lined perimeter for exercise and then canceling it out by pigging out on ice cream sodas and foot-long hot dogs at A&W. "You canceled on me a couple of times. I remember bringing Brittany, and sometimes her friend Vanessa too, just to have someone to walk around with."

"You could have asked Cécile," Norell said sweetly.

Dana knew Norell was trying to be funny at Cécile's expense, but at least she wasn't crying anymore. "Come now, Norell. You know Cécile is too busy hunting down bargains at garage sales or out at the price club buying margarine tubs and cereal boxes the size of Delaware to go to the mall."

They giggled.

"Anyway, then Kenny had his accident," Norell said, "and you couldn't afford to go shopping. I was glad not to have to go to the mall. But Cécile was still a problem. I found it too depressing to be around her and listen to her talk about her family."

All Dana's warm feelings for her friend's situation evaporated like spilled water on a hot street. "You make it sound like my husband's death was the ideal excuse not to have to go to the mall with me," she said coldly.

"Oh, no, Dana. It's not that way," Norell objected. "You know how devastated I was when Kenny died. That was just poor phrasing on my part. I'm sorry."

Dana sighed. Norell had been her rock in those dark days following Kenny's death. She had been so distraught that even now the memories were still fuzzy, but she knew Norell and Vic provided invaluable assistance. She didn't know how she would have managed without them.

"All right," she said. "I guess you're not expressing yourself all that well because you're upset. But you have to realize that Cécile talks about her family because that's what's most important to her.

It's not like she doesn't have any other interests in life, but I suppose everything does revolve around Michael and the kids."

"I know it's not right for me to take out my frustration on her." Norell sighed deeply. "I'm going to call her when she gets back and tell her I'm happy for her. And it's not just lip service, Dana. I really mean it."

Chapter 22

The bowling alley during cosmic bowling sessions reminded Dana of a disco, all loud music and flashing lights. Most of the groups of patrons included children. She bowled two games with Brittany, Gil, and Vanessa, but begged off when the girls wanted to play a third. "Oh, come on, Mom," Brittany said in a wheedling tone. "You promised."

"I'm not saying we have to leave, Britt. I'm just saying I'm not up to playing any more. The rest of you can bowl another game. I'm sitting this one out." She handed Brittany a five. "You already had a snack, so bring my change."

"I think I'll sit this one out, too," Gil said. He reached for his wallet. "Vanessa, go pay for your game quick, before they sell this lane to someone else."

They watched as the girls rushed off to the front counter. Dana turned to Gil and sighed. "Sometimes I think Brittany sees me as someone who's on summer vacation, like she is. It's as if she has no idea that I work eight hours each day, plus an additional three or four hours on my business. Bowling those two games wore me out." She gestured to the tall table and bar stools just beyond their designated lane area. "Shall we sit?"

"How about a nice cold beer? Or a glass of wine if you'd prefer."

"Wine, please."

Gil went off to the bar, then returned a short time later with their drinks, a tall tumbler for his beer and a small wineglass for her. For a few moments they simply watched Brittany and Vanessa roll balls, cheering them on and offering encouragement at those near-spares and almost-strikes.

"So you're working hard these days, are you?" Gil asked, loudly because of the noisy environment.

"Yes, but at least I can see the results fairly quickly. I'm happy to say that business is booming."

"That's wonderful."

"I'll still miss Brittany terribly while she's away, though."

"Why don't we have dinner one night next week?" Gil suggested.

Dana looked at him through confused eyes. "But Brittany is leaving for her grandparents' on Thursday. We'll be busy getting her things together. We couldn't possibly join you and Vanessa for dinner."

"Actually, my invitation didn't extend to Brittany, or to Vanessa either, for that matter. I was thinking more in terms of a one-on-one between you and me."

"Oh! I didn't understand." Dana really hadn't. When Vanessa called Brittany about going bowling tonight, she said her father would be coming along, too. Dana and Brittany arranged to meet them at the bowling alley. It made perfect sense to Dana for Gil to join them, since Vanessa was spending the weekend at his apartment. The unexpected invitation for dinner went right over her head.

As his intent sank in, she suddenly felt shy. Her feet remained firmly planted in place, but inside she was trembling. This could be a dream come true, or it could be a nightmare if Irene found out. "Gil, uh, do you really think that's a good idea?"

"I won't pretend to not know what you mean, but let me ask you this: What does your first instinct tell you?"

Dana quickly decided that only the truth would do. "I'd be inclined to accept. I'd *like* to accept. But as I said, I don't know how wise a choice that would be."

"Okay, so you'd like to go out with me. The fly in the ointment is, I presume, my ex-wife."

"You have to agree it could get rather awkward, Gil. I have a lot of contact with Irene because of Brittany and Vanessa being so close. We help each other out. I've kept Vanessa when she had something to do, and she's kept Brittany for me." Dana specifically remembered caring for Vanessa on Mother's Day while Irene went to dinner with Gil. Irene came for Vanessa afterward, beaming but typically close mouthed. They must have had an amiable meal, but that was all. Gil's invitation to her proved that nothing had come of it.

"Well, for now we're talking about one meal together, so why don't we just do it, and we'll deal with Irene later. Uh, you do have another babysitter you can use?"

Dana let out the breath she hadn't realized she'd been holding. "Yes." It would hardly do to ask Irene to sit with Brittany while she went out with Gil, but her teenage neighbor was usually available. "All right," she said. "Dinner it is."

It was nearly eleven o'clock when Dana got home, but she decided to take a chance and call Norell, whom she knew often worked late. She desperately wanted to discuss Gil's invitation and her concerns about it with someone, and she definitely couldn't call Cécile at this hour. Funny. For years the three of them had managed to have lunch together at least once a month, but since they'd gone into business they'd all been so busy that the only time they managed together was for CDN's weekly staff meetings. Discussion at their meetings was limited to business matters, after which they all returned to their respective home offices to work.

Fortunately for Dana, Norell answered the phone sounding wide awake. "I'm just closing up shop," she said in response to Dana's asking if she could spare a few minutes to talk. "Eleven o'clock is my limit. I want to spend some time with Vic. He's been a little testy lately, says I'm devoting too much time to CDN."

"Oh. That's not good. I wouldn't want CDN to put a strain on your marriage."

"It's not strained," Norell said quickly. "I'm just concentrating on becoming more of a morning person, getting up and starting work early like you and Cécile, so my evenings can be free."

Dana chuckled. "As I remember, when we worked in the office you had trouble getting in by nine."

"Like I said, it'll take some effort. It'll be fine. So what's on your mind?"

Dana told her about Gil. "One part of me is overjoyed that he wants to see me socially, but the other part is a little worried about how his ex will react."

"Isn't she the one you said is kind of cold?"

"I wouldn't call her cold, but she doesn't have the most brilliant personality in the world. She's always been pleasant, but doesn't really have much to say unless it's about the weather or something general like that. I've known Irene for at least six years, and I still don't have a clue about her personally."

"That works in your favor. You'd be right to have second thoughts about going out with Bill if you and Irene were friends."

"Gil."

"Isn't that what I said?"

"No, Norell, you called him Bill." Dana wondered if Norell was drinking. She'd said she'd finished work for the day, but Dana felt concern nevertheless. She knew how unhappy Norell had been lately, in spite of her putting on a brave face and calling Cécile to wish her well. Lately it seemed that Norell's drinking had escalated. She mentioned having morning headaches, and later in the day she seemed a lot more mellow than usual. Dana expected her to be as adamantly against the idea of her dating Gil as she had been with Sean.

"Oops. Sorry. Well, it might be a little uncomfortable when you see the ex-wife, but whether or not you want to cope with that is up to you. But I don't think you're doing anything morally wrong, no."

"What do you mean, you knew it?" Dana said to Cécile.

"This was bound to happen. You were with him at the beach the other week. You were in touch with him when he took Brittany to New Orleans. When you said he was going along with you and the girls when you went bowling I knew something was in the works."

"Well, it looks like you were right. But what do you think about my going out with him?"

Cécile sighed. "Dana, can't you find a man to date anywhere in Jacksonville who isn't connected to your past in some way? You know, start a relationship with a man you've never laid eyes on before."

"So you don't think it's a good idea," Dana said, her voice low with disappointment. She had Norell in her corner—even if her support came courtesy of Smirnoff—and hoped to have Cécile as well.

There was a pause on the other end of the line. Dana imagined Cécile was swallowing those doggone gummi bears again.

"It's not what I think that counts," Cécile finally said. "It's what Brittany and her friend and her friend's mother think. Personally, I don't think any of them will be pleased." Cécile paused. "Of course, if her mother knows you've been present on all these outings, she's probably sensing what's coming herself."

"Come on, Cécile. I didn't plan this."

"You didn't plan Sean, either, did you? And look what happened."

"This is different. Gil isn't like Sean."

"And you know this how?"

Dana sighed. "I just know. My instinct tells me, and I trust my instincts."

"Dana, please don't be offended by this, but it's not your instinct you're listening to. It's that tingling you're getting between your legs."

"I can't deny that has something to do with it. I'm only human, Cécile."

"Yes, but I think your instincts are steering you in the wrong direction." Cécile paused. "You *did* ask what I thought."

"Yes, I did. And you told me, all right." Dana changed the subject to something she'd been thinking about in recent days. "Cécile, why don't you and I plan to go out for dinner with Norell, like we used to? We haven't been out since the day we launched CDN."

"I'd love to, but it's hard to find the time. I'm still working for Precise, and there's Michael, the kids, the baby, and the house hunt."

"Norell mentioned that Vic wasn't happy about all the time she spends working," Dana said. "She tried to make light of it, but I'm worried. I don't want her and Vic to break up over this."

"Break up? Dana, you know how marriage is. It's full of rough patches. Michael was in a snit for weeks when he found out I was pregnant. He's finally accepted it, but most of the time he still makes excuses when it's time to look at houses. He says it takes too much of his weekends, and that when I find one that'll work for us I should bring him to look at it." She sighed.

"Well, I think Michael is being unfair. After all, you didn't get pregnant by yourself."

"Oh, please. If it's not my fault, then it's the doctor's fault who tied my tubes. In Michael's opinion, *he* had nothing to do with it."

"How's the house hunting going, anyway?"

"Lousy. Everything I see that's nice has too high an asking price."

Gil called Dana Sunday night. "How's Tuesday? Surely you can get away for a few hours."

"Yes, I'm sure I can. Brittany is old enough to get her clothes together. I'll just double-check and make sure she's got everything."

"Great. I'll pick you up at six."

Dana's stomach did a somersault. "Gil, you can't pick me up."

"Why not?"

"Brittany might see you!"

"So what if she does? We aren't doing anything wrong, Dana."

"I agree, but I don't feel Brittany needs to know you and I are having dinner together."

"That's foolishness. We're single adults spending an evening together. There is nothing whatsoever inappropriate about that."

Dana felt her resentment building. "Gil, why don't I call you back tomorrow?" she suggested tightly. "I have your card. I'll call you at the office."

"All right."

She resisted the urge to slam the phone down. Where the hell did he get off, telling her what her daughter should or should not know? She glanced at her watch. Eight-thirty. It was a cinch that Vanessa was home with Irene by now. He hadn't even called her to finalize their date until his own daughter was out of the house, yet he wanted to flaunt their date in front of *her* child. It looked like Gil the fantasy held a lot more appeal than the real thing. Well, he had a surprise coming. Tomorrow she'd call and cancel.

Chapter 23

Cécile turned to her stepdaughter. The multicolored balloons tied to the mailbox to mark the party site told her she had the right house. "Here we are. You have a good time, Monet. I'll see you at five o'clock."

"Okay, Mommy." Monet opened the car door and got out, nearly dropping the shorts set they had selected for her friend Daphne, who was turning nine. "Bye!"

"Bye." Cécile waited in the car as Monet got to the front door and rang the bell, not pulling off until the door was opened by a woman she presumed was Daphne's mother. Monet turned and waved, as did the woman. Cécile waved back and drove off.

She usually spent special time with her stepdaughter on weekends when her own daughters were staying with Louis. In addition to missing them, Monet clearly felt left out when Josie, Gaby, and Eleith came back and described the fun things they had done with their father. Cécile grudgingly admitted that Louis did a fine job of keeping the them entertained, bringing them to The Landing in downtown Jacksonville for arcade games and out for ice cream sodas, or to a drive-in movie, a roller rink, a bowling alley, or for go-kart rides.

She and Monet usually went shopping and sometimes went to the movies—choosing whatever film the other girls said Louis planned to take them to see. They also walked for exercise. Michael said that even as a toddler Monet had been on the pudgy side. Through exercise and portion control they had both lost ten to fifteen pounds, but of course Cécile had gained all hers back.

In recent weeks they'd gone shopping for the baby. Josie and

Gaby, and sometimes even Eleith, raved about their little brother, Pierre, who lived with his mother, Louis's girlfriend. Monet, having been the youngest of Michael's children, had never really been around a baby, and she said she wished she had a little brother or sister. Cécile had a feeling that after the baby came, instead of missing her stepsisters, Monet would be delighted to have her new brother or sister mostly to herself.

Cécile smiled. The kids had all been excited about the baby when she and Michael told them the news. Even the boys had been tickled.

She considered dropping in on Dana, since she was near her house. Jacksonville was huge, with over eight hundred square miles; and the implementation of a magnet school system in Jacksonville meant that schoolchildren had friends who lived in different sections of the city. This San Jose neighborhood was a good five miles from their home in the St. Nicholas area of town, but only about five minutes from Dana's house in Lakewood.

Monet's friend Daphne lived in a well-established community with plenty of greenery and well-kept ranch houses whose ages were given away only by the one-car garages that were popular until the emergence of dual-career couples in the late sixties. Most bore signs of upgrading, like storm windows and those elegant wood doors with stained glass in the center.

She saw an "OPEN HOUSE" sign on the corner and on an impulse turned in the direction of the arrow. What the heck, she could see Dana anytime.

The home for sale was on the next street. It was larger than its neighbors, with a second level on the left side and an attractive double front door. Two cars sat parked in the wide driveway, one of which she knew belonged to the real-estate agent.

She rang the bell, which was quickly answered by a sixtyish man with horn-rimmed spectacles who wore a dark suit. "Hello," he said in a soft-spoken way that, paired with his slight build and dark suit, made her think of a funeral director. "Come right in."

"Thank you. I was in the neighborhood and saw your sign. Looks like a nice place."

"Well, let's take the tour," the agent suggested, thoughtfully stepping back so as not to obstruct her view.

Cécile couldn't keep the excitement she felt out of her voice as she recounted what she saw to Michael. "It's perfect for us. It's a real house, not a messy jumble of rooms some nutty architect designed. It has three bedrooms downstairs, one with a full bath, plus a full bath in the hall. All the hallways are nice and wide, and the foyer is large enough for a good-sized console table. And we can get a computer for the kids' use and put it in the hall by the kids' rooms."

"Wait a minute. Three bedrooms won't be large enough for us, Cécile."

"There are three bedrooms downstairs. The owners put a larger master suite upstairs back in sixty-five."

"Sixty-five! How old is this place?"

"It was built in fifty-four."

"Fifty-four! That makes it over fifty years old. It's almost as old as this house."

She tried not to show the frustration she felt. He knew damn well that a newly constructed house would cost more than they could afford. "Yes, but it's a lot larger. The kitchen is huge, and it's been re-decorated, too, in white, red, and black. There's an island, plus the owners have a table for six in the corner, and it fits fine."

"Is that all there is, an eat-in kitchen, or is there a dining room, too?"

"There's a formal dining room. The table in it now seats eight, and there's still room for a bigger one. And the laundry room is big enough to put our freezer in and still have plenty of room for the washer and dryer." She spoke faster and faster, as if she were afraid of forgetting something if she didn't get the words out right away. "Between the dining room and the laundry room is a den. The peo-ple now have a bar, TV, and couch in there, but that could be my of-fice."

Michael looked impressed. "It does sound nice. What's the asking price?"

"One-seventy."

"That's twenty grand more than I wanted to spend." He spoke in a tone that suggested further consideration was out of the question.

"Michael, we won't find anything large enough for that amount, unless you're looking at one of those tiny cottages that's had rooms added here and there over the years and spreads out all haphazardly. In those cases you're paying for the large lots they sit on, because the house itself isn't worth two cents. This is a nice house in a nice neigh-borhood, and it's the best value we've seen, and we can afford it."

"All right. I guess it won't hurt to take a look at it."

She looked at him earnestly. "Michael, my parents told all of us as we grew up that they wanted us to do better than they did. Not only did they want it, they expected it." She chuckled. "I think Micheline may have gone a little overboard on it, the way she loves nice things, but I agree that it's terribly important for each generation to improve their quality of life. I don't want our children to grow up thinking it's all right to live the way we do, all crammed in like crabs in a barrel. It would be different if we barely made ends meet, like my parents. But we both make good money, and from now on there will be extra coming in each year because of CDN. We ought to live in a nice house. And that's going to come with a price tag." Her voice broke as she finished. She'd been looking at houses for weeks now, and in her heart she knew this would be the best deal they would get. If Michael made them miss out on this opportunity because he insisted it cost too much, she didn't know if she could live with it.

Michael put his arms around her and stroked her back. "All right, Cécile. I'm all for upward mobility. Let's go look. We'll go see it before we pick up Monet."

Michael felt the same way about the house as she did, and before they picked up Monet they made a good-faith offer.

"Mrs. Puckett likes us. I think she'll accept," Cécile said as they were leaving.

"What makes you say that?"

"She told me that she and her husband, who died a few months ago, had five kids between them when they got married. They had another one together. That one, the youngest, just got married, and Mrs. Puckett is going to move in with her oldest daughter in Mandarin."

"What'd you do, learn her whole life story?"

"It pays to listen to people. I told her that we, too, have a blended family and that we're having a child together. She seemed very interested. I'm sure it brought back pleasant memories of when she and her husband were young and raising their kids. She's a nice lady, Michael."

"I'm sure she is, but she might decide to sell to someone white. You know how these things go sometimes."

"That's silly, Michael. Monet's friend's family lives on the next street, so there are definitely black people in the neighborhood."

"Yes, but the neighbors might not want any more."

"I don't think so. Didn't you see that picture on her dresser upstairs?"

"What picture?"

"The one with the black baby. One of her kids must have married black. I don't know how she feels about having a black son- or daughter-in-law, but she obviously loves her grandchild, or else the picture would be shut away in a drawer somewhere."

"You don't miss anything, do you, Cécile?"

"Like I said, I think we've got it." Cécile's voice rang with confidence. "She likes us. I know."

Chapter 24

Dana looked at Brittany blankly. "What?"

"Nikki invited me to a sleepover Tuesday night," Brittany repeated. "It's her birthday, and since I'm going to Nassau and she's going to Alabama, we won't see each other until school starts. A couple of other girls will be there as well. We're going to cook out, hamburgers and hot dogs. And Nikki's parents are getting her a limousine, and after we eat we're all going to ride to play miniature golf. Is it okay for me to go?" Brittany looked at Dana pleadingly. "It's Tuesday, so I'll still be able to spend my last night, Wednesday, with you."

"Yes, of course, you can go." Nikki Davis was Brittany's closest friend at school. Brittany and Vanessa started school together and had met in kindergarten, but when Dana and Kenny moved into the house Dana still lived in when Brittany was in third grade, she had to change schools. She'd made new friends easily, but she and Nikki formed a special bond.

Brittany's news that she would not be at home on Tuesday stunned Dana. She found herself rethinking her decision to cancel her dinner with Gil. After all, if Brittany would be at Nikki's she had no reason to. Gil could even pick her up as planned.

But at dinner she would set him straight about a few things.

He showed up on time, complimented her on her outfit—a simple sleeveless sweater, plaid capri pants, and heeled mules that would be cool in the June heat—and opened the car door for her. "I thought we would go to the Fish Camp in Mandarin," he said. "I love their food, but I seldom get to this part of town. They have an excellent selection of steak and pasta if you don't care for seafood."

"I adore seafood, especially theirs."

The restaurant was tucked in a remote corner of South Jacksonville on the banks of a branch of the St. Johns River. Several large boats sat docked near the front entrance.

The inside was all wood, river views, and dim lighting. Dana ordered grilled catfish and vegetables.

"Ooh, this is good," she said after taking her first bite. "Melts in my mouth."

"The food here is wonderful."

"I'm glad we came." She smiled at him warmly. Something in his eyes as he smiled back made her shiver, not in a bad way, and she suddenly knew this would be no one-time dinner. She and Gil would be spending a lot of time together. It wouldn't be too difficult to schedule—with Brittany gone she had no parenting responsibilities—but Dana's thoughts kept going back to Irene Albacete. She'd seemed so happy Mother's Day when she confirmed Vanessa's statement that Gil was taking her to dinner, and later when she retrieved Vanessa from Dana's care. That had been one of the rare times when Dana saw her show any emotion.

But everything hinged on the way he reacted when she pointed out his part in the incident that nearly caused her to cancel their date. "Gil," she began, "there's something we have to discuss. I don't think you were being very fair to insist that you come to pick me up."

"No harm done, was there? I'll bet Brittany didn't even see me."

"No, she didn't, because she wasn't there. She's at a friend's house. They're all celebrating the friend's birthday before they go their separate ways for the rest of the summer."

"Vanessa is going away, too. First she's taking a trip up North with her mother, and then she'll spend a few weeks with my parents in Miami." He noticed her stony expression. "Sorry. I was just making a comment. I didn't mean to take over the conversation. You were saying?"

"Gil, have you told Vanessa that you were taking me out tonight?"

"No. There's no need for her to know."

"Because she doesn't live with you. I noticed the other day that you called in the evening. I guess you waited until after you'd brought Vanessa back to her mother's."

"Well, yes, but—"

"Think about it, Gil. Brittany lives with me full time. There's no sending her to her father's house. It's practically impossible for me to keep any secrets from her, even if a babysitter is present. The only way I can have a sense of privacy is to shield her from anything I don't want her to know. And I don't think it's fair for you to feel you want to keep Vanessa in the dark about us, but take me out openly in front of Brittany." She paused. "Not that Vanessa would be in the dark for long, not if Brittany knew."

He leaned back in his rattan chair and looked at her sheepishly. "I guess you're right. I didn't think of it that way. The whole thing caught me off guard. I mean, you were always the mother of my daughter's best friend. And there I was, not seeing anyone, having difficulty making any special connections, and when I brought Brittany home from New Orleans I kind of saw you for the first time. There you were, a woman who'd been handed lemons by life and managed to turn them into lemonade. You'd lost your husband suddenly, but instead of buckling under you started a business and took in a renter. I admire you for all you've done, Dana. Believe me, there are women out there who've fallen apart over a mere divorce. Of course, there was usually a younger woman involved."

Dana thought of how hurt she'd been at catching Sean out with Micheline. "I'm sure it's not easy being cast aside in favor of a newer model, especially if you've given a man the best years of your life."

"I guess. But that night it occurred to me that you were more than just Vanessa's friend's mother. I saw someone I'd like to get to know better, and since you're widowed there's nothing morally wrong with it." He shrugged. "Of course, even I had to consider that there might be problems. But I'm afraid I thought about it mostly from my own viewpoint. I'm sorry."

She sighed. "As long as we're on the same page. But Brittany will be away for the next month, and at least I won't have to meet you anywhere. You can come to the house freely, and no one will have to know."

His face held mild curiosity. "And when Brittany returns?"

"Well . . ." She hadn't thought that far ahead. "I guess then she'll have to be told. Provided, of course, that you and I are still seeing each other."

Gil reached across the table and covered her forearm with his hand. "I've got a very strong feeling that we will be."

Chapter 25

"Dana, I just got off the phone with Vic's lawyer, and he said he could throw some legal transcription our way," Norell said into the phone. "Jessica did such a good job with that real-estate project, she should be able to handle this as well."

"I don't know, Norell. Real estate is one thing. Legal is something else. They have their own vocabulary that's probably nearly as extensive as ours. Jessica might not be able to handle it. A court reporter might be better suited."

"Oh, there isn't much to legal work. A writ there, a codicil there. It's a cinch."

"Why don't we discuss it at the next partners' meeting?"

"All right."

"You must have eaten your Wheaties this morning, Norell. You sound so energetic."

Norell gulped down a multivitamin. "Well, I got a good night's sleep. I feel great!"

"Uh, how's Vic?"

"He's fine," Norell replied dreamily.

Dana instantly understood. Norell had had a good night with Vic. No wonder she felt so up this morning.

As she hung up the phone she felt a little envious of Norell. She and Gil had been seeing each other regularly the last few weeks, with kisses that grew more and more ardent at the end of each evening. Having Gil in her life had gone a long way toward filling the hole in her life caused by Brittany's absence.

But at least Brittany was having a good time. She had her own set of friends down in Nassau that she'd grown up with, and Kenny's parents were delighted to see her. Thank God for them. If it were left up to her own father, Brittany would never know how it felt to have loving grandparents.

Dana remembered the incident that forever altered her relationship with her father like it just happened last week. Even if the incident had never happened, she would never forget the pain of that day when her mother and sister were buried. Hearing her father say that he would rather she had died so her mother and sister could have lived, that he wished it was she who lay cold and dead in a metal casket, came as a shock almost too great to bear. She'd been as devastated as her father at the loss of half of their family, but she would never have been willing to sacrifice her father to keep her mother and Gail.

Her eyes became damp. She would never forget how she began each day at her Aunt Joan's with a prayer that today would be the day her father would come for her. Every night brought aching disappointment, and even more unsettling was the haunting certainty that if her mother and sister had survived the crash and she had been the one who died, life would have gone on as usual. No one would have been sent anywhere. It would never stop hurting her heart to know that her father valued her less than he did her mother and Gail.

It would be another three years, time filled with grief counseling, high school, and college classes, before she would meet Kendrick Covington and embark on the happy home life she'd always dreamed of, with no way of knowing it would only last fifteen short years.

But now there was Gil. Dana's life was still far from perfect—she worked many hours and still had to watch each penny she spent—but she was happier now than she'd been in over a year. And she knew Gil Albacete was the reason why.

Cécile fidgeted in discomfort under Norell's steady stare. They were at Dana's for their partners' meeting, with Dana speaking about physician complaints, but Cécile wished she could cover her stomach, for that was the focus of Norell's gaze. She was well into her fourth month and just beginning to show. She'd been pleased to get a call from Norell after returning from her aunt's funeral in South Florida to congratulate her on her pregnancy, and even thought that perhaps everything between them would be all right after all. But now she had to cope with having Norell look at her belly like it had suddenly sprouted flowers for another four and a half months. She didn't think she'd be able to take it.

Dana, sitting in a chair opposite Cecile, cleared her throat. "Hey guys, y'all aren't even listening. What's more important than CDN?"

Norell quickly recovered, finally tearing her stare away from Cécile's stomach. "Sorry. I was just thinking about something."

Cécile met Dana's gaze and momentarily raised an eyebrow. Dana's raised chin showed she got the message.

"Did y'all want to reschedule this meeting?" Dana asked.

"We don't have time," Cécile said in protest, instantly regretting her silent signal. She'd merely wanted to let Dana know that Norell was hung up on this baby thing again, not to prompt Dana to offer to reschedule.

"I'm sorry. This is all my fault," Norell said. "I'm afraid my mind just isn't on business this morning. Go ahead, Dana. I promise to pay attention this time."

Dana continued with her presentation. The bottom line was that CDN's clients had few complaints, and most of them were about getting their completed work back late. Others related to errors made in transcribed records, errors that could have easily been avoided by a careful read-through of the work before sending it to the client.

"I've determined that Linda Blake isn't proofing any of her reports," Dana continued. "I think we should let her go."

"Can we afford to lose a full-time MT?" Cécile asked.

"We can't afford to keep her."

"I agree with Dana," Norell said. "We can't have contractors who are only interested in producing as many lines as they can so they can collect big paychecks each Friday. If they're putting out garbage, it's going to reflect on us and may cost us clients. Let's get rid of her."

"But what if she gets mad that we fired her and wants to get back at us?" Cécile asked. "I mean, what's to stop her from getting into the system and doing real damage?"

"Once we turn off her logon she can't access the system," Dana said. "Now, aren't you glad we spent that money on a consultant to personalize our software?"

"Hmph. I'm just glad we're finished paying him."

"I wish we were finished paying Pat Fairfield all that money we owe her," Norell said.

"Come on, Norell," Dana said patiently. They had gone over this many times before. "We did take over all her clients. It's only fair she be compensated for that. Those clients were what got us started. It can take years to build a base like that."

"We were lucky Pat agreed to our terms of a large down payment and the balance in monthly installments," Cécile added.

Dana nodded. "Yes, we were. But partners, we're facing a crisis if we can't hire more people. Remember, we're contracturally bound to bill at a lower line rate if we can't deliver on time, so every time we fall out of turnaround it costs us money. And I'm reluctant to take on any new clients if we don't have the staff. Any suggestions?"

"I've already talked to Michael about going part time for Precise after my maternity leave. That'll give me more time to work on CDN's clients," Cecile offered.

"Won't going part time make you lose your health insurance?" Dana asked.

"We're all covered through Michael's job. As long as I can collect a weekly paycheck for the lines I produce, just like any other MT on the payroll, it'll work out fine. I know I'm a partner, but my family depends on my income, and we won't be splitting any profits until the end of the year.

"In other words, I don't want to sound like a cheapskate," Cécile said firmly, "but I wouldn't want anyone to feel that my pay can be deferred in case of a cash crunch."

"That won't be a problem. We've never had a cash crunch before," Dana said confidently. "We would never take advantage of you that way."

"That's great, Cécile, and we definitely need the extra effort, but it's not an immediate solution," Norell pointed out. "You're not into your fifth month yet, and then after the baby is born you'll need six weeks of recuperation. We're talking something like another five or even six months. CDN needs help *now*."

Cécile frowned. "Well, it's not practical for me to leave Precise now. I've already hinted that I might not be coming back full time after the baby. It wouldn't be fair to them for me to leave earlier. Besides, there's a lot going on in my life right now." Mrs. Puckett had accepted the offer she and Michael made on her house, and now they were all working to get their current home ready to show prospective buyers. Even the kids were doing their part, straightening out closets and moving excess belongings to the garage so the house wouldn't look so crowded. She didn't want to tell Dana and

Norell about their new house because only half the process was complete. They still had to sell the house they lived in now, and she didn't want anything to jinx it. Cécile had a superstitious nature, and she felt Norell's envy could send out some bad vibes. "But I'm not about to sit around for six weeks after the baby comes. Precise doesn't have any short-term disability benefits, other than what paid time off I've accumulated. Once that runs out and I don't work, I don't get a check."

"You're planning on working as soon as you get out of the hospital?" Norell sounded incredulous.

"Sitting in a comfortable, ergonomically designed chair and transcribing for a living hardly takes the effort of being a lumberjack chopping down trees in the woods, Norell," Cécile pointed out. "After the baby is born I'll be back at work in two weeks, max. And all the work I do will be for CDN. Since my status is that of employee, not independent contractor, Precise wouldn't even let me work until the doctor clears me after six weeks."

"We wouldn't want you to overexert yourself, Cécile," Dana said.

"I appreciate that, but you do what you have to do. Remember how quickly Norell went back to work after they took out her appendix? What'd you take off, Norell, three days?"

Norell nodded sheepishly. She had known the hospital bill would be huge, so she'd returned to work after just a few days.

"Yeah, three days," she said. "But I wasn't married then," she added. "I had no choice but to go back to work."

"I'm married," Cécile said, "but I've got to be realistic. I'll have seven kids and probably a much bigger mortgage. Michael won't be able to do it all by himself." She confidently patted her heavy thighs. "I appreciate you guys being concerned about my health, but I'll be fine. There's nothing to having a baby." At Norell's stricken look Cécile withdrew her breath audibly. "I'm sorry. That was a thoughtless thing to say."

Dana sighed and, in a significant gesture, quietly closed her notebook and placed it on the coffee table.

For about ten long seconds, Norell sat still as a statue, then she hastily leaned forward to collect her purse from the floor beside her chair. "I have to go," she said, her voice sounding strained and unnatural.

"Norell, no. Wait for me, please." Cécile struggled to get to her feet. She grabbed her shoulder bag. "I'll see you later," she said to a worried-looking Dana as she rushed to the backdoor, where Norell stood outside lighting a cigarette with an unsteady hand.

Cécile panted as she closed the door behind herself. "Thanks for waiting."

"You obviously wanted to say something, so go ahead."

"I wanted to tell you again how sorry I was for being so inconsiderate." Then the words began pouring out straight from her heart. "Norell, I wish you weren't having such a hard time. I'd give anything if you could—if things were different for you. But it's not up to me. I hate what it's done to us, to our friendship."

"I know I'm not being fair to you, Cécile. I'm sorry. I just can't help being a little jealous. You've got everything I wanted, a husband who loves you and children."

Cecile didn't know what to say. She hadn't expected Norell to come out and admit her jealousy, although Cécile felt it whenever they were in each other's company. "Vic loves you, Norell. You should never underestimate the value of a good husband. Look at what happened to poor Dana, losing Kenny so suddenly. Besides, you're reasonably well off." She thought of Michael's reluctance to trade a small mortgage for a much larger one, and of how difficult it would be to raise seven children in this day and age. "That's something else you don't ever want to take for granted."

"Money helps, but what they say is true. Money can't wrap its arms around you at night or give you a hug. I know things aren't easy for Dana, but I'm sure if you asked her if she'd rather have Brittany or plenty of money, she'd choose her daughter." Norell stubbed out her cigarette with her shoe.

Inside, Dana wished she had a way to hear what Norell and Cécile were saying. She went up to her bedroom, which overlooked the patio. The only thing that stopped her from opening the window was the fear that her friends would recognize the sound. She'd be so embarrassed if that happened. But she couldn't hear a thing with the window closed, damn it.

She stood in the shadow of the sheer curtains and peeked out through a slit in the built-in white wooden shutters. Norell stubbed out a cigarette and said something to Cécile. They both looked pretty calm, no twisted faces of anger, thank God. Dana watched as they stepped off the patio and around to the front of the house. She guessed they were done. Surely both her friends would call later and fill her in. She hoped they had come to a real understanding and not just a temporary fix.

The ringing phone made her jump. Then, realizing how foolish she had been to allow herself to be startled in her own bedroom, she chuckled. She still wore a smile as she picked up the receiver and said hello.

"Hi, it's Gil."

Dana immediately forgot all about Norell and Cécile. "Hi!"

"I didn't interrupt your meeting, did I?"

"No, it's all over. The girls just left. We're all busy little bees, making money day and night. What's on your mind?"

"Do you think you might be able to take a few days off? I thought it might be nice to get out of Jacksonville for a few days."

"Oh? What'd you have in mind?" She reclined against the pillows, stretching her upper body and feeling quite sexy.

"Savannah. It's a pretty city, conveniently located, historic, romantic."

Dana couldn't care less about the history, but a romantic setting definitely appealed to her.

"What do you say? I know it's short notice, but there's not much time until Brittany returns. If we're going to get away, we probably need to do it this weekend."

"Yes, Brittany comes back a week from Thursday. What about Irene?"

"There's no need for her to know my whereabouts. Vanessa is still down at my parents'. I'm in touch with her directly."

"Do you plan to tell her about us?"

"Yes, eventually. I'm still trying to work it out in my head. Don't worry about her, Dana." He paused. "So, should I make a reservation for this weekend?"

"Sure." She saw no reason to be coy about it. When a man asked a woman to go away with him for a weekend, that meant sex.

She couldn't wait.

Chapter 26

Norell breathed deeply as she accelerated away from Dana's house. CDN held their partners' meetings at ten A.M. so that traffic conditions would be more favorable. Cécile lived reasonably close to Dana, but she had to drive in all the way from the beach, and all the way back. That commute always cut into her output on meeting days.

It was only eleven-twenty, but Norell felt like she'd already put in a full day. Confessing her true feelings to Cécile had felt almost therapeutic, but it also drained her emotionally. And it didn't take the pain and resentment away. She doubted anything would.

At least she had helped mend her fractured relationship with Cécile. Two of Norell's relationships were in need of repair: those with Vic and Cécile. She felt optimistic about both. She and Vic had enjoyed a good weekend together. Saturday they worked side by side in their spacious gourmet kitchen and made a surf-and-turf dinner, complete with giant baked potatoes and salad containing a little of everything. With their dinner she drank only two glasses of red wine. When they went out yesterday afternoon for an early, informal dinner against the background of live music at a local restaurant, she had only two drinks. Last night they'd made love and fallen asleep in each other's arms, and they had a quickie again this morning, a rarity for them. They had plans to meet in town for dinner at six tonight.

That would present a challenge. She wouldn't get home for another twenty minutes, but she still had a full day's work to do. She'd have to get cracking the moment she walked in the door. To meet Vic by six she'd have to be dressed and on her way downtown by five-fifteen, and that time would be here before she knew it.

But she just had to have something to calm her nerves after the confrontation with Cécile. She knew that the three-quarter liter bottle of Smirnoff at home had only a few drops left.

I'll have one drink before I start my work, she promised silently as she pulled into the parking lot of the liquor store. *Just to take the edge off. Then I'll be fine.*

Vic looked at his watch impatiently. Twenty after six already. Where the hell was Norell?

His cell phone began to ring, and one look at the originating number and he knew the reason for the call. "Yeah," he greeted without enthusiasm.

"Vic, I'm so sorry—"

"Don't bother, Norell. I know what's coming. You're busy with your work, you lost track of the time. Why don't we just forget it? I'll be home soon." He broke the connection before she could respond.

Even as he said the words, Vic knew he wasn't going home, at least not right away. Let her worry about *him* for a change . . . if she even noticed his absence.

He signaled the bartender for the check. He'd finish his beer, then have a good dinner at that seafood place upstairs, where he'd planned to take Norell.

Micheline moved with quick steps. Her coworkers were getting together for drinks at The Landing after work, but she'd stayed late to finish some research she was doing with a source in Texas, where it was an hour earlier. She hoped the others were still there.

They were, but they were about to leave. "I'll have to catch y'all next time," she said.

"Are you going home?" someone asked.

"No, I think I'll get some dinner to take out."

Micheline walked around The Landing, a large wharflike structure with shops and restaurants on the banks of the St. Johns, trying to decide what to get for dinner. She was familiar with the fast-food stands on the upper level facing the street. Sit-down restaurants lined the side of the building facing the river, offering both indoor and outdoor seating. She knew from her coworkers that new restaurants came and went all the time. Hooters was one of the few long-term tenants, but she didn't feel like eating chicken wings while those Hooters girls, flinging long blond tresses, strutted around in their too-tight T-shirts and bright orange shorts, so short that their flat little butt cheeks hung out. They should hire more sisters if they wanted nice round behinds.

Hmm . . . The menu the seafood restaurant posted outside its entrance made her mouth water. That was it.

She approached from behind what appeared to be a middle-aged black man who, judging from his slim torso and flat belly, worked hard at keeping himself in shape. He must have sensed she was behind him, because he glanced around and smiled at her, then held the door open for her to walk through.

"Thank you," she said graciously, noting that not only did he take care of himself, he was handsome as well, in an older man type of way.

The hostess approached and smiled at them. "Table for two?"

Micheline and the stranger looked at each other and laughed. "No," she told the woman. "Actually, I just wanted to see a menu so I could place a takeout order."

"I need a table," the man said. "But could you give us a minute?"

"Certainly." The hostess promptly disappeared.

Micheline looked at the stranger with an arched eyebrow, although she knew the question about to be asked.

"It seems a little silly to dine alone if I can have some company," he said. "My wife stood me up. Would you join me? It's just dinner."

Micheline shrugged. He had a point. Joining him would be harmless. Besides, it would be more fun to eat with someone than to eat alone, even if the someone was old enough to be her father. He might even pick up her check. "Why not?"

When the hostess returned she didn't seem in the least surprised that they would need a table for two. She led them to a table with a view of the St. Johns, an unusual river in that it flowed from south to north. Several boats bobbed in the water, their owners having turned off the motors to allow them to float in the tide. A water taxi ferried back and forth between The Landing and the St. Johns River's south bank, the home to more hotels and restaurants.

"I'm from South Florida and have only been here a few months, but Jacksonville is a nice city. I think I'll stick around awhile," Micheline remarked after they introduced themselves with first names only. His name was Vic.

"You make our city much prettier."

"You're charming, Vic."

"What is it that brought you to the First Coast?"

"I wasn't happy in West Palm anymore. Except for a few years spent in New York right after college, I'd lived there my whole life. I have a sister here, so it seemed logical. I applied for a job here and they offered it to me, so that makes life a lot more pleasant. I'm a paralegal at Mills and Conrad."

"Are you bilingual?"

"I speak French, but I don't use it in my work."

"Oh. I thought you might speak Spanish."

Micheline smiled. She had heard this many times. She didn't agree, but many people thought she looked Latina. In West Palm people were always coming up to her and babbling in Spanish. She had learned to say "No hablo Español" to get rid of them.

They took a few minutes to study the menu, and the waitress approached and, apparently alerted by the hostess that they were not together, asked, "Will this be separate checks?"

"You can put both on mine," Vic said easily.

Micheline merely shrugged, as if it didn't matter, although secretly she was delighted. She calmly gave the waitress her order, followed by Vic.

She waited until the waitress left before saying, "That was sweet, but you didn't have to do that, Vic."

"It's all right. I was going to buy my wife dinner, anyway."

"Is she all right?"

"She's fine. She's just very busy. She operates a home-based business."

"My sister works at home, too. Personally, I don't know how she does it. I'd be bored to tears, staying in the house all day long. But she's got kids, and she swears it's worth it for the convenience."

"I can't argue with the logic of having someone in the house during business hours. It makes it nice for deliveries and home services. But I'll say this much: My wife never stood me up when she worked for somebody else."

Micheline discreetly lowered her gaze. She picked up on a definite note of discontent in his voice. This would bear closer inspection . . . there might be something in it for her.

Over the course of dinner they spoke about their work. Vic worked as a bail bondsman, and he amused Micheline with stories about some of the more frivolous charges his clients had been jailed for. In turn, she spoke about the interesting cases she had worked on.

They were just finishing up when Vic's beeper went off. As he reached for the gadget he hoped Norell was calling to ask when he would be home, but his hopes dissolved when he saw a familiar number in the display.

"Is everything all right?" Micheline asked, thinking the little woman wanted to know what was taking him so long to get home.

"Yeah, it's a regular customer. And since there's still time to post bond and get him hatched tonight, I'll have to get right on it."

"At least they didn't interrupt your dinner." Micheline demurely dabbed the corners of her mouth with a napkin.

"True. My cell phone's in the car, so I'll just take care of the check and be on my way. Will you be all right?"

"Oh, sure." She got to her feet and held out her hand. "It was a very pleasant dinner, Vic."

"I enjoyed it, too. Thank you for dining with me."

"It was my pleasure. Good night."

Micheline headed toward the exit. She longed to turn around to see if Vic was watching her, but couldn't think of a way to do so without appearing obvious.

She got her chance when she came upon the hostess, who bade her farewell in that cordial tone hostesses use, but Micheline knew the woman was surprised to see her leaving alone.

She turned around to exchange pleasantries with the hostess and saw Vic rising from the table. If he had been watching her at all, he certainly wasn't now. She turned and left. There went a man obviously very much in love with his wife. She hoped the wife realized it, because even the most faithful husband had a breaking point. She shrugged. It wasn't like she'd wasted her time; she'd gotten a nice dinner out of it.

When she stepped into her dark apartment she saw the orange blinking light on her cordless phone, indicating someone had left a message. She took her time getting to it. It had been a long day, longer than she'd planned on, and she wanted nothing more than to get out of her business clothes and relax.

She changed into a terry-cloth halter dress and booties, and poured an Arizona chocolate soda over ice before finally picking up the phone to see who had called. She hoped it wasn't Cécile. Her sister called at least twice a week. Their relationship had been strained since that unpleasantness with Sean Sizemore, but Micheline had a hunch that Cécile kept an eye on her for the benefit of their parents, whom she knew worried about her living alone in a strange city.

But it was a deep male voice that greeted her. "Hey Michie, it's Errol. I was just thinking about you and wanted to hear your voice. I'll try you again about nine."

She smiled, glad she'd missed his call. Surely his curiosity had been aroused about her possible whereabouts on a Monday night, and that was fine by her.

A second message had been left as well. "Michie, it's Yolanda. I haven't talked to you in a while and thought I'd say hello. I hear from Rob that things are going pretty good with you and Errol. Any wedding plans?" She laughed heartily before hanging up.

Micheline disconnected from voice mail and reached for the remote control as she stretched out on the sofa, carefully cocooned in a blanket she kept handy to protect the white cotton upholstery. Micheline didn't believe in tying herself down with a lot of material things, but everything she owned was the best she could afford.

She'd loved the openness of the apartment's layout from the very first moment she saw it. Micheline planned to stay here a while, probably until she married. At that time she expected to go directly into a house, and a nice one, not one like that awful little place Cécile had. She wanted a place even nicer than Dana's or Yolanda's.

And if she could keep Errol interested despite the no-sex edict, she had a good shot at making it all come true.

"I thought you'd be home before now," Norell remarked.

Still working, she had left her office to go downstairs when she heard him come in. Vic sat in the living room watching TV. His eyes didn't move from the screen. "I didn't think you'd miss me."

"I'm sorry, Vic. I had that meeting at Dana's, and then one of the doctors is getting ready to go on vacation, and he tied up all the loose ends before he left. Patients he's seen but forgotten to dictate, things like that. We notify them every day which patients are missing, but they always wait and do them all at one time, even if it's three months' worth. He insisted on getting them in today so he could sign off on them before he left. If I'd known he was going to do that I'd never have agreed to meet you for dinner." She deliberately omitted mentioning the fact that she'd had five vodka-and-grape-fruits and was knocked out for two hours.

"I'm glad you're taking your work seriously, but I'm getting tired of this, Norell. You're not second to *my* work. I don't like being second to yours."

"It's a one-time incident. Look at the wonderful weekend we just had."

Finally he turned to her. "I know you're trying. I think you might be putting too much on yourself. Why don't you girls hire more help?"

"We have. We hired two people the other week. But now we have to let someone go. It's hard to find qualified people, Vic." Vic, like so many other people, didn't really grasp what medical transcription was all about. He felt that anyone who knew the keyboard could sit down and transcribe a cataract extraction or a heart bypass.

"You must not be trying hard enough."

"We run an ad continuously on the Internet. The response has been wonderful, but when we test people they can't spell or they use the wrong words. We can't have people like that working for us, Vic. Our service would go out of business in a heartbeat if our quality was that poor."

He silently turned back to the television, and after a few moments she went back up to her office with leaden steps, her heart feeling as heavy as her feet.

Chapter 27

Dana's forehead wrinkled. Why did she always imagine she heard a ringing phone whenever she vacuumed? Sometimes she stopped to shut off the vacuum as many as two or three times to investigate. She told herself she had merely imagined the sound and continued moving the vacuum back and forth. But the sensation persisted, and she finally shut off the motor just in time to hear the tail end of a ring.

She jumped onto the bed and reached for the receiver on the nightstand. "Hello."

"Hello, Dana. Irene Albacete."

Dana's shoulders grew rigid. *She knows.* "Hi, Irene," she said, forcing herself to sound natural. "What's up?"

"Vanessa is down in Miami with her grandparents, and she thinks she might have left her jeans skirt at your house. She really wants to wear it while she's there. I know Brittany is away too, but I was hoping that maybe you'd seen it."

Dana's body immediately relaxed. "Yes, I sure did. It was in the wash, and I knew it wasn't Britt's. It's all ironed and folded."

"Oh, good. I hoped she hadn't lost it. I was about to run some errands. Would I be able to come by and pick it up? I promised I'd mail it to her."

"Yes. I'll be here."

"Here it is, all ready to wear," Dana said to Irene twenty minutes later as she handed her a plastic supermarket bag containing Vanessa's skirt. They stood just inside Dana's front door.

"Thanks so much, Dana." Irene smiled. "I guess you miss Brittany as much as I miss Vanessa."

"I really do. Have you been enjoying your summer?"

"Oh, yes. Vanessa and I went up to New Jersey to visit with family. I got one of the special deals where you drive a rental car up and leave it there. It only cost fifteen dollars a day to rent a Ford Taurus. I could have gotten away with ten bucks if I wanted to rent something smaller. We used the car while we were there, and then we dropped it off and took the train back."

"They're trying to move their fleet back up North for the fall. By the holidays they'll be offering the same deal for one-way drop-offs in Florida and other warmer climates. Usually you can't get those rates this late in the year, so I consider myself lucky." Irene smiled and patted the skirt. "Thanks a lot, Dana. I'll get this off to Vanessa right away."

"You're very welcome. I'm glad I could help." Dana hadn't seen Irene since before Brittany had left for Nassau. She seemed so friendly and warm.

An impulse hit Dana like a bolt of lightning, and she acted on it before thinking it through. "Irene, do you have a minute? There's something I'd like to talk about with you."

Irene nodded and followed Dana into the living room, where they took seats. "Do you have another special date?" Irene asked with a smile.

"Uh, no. It's something else. I've been wanting to talk to you for a couple of weeks now," Dana began.

"Really? What about?" Irene sounded more curious than anything else.

"Well . . . I'm not sure where to begin. It's about Gil."

"Oh?"

Irene's tone had become a tad chilly, and Dana considered that she might have made a mistake in thinking she could share the confidence of her relationship with Gil. But she couldn't back out now. "You know he helped me with my business loan," she said.

"Yes, I knew about that."

"We worked very closely together, and he put in a recommendation for me. I think Gil wants us to succeed as much as we do ourselves." Dana knew she was chattering, but now she dreaded completing what she'd started.

"Dana, what did you want to talk to me about?"

Naturally Irene would ask her to get to the point. The woman had things to do. "Well, like I said, we've worked together closely, and one thing kind of led—Irene, would you be terribly upset if we went out?"

"You mean if you and Gil started *dating*?" Irene asked incredulously.

"Something like that." No way would she let on that they already had.

Irene stood up. "Dana, I find it odd that out of all the men in Jacksonville, you can't find anyone to date other than my husband." She turned and left, closing the front door behind herself with more force than required.

Dana had stood, too, and she went to the window and watched, stunned, as Irene rushed to her car at the curb and drove away. It all happened so fast, she hadn't even had time to point out that Gil was Irene's *ex*-husband.

Dana fervently wished she could take back the whole conversation. What had seemed like a good idea in the beginning now seemed like a terrible error in judgment. Gil would be furious. She dreaded telling him.

She puttered around for a few minutes, wanting to put off the inevitable as long as possible. When she had summoned her courage she finally picked up the telephone and dialed him at home.

He answered on the first ring with a terse, "Hello." When she identified herself he responded with an equally abrupt, "I'm on the other line. I'll have to call you back."

Dana hung up, dazed. Was he upset with her, or was she merely being overly sensitive?

She jumped when the phone rang two or three minutes later. She immediately picked it up and uttered an anxious-sounding greeting.

"Dana, what were you thinking?" Gil asked incredulously without preamble.

"Irene called you already?" So she hadn't imagined his annoyed tone.

"From her cell phone. Reamed me out. This wasn't how I wanted to handle this, Dana. You know I haven't even told Vanessa yet. Now Irene will probably beat me to it."

"I'm terribly sorry, Gil. It was an impulse, a bad one. But in my defense, let me point out that Irene would have found out eventually anyway."

"Yes, she would have. And she wouldn't have been happy no matter who I got involved with. I can live with that. It's Vanessa I wanted to protect. I wanted to get her first, honest gut reaction to us, not one that's first been poisoned by Irene's venom. But now that won't be possible."

Dana didn't know what to say. She knew she'd blown it. "What happens now?" she asked.

"I guess we'll have to wait and see. I'll be talking to Vanessa every day while she's at my parents', and I'll see her when she comes back. I don't think Irene will tell her until she returns. Maybe I can meet her plane and head Irene off."

Dana hoped so, too. For Gil's sake, and for Brittany's as well.

Dana and Gil left for Savannah right after work on Friday. Dana dozed off somewhere after Brunswick, Georgia. When she opened her eyes they were thirty miles outside Savannah.

"I'm so embarrassed," she said, her palm cupping her chin and jaw. "I didn't mean to go to sleep like that. It's just that I've been up late the last couple of nights trying to stay on top of my work so I won't come home to a huge backlog."

He reached across the console and patted her hand. "It's all right, Dana. I know how hard you work and how last minute this all was, and I'm grateful that you were able to get away." Then he squeezed her hand. "And if I had a choice between you being tired now or tired later, I'd rather you be tired now."

Her breath caught in her throat, and a twirly sensation made its way to her stomach. In just a few hours she would be intimate with Gil for the first time. She'd been so eager before, but now she began to feel nervous. What if Cécile had been right and the same thing happened with Gil as had with Sean? Would Gil lose interest in her after they slept together? Would he go after some woman in her twenties with a better body, like Sean had?

When they arrived in the city, Gil checked them into the hotel. Instead of going up to their room, they left their luggage at the front desk, parked in the hotel garage, and set off on foot for a look at the historic district.

Dana was glad she hadn't had to look at their hotel room too soon. Her nerves had become as limp as cooked pasta as she considered that perhaps she'd made a mistake.

Spending time with Gil out in the open—simply walking down the street, with no huge bed in the background—turned out to be just what she needed to relax. Dana quickly became engrossed in her surroundings. She had never been to Savannah before. She liked the pulse of the city, all the people walking around, the street performers, the music drifting out of the bars. It reminded her of New Orleans, but with different architecture. "I see why you like it here," she remarked. "It's very different from Jacksonville, much more lively."

"Jacksonville is a great town, but it doesn't have a real personality. It's kind of bland. I like the beach atmosphere and enjoy living there, but I'm ready to purchase property, and I can't afford to buy out there."

"So you'll be heading further inland, huh?"

"Yeah, probably one of those new town houses they're putting up all over town. I've always liked the convenience of having a pool and a fitness center available for my use, and not having to mow my own lawn. That's why I bought a town house years ago, the one where Vanessa lives now."

How considerate of him not to mention Irene, she thought. "I know what you mean," she said. "My pool requires a lot of work. Usually I let Brittany do it, but since she's been away it's fallen on me. I do keep an exercise bike and a glider in my garage. It used to look like a gym in there, before I sold . . . before I sold the biggest piece of equipment." She hadn't thought of the weights that ultimately killed Kenny in a long time, and those thoughts had no place during a romantic weekend with Gil.

He reached for her hand. "We've been walking for a long time. How about going back to the hotel and getting some dinner?"

"Are you sure you wouldn't rather eat at one of the places we've passed?"

"For lunch tomorrow. The package I bought includes breakfast and dinner at the hotel. The food there is excellent, by the way."

Dana's spirits sank. "So you've stayed there before." *With Irene.*

"Many times. But that has nothing to do with you and me." He squeezed her hand. "Dana, I guess this is as good a time as any to talk about this. Our room has a separate sitting area with a couch and some very comfortable chairs. I don't want to pressure you into doing something you're not ready for."

She smiled. "Somehow my picture of a romantic weekend in Savannah didn't include you sleeping on the couch."

He stopped walking and looked her in the eye. "Are you sure, Dana?"

"I'm sure."

It was nearly seven o'clock when they returned to the hotel. By then Dana felt completely at ease, and the sight of the king-size bed in their room filled her with anticipation, not dread. In addition to the sitting room, their quarters also had a tiny patio barely large enough for two chairs and a small table. They could sit outside and watch the street scene below. Gil certainly hadn't skimped on this weekend. She would do all she could to make it memorable.

They took turns showering and changing in the privacy of the bedroom, then went down for dinner. Dana thoroughly enjoyed her veal piccata. The atmosphere of the restaurant set a romantic mood, with dim overhead lighting, candlelight, flowers, and soft music.

Gil lifted his wineglass. "Here's to good food, good drink, and the other pleasures of life," he toasted.

Dana knew he was offering her one last out. All she had to do was amend his toast. Instead she touched her glass to his. "Here's to new beginnings," she said. She sipped her wine, her eyes boldly meeting his and the corners of her mouth slightly upturned. Suddenly it didn't matter who Gil had been there with before. This time it was just the two of them.

Gil unlocked the door to their room. "That was a great meal," he said, rubbing his belly. "What do you say we sit and chill for a while, let it digest?"

"Sounds perfect." Right now Dana was too full to think about romance.

They sat on the couch in the sitting room, Dana all too aware of the king-size bed just beyond the double doors a few yards behind them. Gil found an interesting movie on cable about a wealthy man whose wife and her lover left him stranded in the desert, with a broken leg, yet. They quickly became engrossed in the film, and as they watched they shifted positions. Originally they sat next to each other, but by the time it started to look like the unfortunate but resourceful man would survive his ordeal, Dana was reclining between Gil's legs, her back against his chest. His arms went around her waist and rested comfortably before one hand eventually wandered to her breasts, squeezing them through the fabric of her halter dress, then boldly slipping a hand inside. Dana moaned as he rubbed her hardened nipple between two of his fingers.

"You feel good," he murmured. She felt his lips on her jaw, then on her throat, and his other hand fumbled with the full skirt of her dress until he found her underwear beneath. Dana gasped with pleasure when he reached inside her already-damp panties. She forgot all about the problems of the man on screen, concentrating instead on her own pleasure.

Gil brought her to orgasm with his fingertips. Hands on her shoulders, he pushed her up. "Let's get in bed. We can be more comfortable."

They walked to the bed. When they stood before it Gil reached out and untied the sash of her halter. As the straps fell, exposing her upper body, he smiled gently. "You don't know how badly I ached to do that, from the time you came out of the bedroom in that dress."

"And now you've done it."

"Yes," he said, "now I have." With those words he proceeded to make love to her until her entire body shook with satisfaction and she moaned uncontrollably.

And, when she regained her strength, she did the same for him.

Chapter 28

On Tuesday afternoon Dana drove down to the Orlando airport to meet Brittany's return flight. It delighted her that Brittany was as happy to see her as she was to see Brittany.

"Mom, you look really good," Brittany said as they waited at the luggage carousel for her bags to appear. "Things must be going well with the company."

"Not really," Dana admitted. CDN was faced with a difficult situation. One of the local medical centers had approached them about doing overflow work. She hadn't wanted to accept the contract because she feared they wouldn't be able to keep up, but both Cécile and Norell voted against her, not wanting the growth opportunity to go to one of their competitors. It was the most heated argument the three partners had had yet, and Dana still felt very apprehensive about how they would manage the workload.

"But I do have some good news," she said. "We have a new tenant. She'll be moving in next month. A junior at UNF. She—or I guess her parents—are paying for the whole semester up front. Isn't that great?"

"That's good, Mom. I figured you'd get another tenant when college classes started."

Brittany had all the latest news about Kenny's cousins and childhood friends, and she chattered all the way home from the airport.

"So what've you been doing while I was away?" she finally asked as they entered the house with her suitcase.

Dana took a deep breath. "Brittany, there's something I have to tell you."

"What is it, Mom?"

"While you were away I started seeing someone."

"I thought you were through with stuff like that. You went out a couple of times with some guy back in May, and then you stopped all of a sudden."

Dana suppressed a smile. When she was Brittany's age she, too, would have thought people her parents' age too old for "stuff like that." "This is different, Britt. That other time was just a couple of dates. This one has already lasted longer. There's no such thing as a standard relationship. Each one is different."

"So do I get to meet the guy this time?"

"You already know him. It's Mr. Albacete."

"Vanessa's daddy?"

Dana smiled. "You know another man named Albacete?"

"Wow, Mom. You and Mr. Gil? I can't picture it. It's been a long time since he was with Miss Irene, but I still remember. It seems weird that he's with you now."

"Well, Mr. and Mrs. Albacete were married, so the term 'with' has a different context altogether," Dana said dryly. "He and I are just dating. We're having a lot of fun together. But we didn't plan for it to happen. We realize that the situation has a high degree of sensitivity, and that there are other people involved."

"Miss Irene might not like it, but I think it's okay."

"Oh Britt, do you really?"

"Sure, Mom. It'll be hard to see you go out with somebody other than Daddy. . . ."

Guilt stabbed at Dana.

". . . but at least I know Mr. Gil. I think it was harder when you were going out with some strange man. I used to imagine you with a real big, ugly dude, like Brutus from Popeye."

Dana laughed.

"So," Brittany said with wide-eyed curiosity, "do you think you two will get married?"

"No, Brittany, I don't. Like I said before, we're just having a lot of fun together. Marriage is something that comes after you've known a person for a long time. You don't go out on a few dates and then decide to get married."

"Okay. I was just thinking that if you and Mr. Gil got married, me and Vanessa would be sisters." Brittany flashed a slightly crooked grin. "Wouldn't *that* be neat!"

* * *

Gil called before she'd been home an hour. "I just wanted to make sure Brittany got in all right."

"Oh, yes. She's fine. It's good to have her home again. I, uh, told her about us."

"You did?"

"I hadn't planned to, but she gave me an opening, and I stepped into it. She took it surprisingly well."

"That gives me hope that Vanessa will do the same. Listen, I know you're tired after that long drive to Orlando and back, but I hope I can see you tomorrow. We could have an early dinner after work, and you'll be home well before dark."

"I'd love to. Where shall we meet?"

The line went silent. "Meet? I thought that since Brittany knows about us—"

"That you would come to the house and pick me up," Dana finished. "I understand, but I'm not quite ready to do that yet. I don't mind telling Brittany that I'll be out with you, but just because she says it's okay with her for us to be dating doesn't mean she's ready to actually see it."

"I don't get it, Dana."

She hesitated. "She said something about it being hard to imagine me with anyone but her daddy. I want to go slow, Gil. Brittany has accepted the finality of death, but I'd like to prevent her from having any delayed grief reaction from seeing you and me together as a couple."

"You say that like you know a little about it."

"I've accepted that Kenny is gone, Gil." Dana thought it best not to say how she still got the blues, the if-Kenny-were-still-here-everything-would-be-all-right lament, especially when money ran tight. Gil wouldn't understand that it stemmed from the struggle to make it on her own. He would see it as her still being in love with her deceased husband. Well, part of her would always belong to Kenny, but she'd been touched by death enough times in her life to know it was permanent. "But I grieved off and on for years when my mother and sister were killed. I was younger then, and when you're younger it's harder. Besides, I'd lost my *mother*. I didn't get to have her around for the important events in my life. Getting married, having Brittany, things like that. As happy as Kenny and I were together, there's always been a hole in my life because she wasn't with me."

"I think I understand. I'm forty-two and know I'm lucky to still have both my parents. All right. Why don't we meet down in San Marco? That's convenient for you, isn't it?"

"Yes. How about La Nopalera?"

"La Nopalera it is."

Dana hung up with a satisfied sigh. Things were looking up. Not only did Brittany accept her relationship with Gil, but Gil understood her reasons for not wanting to flaunt their affair in front of her. His stubbornness on the same subject had almost prevented their relationship from ever getting off the ground.

But she knew that the key to her continued happiness rested with a thirteen-year-old child, for if Vanessa Albacete wasn't happy with Dana's involvement with Gil, things were about to get very unpleasant.

Chapter 29

At six o'clock Norell poured herself a vodka and grapefruit juice, her second drink of the day. She'd poured herself one at four o'clock just to reward herself for getting so much done. Now she took a second break after marinating two ribeye steaks, preparing a tossed salad, and scrubbing two Idaho baking potatoes in preparation for microwaving. Vic usually called just before he left the office, and that advance notice allowed her to have dinner practically ready when he walked in.

This drink was to congratulate herself on staying on top of it all.

She managed to get another half dozen documents proofed before Vic called to announce he was on his way home.

By the time he arrived Norell had just removed the steaks from the broiler, the potatoes had another three minutes to go in the microwave, the salad sat in a glass bowl on the table, and she sipped her third drink.

After dinner, Vic said, "That was great, Norell. I like that marinade."

"Caribbean jerk, I think it was. I'll have to look at the bottle. Hey, did we have anything planned for Friday night?"

"Not that I know of. What were you thinking of doing?"

"Would you mind if I invited Dana and Cécile and Lynn over Friday night?"

"Who's Lynn?"

"Lynn Phillips, my old friend from when we were kids. Remember, her father died a couple of weeks ago and you went to the wake with me?"

"Oh, yeah, now I remember. No, I don't mind. What's the occasion? Is it somebody's birthday?"

"There isn't one, other than I haven't gotten together with my friends in ages. When I said good-bye to Lynn I promised I'd call her soon. It's been three weeks, and I haven't done it yet. I think it would be nice to invite her over. And since I'm having her over, I figure, why not invite Dana and Cécile as well. Our relationship has changed since we started CDN. We've become less friends and more business partners. I think we need to spend some social time together, like we used to."

"Are you sure you want to be around Cécile?"

She bristled. "Why wouldn't I?"

Vic sighed. "Don't give me that BS, Norell. I know it's hard for you to be around Cécile because she's having a baby and you can't."

She flinched at his blunt assessment. Now she wished she'd gone along with the program instead of pretending she didn't know what he meant. They'd already been over it during a recent argument, in which Vic pointed out that her drinking had accelerated since she'd learned about Cécile's pregnancy, and she couldn't bear hearing that again. "I'm fine with it," she said. "We had a nice talk the other week at Dana's. We kind of called a truce. Cécile and I have been friends for a long time, Vic. I was there when her first marriage broke up. She was there when my mother died. Yes, it's hard for me to see her having another baby when I can't even have one. But I have to learn to live with it."

"I agree. Go ahead and have your friends over. I'll probably go out and play cards with the guys or something so I don't have to listen to a bunch of women cackling."

She pretended to be insulted. "We don't cackle. We laugh like ordinary people. But I'll understand if you'd prefer not to be around us."

"I hope you're finished for the day," he said as she brought their plates to the dishwasher.

"I thought I'd go back up and work for another hour or so. The new hires are helping a lot, but we really need more staff." She noticed his frown. "I know you don't like it when I work after dinner, Vic. It can't be helped, at least not right now. We've got to stay on top of our work so we can accommodate the new hospital account."

"I don't see you all day, Norell. I don't think I'm asking too much for you to spend your evenings with me."

"I'm trying to be more of a morning person, wake up before dawn like Dana and Cécile do, but I've never been an early bird."

"You might find getting up earlier easier if you laid off the Smirnoff."

Her lower lip set determinedly. "You make it sound like I'm a lush or something. I resent that, Vic."

He rose from the table and stood on the other side of the counter so he could face her. "Norell, I know you're drinking more these days. Three months ago you worked a lot and drank a little. Now you work a lot and drink a lot. Like I said before, it started getting real bad when you found about Cécile's pregnancy."

"This is only my second drink today." Norell stated the lie boldly, but she didn't know what else to say in her defense. Damn it, Vic just wouldn't let up on her. Couldn't he see how hard she was trying to cope with Cécile's coming baby? Why did he try all the time to get her to admit how much it hurt that Cécile, who already had more kids than she knew what to do with, was having yet another while she had none, nada, zilch? Didn't he know how much it pained her?

"Maybe," he said. "But by the time you go to bed tonight a third of the bottle will be gone. I'll come to bed feeling amorous and you're . . . Well, I can't say you're out of it, but it would be nice to know that you realize it's me who's making you feel so good. Two complete strangers can fuck each other and feel like a million, Norell. It's the intimacy between them, their bond, that makes it special. With you lately there's been none."

She tossed a crumpled napkin into the trash. "I'm glad you let us enjoy our dinner before you started in on me."

He slapped the countertop with his palm. "Damn it, Norell, why don't you get that I'm not your enemy?"

"I've got work to do," she said coldly. "I'll clean up here later." She headed for the stairs on slightly wobbly legs.

When she returned an hour and a half later he was gone. She had a pretty good idea of where he'd gone. The Beaches area had no shortage of bars. It was just a question of which one. Not that she was about to go running after him.

Norell knew she'd driven him away. She hated it when she acted like this. She felt so useless. Sure, CDN was thriving, but it would never be anything more than a regional transcription service, providing her with a moderate income. But even if she were to become wildly successful, like the industry giant MedQuist, it wouldn't be enough to fill the hole in her heart. And Vic would never understand.

Norell loaded the dishwasher and did a quick wipedown of the counters and microwave. Before starting the dishwasher she tossed in the kitchen sponge. The dishwasher hummed, and the kitchen smelled lemony clean. But she was all alone, for Vic hadn't returned.

She took a fresh highball glass from the cabinet and poured herself another drink.

A double.

Chapter 30

Dana awoke feeling anxious the day Vanessa came home from Miami. Gil had arranged to meet her at the airport with Irene. She waited as long as she could stand it before calling him at home. He had to be back by now. "So, how'd it go?" Dana asked Gil.

"Her flight was on time. She had a good time—"

"That's not what I meant, Gil."

"The minute Vanessa went up to her room Irene asked me if you and I were still seeing each other."

"And?"

"She didn't like my answer."

"Oh."

"I'm sorry, Dana. I know this makes things difficult for you because of Brittany's friendship with Vanessa."

"It's not your fault. I was the one who blurted it out about us to Irene in the first place."

"Yes, but from the way she's behaving, I really don't think it would have made a difference in her reaction whether she learned earlier or later."

Dana began to wonder if she should be more concerned about Irene than she was. Gil made it sound so serious. "Come on, Gil. Don't you think she'll get over it after a few weeks?"

"No, Dana, I don't think so. I was married to Irene for a long time. I know how she is."

"Well, did you get to talk to Vanessa at all about us?"

"I had to tell her in front of Irene. She wouldn't give me a moment alone with Vanessa."

Dana's heart thumped so loudly she thought it would come out of her chest. "How'd she take it?"

"It was definitely a surprise. She asked Irene if this was the surprise she'd told her about."

"So all Irene told Vanessa was that you had a surprise for her."

"That would be too simple. She intimated it wasn't a good surprise, so the seed has already been planted. Vanessa said she thought her mother and I were going to get back together. She asked why I was going out with you."

Dana swallowed hard. "Why did she think you and Irene were going to reconcile?"

"Because Irene has been sharing her hopes with our daughter. Imagine, a grown woman confiding in a child. I think she needs to remember that Vanessa is her daughter, not her friend."

"So Irene does want you back."

He sighed. "I don't want to sound like an egomaniac, but Irene fought the divorce from the very beginning. She's a very controlling, manipulative woman, Dana. Always has been. The only reason we got married in the first place was because she got pregnant with Vanessa, accidentally on purpose, as they say.

"I tried to make the best of it," he continued. "But being with someone out of a sense of duty isn't the same as being with them because you're madly in love. As time went on I felt more and more unhappy. I'm afraid I wasn't faithful. Irene sensed it, and she became more of a shrew. She said that if I left she'd make me pay through the nose for Vanessa. That's a natural reaction for most women when they've been hurt, to strike back at their husbands in the pocketbook. But most women don't stay angry for long. Irene does."

"Hell hath no fury," Dana said quietly.

Dana noticed Brittany's dejected expression right away. "What's wrong, Britt?"

"I called Vanessa again. I've been trying to reach her since she came back from her grandparents', but she always said she couldn't talk because she was busy."

Apprehension stabbed at Dana's gut. "Oh? That sounds strange."

"I thought so, too. So I called her again, and she said she doesn't think she can be friends with me because of what you've done to her mother."

"What I've done?"

"Vanessa says that you've taken Mr. Gil away from her mother, that he and her mother were about to get back together until you came into the picture."

Dana withdrew her breath sharply in shock. "No, Brittany, that's not true. Vanessa's parents were divorced well before Gil and I looked at each other. Irene may have convinced herself that reconciliation was right around the corner, but Gil had no intention of going back to her. We discussed it, and I believe him."

"Well, I don't think it's fair for you to go out with him if it means Vanessa and I won't be friends anymore." Brittany half spoke and half cried the words.

Dana held out her arms. As she stroked her daughter's hair she said softly, "I'm so sorry, Brittany. I didn't mean for any of this to happen. You see, Gil and I agreed that he would be the one to tell Irene about us, and I blabbed it to Irene when she came over one day to pick up a piece of clothing Vanessa left over here. I thought she would take it well, but she was furious.

"Vanessa is in a difficult situation," she continued. "She sees her mother is hurt, and she blames me, largely because her mother told her it's my fault, even though it isn't. So try not to be too hard on her. I'm sure she'll come around."

"But we've been friends our whole lives, Mommy! It isn't fair for her to not want to be friends anymore because of you and Mr. Gil. Can't you just stop seeing him?"

Dana pulled back a little and forced Brittany to look up. "I can't do that, Britt. You see, Gil and I have come to care for each other quite a bit."

"You mean love? Like with Daddy?"

"I don't think I'd say I'm in love, but I feel I owe it to myself to find out what might happen."

"But what about me? I haven't done anything wrong. Why should I lose my best friend because of what you're doing?"

Dana swallowed hard. "Brittany, I'm not doing anything wrong, either. Gil and I are both single adults. We're free to see each other. Vanessa has simply been manipulated by her mother into breaking off her friendship with you. I know it's not fair, but all I can ask is that you be patient. Vanessa will come around. In the meantime, you do have other friends."

"But it won't be the same, Mommy!" Brittany sobbed.

Dana's arms tightened around her daughter, and she breathed

deeply. For a moment she considered breaking it off with Gil, but then she realized that really wouldn't help Brittany. The damage had already been done. Vanessa wouldn't suddenly come prancing back into Brittany's life if she stopped seeing Gil.

Maybe she shouldn't even tell Brittany that Vanessa would come around, because she might not. A friendship that seemed destined to last a lifetime might be over for good.

She didn't know how she could live with herself for the part she had played in its end.

Chapter 31

Vic sat alone at a table on the upstairs deck of Bukkets at the Beach, listening to a blues band. Funny how blues had caught on with the white boys; these dudes' music sounded pretty damn good to his ears.

He needed something soothing. His own wife always had something to do, either something for her transcription service or for her damn friends. She hardly ever even cooked anymore. Except for one steak meal she made early in the week, every other dinner they'd had came from either the supermarket deli or from restaurant takeout.

Vic glanced around at the women in attendance. Jacksonville and its beaches were crawling with single, unattached women, but none of them were here tonight. The women here were all young and white. Too bad. His male ego was crying out for some feminine attention, but he'd never felt the urge to go that route. Maybe he should have held on to the phone numbers of the women he'd dated in between his marriages. But it had been too long, and he was sure none of them were still available. Too bad. The terms of those relationships had been perfect for him: Dinner, movie, and then back to their place for sex. He might have been able to convince one of them to skip the dinner or the movie and hit the sheets for old times' sake. He wouldn't mind a little meaningless sex right about now, as long as his partner was someone other than Norell.

She had turned their marital relations into something meaningless. At this point he'd had it with her, her company, her friends, and her drinking. He'd tried to give her everything, but all she could do was bemoan the fact that she couldn't get pregnant. Plenty of other joys in life existed besides having babies. The funny thing was that if, by some miracle, Norell did get pregnant, she'd probably complain about having to get up in the middle of the night to tend to a bawling baby. The grass was always greener.

After an hour and three beers he began to get bored. He decided to go check on the rental condominium he owned—the last vacationers who rented it had just returned home two days ago—and then just go home, unless he decided to hang around the condo and listen to some music. Hell, maybe he'd even spend the night there, just to get Norell worrying. If she thought she might lose him, maybe she'd get her ass in gear and stop working so much.

The band finished a number, and the crowd applauded wildly. Vic was surprised at how rowdy they had become. It had to be the alcohol. He leaned forward a little so he could scan the crowd without straining his neck muscles. A brown face jumped out at him, and not just any old face. She looked like that woman he'd had dinner with at The Landing a couple of weeks ago. What was her name? Damn, he couldn't remember. Wait a minute. Didn't it sound something like a tire?

She sat at a rear table with two young white women, whom he surmised were friends from work. Judging from her expression, she felt as bored as he did. Vic quickly signaled a waitress. "I want you to deliver a drink to the young lady at the table back there. She's African American, has light-colored hair, and is wearing a tan blouse," he instructed.

"Right away, sir."

The waitress, a blonde in her mid-twenties, immediately approached Micheline's table. "The gentleman sitting up ahead would like to buy you a drink, miss."

Micheline craned her neck to see through the tables separating them. She only saw the back of a head, but the gray in it and the way it was cut told her it had to be that old guy, Vic, from The Landing. She wondered if his wife had stood him up again. "Thank you. I'll have another green-apple martini. But you can deliver it to his table." She picked up her purse. What perfect timing. She had just been about to ditch this joint anyway. The music wasn't bad, but the company left much to be desired. She only came out in the first place because she didn't want to be home. She knew Errol would call, and with a man you never knew when he might drive past your apartment and look for your car, so it wasn't enough to merely turn off or ignore the phone. She wanted Errol to realize that she had a life outside of the time they spent together. If she looked boring and predictable to him, he'd lose interest. She had to be elusive, especially after holding on to him this long. He'd invited her to have dinner with his parents on Sunday, so she had to be doing something right.

"Excuse me, girls," she said to her companions. "I see an acquaintance of mine. I'm going to go and have a drink with him. I'll be back in a bit." She had no intentions of rejoining them, but she felt it sounded nicer to say she would.

She ignored the admiring glances she received from most of the men she passed, all of whom were white, and most of whom were there with dates. "Hi!" she said as she sat down next to Vic. "Fancy meeting you here."

"Hi. It's funny. I just happened to turn around, and there you were."

"I don't know how I missed you when I came in."

"Sometimes if you're not expecting to see someone you don't really notice they're there. How've you been . . . Micheline?" Silently reciting all the brand names of tires he could think of had suddenly restored her name to his memory.

"Pretty good, Vic. How about you? Don't tell me your wife stood you up again?" *Might as well find out the deal from the jump*, she reasoned.

He chuckled. "No. Actually, she's entertaining a group of her girlfriends. They're going to tie one on, and I just didn't feel like being around a bunch of cackling, slightly intoxicated females."

"Oh, I see." Micheline supposed a bunch of women over forty-five getting drunk and loud wouldn't be a pretty sight.

They sat back in their chairs, temporarily foregoing conversation in favor of the music. The waiter delivered Micheline's drink, and Vic raised his beer glass in a silent toast.

After two more numbers the band announced they were taking a break. "They're really good," Micheline remarked when they left the bandstand. "But when the girls said they were going to see a blues band, I thought there would be more black people here."

"Blues is big here at the beach. The white folks love it. I'm not sure why they don't have more black clientele. Maybe people don't realize they're out here."

"Maybe. It's too bad."

Vic glanced at the two women Micheline had been sitting with, who had now been joined by a man. "I hope I didn't interfere with your evening."

"No, not at all. We just met out here after work and had dinner."

"Didn't you say at dinner last time that you lived off Touchton Road? You're kind of far from home, aren't you?"

"Not that far. I like it. At one point I considered moving out here, but I decided it would be more convenient to live closer to town. Plus, I can't really afford hurricane insurance. Just because there hasn't been a major storm since sixty-four doesn't mean one won't hit soon."

"Yeah, I remember that. Hurricane Dora. She tore up the beaches."

"You remember that? It's been more than forty years."

He smiled at her. "You're being kind, but yes, I remember. Of course, I was just a kid at the time, but I remember a lot of things from that era. Hell, I remember when you and I couldn't be served in a restaurant like this. There were 'WHITES ONLY' signs everywhere."

"Wow."

"I'll never forget it. Sometimes I'm amazed that I still live here, but then things began to change and this city got a lot friendlier, even if a lot of white folks did rush to get their houses on the market when the first black family moved into their neighborhoods."

"It looks like you've done pretty well here."

"I haven't done too badly, I guess." He drained his beer. "I was about to take a ride over to my condo and check it out. Since my house is full of my wife's friends, this seems like a good time to do it."

"What's that, a second home?"

"Rental property, on First Street. It's not rented this week. Even though I have a management service that arranges for cleaning after each guest leaves, and takes inventory and reports damages, I still like to check on it after they've been through it." He noticed the sparkle in her eyes and knew she was thinking she had struck pay dirt; that she'd found a man who had a few dollars to spend on her. "Want to come along? You can follow me in your car."

"Yes, I'd like that. I'll just take me a few minutes to finish my drink."

"Take your time." No, that wouldn't do. He wanted to leave first so he could stop at a convenience store and get some condoms in case she could be easily convinced to give him some. "Maybe I should leave now, just to make it look a little better, since you know people here."

"Good point. I don't believe in letting my coworkers know my business."

He scribbled the address on a piece of paper and handed it to her. "Finish your drink. Wait ten or fifteen minutes. I'll see you in a bit."

"All right, Vic."

Micheline's foot began to tap with a spring that hadn't been there before. So, Vic owned property on First Street. She knew enough about Beaches geography to know that was just a block from the beach. Vic might be the perfect man to suit her needs. She still saw Sean fairly regularly, but that relationship had long since lost its luster. He'd become such a cheapskate since he'd gotten his own place. All he wanted to do was come over with some KFC or cheap Chinese food and then get her in the sack.

Errol Trent continued to try to get her into bed, but she demurely refused, saying she didn't believe in premarital sex. The poor slug had no idea of what went on between her and Sean.

Micheline often satisfied her sexual appetite with the men she had no interest in marrying while putting off the ones who pursued her. Married men were particularly useful for this purpose due to their off-hours availability. The fact that they often felt compelled to buy her gifts to soothe the disappointment they mistakenly believed she experienced when they couldn't be with her was an extra benefit, and the more money they had, the nicer the gifts.

Vic certainly had a few bucks. He appeared older than any of the men she'd had affairs with, but he looked like he not only had it but knew how to use it to prime advantage.

She was about to find out.

The ground floor one-bedroom condo smelled fresh and clean. The pine wood furnishings with their natural dark stains successfully stuck a balance between homey and impersonal.

After Vic showed it to her they returned to the living room and listened to smooth jazz on the radio. He had a little difficulty pinpointing the station and turned away from her while he adjusted the radio dial. Micheline took that opportunity to stretch out seductively on the floor pillows. "So tell me, Vic," she asked when he turned to her, "have you ever cheated on your wife?"

* * *

Vic was on the verge of a monster orgasm, his third of the evening. He gripped Micheline's hips and pumped like crazy. God, she felt good. She actually reminded him a lot of Norell in the good old days before she became a business owner.

He cried out when he felt the beginning of his climax, and she met him with a shout. Afterward they collapsed on the bed. "My God, you're gonna give me a heart attack," he said between gasps.

"If I do, you'd better hope you die. Your wife will never forgive you if she finds out what you were doing."

He laughed. "You got that right."

"It's getting late. I should be getting home."

"I'll be happy to drive you if you're tired."

She gave him a Mona Lisa smile. "And how will I get my car back?"

"I can bring you to get it after you've had a chance to rest." She was still smiling, and he knew why. "I know what you're thinking. You think that if I knew where you lived I'd become a pest and start showing up at your door every five minutes, but I'm not. I'm not in the habit of doing this, Micheline." It was true, at least partially. He had cheated regularly on Phyllis after she put on the first forty pounds, but this was the first time he had stepped out on Norell. It had been strictly for his ego; it really didn't mean anything. He'd just gotten fed up with feeling like he ranked last on her list of priorities.

"I appreciate that. I can drive myself, though. Ooh."

"What's wrong?"

"I feel something." She sat up, her fingers disappearing between her legs. "It's the condom. It must have unraveled. Oh, no."

Vic sat up. After a quick glance downward he said, "I didn't even realize it was gone. Can I help you get it out?"

"No, I've got it." Micheline removed the prophylactic, which had actually torn. This had never happened to her before. She felt a sudden sense of urgency. She'd better get home quickly so she could douche.

"I'm sure it'll be all right. I am sorry about that, though." He'd forgotten how refreshing sex was when there was no agenda. Even after the unfavorable results of her fertility workup, Norell—when she wasn't drunk, that was—still put her legs up with her feet against the wall or bent her body in favor of her tilted uterus, trying to give Mother Nature a helping hand.

Micheline got into her clothes. "It was nice, Vic, but I've got to go."

"Wait; I'll walk you to your car."

"Not necessary. I parked right outside."

She wasn't messing around, he thought. Probably just as well. He couldn't go outside naked, and he'd really prefer taking a shower before he went home, so Norell wouldn't pick up the scent of another woman on him. He would come back tomorrow and toss the bed linen in the washer. And he knew where she worked if he wanted to contact her for another go-round in case things stayed bad between him and Norell.

Micheline gave him an impersonal peck on the lips. "Good night, Vic. I enjoyed it."

He watched her run to the door. He didn't even know Micheline's last name, but one thing he did know: She was a cheating man's dream woman.

Chapter 32

Norell poured champagne into everyone's glass. "Here's to spending a pleasant evening with my friends," she said, "old and older."

Her guests laughed. "Well, I like that!" Lynn Phillips exclaimed.

"I didn't mean you were old, Lynn. I meant that we've known each other since grade school. And of course, I've known Dana and Cécile for about ten years now."

"I guess now that we're getting close to forty I'm a little sensitive about the word 'old'," Lynn conceded with a smile. She held up her glass. "One more toast. Here's to reconnecting with old friends. It makes the pain of losing a loved one a little bit easier."

They all clicked glasses a second time. "And let's drink to Michael and me," Cécile added. "Not only did we find a new house, but we sold our old one!"

"You did!" Dana exclaimed. "How wonderful. Tell us all about it!"

Cécile first took a moment to fill Lynn in on her housing dilemma, then described her new house. It sounded marvelous. Norell listened and tried to smile. She was glad that Cécile had found a larger place for her growing family, but it only made her own situation appear that much bleaker. She drained the rest of her glass, and the rush of the champagne spread warmth throughout her body. It embraced her like an old friend.

It would get her through the night.

Vic arrived home just as Norell's guests were leaving. He greeted Lynn cordially and briefly hugged Dana and Cécile, whose pregnancy was really causing her to blow up all over. "Did you girls have fun?" he said to Norell after they all drove off.

"Yes, it was real nice. Cécile and Michael found a new house over in San Jose, nice and big, from what she described. They sold their old one, too, so they'll be moving soon."

Her voice sounded casual, but Vic watched as she went to the wet bar and poured Smirnoff into a highball glass. The hand that held the bottle shook slightly. He knew then that she was just putting up a front, and now that her friends were gone she'd be drinking herself into a stupor.

Any guilt he'd had about sleeping with Micheline evaporated like a puddle in hundred-degree heat.

Micheline felt fairly confident that none of Vic's semen had spilled out of the condom when it rolled back, but she was anxious to get home and douche just in case. She'd stop at that twenty-four-hour Walgreens and get a medicated douche. Vinegar and water wouldn't be strong enough. She wanted to get something with chemicals in it, something that could kill any runaway sperm.

At the store she noticed a display of early pregnancy tests near the boxes of douche products. She reached out, about to look at the box, but then pulled her hand back. She had no need for early pregnancy detection. All she had to do was douche, and she'd be fine. Her period would come on time, and her life would go on according to her plan.

And if she did well tomorrow with Errol's parents, she might be married by this time next year.

Chapter 33

"May I help you, Mrs. Trent?" Micheline offered.

"Oh no, dear. It's all on the table. You all come on now and sit down."

Errol offered Micheline his arm. She took it, and he escorted her to the dining room, where she saw the table had been set for four.

"What a lovely table, Mrs. Trent," Micheline said as she lowered her hips into the chair Errol pulled out for her. No tablecloth covered the washed oak table; instead, attractive multicolored wood place mats held plates and silverware. Ice water had been poured into goblets, and each setting also included tall iced tea glasses and wineglasses. An arrangement of fresh yellow gladiolas made a lovely centerpiece, and tall vanilla candles in silver holders graced the table as well.

"Oh, thank you, Micheline. That's such a lovely name, by the way. Is it French?"

Micheline wondered if Errol had told his parents all about her, and Mrs. Trent was simply making polite conversation. "Yes. My parents came from Haiti."

"Ah, Haiti," Mr. Trent said. He'd been busy grilling steaks and chicken out on the screen-enclosed patio. "I've never been there, but I understand it's a lovely island."

"I've never been there myself." Micheline's parents had each gone back at different times to visit family members, but she had no interest in seeing people barely scraping by.

"Really?" Mrs. Trent said. "So you were born in the States, then?"

Micheline picked up on the approval in the older woman's voice. She and Mr. Trent probably had a long list of desired attributes for the future wife of their only son, and being born on a poor, strife-torn Caribbean island probably ranked among the no-nos. "Yes. My family settled in West Palm Beach."

"What do your parents do?"

She'd been waiting for that one and had her answer all ready. "My father owns a landscaping service. His employees tend to many of the Palm Beach estates. And my mother is a caterer." Claude Mehu had hired himself out to do landscaping for a long time, but he owned no business. And Catherine, after leaving the hotel and get-ting a job cleaning offices in the evenings, sold sandwiches and potato salad to the hungry lunch crowd at a nearby factory. They both would be shocked if they could have heard their daughter describe how they earned a living, but Micheline wasn't about to tell the Trents the truth.

One look around was all it took to determine that Errol was no son of a bus driver or mailman who'd made good by becoming a dentist. His parents had an older ranch house, but it sat on the banks of the Ribault River, was impeccably furnished, and the driveway was populated with a Cadillac sedan and a Navigator SUV. She could hardly tell people of this caliber the truth about her family background—that she'd grown up in a rented house a few steps above a shack in Riviera Beach, and that not a single one of her fam-ily members had done anything to set the world on fire. Her brothers all labored at average jobs, like selling stamps at the post office or driving for UPS. As for Cécile, putting on a T-shirt and a pair of sweatpants and typing all day hardly qualified as professional work. Maybe you had to know a few special words here and there, but anyone with half a brain should be able to do well in that field.

"Oh, they're entrepreneurs," Mr. Trent said with a nod of ap-proval. "That's the backbone of the economy, and it can also be a wonderful way to build wealth."

Micheline pounced on this like a dog on a bone. "Oh, my family have always been strong believers in being their own boss. My sister also owns a business. She provides transcription services for doc-tors." So what if Micheline wasn't impressed by Cécile's business venture? If it would help her out with the people she hoped would be her future in-laws, she wouldn't hesitate to use it to her advantage.

"Our family has a long entrepreneurial history," Mrs. Trent

remarked. "My parents owned the African-American funeral home in Crescent City. And my husband's father ran a moving-and-storage service."

"Were you bitten by the entrepreneurial bug yourself, Micheline?" Mr. Trent asked.

"I'm afraid not. I'm a bilingual paralegal for a law firm downtown."

"Do you plan on becoming an attorney?" This from Mrs. Trent. Micheline felt like a tennis ball being volleyed back and forth. She wondered if the Trents realized that their questions were being asked in an alternating rhythm. *No, I want to marry your son and have his baby.* "I considered it at one time, yes," she said, "but I do so enjoy my career. Working full time and going to law school at night would be, if you'll excuse my bluntness, hell."

"I'm sure it would be."

"We went the safe route ourselves," Mr. Trent remarked. "I'm District Counsel for the Small Business Administration, and my wife is a department head at the Internal Revenue Service."

"But of course Errol is self-employed," his mother said proudly. "He started his own business from the ground up. It's a huge undertaking, but in the long run it'll be worth it, even if it means waiting years before he can settle down."

Micheline discreetly lowered her lashes. Her first reaction was to scowl at what she recognized was Mrs. Trent's message to her not to expect marriage from Errol this soon in the game. "I'm sure," she murmured.

"Have you ever been married, Micheline?" Mr. Trent asked.

"No, I haven't. I'm still looking for my Mr. Right." Micheline enjoyed the look of shock on Juanita Trent's face. *She thinks I want to marry her precious son? I do, but let her think that I'm not so crazy about him.*

"And do you have any children?" Mrs. Trent asked demurely, wiping the corner of her mouth with a cloth napkin.

"Mom," Errol said, his tone indicating she'd gone too far.

"Oh, no," Micheline said, looking properly taken aback. "I'd never want to have a child unless I was in a happy, secure marriage." With a man who could support them. She didn't know what she'd do if she ever found herself a single mother. Most of them struggled to get by. Look at Dana Covington. Surely she wouldn't be taking in boarders and working full time in addition to all the hours it took to run a business if her husband had provided for her decently.

She should have known Errol's parents would want to know about that. It was a cinch they wouldn't want him to get involved with anyone who had children, and it wasn't limited to just children out of wedlock. Errol could be forty and dating a thirty-five-year-old divorcée, or even a widow like Dana, but the Trents were certain not to like it if she had kids.

"Mom, Dad," Errol pleaded. "Do you think we can stop the investigation of Micheline and have a nice, pleasant conversation?"

"Well, we're sorry," Mrs. Trent said with a touch of indignation. "But you can't blame us for being a little curious. You announce you're bringing a young lady over for dinner and don't tell us anything about her. We don't even know how long you two have been seeing each other." She smiled at Micheline. "You see, my dear, when my son brings a girl home to meet us, that usually means she's very important to him. So naturally we want to know all about her."

Errol broke in again. "Mom, please. You're embarrassing me."

Micheline placed a hand on his forearm. "No need to be embarrassed, Errol. I think you're pretty special, too." The Trents beamed at her, and she flashed a smile as wide as Broadway.

When Errol brought her home he made his usual play for her. Usually his kisses struck her as incredibly sensual, but tonight they simply seemed wet and sloppy. Micheline pushed him away. "I'm awfully tired, Errol. Remember, tomorrow's a workday."

"I know, I know," he said, his hands grasping her buttocks. "Just give me one more minute of heaven."

He nuzzled her neck until her heavy sigh stopped him. "Micheline, what's wrong? You've been so quiet ever since we left my parents'. Don't you feel well?"

"I'm just a little tired, that's all."

"My parents liked you, you know."

"I liked them, too," she lied. The Trents had the same effect on her as most people: she was indifferent to them. They mattered only if they interfered with her plans. "But Errol, I'd really like to get ready for work tomorrow and go to bed."

"All right. I'll go. But I'm going to call you when I get home. I want to make sure you're all right." He kissed her cheek, then slipped out the door.

Micheline latched it behind him. She knew she'd managed to charm the Trents, and it surprised her that she didn't feel happier about it than she did.

It had been a very stressful weekend for her. She'd had to anticipate Errol's parents' questions and have her answers ready, as well as turn on the charm; and despite her best efforts, that incident with the torn condom Friday night still worried her.

She kept telling herself she had nothing to worry about, that everything seemed to be working just the way she planned. Instead of worrying—an emotion foreign to her—she should be rejoicing.

Micheline thought of the look on Mrs. Trent's face when she stated she was still searching for her Mr. Right. She didn't know if they believed her or saw through her bluff, but she hoped she'd convinced them that she regarded their son as very sweet, but nothing special.

The triumphant feeling didn't last long. By the time she pulled back her bed's top sheet and slid in, the uneasiness had returned. She'd already checked her calendar. Her period wasn't due for another two weeks. In her heart she knew she wouldn't truly relax until she knew for certain.

It would be a very long two weeks.

Chapter 34

Irene sat in her Grand Am a few houses down from Dana's. She didn't know what she expected to see on this quiet block. Tuesday morning at ten-thirty A.M. was an unlikely time for Gil to be at Dana's. He'd be at work this time of day. Normally she would be as well, except for a dental appointment for a teeth cleaning.

Dana, on the other hand, was sure to be inside. Irene knew from general small talk with Dana that she began work before dawn, transcribing documents for her full-time job, before devoting time to running the business she owned with a couple of partners.

In her rearview mirror, Irene caught sight of a mail truck a few houses behind her. Whoever had this mail route didn't have to do much walking. The carrier merely deposited mail into the curbside mailbox, and then drove a few yards to the next house and did the same thing. Knowing the mailman had seen her loitering prompted her to make her move. She drove down the street until she was right in front of Dana's driveway, where she recognized the Camry Dana drove. She pulled into the driveway until her car was right behind Dana's.

Irene walked with brisk steps up the short front walk. She rang the doorbell and waited, deliberately standing close to the door so that Dana couldn't see her from the office window upstairs.

Irene heard footsteps bounding down the stairs and then a pleasant voice calling out, "Who is it?"

"Irene Albacete, Dana."

The door immediately opened. Dana stood inside, wearing jeans, a T-shirt, and a surprised expression. "Irene."

She struck a perfect balance of congeniality, polite without being overly friendly, Irene noticed. "I had an appointment over this way this morning, and I found myself stopping over here. I hadn't planned to."

"You must want to talk to me about something. Why don't you come in?"

"Thanks." Irene stepped inside and sat down in a stiff-backed chair in the formal living room. She waited for Dana to settle in a corner of the floral-print sofa before speaking. "I wanted to ask you to consider not seeing my husband anymore."

Dana had never looked entirely comfortable from the time she first opened the door, but now her features hardened. "I think maybe your coming over wasn't such a good idea, Irene."

"In other words, you won't do it."

Dana leaned forward earnestly. "Irene, no one set out to deliberately hurt you. Sometimes things just . . . just happen. No laws are being broken, nor is anything morally wrong. You and Gil are divorced. I've noticed you like to refer to him as your husband, but he isn't. He's your *ex*-husband."

"I call him my husband because I know he still loves me. You're interfering with my family, Dana. We're trying to heal after a difficult period for all of us."

"The healing will come from accepting your marriage is over, Irene. I don't believe Gil is still in love with you. He respects you as the mother of his child, yes, and he probably does still love you in a special way, but not the way a husband loves a wife. Insisting that I'm destroying your happy home is just nonsense."

Irene stood up. "If you're not willing to listen to reason, I guess there's no point in continuing this conversation."

Dana stood as well. "As long as you're being unreasonable, I guess there isn't." She crossed to the front door and held it open. "Good-bye, Irene. I'm sorry you're so unwilling to see things as they really are."

"Well, just remember, God don't like ugly," Irene said as she swept past Dana, using an expression she'd heard one of the girls at work say. Seconds later she heard the door close behind her, none too gently.

Well, she'd tried. Dana refused to leave Gil alone, refused to let him come home to her and Vanessa so they could be a family again.

All Dana cared about was herself. She didn't care who she hurt, whose life she made miserable.

Irene slowed down as she approached Dana's mailbox. The mail truck had moved a half block down the street. She turned quickly and scanned the front windows of Dana's house. No sign of her.

Irene made her choice quickly. She opened the box, pulling out a sale circular from JCPenney, a utility bill from JEA, and a couple of envelopes addressed to CDN Transcription. The latter two she found most intriguing, and she held on to them and quickly closed the box. She'd open them when she got to work.

As soon as Irene removed her keys from the ignition in front of the small consulting firm where she worked as office manager, she tore open the envelopes. To her delight, they both contained checks, one for six hundred dollars and the other for eighteen hundred.

Irene smiled triumphantly. Her little hunch had paid off.

Now let *Dana* feel some interference in her life and see how she liked it.

Dana glanced through the curtain at Irene's retreating form. What nerve. The woman must be crazy with the statements she'd made about her husband and her family. *She makes it sound like I started seeing Gil when he was still living with her as husband and wife.* She'd go call him now and tell him about it.

Dana turned and walked away from the window, missing Irene's pause by her mailbox. Gil had to know about this right away.

"And then she had the nerve to say to me on her way out that God don't like ugly," she said to Gil. "Can you believe that? Like I'm some temptress getting you to commit adultery."

"Irene has been trying to get back with me ever since I left. And I'm not saying that because I want to build up my ego, Dana. It happens to be the truth. I think she's convinced herself that you're the obstacle to reconciling with me. I'm sorry. If you don't want to see me again, I understand."

"Don't want to see you again? Because of one little visit from your ex-wife? You're being silly, Gil."

"I'm not so sure."

Dana had resumed her work when Cécile called. "Do you mind if I skip next week's partners' meeting? Michael and the kids and I have plans to go through everything in the house and the garage this weekend. We're going to pack up whatever we can get by without."

"When do you close on the new house?"

"Next month. The closing on this house is scheduled for a week later, so we'll have plenty of time to get moved out and come back and straighten up here."

"I'm happy for you, Cécile. I haven't moved in a long time, but with the size of your family it must be a real nightmare."

"Oh, it'll wear me out, all right. But I can deal with that. What I'd like to avoid is having Norell stare at my stomach like she wishes it would explode."

"Come on, Cécile. Surely she's not still doing that, not after you guys made up."

"She doesn't stare like she used to, but I still caught her eyes latched onto my belly a couple of times yesterday when she thought I wasn't looking. It's never going to go away completely. That's what makes me uncomfortable. I feel like she's going to bring me bad luck."

"We have to try to be patient with Norell, Cécile. After all, it probably would have just about killed me if I'd been told I couldn't have children. Brittany was the one reason I had to keep going on when Kenny died." Dana drew in her breath, immediately recognizing that for the first time she had admitted Kenny was dead, not merely the victim of an accident. "And look at you. Your kids are your life."

"Dana, you'd been through a major psychological trauma, losing your mother and sister, and then hearing your father say what he did. God wouldn't be that cruel to you to deny your having a child. And as for me, my whole life, all I knew was taking care of kids. Since I was the second oldest and the oldest girl, I was my mother's right hand growing up. I always knew that I'd have my own kids one day. Not this many, of course," Cécile added with a laugh.

"Most girls dream of having kids when they're growing up. Norell's no different. It's hard for her to see you and me with our children, that's all. She doesn't want anything bad to happen to us." She chuckled. "After all, I've made her Brittany's official guardian in case I die or become incapacitated."

"I'm glad you've made plans for Brittany's sake, but I'd watch my back around her if I were you. She's likely to drop cyanide tablets in your soup."

"Cécile, you're exaggerating. But I understand your being uncomfortable around her. Once you have the baby it'll go away, and Norell will hold it and coo at it and make silly faces just like everyone else. So you go on and get your packing done. Don't worry about missing the meeting. I'll fill you in on everything that happens and e-mail you a copy of our freshly updated financials. I'm expecting a couple of checks this week."

Although a few other checks did arrive, by Friday nothing had come in from either the sports-medicine clinic or the dermatology practice. This struck Dana as unusual. Both always sent their checks within days of being invoiced, and the invoices had gone out ten days before. She made a mental note to give both offices' bookkeepers a pleasant nudge if the checks weren't in Monday's mail delivery.

Monday's mail contained no checks, but both bookkeepers she spoke to insisted that they'd mailed their checks last week. She should have had them by now. CDN kept a post office box as their official mailing address to meet home-business regulations, but she, Norell, and Cécile all agreed it would save time if they used Dana's home address on the envelopes they enclosed with clients' invoices. This allowed payments to be promptly received and deposited without having to make extra trips to the post office to retrieve checks. Now she was faced with either waiting for a delayed delivery or going through the further delay of requesting that the clients issue a stop-payment order on the checks.

She discussed the matter with her partners. "Give it until the end of the week," Cécile said.

"How much money are we talking about?" Norell wanted to know.

"About twenty-five hundred, total."

"In that case I'd ask for a stop payment now," Norell advised. "It'll probably be at least two days before they can reissue the checks. This way you'll have it wrapped up by the end of the week."

Dana sighed. "Maybe I should. Cécile thought I should wait until the end of the week."

"Cécile wouldn't be so patient if somebody owed her twenty-five hundred dollars personally."

"You're right, she wouldn't. Okay, I'll call."

"Let me know what happens." Norell hung up the phone. It rang again before she could reposition her fingers over her ergonomic keyboard. "Hello."

"Hey, beautiful."

"Well, hello to you, too, handsome," she said, immediately falling into the flirtatious mood Vic set.

"I was thinking, how'd you like to have dinner at Harry's tonight?"

"I just put a roast beef in the oven."

"Well, save it for tomorrow. Or better yet, slice it for sandwiches."

She laughed. Her first thought had been to say, "Vic, I can't," and she was glad she'd caught herself. He'd been so sweet these last couple of weeks, coming up with spontaneous suggestions for dinner or the movies. He hadn't squawked once when she announced after dinner that she had work to complete. CDN now did overflow transcription for a local medical center. They had hired three part-time MTs, women with families hoping to make a few extra dollars. Between them they got in maybe seven hours of work a day, but even that made a dent in the hospital account. At least the director of medical records, who had hired them, was pleased with their work.

Best of all, she and Vic were getting along now like they had in their early days together. All she'd ever wanted was for him to give her emotional support, both with CDN and with her infertility struggle. He'd been way too slow to react to both, something she still found hurtful.

But at least their marriage stood on firmer ground these days. That's all it took: a little understanding, and a little extra effort on both their parts.

"Just tell me what time you want me to be ready," she said.

"I'll be home at around six-thirty, six-forty-five, so why don't we plan on seven?"

"That'll work. I started work early today, and I think I can reach my goal for the day before then. That means I won't have to work when we get home. And if I don't reach my goal, I can get up early tomorrow and finish first thing."

"Yeah, well, I wouldn't plan on getting up *too* early if I were you," he said suggestively.

Another bonus of their combined efforts. Lovemaking was happening in their bedroom, a lot of it. Sessions that stayed in her memory vividly and weren't lost forever, like an empty liquor bottle. "You'd be surprised how well I sleep on nights we make love. I can sleep for six hours and it'll feel like ten. It gives me energy just thinking about it."

"In that case I'll let you get back to work. I'll see you later." Vic hung up the receiver and leaned back thoughtfully in his chair.

He sensed Norell's almost childlike eagerness as she tried to accommodate his wishes, and her simple efforts made him feel ashamed of his behavior.

He'd felt guilty ever since that night at his rental condo with Micheline. He resolved then to make more of an effort to work with Norell. It worked, and they were happier now than they'd been in a long time.

Vic knew it shouldn't have taken his sleeping with another woman to bring him to his senses. He knew he'd thrown the adult equivalent of a temper tantrum and been generally uncooperative with Norell's efforts to do her share in the business she co-owned. He found it difficult to accept that the no-responsibility woman he married had evolved into a hardworking businesswoman. Too bad it took an act of adultery to wake him up.

But it looked like it might have worked out for the best. After all, it wasn't like he'd ever see Micheline again.

Chapter 35

"Brittany, I'm going to go out for a little while on Saturday," Dana said.

"You going out with Mr. Gil?"

Dana didn't like the smart-alecky tone in Brittany's voice. She never missed an opportunity to express her unhappiness about Gil ever since it had cost her her best friend. "Who I'm going out with isn't really any of your business," she snapped. "I'm just giving you a heads-up that Tina will be over to sit with you."

"You gonna stay out all night?"

"That's *enough*, Brittany." Dana hadn't spanked Brittany since she was a very little girl, but one more remark like that, and she'd get her face slapped. Brittany knew damn well that their neighbor Tina, a junior in high school, only babysat until midnight. Because of the friction between Brittany and Vanessa, Dana had decided against allowing Gil to pick her up. Brittany considered Gil the reason for the debacle with Vanessa. She definitely wasn't ready to see the two of them together as a couple.

"All right, since you insist on making my life miserable," Brittany muttered as she tucked her long hair into her swim cap and went out the backdoor to the pool.

Dana rolled her eyes. Although she wanted to convince herself that Brittany was merely being overly dramatic, she knew how important friends were at thirteen years old. She wondered if she'd make a mistake in getting involved with Gil. But how could something that felt so right possibly be wrong?

Brittany rushed back inside. "Mom, come quick! You've got two flat tires!"

Dana followed her outside. Her Camry sat in the driveway right in front of the garage, leaning to the left because its weight on that side rested on its rims. Both tires were completely flat. "Well, that's odd," she said. "I just had the pressure checked with the oil change I had last week, and I don't remember running over anything that would flatten both tires." She walked around to the other side of the car. Those tires were fine, and so were those of the yellow Saturn belonging to Jennifer, her college-student tenant.

"Look, Mom," Brittany said. "There's a big hole in the tire right here. I'll bet there's another one just like it on the other one."

Dana came back around in time to see Brittany slip her index finger into a gash in the rubber that she estimated was three inches long. Then Brittany moved to the rear tire and found similar damage.

She drew in her breath. "I wonder if any other cars on the block had their tires slashed." But even as Dana said the words she had a feeling her car would be the only one. Why slash her tires and leave her tenant's wheels unharmed? "I'm going to call the police," she said.

"Mrs. Covington, none of your neighbors has been victimized," the uniformed officer informed her. "That tells us this probably wasn't just a random act of vandalism. Is there someone you suspect might act on a grudge?"

"I can't think of a soul."

"Where is Mr. Covington, if you don't mind my asking?"

"He's dead," she said quietly. "He died in an accident over a year ago."

"I'm sorry. What about work? What type of work do you do?"

"I own a medical-transcription service with two partners who happen to be my best friends. It's an amiable working relationship."

"Employees? Anybody let go lately?"

"Well yes, but I'm sure she wouldn't—"

"We'll need her name and address. What about your social life? Have you recently broken off with someone who didn't take it well?"

"I'm involved with someone, and it's going fine."

The officer nodded. "You might want to go over every relationship you have. Something might come to you. In the meantime, I'd suggest that you put up some motion detectors throughout your property. They're surprisingly effective against vandalism."

"So what do we do now, Mom?" Brittany asked after the police left.

Dana sighed. "The first thing I need to do is get new tires. I'll have to get the auto club to tow the car down to Allied. While that's going on, you and I are going to have to rearrange the garage so I can park in there. That's about it. I can't afford to get motion detectors installed right now."

"What about the patio lights? Can't we use those?"

"Those will disturb Jennifer and our other neighbors. They're meant to be used if we're entertaining after dark, not to stay on all night. That's the nice thing about motion detectors. They'll go on for a minute or two whenever they sense movement. That will alert us that someone is outside."

"So like when Jennifer gets home at night, lights will come on outside my window?"

"Just for a minute, and then they'll go off. I'm sure you won't be disturbed, Britt. You sleep like a rock. After all, you didn't hear anyone come around last night, did you?"

"I wish Daddy were here. Bad things like this never happened when he was here."

"Brittany, I know it's hard for you to accept, and God knows you shouldn't have to at your age, but Daddy isn't coming back. We're going to have to get by all by ourselves."

Brittany's face puddled up. "Sometimes I can't believe I'll never see him again."

Dana embraced her daughter tightly, her eyes shut. She, too, would give anything to hear her mother's voice one more time. "I know, honey," she said. "I know."

Dana sluggishly moved into a sitting position in the bed. Gil was already getting back into his clothes. They'd just spent their lunch break making love.

No man had set foot in her bedroom since that one time she'd allowed Sean Sizemore to come over, just days before she learned he was seeing her tenant Micheline behind her back. Funny, but even then it hadn't felt right. Maybe in her heart she suspected that Sean didn't belong in her bed. He didn't deserve to be there. But she had no such bad feelings about Gil.

"I don't know what we're going to do," he said as he tied his tie with swift-moving fingers. "Vanessa cutting off her friendship with Brittany, your still not wanting me to pick you up—"

She sighed. "Gil, that just can't be helped. I was all for it after I spoke to Brittany about us and she was so receptive. It would be different if Vanessa and Brittany were still friends, but under the circumstances it's like rubbing salt into an open wound. Brittany is hurting over Vanessa, really hurting." She didn't want to add that Brittany had also experienced a delayed grief reaction as a result of the incident with the car tires. It frightened her daughter to know that someone had crept onto their property just below where she slept and her daddy wasn't there to protect her.

"I've really made a mess of things for you, haven't I?"

Dana didn't know what to say to that. She couldn't deny that her problems with Brittany wouldn't exist if it weren't for Gil. She pulled her T-shirt over her head while she searched for something to say. "She's mad at both of us, you know."

"I guess she feels that if you and I were to stop seeing each other, Vanessa would be her friend again, just like that."

"I told her the damage has already been done, but naturally she doesn't believe me." Dana sighed as she slipped into her cutoffs. "I kept hoping Vanessa would come around, but the longer this goes on the longer it seems like that won't happen."

"Vanessa doesn't know it, but she's being manipulated by an expert," Gil said as he ran a comb through his close-cropped sandy hair. "Irene missed her calling. She should have been a lobbyist."

Dana laughed. "You make me feel good, Gil. Lord knows I don't have much to laugh about these days. This thing with Vanessa and Brittany, my tires, the mail—"

"What about the mail?" Gil asked abruptly.

"A couple of checks I was expecting from clients didn't come. We use a post office box for our mailing address, but to save time we used my home address on the return envelopes, so checks would come directly here. It's perfectly legal. But the checks never came. Almost twenty-five hundred dollars. I had to ask the clients to stop payment on the originals and issue new ones."

Gil paced the floor, his hands in his pockets. She looked at him, suddenly worried. "Gil, what's wrong?"

He stood with his back to her. She watched his body language, watched as his head bowed. Clearly he knew something he didn't want to tell her.

She waited patiently, knowing he would tell her eventually.

Finally he turned. "Dana, I've got to tell you this. I think Irene is behind this."

"Irene?"

"Let me explain. After I moved out I started dating a very nice lady. I didn't hide it, like I had when I was stepping out and still living at home." He noticed her frown. "I know that it probably wasn't right—I was technically still married, even though I'd already filed for divorce.

"Anyway, strange things began happening to the woman I was seeing. Her job got calls that suggested she was under some kind of investigation. Somebody threw a brick through her windshield. She received threatening letters."

"The letters mentioned you?"

"No, my name never came up. If it had, it would have been pretty easy to determine where they were coming from. But I suspected Irene all along, and I had to tell the woman what I thought. She broke up with me." Gil shrugged. "Nothing was ever proven, but the minute she stopped seeing me, the harassment stopped. So what does that tell you?"

"But how could she have known all of your girlfriend's business? Where she lived, where she worked, all that?"

"Dana, you're being naïve. It's easy. All she had to do was follow me on a Saturday night and see where I went."

"Gil, come on. You wouldn't notice Irene's car following you, even in the dark?"

"Not if it was a rental. And she probably wasn't directly behind me."

Dana raised an eyebrow. It all sounded so shady, almost comical, the idea of renting a car and setting out to trail Gil. What did Irene do, put on a tan trench coat and matching fedora, like Sam Spade in the movies? But at the same time it was a little spooky.

"Once she knew my friend's home address," Gil continued, "all she had to do was wait for her to leave for work and follow her there. I'm not sure how she found out her name, but she did."

"I don't know what to make of all this, Gil. I mean, if Irene is really behind all this that means she's tampered with my mail, which is a federal offense. And slashing my tires! It sounds like she's already gone off the deep end. Who's to say that she won't come to my door one day with a shotgun and blast me in the face? Or, God forbid, my child?"

"I think I know what's coming next," he said sadly.

"Gil, much as I care for you, I'm not willing to put my life or Brittany's at risk because Irene can't accept the idea of you being with someone else. If we could prove it was her and have the authorities deal with her, it would be different. I'd feel safe if she were locked up." Dana studied his face carefully. She feared he wouldn't like the idea of her pressing criminal charges against the mother of his child.

But all Gil did was nod. "That would certainly take care of all my problems. If Irene were in jail, I'd get custody of Vanessa.

"Let's do this," he suggested. "We won't see each other this weekend. Now that I'm sure this was no random act of vandalism, it would be better if we didn't meet. It might not be safe for you going home." He saw her wince. "Let me take care of this."

"What're you going to do?"

"I'm going to put a stop to all this foolishness." He kissed her quickly. "I've got to run. Come down and put the latch on behind me, all right?"

As Gil drove back to work he formulated a plan. No way would he allow Irene to destroy what he'd built up with Dana. Not only did he have to stop Irene's harassment, but he had to find a way to get Vanessa and Brittany to reunite. He couldn't call himself a man if he couldn't stop the havoc his ex-wife wreaked on his personal life.

He thought of the frightened look on Dana's face when he suggested she might not be safe after meeting him for a date. He thought of how sad she seemed whenever she talked about how hurt Brittany felt by Vanessa's rejection. He wanted to protect Dana, to make her happy. He'd fallen in love with her.

And, determination burning in him like a raging forest fire, he thought that nothing and no one would make him give her up.

Chapter 36

"Well, isn't this a nice surprise. To what do I owe the pleasure?"

Gil faced his ex-wife. Even a deaf man could sense her sarcasm, if not by hearing it in her voice, then by her sardonic expression and the hostile way she crossed her arms over her chest. Not that he'd expected her to be cordial.

"Irene, we need to talk," he said. He instantly recognized a glint of hope in her eyes, but she tried to be nonchalant.

She waved her hand across her body, inviting him inside in a grand gesture. Gil glanced around at the town house condominium where he had once lived with Irene and Vanessa. It looked exactly the same as it had when he lived there. Of course, he hadn't been gone long enough for Irene to have time to make changes.

As he sat on the familiar rust-colored velvet sofa, he realized that Irene probably had no interest in changing anything. She wanted things to be the way they used to be, him living here with her as husband and wife. It wouldn't happen, and he had come here tonight because her attempts at getting him back had gotten out of hand.

Fortunately, she sat in the matching chair opposite him. He didn't think he could stand it if she sat close to him. He'd probably have to get up and change seats. "So what's on your mind?" she asked, a smug look on her face, like she was about to receive good news.

"Irene, I know you're behind the problems Dana's been having."

"What problems?" Her face contorted into a scowl. "What are you talking about, Gil?"

Damn, she was good. If he didn't know in his gut that she was guilty, he might have had second thoughts.

"You know exactly what I'm talking about. Her slashed tires. The checks you stole from her mailbox. That's a federal offense, you know. And when you're caught, federal crime or not, Dana is going to press charges against you."

"I'm sure you'd love that, but you're forgetting something, Gil. I haven't done any of the things you accused me of. That makes catching me for doing something impossible."

"Well, just remember this while you're denying everything: It'll be very easy for me to get custody of Vanessa once you're formally charged with harassing Dana."

That got a reaction out of her. The color faded from her face, and she couldn't prevent a gasp from escaping from between her lips.

"I want you out of here," she said, jumping to her feet. "I know what this is all about. This is about intimidation and control."

"No, Irene," he said calmly. "This is all about your trying to get me back. It's over between us, but we'll always have contact because we have a daughter together. The way I see it, one of two things can happen now. We can be civil and get along for the sake of our daughter, or we can threaten and harass and argue with each other. I vote for the former, but it's up to you.

"But whatever you choose, remember this," he said, rising. "I want you to stay the hell away from Dana."

Chapter 37

Micheline brushed her hair into place. Sean didn't have a mirror in his bedroom—hell, he didn't even have a dresser, just a mattress and box spring resting on the floor, and a plastic Parsons table on one side to hold an alarm clock. At least the shabby decor fit the neighborhood. If anyone broke into his apartment they wouldn't get much, just a TV set, a boom box with CD player, and a nice collection of CDs. She certainly wouldn't miss coming to this low-rent district.

She should have known that when Sean finally got around to renting a place of his own, it would be old and unpleasant. But they usually had their trysts here. Micheline wanted to avoid any potentially embarrassing encounters in case Errol decided to drop by her apartment uninvited. She also preferred staying in, afraid someone she knew would spot her with Sean, and it would get back to Errol. Sean usually ordered in. She found the arrangement satisfactory, even if the surroundings were dismal.

The best thing she could say for this apartment complex was that the tenants were quiet. The two-story pale blue brick buildings couldn't be more plain. No ground-floor patios or second-floor balconies, no individual entrances, just dimly lit hallways with dirty gray carpet and dark green apartment doors. Only losers lived in a place like this, people who drove fifteen-year-old vehicles, or laughable new cars like those little three-cylinder deals, the ones that folded up like paper fans in collisions.

She put her brush in her purse with a little sigh. The time had come to tell Sean she wouldn't be back. A simple suggestion from Errol had changed everything.

Micheline found Sean in the living room, sprawled out on the black imitation-leather sofa. An almost-empty pizza box sat on the coffee table—he had no dinette set, which made perfect sense, since the tiny efficiency apartment had no dining area. "You about ready to go?" he asked.

"Yes."

"I'll walk you out." He sat up and reached for the old gym shoes he used for quick trips to the laundry room or to the trash dump, their backs permanently flattened from being constantly walked on.

"If you could wait just a minute, there's something I have to tell you."

He looked up with a nervous expression. "Oh, shit. You're not gonna say you're pregnant, are you?"

"Of course not. What makes you think that?"

"Maybe you haven't noticed, but you've put on a few pounds."

She lowered her chin to her chest and glared at him. "I have not!"

He shrugged. "Have it your way. What did you want to say?"

"Just that we've had a lot of fun together, but I'm afraid we've come to the end of the road."

"You're dropping me, huh? What happened, did he propose?"

"I don't know what you're talking about." Micheline managed to project genuine indignation. Truly believing one's own bullshit, she found, helped prevent facial expressions or coloring from giving one away. Her fair complexion used to lose color or brighten, until she learned to control her thinking.

"Yeah, whatever. I'm not stupid, Micheline. I know you're not going to settle for takeout pizza or Chinese. I'm sure you've been seeing somebody on the side, and from how aggressive you've become in bed lately, you probably aren't giving him any. I guess that's why you kept on seeing me."

"Well, that's all very interesting, Sean, but you and I never had any exclusivity factor. I'm sure you're seeing someone else, too, somebody you're spending more money on than the cost of a barbecued chicken and sides from Sonny's." Her eyes scanned his barren apartment. "I'm sure that lead IT technicians are reasonably well paid, and you certainly aren't spending anything on this place."

"Okay, so I'm seeing somebody. But at least I'll admit it, which is more than I can say for you." He looked at her, shaking his head in amusement. "Micheline, I saw through you the first time you insisted I come and pick you up, even though I told you your living in Dana's guest house made it awkward for me."

"Oh, you mean because you *used* to date her?"

Sean lowered his eyes for an instant, then met her gaze defiantly. "All right, all right. We both know I wasn't honest about that. After I found out where you lived I regretted having made a date with Dana. That's right, Micheline, you were my preference. But I didn't want to hurt Dana, and I was sure it would have been very painful for her if I canceled our date."

She raised an eyebrow.

"Not because I think I'm all that, Micheline. Because Dana had just begun to go out again after losing her husband. I don't believe you can empathize with how difficult that is for a person who had a long-term relationship. I'll never forget the look on your face when she caught us together at the beach. After your initial shock, you looked like you got a kick out of the whole thing."

A yawn inadvertently escaped from Micheline's mouth. "I'm sorry," she said. "I don't mean to imply you're boring me. But all this is old stuff. We've had a good couple of months together. Why not end it on a high note instead of criticizing each other? It's not like we ever expected we'd be together the rest of our lives. We had fun for a few months, and now it's over."

"You're right. I've enjoyed knowing you, Micheline." He held out his arms, and she stepped into them. For a few moments they stood in a friendly embrace, then he pulled back and offered her his arm. "I knew I never stood a chance with you," he said softly as they walked outside. "But I'm not as pitiful as you think I am."

"I don't think you're pitiful, Sean." Perhaps he wasn't the most ambitious man she'd ever met, but she wouldn't bother with anyone she truly considered pitiful, no matter how convenient it might be.

"I hope you don't," he said. "I never told you this, but I took this apartment so I could live cheaply and save some money for a few months. I've been banking as much of my checks as I could since I left my wife. I got my divorce through one of those legal clinics so I wouldn't have to spend money on an attorney. The minute the papers were signed, I put thirty thousand down on one of those new town houses they're putting up near Southside Boulevard."

Micheline perked up, like she always did, at the sound of money. "That's a nice down payment."

"I wanted to make a big one. This way my mortgage payments will be affordable. I got a preconstruction price and signed a seven-month lease here. My unit should be ready to move into by the time it's up. Then I'll invest in some furniture."

"That's wonderful news, Sean. I'm happy for you." Micheline unlocked the door to her Bug and got behind the wheel. She smiled at him with genuine fondness, but no sentiment. Sean represented just one of the many people who would pass in and out over the course of her life. She never had problems saying good-bye. "I'll probably see you around town. You be good, huh?"

"You, too. Take care."

She started the engine and backed out of the space, stopping to wave at him before she drove out of his life forever. She was truly glad to hear Sean had plans for his future. She'd seen those condos he talked about. One of the major builders had them under construction all over town, and they weren't bad. But if she was lucky, better things awaited her.

Errol's casual suggestion that they spend a few days down in Key West and stop off in West Palm to visit her parents had spurred her to take action and drop Sean. She'd gotten tired of him anyway, and she suspected that some other woman was getting the invitations to dinners, concerts, and shows that she used to get. It annoyed her that he'd seen through her, had known she wanted him just for sex and good times. He hadn't even seemed particularly surprised when she broke it off, much less hurt.

Maybe Errol really did plan to propose. Wouldn't that be wonderful? She, Micheline Mehu, married to a dentist, getting mail addressed to Dr. and Mrs. Trent. She would have much preferred a medical doctor in an especially lucrative field like plastic surgery or cardiology, or even a high-powered lawyer, but nevertheless her parents would be proud, her brothers impressed, and she could probably even get Cécile to stop talking about that damn house. She and Michael had suffered a setback when their original buyer's financing fell through at the last minute, but after six or seven weeks they'd found another buyer for that awful little place. They'd move into their new place just before Thanksgiving, more than two months after their original plan. The way Cécile went on and on, you'd think they were moving into Buckingham Palace.

*   *   *

Michline struggled with her zipper. At first she thought maybe the dry cleaner had managed to shrink her clothes, but these slacks were washable. She wasn't imagining things—she really was gaining weight. Even Sean had noticed it.

She didn't understand how that could happen. Her eating habits hadn't changed. Maybe her metabolism had slowed. She did feel more sleepy these days. Both Saturday and Sunday she'd had to lie down during the day, something she never did. She found it harder to get out of bed in the morning, and sometimes after lunch at work she had to force the heavy-lidded feeling of sleepiness away.

Micheline could just see Cécile now, gloating over her weight gain and saying something inane like, "That's what happens when you get older." That was just plain ridiculous. *I'm not older. I'm twenty-seven.* And she had no intention of getting fat like Cécile. Micheline always told herself that even after her one future pregnancy, she would get her figure back even if it meant being near starvation to do it.

The thought of eventually having a baby filled her with anticipation. Micheline always wanted to be a young mother, and at the rate she was going she had a chance to become a parent by age thirty.

In her spare time she often wondered what Errol had in store for her when they took their vacation next week. Maybe all that interest she'd shown in listening to silly tales about women who wore thick coats of lipstick to dental appointments and young folks with meth mouth—rotten teeth due to abuse of crystal meth—had finally paid off.

Micheline knew there was more to landing a man than merely trying to tantalize him sexually. A woman had to show interest in her man's work, his hobbies, whatever interested him. That was especially important if she didn't plan on sleeping with him until she had him hooked.

Errol still regularly tried to get into her pants, without success. Micheline worked very hard to keep his interest piqued. She usually gave him more liberties with her body as time went on so frustration wouldn't lead him to seek satisfaction elsewhere. But he wouldn't get the grand prize until he had at least an engagement ring on her finger, a good-sized diamond she could keep just in case things didn't work out.

She'd had the best of both worlds: old-fashioned necking and good-girl fun with Errol, and great sweaty sex with Sean. That roll in the hay with that guy Vic back in July had been like getting a bonus.

Micheline smiled. How appropriate a word to describe Vic in bed. She had no idea a man his age—he had to be in his early fifties—could be so exciting. She wondered if he'd taken a Viagra when he left Bukkets that night. Sex with him had been like finishing the whole sundae, complete with the whipped cream and the cherry on top. With Sean she only got the ice cream and syrup. But it was enough to keep her satisfied.

Micheline tried to adjust the waistband of her slacks to a more comfortable position. She ultimately decided they would pinch no matter how she wore them. She would start a rigid diet tomorrow.

She had too good a thing going to let some extra weight spoil it for her.

Chapter 38

"So, in answer to your question," Dana said, "that's why I don't see my father." She turned onto her side to face Gil. Light filled her bedroom, but by now the strongest rays the room received in the morning had faded.

In another half hour it would be noon. Gil had an off-site meeting at nine, and when it ended he came directly to her place. This private time with him gave Dana the only outlet she had, and it thrilled her to know they still had another hour and a half to be together before he had to return to the bank. It meant working later into the evening than she preferred, but the opportunity to be with Gil made it worth it.

"Wow," Gil said. "I can't imagine saying that to Vanessa. I can't argue that if I had to lose one of them, I'd rather it be Irene, but it's not something I would say aloud to either of them. Some feelings are so painful to admit that you never want to share them." He positioned his arm so that his hand rested on her shoulder. "So what happens now? Do you think you'll ever talk with him again?"

"It's not like we don't talk, Gil. We just haven't had much of a relationship since that day. I know from the therapy I've had that he's ashamed that I heard him say he wished I'd been the one who died. But he's never come to me and apologized, never acknowledged that he spoke out of grief. Nothing. I can't tell you how much that hurts. He'd rather let me out of his life completely than admit he was wrong."

"Maybe he's too embarrassed, or ashamed, to bring it up. Have you thought about calling him or going to see him to talk about it? That was twenty-some years ago, Dana. He's got to be well into his sixties by now. You'll never get those years back, whether you make up or not."

Dana made a face. "Quite honestly, Gil, I've learned to live with it. Besides, he had a perfect opportunity to reach out to me when Kenny died." She blinked, aware that she'd said *died*, not *accident*. This made the third time. She'd said it to Cécile, then to the officer who investigated her slashed tires, and now to Gil. Her subconscious had finally accepted Kenny's death.

"But he didn't," she continued. "He came to the funeral, expressed condolences, and I haven't heard from him since. Unless you count the Christmas card he sent, and that was written out by his wife, so I don't think that counts."

"I guess I can't blame you, but let me ask you this: How would you feel if you learned today that he had died?"

"I'd take Brittany and go to the funeral, and then that chapter of my life would be closed for good."

Gil's arm tightened around her. "Dana, you might deny this, but I can tell you're still hurting."

"Damn right it still hurts. It'll always hurt. But like I said before, I've learned to live with it. He obviously isn't going to have any change of heart."

They lay quietly for a few moments, and then Gil said, "I'd like to be back at the office by one-thirty. What say we get dressed, and I'll take you to get something to eat?"

"Sure. Just give me a minute. I'm way too comfy to just hop up and start getting dressed." She yawned. "Excuse me."

"You've had no more problems with vandalism?"

She shook her head. "Everything has been fine. The clients reissued the checks, and the motion detectors only came on once because of a stray cat wandered near the house." She paused. "I still feel guilty for letting you loan me the money to pay the electrician for installing the lights. I have a credit card, but it's hard for me to bring myself to use it. Kenny and I never charged anything unless we absolutely had to, and then we paid the bill as soon as it came in. It's always in the back of my mind that if I'd been saddled with credit-card debt on top of my living expenses, I never would have made it on my own. I'm terrified of spending money I don't have."

"Don't feel guilty, Dana. That's a good policy to follow."

"It wasn't so much the cost of the lights themselves as the labor costs. I promise I'll pay you back when I get my next paycheck."

"I told you before, Dana, don't worry about it. It's important to me that you and Brittany are safe. In fact, you might want to consider getting an alarm system. Monitoring fees are only about twenty-five dollars a month, and the bigger companies will do free installation if you sign a two-year contract."

"Well, we'll see what happens after I get my split of CDN's earnings next June." She rolled over on her back and stretched her body, from the tips of her raised fingers to her toes. "I'm just relieved that my troubles seem to have stopped."

"I think I put the fear of God into Irene. She put on a brave front, claimed to be innocent, but she couldn't hide her emotions. A reaction of a second's duration was sufficient to give her away."

"That's wonderful, Gil. Do you think she'll just give up?"

"I like to think so, but I'm not sure. In the meantime, let's continue doing what we've been doing. I don't want us to be out together at night unless I can bring you home."

"Oh, Gil." Her shoulders slumped with disappointment. "I feel like we're still at Irene's mercy."

"Just hold on a little longer. I've got a plan to put a stop to this as well." He playfully slapped her butt. "Okay, that's enough relaxing. Let's get some lunch."

Chapter 39

Micheline made sure she arrived at Bennigan's and was shown to a table before Cécile showed up. She felt that the table helped hide her weight gain, but Cécile's sharp eyes didn't miss anything. Right after the waitress delivered their entrees Cécile cast a curious glance at Micheline's upper arms, which had grown in size. "Micheline, have you gained weight?"

Micheline silently cursed herself for not wearing long sleeves, but in Northern Florida in early November, the afternoon temperatures hovered around seventy. "Yes, I have," she admitted. "I don't know what's wrong with me. I'm not eating any more than I usually do, but I'm getting heavier and heavier, especially around the middle. I made an appointment to see the doctor next week."

"Are you sure you aren't eating more? I'm sure you were disappointed when Errol didn't give you an engagement ring."

"I wasn't expecting a ring from Errol, Cécile." Micheline lied like a sleeping dog, but damned if she'd tell Cécile how dashed her hopes had been when she and Errol returned from South Florida and she had no proposal and no large diamond for the fourth finger of her left hand. "So I have no reason to drown my sorrows in food. But I am getting concerned about my health. Not only am I putting on weight, but my boobs have gotten tender and a little swollen." She chuckled. "If I didn't know better, I'd swear I was pregnant."

Cecile calmly took a bite of her salad. "Don't be too sure you're not."

"That's ridiculous, Cecile. I haven't missed any periods." She still remembered the day her period came on time, two weeks after the condom incident with Vic. She'd treated herself to a sinfully rich piece of chocolate cheesecake to celebrate.

"If you're like Mama and me you don't have to. I had my periods all through my pregnancies, and so did Mama."

"Periods through pregnancy? What kind of freaky thing is that?"

"It's not so rare, Michie. Haven't you read articles about women who went to their doctors for what they thought was indigestion, when they were actually in labor? The only way to go through nine months of pregnancy and not know it is if your periods continue the whole time."

"And to have a damn big stomach," Micheline muttered.

"Well, that too, I suppose. When I got pregnant with Josie I figured something was going on because I was tired all the time, and nauseated. The smell of coffee brewing first thing in the morning made me vomit. That sent me to the doctor."

"Well, I'm never nauseous."

Cécile looked at her with a smile, like she was enjoying the whole thing. "Every woman is different. But do you find you get tired easier, and that you sleep longer than you used to?"

"Well, yes. But I'm sure I'm not pregnant," Micheline added quickly.

"It wouldn't be such a bad thing, would it? You and Errol have been dating for what, six months now?"

Micheline dropped her eyes to look at the roast beef au jus sandwich she'd ordered. The hearty aroma of the sauce floated up toward her nostrils, but she'd just lost her appetite.

Vic drummed a pencil on his desk. He couldn't imagine why Micheline had called him this morning and requested to see him. Three or four months had passed since their little fling out at the beach. At the time he'd made a mental note of the name of the law firm she worked for in case he wanted to contact her again, but once he came to his senses he knew the only one he wanted was Norell. Their marriage had survived its rocky period and was now back on track.

His gut told him something was wrong, but he couldn't figure out anything else. Why would any woman want to contact a man she'd slept with months after the fact? She couldn't be pregnant, or else she would have told him before. Did she want to have a second go-round? Sure, that possibility appealed to his male ego, but that didn't make sense, either. She'd gone through a considerable amount of trouble looking for him in the Yellow Pages. The only way she'd been able to do that was because he'd told her his profession.

He began to relax. Maybe she knew someone who'd gotten locked up and wanted to arrange bail. It could be that simple, and probably was. He needed to stop overreacting.

Vic put down the pencil and got back to work.

"We have a problem," Micheline announced the moment she crossed into his office.

He quickly got up and went to the door. Bertha Franklin, his assistant, had heard Micheline's statement, judging from her curious expression. Seventy-six years old and sharp as a tack, the widow of a bail bondsman, she worked twenty hours a week keeping his office running smoothly. "Excuse me, Bertha," he said as he closed the door. He turned to Micheline and gestured for her to sit, then strode around to sit behind the large, cluttered desk. Micheline sat in one of the two chairs facing his desk. She watched as he passed the vacant chair to move behind the desk, wondering if he felt safer with the large piece of furniture between them.

"What's on your mind, Micheline?" he asked easily.

"It's not what's in my mind that I'm concerned about. I'm pregnant, Vic."

His forehead wrinkled slightly. "I don't get it. Why are you sharing this with me? It's been months since you and I were together that one time."

"The night the condom broke."

That got a reaction out of him. His lazy grin dissolved. "Yes, but again, that was months ago. If you'd conceived then you would have known a few weeks later."

"That's what I thought, too. But apparently there's a family trait I didn't know about. Women in my family don't miss periods, even when they're pregnant."

Vic's mouth dropped open. "You mean you got pregnant that night, and you're just finding out about it now? Doesn't that make it too late to do anything about it?"

"That's why I'm here."

He got up and walked around to the front of the desk, sitting on its edge as he faced her. "I don't mean to sound harsh, Micheline, but somehow I don't think I'm the only man you went to bed with. So why do you think I'm the one with the guilty sperm?"

"Because you were the only one with a broken condom. I'm not trying to sell you a bill of goods, Vic. And in case you're thinking of having me followed, I'll tell you straight out that I'm seeing one other man, and I've never slept with him."

He could just imagine why. The unsuspecting slob was probably loaded. *She's holding out for the gold, the little slut.*

"Of course, we can always have tests done. I can't say that I'd blame you."

"Damn, Micheline! I don't want a baby, and I'm pretty sure you don't want one either."

"This is a huge inconvenience, but I don't see where there's much I can do about it this late in the game."

"Do you plan to keep it?"

"Of course not," she said impatiently. "Once the little devil is born I'm through with it."

Vic's senses suddenly perked up as an idea began to form. "Have you made any arrangements for the baby's care?"

"I haven't done anything. I just found out, and I wanted to find you. Thank goodness you told me what you did for a living, or else I would've had to hang around The Landing and hope you showed up, or place a personal ad in *Folio*, which you probably never would have seen."

"Listen, Micheline. If you plan to give up the baby, give it to me."

"What?"

"Let me adopt the baby."

She looked at him suspiciously, like she was trying to figure out his angle . . . and what was in it for her. Micheline was the type to always think someone had an angle.

"Why would you want to adopt this baby?" she asked.

Vic decided she deserved to know. "My wife hasn't been able to conceive," he said. "It's pretty much a hopeless case. It's been very painful for her. She's been burying herself in work and in alcohol, and it hasn't done our marriage any good. A baby would solve all our problems."

"And you plan on just waltzing in and announcing, 'Look, honey, at what I found on the doorstep?'"

"I haven't worked out the details, but why shouldn't we have a baby that's half mine?" At the dubious look she shot him he added, "Micheline, I'd be willing to have a contract drawn up laying everything on the line. I'm talking about paying reasonable expenses, like your out-of-pocket medical expenses and even your living expenses if you want to take a leave of absence from work."

She shrugged. "And what do I get out of it?"

"I'm not going to haggle with you, Micheline. If you don't feel that knowing your baby is in a secure, loving home is worth anything, this won't be a good idea." He didn't like the glint in her eye, like it had just occurred to her that she could show her soon-to-be bulging belly to desperate couples and take bids. "I won't lie to you. My wife will never be completely happy unless she has a child to call her own. You might not believe this, but I really do love my wife. It's not my nature to go out and pick women up in restaurants. I'd never done it before that night with you, nor have I done it since. I'd like to save my marriage, and this is just what it needs. It's rare for black women to give up their babies, even if they're mere teenagers.

"But I won't be taken advantage of," he added. "If you don't want to cooperate, I guess my wife will keep working like crazy until she can get every doctor in Jacksonville subscribing to her transcription service." He noticed a strange look come over her and realized she probably didn't know what he was talking about.

"My wife transcribes medical records," he explained. "Apparently there has to be a written record of each patient visit and everything that happens during a hospital admission. It's a booming business behind the scenes."

"Oh, I see." She sighed, an action that even under the circumstances Vic found sexy. "I need some time to think about your offer, Vic."

He quickly forced himself to remember that the sexy woman across from him couldn't be trusted. "Of course. I'm not rushing you. But if you're going to give up the baby anyway, wouldn't you feel better if you knew at least one of the people who would be raising him or her?"

"That does offer me a degree of comfort, yes."

The hell it does. Vic knew that air of reluctance Micheline gave off came from hopes of getting him to sweeten the pot. "I'd like to consult an attorney and see what is standard in these cases. But there's something we need to settle right now, or else there's no point in going forward."

"And what is that?" Micheline's tone held an element of surprise, the way people look when they think they've got you by the balls. But while he might consider any reasonable counteroffer she made regarding her expenses, he wasn't budging on this point. Vic figured if it wasn't meant to be, it wouldn't be. Micheline might think she held all the cards, but she didn't.

He looked her dead in the eyes. "I want you to give up all parental rights to the baby at the time you hand him or her over."

She appeared unruffled. "I'm pretty sure the law says I have six months. What puts you above the law?"

"I may not be above the law, but that's the way I want it. I don't want my wife getting attached to an infant and considering it to be hers and then have you waltz in and say you want him back. It would kill her."

Micheline took a moment to digest that. "Here's my cell number," she said, scribbling a number with no name on a sheet of notepaper on his desk. "Do what you have to do and let me know the deal, and we'll go from there."

"All right. Give me a week." He helped her up, thinking how strange it was that one night of intimacy between strangers resulted in their becoming parents together. He cared nothing for Micheline. Yeah, she was pretty. Yeah, she was sexy. And she'd been great in bed, but overall she had just been a way of getting back at Norell for putting her work first. The whole thing had been pretty childish of him.

But if all went well, that one case of poor judgment might provide the missing ingredient in his marriage.

Chapter 40

Micheline's excitement grew as she drove home. Her chat with Vic had proven to be quite enlightening when he mentioned that his wife owned a medical transcription service.

She'd never known the last name of Cecile's friend Norell, but now she was sure it was Bellamy, as in Bellamy Bail Bonds.

From what Cécile said, Norell had married an older fellow who had a few bucks. Cécile hadn't mentioned his name, but she'd put Norell in her mid to late thirties, so Vic would qualify as an older man. And Cécile also said that Norell lived out at the beach. Surely Vic's wife who couldn't have babies and who ran a medical transcription service and Cecile's friend Norell were one and the same.

Micheline found herself envious of Norell's position. She knew enough about men to know that those few hours Vic spent in bed with her meant nothing. The sex satisfied them both, and that was all. Yeah, so Vic had cheated on Norell, but he didn't have the cocky attitude of a habitual cheater, an attitude Micheline knew well. On top of that, he certainly sounded sincere about wanting to save his marriage. Norell was a lucky woman; her husband truly loved her. Just think, if it hadn't been for that torn condom, Micheline never would have had the need to seek him out and never would have learned of the connection.

But it had and she did. She might be able to benefit from it, but not without paying a price. The relationship with Errol that she'd so carefully cultivated like a prize-winning garden was about to go to seed. Even though he hadn't proposed, they'd grown closer than ever since their vacation together—a vacation spent in separate rooms.

He'd felt right at home in her parents' simple abode. In Key West they'd taken long walks on the beach, hand in hand, and she'd tearfully confessed that she'd exaggerated her parents' occupations out of fear that his parents wouldn't feel she was good enough. He assured her that he was his own man and couldn't be influenced by his parents. He'd even acknowledged last week, when kissing her good night and grasping her buttocks, that he'd probably have to marry her before she'd give him any . . . and he'd only been half kidding.

If she had to let Errol go she'd be alone once more, while Cécile's friend Norell got her marriage back on track and a baby to boot— *her* baby. Damn it, that wasn't right. She would have to give this some serious thought before agreeing to any terms.

It annoyed Micheline how everything always worked out for Cécile and her friends. Hell, even Dana seemed to have gotten over the trauma of her husband's accidental death and Sean Sizemore's duplicity and was involved in a thriving relationship, according to Cécile. As for Cécile, she and Michael would soon be moving into a nice large house where they and their kids could live comfortably, and Norell's dream of being a mother would come true, or at least it would come true if Micheline went along with Vic's proposition. Well, screw Norell. *She* should be the one to come out on top.

Micheline pressed her lips together and ran her tongue over them. Adrenaline raced through her veins, and she realized she still had a way out. If she couldn't have Errol, why not go after Vic? Okay, so he was a little old for her, but sexually he could curl her toes, and he could support her. She wouldn't have to work. She could be just like her friend Yolanda.

The more she thought about it, the better it sounded. Vic would never have reason to turn to another woman with her around. His wife might be all down in the dumps, but Micheline had never been depressed a day in her life. She could dangle the thought of their coming child in front of his eyes like a gold carrot and say that she had fallen in love with him and wanted nothing more than to be with him and their child. Surely his concern about preserving his marriage to Norell by adopting his own baby would evaporate once he learned *she* was available. After all, she was younger than Norell, and prettier. Let Norell just move on down the hard path of a sixty-hour-workweek business owner she'd chosen. In the meantime she, Micheline, would quit her job and move in. She felt confident that Vic would never look back.

* * *

"So that's it in a nutshell," the attorney—Micheline believed his name was Nelson—said in conclusion. He had just presented a proposal to Micheline of behalf of his client, Vic.

She'd been surprised when the attorney's secretary called to set up the appointment. That suggested Vic had no interest in seeing her, that all he wanted her to do was give birth and hand over the baby to him and that depressed wife of his. That didn't bode well for her plan.

She'd dressed spectacularly for the event in her best suit, a Le Suit she'd gotten on sale at Dillard's. But to her disappointment, Vic didn't show up. She met with Nelson, who apparently served as Vic's intermediary.

"Do you have any questions, Miss Mehu?" Nelson inquired.

"Not really. Your explanation was very thorough, and I work at a law office myself, so I've got more knowledge than your average person in these matters."

"Oh? What do you do?"

"I'm a paralegal. Mr. Nelson, I'd like some time to go over this contract."

He followed her lead and spoke in a businesslike fashion, dismissing all attempts at personal conversation. "Of course. It's a lot to absorb. I do hope you'll keep under consideration that you'd be doing a couple a great service, and that your child would be placed in a wonderful home and is all but guaranteed a happy life."

God, not another speech about doing a good deed and the rewards it would bring for her child. Micheline didn't even acknowledge it. Instead she said, "And I'd like to speak with Vic directly."

"Well, he did authorize me to handle this matter for him," Nelson began, "but I'll relay your request to him and I'm sure he'll be happy to telephone you directly."

She stood, with him following suit. "Thank you," she said. "I'll be in touch."

Vic called her at home at seven o'clock that night. "Henry tells me you wanted to speak with me. I'm sure if there's something you're not clear about, he could clarify it for you."

"That wasn't it, Vic."

"Then what was it?"

He sounded impatient. Damn, she'd have to be awfully convincing. "I was hoping you and I would get a chance to talk."

"What's there to talk about, Micheline? I came up with an idea that will solve all your problems, and mine too. Any questions can be answered through my attorney. All that's left to do is say either yes or no."

"I need to see you, Vic. There's something I have to say, and it can't be done over the phone. Can you come over?"

"Where do you live? I was just about to leave for the day, but I don't want to go out of my way."

Micheline understood. With a land mass greater than eight hundred square miles, Jacksonville ranked number one among U.S. cities in terms of area. Someone had told Micheline that the towns of Mandarin, San Marco, Arlington, Wesconnett, and others, which were now mere sections of Jacksonville, had consolidated to form one large city to diminish the effect of the black vote. She didn't know if that was the entire truth, but she did know Jacksonville was one hell of a huge city.

"I'm in the southeast corridor, off Touchton Road," she said.

"All right. I pass that exit anyway on my way home. Give me the particulars."

By the time he rang her bell thirty minutes later, Micheline was sitting in her prettiest peignoir, fully made up. She opened the door almost shyly. "Come in, Vic."

The admiring look on his face disappeared quickly, but she knew he'd been impressed by the way she looked. She chased away her smile as she closed the door.

"Nice place," he remarked, sitting on the white cloth sofa.

"Thanks. Can I fix you a drink or something?"

"Thank you, but no. I really want to get along home. What can I do for you, Micheline?"

She gulped. What the hell was the attraction at home? Norell and her sorry can't-have-babies self? Him and his big hurry were throwing her off, making her nervous.

"Well," she began, taking a seat near the opposite end of the sofa, her hands resting on her thighs, "I felt you should know that I've given a great deal of thought to what's been happening lately. Vic, you and I have created a child together. In a few months it'll be a living, breathing individual."

"It happens all the time."

"Not to me is doesn't. I lie down at night with my hand on my belly, and the thought of giving up my child, even to its father, has suddenly become reprehensible."

"You're saying you want to keep the baby and raise him yourself?"

"Vic, what I'm saying is that I have this picture in my head of you and me raising him or her. Together, as a family."

"Wait a minute. You want me to leave my wife and marry you?"

Micheline didn't have to pretend to be insulted. "Is that really so distasteful to you, the idea of being with me? This isn't easy for me to say, Vic. I've fallen in love with you—in hindsight, I felt something from the very beginning, that day at The Landing. I kept hoping you would call me at work. Then when I saw you again at Bukkets, I felt my prayers had been answered. I'm not accustomed to being picked up in restaurants, but I felt this incredibly strong attraction to you. I wanted to be with you. I kept hoping you would call me after that night we spent together. For all my bravado the day I came to see you at your office, I secretly hoped you would tell me you wanted me and our baby, too." She sniffled. "I can't believe this. I open up to you, and you practically tell me to get lost."

He reached out and took her left hand, which was closest to him. *Finally, some progress,* she thought triumphantly.

"Micheline," he said gently, "what you feel for me isn't love. It's the idea of a happy ending that you keep thinking about. I'm part of your thoughts only because I planted the seed.

"Yes, I think it's a beautiful thing for a man and woman to create another life together, when they're in love. I had that experience with my first wife, and I wouldn't trade it for anything. But what you and I had was a one-night stand. The only woman I want to raise a child with is my wife. I'm sorry if that hurts you, but it's the truth, and it's not going to change."

"I see." Micheline didn't want to admit how embarrassing she found Vic's rejection, so she let anger take over. How dare he reject her like that? Her first instinct was to tell him to just forget about the baby, that he'd never see it. Something she couldn't identify stopped her. "In that case, there's nothing to talk about." She got to her feet, and he followed. "Thanks for coming by."

She went to the door and opened it, waiting for him to plead with her not to withhold the baby, to stress again what good parents he and that silly wife of his would make. She wanted him to grovel.

That would make up for the humiliation she'd felt just a few minutes before and even the score.

Vic reached out and laid a hand on her shoulder. "I didn't mean to hurt you, Micheline," he said gently. "If I did, I'm sorry. But I think it's best if we're honest with each other. If you decide not to accept my offer, I understand."

"Good night, Vic," she said icily. It infuriated her that he didn't beg her to reconsider. But Vic Bellamy didn't have the best of her. She still had one trump card to play.

Chapter 41

Gil faced his ex-wife's stony expression. "She's almost ready," Irene said sullenly. "And I hope you don't get any ideas about bringing her out with Dana. I don't want her exposed to your sordid little sex life."

"I think it would be better if I wait outside," he said abruptly. He didn't feel like getting into a stink with her about his relationship with Dana.

Dealing with Irene had become intolerable. He wished she wouldn't even bother to come to the door these times when he picked up Vanessa. He didn't spend as much time with Vanessa as he used to. She had chosen to not spend the entire weekend with him any more. They just went out Saturday afternoons, usually to the bowling alley or the movies, then had dinner, and he brought her home. The change had been her idea, not his.

He leaned against the driver's side of his Murano, his hands in his pockets. He could see Irene standing at the window watching him through the open blinds and sheer curtains. He promptly turned and walked around to the back of the truck. He could see Vanessa when she came out, but Irene couldn't have a very good view of him. Let her focus on something else.

His jeans-clad daughter emerged from the town house, her pony tail bouncing behind her. She'd inherited Gil's light brown complexion, but her mother's dark hair. Gil emerged from the rear of the truck. "Hey."

"Hi, Popi!" She ran toward him, her arms outstretched.

Relief flooded through him as he embraced her, as it always did. He'd secretly been afraid that Vanessa would turn her back on him, cut him off like she'd done to Brittany, but while their relationship had changed she clearly still loved him.

He decided to try to get her to change her mind. "How about spending the night? All you have to do is go in and get a change of clothes."

She sighed. "No, Popi. Let's just go out tonight."

He gestured for her to get in the truck. "You know, you never explained to me why you cut back on our visits. It has to do with Dana, doesn't it?"

"Do we have to talk about this, Popi?"

"Yes, I'm afraid we do. I only get to see you two weekends a month, and now it's down to two afternoons a month. I'm not happy about that, and I'd like to know why."

"I can't leave Mama, Popi. She needs me."

"I need you, too," he said quietly.

"But you have Miss Dana. Mama doesn't have anyone. Except me."

Gil gripped the steering wheel tightly. It enraged him that Irene presented herself as so needy to their daughter. He'd always encouraged Irene to make friends, from the time they'd arrived in Jacksonville from South Florida when Vanessa was just a toddler, but she hadn't taken his advice. Instead she'd built her entire existence around him and Vanessa. No wonder she fought the divorce the way she had. If Irene chose not to have a life of her own that was her own decision, but damned if he would let her ruin Vanessa's life. If Irene wasn't stopped, years down the road she would stand in the way of Vanessa going to college, of her dating and wanting to have a life of her own.

He decided to put off forcing a reconciliation between Vanessa and Brittany.

Vanessa's future took precedence.

He went inside with Vanessa after they came home from dinner at Chili's. Irene sat in the fabric-covered, high-backed rocker in the dimly lit living room, watching a movie on cable. Gil felt she'd carefully orchestrated the scene to emphasize her solitary state and to incur guilt in Vanessa for going out for a few hours.

He watched as Vanessa rushed to Irene and threw her arms around her. Irene whispered something, and Vanessa shook her head.

"Vanessa," he said, "I was wondering if you'd give me a few minutes alone with your mother."

"Sure, Popi," she said, her eyes shining like stars in the night sky. "I'll be in my room."

She thundered up the stairs, and Irene looked at Gil expectantly. "You wanted to talk to me?"

"Irene, I want you to think about what you're doing to our daughter. Not only has Vanessa terminated her most longstanding friendship at your suggestion, but she's also afraid to leave you alone for any period of time. She spends an afternoon with me and comes home to find you sitting in a rocking chair like Whistler's mother. What type of effect do you think that's going to have on her?"

"Don't you start with me, Gilberto Albacete. I haven't done anything to Vanessa. She made up her own mind not to be friends with Brittany. And her not spending Saturday nights at your place probably has less to do with her not wanting to leave me and more to do with your new girlfriend."

"Yeah, well tell me this, Irene. Did you ever once discourage her, tell her that her friendship with Brittany has nothing to do with my relationship with Brittany's mother, or that it's okay for her to spend as much time with me as she always has?" She simply stared at him, and he nodded. "I thought not. You're manipulating her into behaving the way you want her to, with no regard for what's best for her. She's a thirteen-year-old child, and she's not emotionally equipped to be your confidante. If you want someone to tell your troubles to, find a friend. Or see a counselor. But don't put all your fears on your child."

Irene stared at him coldly. "I find it amazing that you always find a way to put everything back on me. You're the one who got Vanessa all confused by getting involved with her best friend's mother."

"Irene, you've allowed your jealousy to turn you into a bad mother. I'm not going to stand for it. I'm going to see my lawyer about custody."

She rocked calmly. "You do that. All I have to do is tell them who you're sleeping with. You don't stand a chance."

"You really are despicable, Irene. You're willing to fight for custody of Vanessa so you can project your own neediness on her. What you need to do is get a life." He glanced at the stairs. "I'm leaving. Tell Vanessa I'm sorry I didn't say good-bye, but I'll call her tomorrow."

He went out the door with a slam.

Chapter 42

Micheline tossed her supermarket purchases in the trunk of her Bug. As she lowered the top of the trunk she wiped sweat from her brow. This heat was really starting to get to her. Two weeks from now Americans everywhere would be sitting down to Thanksgiving dinner—when would it start to cool off?

She forced herself to calm down, knowing pregnancy made her grumpier than usual, griping about the Florida heat she'd known all her life. She'd put off getting back to Vic. Let him sweat a little. Besides, she knew they had a connection, and he didn't. He didn't seem to be the type to be susceptible to blackmail, but surely she could do something with that information.

"Hey there, Michie!"

Micheline looked up, immediately recognizing Cécile's voice. Her sister approached, looking unwieldy in her pregnancy. Her belly led, and the rest of her followed. Micheline pressed her lips together to keep her upper lip from curling in disgust. *My God, is that how I'll look four months from now?* "Hi. I didn't know you shopped in this neighborhood," she said.

"The stores over by me are crummy, all dingy and dark. I like this one. So what's up with you? Long time no see."

"I've been busy," Micheline said lamely.

"Yes, I'm sure you have. Ah, the life of a single girl trying to snare a husband." Cécile made it sound like the worst thing in the world, which did nothing to help Micheline's mood. "Anyway, we're planning on moving next week. Would you be able to help out for a couple of hours? You never know how much stuff you've got until it's time to move. We could use all the help we can get."

Micheline decided this was a good time to spill her secret. Cécile needed to have her cheerful little bubble burst. "I'm sure I can be of some help to you," she said sweetly, "but I won't be able to do any heavy lifting."

Cécile drew in her breath. "You're pregnant!" She spoke softly because they were in a parking lot with people occasionally passing by, but the news clearly came as a delight.

"Yes."

"You really are!" Cécile exclaimed. "I thought you might be, but you seemed so sure it wasn't possible."

"I'm four months pregnant, Sis."

"Well, congratulations!" Cécile paused. "So are you and Errol going to get married? You know, Mama couldn't stop talking about him. I'd love to meet him myself," she hinted. "But Mama and Papa will be thrilled, even if the conception came before the ceremony."

"No. He's not the father. I haven't even slept with him." Micheline saw the confusion in Cécile's eyes, watched as she groped for an appropriate response.

"Well, does the father know?" she finally said.

"Yes. He wants to adopt the baby."

"He does? Why?"

"Because his wife can't get pregnant, and he feels that a baby is just what she needs."

"Does he plan on telling her it's his baby?"

"I really don't know. I don't know all that much about him. He's an older guy, about fifty-one, fifty-two, in really good shape. He's a bail bondsman, he lives out at the beach somewhere, and he's got a wife who's a basket case because she can't get pregnant. I presume she's younger than he is. If she's his age and wants a baby, she should be a psychiatric patient." Micheline waited for the bomb she just dropped to detonate.

"He's . . ." Cécile grew silent as her mind digested these facts. Then she demanded, "What's his name?"

When Micheline heard that uncharacteristic command, she knew Cécile had put it together. "What difference does it make?" Her insulted tone disguised her delight.

"I'm not kidding, Michie. What's his name?"

"Vic. Why?"

"My God!" Cécile hissed, glancing around to make sure no one stood within earshot. "Michie, do you bother to learn anything about a man before you fall into bed with him? I'll bet you don't even know his last name!"

"His last name wasn't important at the time, Cécile. I wouldn't have needed to see him ever again if the condom hadn't torn. Actually, I thought I was safe until I found out about that little twist in the female history of our family. By then I'd passed my first trimester, making it too late to do anything about it."

"Well, it just so happens that Vic Bellamy is married to my friend and business partner, Norell." Cécile shook her head and continued to speak in a loud whisper. "My God. I thought that your going out with Dana's boyfriend behind her back was the worst thing that could happen, but this is worse. You must really hate me."

Micheline didn't bother to claim innocence. "Oh, please. Why must everything always be about you?"

"Pardon me. Everything's always supposed to be about *you*." Cécile stared at her incredulously. "So what are you going to do?" she hissed. "What about Mama and Papa?"

"They don't have to know," Micheline said quickly. "No one has to know. Vic's made me a good offer. He'll pay my living expenses from the time I begin to show until six weeks after I give birth. That means I can put in for a leave of absence at work, and no one has to know my business. I can say I've got a family emergency or something, come back four months later, and resume working, like nothing ever happened."

"And what about Errol?"

"I've got it all planned. I'm going to disappear for a few months and have a vague explanation."

"And he'll be content to just have you disappear from his life? That doesn't say a lot for how much you mean to him."

"Believe me," Micheline said confidently, "it'll work out fine."

Cécile stood with her hand on her swollen belly, her forehead wrinkled and her mouth forming a scowl.

"Am I to understand this correctly?" she said. "My friend Norell will raise your baby, my niece or nephew, as her own." Cécile shook her head. "Norell and I barely managed to stay friends after a very difficult period for us, and now you've made me part of a lie that will destroy our friendship forever if she ever learns the truth. Do you realize the position that puts me in, Micheline? And do you care?"

She shrugged. She could tell Cécile was pissed, for she never used her full first name. "I don't know what Vic plans on telling Norell about where the baby came from, but I'm pretty sure he won't tell her it's his."

Cécile pressed a palm into her forehead and closed her eyes. After a few moments she removed her hand and opened her eyes. "You've got me so upset I can't even shop. I'm going home. I'll send Michael to the store later."

"Suit yourself. I'm sure it won't hurt you to miss a meal." Micheline calmly got behind the wheel of her Bug.

Cécile glared at her.

Vic looked up in surprise. "Hey, Cécile! I didn't expect to see you here." Then it dawned on him that she might have a problem at home. God forbid Michael or one of her stepsons had been arrested. "Is everything okay?"

"No, Vic, it's not." She glanced back at Bertha. Vic couldn't see his assistant from where he stood, but knew she was eyeing his very pregnant visitor with interest. "Is it all right if I close the door? I need to speak with you privately."

By now Vic had risen from his chair and walked over to where she stood. "Of course." He closed the door and gestured for her to sit down. Two irate females entering his office for private talks in as many weeks, one of whom was visibly pregnant. Bertha's curiosity must be boiling. He had a strange sense of déjà vu himself. "Now, tell me what's wrong."

"You like to live dangerously, don't you, Vic?"

His head jerked back. He'd thought she had a personal problem she wanted to discuss with him. What the hell did she mean by questioning him about his behavior? "What's this about, Cécile?" he asked, not bothering to hide his annoyance.

"Do you realize the spot you've put me in? My sister told me about the baby."

Panic rose in his throat like a tide. "Your *sister?*"

"Micheline."

"Micheline is your sister?"

"Yes, Vic," she said calmly. "We're often told we look alike. Our coloring is a little different, that's all."

He looked at her carefully. Her eyes *were* shaped like Micheline's. Her nose, her mouth . . . my God, Cécile was a shorter, darker, heavier version of Micheline. Why hadn't he noticed it before?

"So?" she pressed. "Don't you have anything to say for yourself?"

"Cécile, you've got to believe me when I say I had no idea."

Her stern stare softened, and for a minute she appeared to be at a loss for words. But when she finally did speak, she sounded just as unforgiving as she had earlier.

"That doesn't make it easier for me, does it? I mean, not only does my friend's husband cheat on her with my sister, but he knocks her up." She slapped the arm of her chair with her palm. "Some things you'd rather just not know, if you know what I mean."

"Yes, I understand how awkward this could be for you." His mind raced. It shouldn't be too bad. It pained Norell to be around Cécile in her pregnant state, to the point where she could barely stand being around her. The two women not seeing much of each other would make things easier for him.

"All right Vic, so what happens now? Are you really planning on adopting your own baby and passing it off as a stranger?"

"Cécile, listen to me. Norell wants a baby more than anything in the world. I believe she'd trade me for one if given the choice. Doesn't this seem like a wonderful chance for her to be a mother?"

"That's sweet, Vic, but it doesn't answer my question."

Damn, she was hard. Who knew sweet little Cécile had it in her? "I haven't worked out all the details yet," he admitted. "At this point Micheline hasn't even consented to give me the baby."

"She told me she was going to accept your offer to pay her living expenses for six months."

"That's all well and good, Cecile, but until she signs the papers, it's meaningless. And in the meantime, even though I know I'm putting you on the spot, I have to ask that you not mention any of this to Norell. I can't tell her about the baby unless Micheline signs the papers, and even if Micheline signs, I doubt I'll say anything to Norell right away. March is still four months off." He didn't want to say he didn't trust Micheline.

"I won't. But I don't like this, Vic. I don't like being privy to a secret that could devastate my friend. I don't like knowing that I'm a blood relative to the baby she's going to adopt. Norell and I have been friends for ten years. We've cried on each other's shoulders through all types of crises, but she hasn't been able to cope with the fact that I can get pregnant easily and she can't. We've had a rift over the last year, year and a half, and my baby"—she patted her belly—"has only made it worse.

"You realize," Cecile continued, "that if the truth does come out and Norell finds out I knew about it, she'll probably be more mad at me than she'll be with you, just because I've become a target for her temper. But I do hope everything works out, for her sake."

"You're a true friend, Cécile. I'll make sure Norell realizes that."

"Thanks, but right now you've got more pressing problems. It'll be awfully hard to convince Norell that baby belongs to a stranger if it comes out with your face." With that she grabbed her purse, stood up, and left, opening the door of his office so hard that it banged against the wall.

Vic leaned back in his chair, his hands clasped behind his head. "I'm fine," he said when Bertha Franklin appeared, as he'd known she would. He waved her off.

He still couldn't believe Cécile and Micheline were sisters. Their personalities couldn't be more different. Cécile had such a kind, considerate nature, while Micheline possessed a what's-in-it-for-me attitude.

He hoped Cécile knew what she was talking about when she said Micheline had decided to take his offer. It might be more of Micheline's bullshit, like that ridiculous story about how she'd fallen in love with him. Hell, she didn't even know him. They'd seen each other exactly twice. Micheline probably figured she'd settle for whatever he could give her, since her pregnancy interfered with any other action she had going. After a few years she would have divorced him and tried to get a big chunk of everything he owned. She'd probably jump off to lie with somebody the minute he left for work. Hell, he deserved to be two-timed if he was dumb enough to fall for that, which he wasn't. How many times had he scoffed at photos of those old Hollywood actors in those magazines Norell subscribed to, with shapely, attractive women a generation younger than they? What saps, he thought. Didn't they know the chicks were after their bankrolls? If Norell had been a just few years younger he would've been suspicious of *her* motives.

His expression softened at the thought of his wife. All Norell needed was a chance to be a mother, and she'd be complete. But he had to come up with a believable explanation of where the baby came from.

Which might be difficult if, as Cécile pointed out, it came out looking like him.

Cécile fumed as she threw her purse on the passenger seat of her car. Damn that Michie! Never doing what she was supposed to do, and not doing the expected.

Cécile expected Vic to know all about her relationship to Micheline. She thought Michie would spill the beans the first chance she got after their encounter in the Publix parking lot yesterday, but that look of shock on Vic's face had been genuine. He'd had no idea. That told her Michie's scheming nature was in play.

She had something up her sleeve.

Chapter 43

"Do you really like it?" Norell patted her hair. After two years of having it bleached a reddish blond, she had returned to her natural dark brown.

"I think it looks great," Dana said. "It's been so long since you've been a brunette. You almost look like a different person."

"I decided I was spending too much time at the salon. Between touch-ups, coloring, manicures, pedicures, eyebrows . . . At least this way I won't have to run back to them two weeks after my touch-up to have my roots bleached."

"Besides, all that bleach really isn't good for your hair," Dana added. She turned to Cécile. "Doesn't Norell's hair look nice?"

Cécile agreed, but Norell noticed that she quickly averted her gaze. She'd been doing that ever since their partners' meeting began. What was the deal with her, anyway? It didn't make sense. After everything they'd been through, all of a sudden Cécile couldn't look her in the eye. She thought they'd put all the bad stuff behind them the other week. She'd had a hard time hearing about Cécile's new house, sure. Hell, she was only human. It was perfectly natural to feel a little envious watching someone's dreams come true when you had the same dreams, and yours hadn't. She knew it was wrong, but nevertheless it gave her a small degree of satisfaction to know the Rivers family lived in cramped quarters. She reasoned that they had already been blessed with six children, soon to be seven; why should they have a nice spacious house, too? But the twinge had passed, and now she was happy for Cécile and Michael. She and Vic had even offered to help them with their move next week.

So she just didn't understand why Cécile acted so strangely, like she wanted to avoid her.

"If that wraps up our business, I'd like to make an early exit," Cécile said, rising. "I'd like to get some more packing done, and of course I've got to finish work."

"Sure, we're done," Dana said. "Run along. And try to take it easy, Cécile. You're doing a hell of a lot these days."

"Oh, I'll be fine. I'm healthy as a horse. But that first buyer losing his financing at the last minute really hurt us, time-wise. We should have been in and settled by now. This is going to make for a haphazard Thanksgiving. Michael and I are seriously talking about skipping the big dinner and just sending out for pizza." She chuckled. "See you guys later."

Dana waited until the front door closed behind Cécile. "Is it me, or is she wired?"

"She's wired," Norell said. "But like you said, she's got a lot on her plate, plus she's eight months pregnant. But at least she'll look you in the eye. Whenever she had to look at me from the time she got here she focused on something just beyond the top of my head."

"I didn't notice. I thought all that uncomfortable stuff was over with you two."

"So did I. Ever since she and I had that heart-to-heart on your patio. I don't understand it. I almost want to ask her what's wrong, but I'm sure she'll deny there's a problem."

"Maybe she just feels a little guilty at being pregnant around you."

"Maybe. But it's awfully strange timing to feel guilty less than a month before her due date, don't you think?"

Norell looked at the brochures Vic had brought home. "A cruise, Vic? That's wonderful, but the timing is bad. You must have forgotten we promised to help Cécile and Michael move into their new house next week."

"They can manage without us. I thought it would be nice to be away this Thanksgiving."

"And what about my work?"

"That's one reason why I chose this week to surprise you. Doesn't the workload drop over the holidays?"

"Traditionally, yes, but—"

"But nothing. You deserve a vacation. I got a great deal on seven days in the Southern Caribbean, but we have to leave from San Juan. The ship leaves next Sunday. I made arrangements for us to fly to San Juan on Saturday."

"I just wish you'd talked to me about it before you booked it, that's all."

He moved in close, wrapping his arms around her and reaching down to cup her buttocks. "But then it wouldn't be a surprise."

She giggled, slipping her arms around his neck. "Oh, Vic. It does sound wonderful. I guess Dana and Cécile can manage to keep CDN running. I just feel kind of bad about reneging on Cécile and Michael."

"Like the two of them can't afford three or four hundred bucks to hire a moving van to bring their belongings a few miles. Believe me, Norell, they'll understand that you'd rather take a seven-day cruise than stay in Jacksonville to help them move. They'll even be a little envious. With all those kids they've got, the only vacation they'll get to take for the next fifteen years will be going to theme parks."

"Vic, you are so bad." She giggled.

To Norell's surprise, Cécile didn't seem particularly disappointed when she broke the news in a phone call the next day. "Wow, a cruise! What ports will you be visiting?"

"Oh, Saint Maarten, Antigua, Barbados, maybe one other place. I'm not sure."

"That's wonderful, Norell. I'd grab it in a minute." Cécile sighed. "I've got a secret vacation fund to surprise Michael with. I'd really like to get out to Las Vegas. I figure there's plenty out there for the kids to do during the day, and for Michael and me at night. Of course, it'll probably take three or four years to get enough money for all of us to fly."

"It would probably make a great drive, Cécile. Just think of all you and the kids would see. And in a few years Jonathan and Damon will have their driver's licenses, so they can help drive."

"You might have something there. Getting a second hotel room every night we're on the road should still be cheaper than buying nine round-trip airline tickets."

"Just picture yourselves driving through the desert, looking at all those rock formations with the theme to *The Good, the Bad and the Ugly* playing on your CD player. It won't be that long, either, before you can afford it. Remember, you'll be getting an annual check for your share of CDN's profits starting next year. Why not treat your-self?"

"Yeah, maybe. I'll have to see how things work out."

"I'm glad you're not angry with me for backing out, Cécile."

"Hey, it's fine."

Cécile chuckled as she hung up. So Vic had booked a cruise to prevent him and Norell from spending an afternoon in their company, which would be uncomfortable for him. His expenses were racking up like the shell of a skyscraper. Seven-night Caribbean cruises over the holidays didn't come cheap, and he'd already agreed to fork over thousands of dollars to Micheline for her living expenses.

Keeping his dirty little secret a secret just might bankrupt him.

Chapter 44

One look at Norell, and Vic could tell something had upset her. She sat on the sofa, her bare feet resting on the coffee table. The immaculate kitchen showed no signs of cooking activity. When he came home from work he always found her either working in the kitchen or upstairs in her office. Her state of just sitting, listlessly staring into space, suggested she'd received bad or shocking news.

"Something wrong?" he asked.

"No. I'm just sitting here thinking." She sighed. "Cécile had another girl. Eight pounds, three ounces. They named her Regine."

"Hey, that's great! She'll be home in plenty of time for Christmas."

"Yes, today's only the eighteenth."

"You want to go by the hospital to see her?"

"No," she said quickly. "I'd rather wait until she goes home. They'll probably release her the day after tomorrow." Her eyes grew wide as he stood opposite her and beckoned with his index finger. "What?"

"I think you need a hug, and I can't give you one if you're sitting down."

She swiveled her feet off of the coffee table and stood up. Vic felt her relax against him.

"You're right," she said. "I needed that."

"Norell, I was saving some news as a surprise for you, but I know how hard it'll be for you to watch Cécile holding her new baby, so I think I'll tell you now."

"What?"

"I put out some inquiries through Henry Nelson."

"Your attorney? What kind of inquiries?"

"Baby inquiries. I'm sure that somewhere out there is a female, whether a frightened young girl or a mature woman on the verge of menopause, who is coping with an unwanted pregnancy and would be interested in giving up her baby for adoption."

"That's noble of you to try, Vic, but I'm afraid you're unlikely to meet with any success. In black families, if someone is unable to raise their child, somebody else usually steps up to help. A mother, a sister, an aunt . . . even a grandmother. We don't like the idea of giving up our flesh and blood." She looked at him strangely, realization dawning. "Wait a minute. Did you say you had a surprise for me? Have you actually found someone willing to give up her baby?"

"I did. The baby is due in April. I've been paying her living expenses, including her deductibles on her insurance, for the last couple of weeks."

Norell's heart swelled with excitement. "Oh, Vic, that's fabulous news! What was it, a change-of-life baby? A woman past forty-five would probably have a harder time finding a family member to help her, because they're all older, too."

"No, it's actually more of an inconvenient pregnancy for a younger woman who didn't have it confirmed until her second trimester. I think Henry said she's in her mid-twenties."

"It sounds like she just wants to have the baby and turn it over so she can get on with her life."

"It sounds that way, but Norell, before you get too excited, you have to keep in mind that these types of arrangements are never carved in stone. The terms of the contract state that she will hand over the baby and disappear forever, but if she changes her mind and wants the child back, judges just about always give the birth mothers custody. The only thing I might be able to enforce is financial restitution. I had it put into the contract that if she reneges, she'll have to pay me back every cent I put out for her." It pained him to watch the joy fade from Norell's face. "It's just a possibility you have to be aware of, Norell. When it comes to adoption, nothing is a sure thing. The birth mother can come back for a period after placement and demand the baby back. I think it's something like six months. Henry will know for sure. So you might want to hold off on telling your girlfriends, or if you do, tell them there's a chance that it might not work out if the birth mother changes her mind. It doesn't hurt to have a couple of friends pulling for you."

Norell rose from her seat in the hospital lobby when she saw Dana approaching. Since Vic had revealed his surprise, she didn't feel fazed by visiting a neonatal unit full of newborn infants. Four months from now she'd have an infant of her own to care for. "Isn't Brittany with you?" Norell asked as she fell into step alongside her friend.

"No. She wants to get her homework done. Tomorrow she has a sleepover at one of her friends' houses."

"Oh, did she and Gil's daughter make up, finally?"

"No," Dana said sadly. "She'll be at the home of another one of her friends from school."

Hearing the down note in Dana's voice made Norell regret having brought up the topic of Brittany's broken friendship. "I'm sorry, Dana."

"Gil says to give it time. He says Vanessa is a very confused young lady right now. But at least Brittany is thriving with her other friends. She's on the phone a lot, and on weekends she's always going to the movies."

They got into the elevator and headed for the third-floor maternity unit. Cécile sat in her hospital bed, bottle feeding a wizened-looking infant. "Look, Regine," she said when they entered the room. "It's Auntie Dana and Auntie Norell come to see you."

Norell thought the baby looked like a little gnome, much less cute than Cécile's other daughters, but she oohed and aahed appropriately.

"She's beautiful, Cécile," Dana said wistfully. "I remember when Brittany was a newborn. It seems like yesterday."

"It's good that she came early and you didn't have to spend Christmas in the hospital," Norell added.

"I knew she wouldn't let me down. She's my good-luck baby," Cécile said. She removed the bottle from Regine's mouth and studied the fill line, then placed the bottle on her bedside table. "That's it for you, young lady." She lifted the infant to burp her. "We're going to have a nice holiday," she said. "My parents are coming up to stay with us, to see Regine and the new house. But if we were in the hospital, it wouldn't be the same, would it, Precious?" She directed her question to baby Regine.

Norell could stand watching Cécile fawn over her infant no longer. "Guys, I've got to tell you something. Vic has arranged for us to adopt a baby."

Dana squealed so loudly that Regine began to cry. "That's right, frighten my child half to death," Cécile hissed. Still speaking in a stage whisper as she patted her baby's back, she said, "That's wonderful, Norell! Tell us about it."

"When will this happen?" Dana asked with excitement. "And do you know if it's a boy or a girl?"

"The baby is due in April. But listen, guys, there might be a complication. I need you both to pray for us."

"What kind of complication?" Dana asked.

"Vic isn't entirely convinced that the birth mother won't change her mind at the last minute."

Dana spoke again. "Oh, gosh. I guess I could see how that could happen."

Norell knew Dana meant no harm, even though the words stung. She looked at Cécile, hoping she would say something more positive, but Cécile wore a strange blank expression as she almost mechanically patted Regine's back.

Dana continued talking in almost a trancelike state. "If she holds the baby just once, she might decide in that instant she just can't give it up." Then she drew in her breath, obviously realizing how painful her assessment sounded to Norell. "God knows I hope that doesn't happen in this case."

"I'm sure it won't," Cécile said, suddenly springing to life. "I'm very happy for you, Norell. Babies bring good luck. I know my little Precious did."

"She looks different from Josie and Gaby and Eleith, doesn't she?"

Cécile didn't like the amused smile on Micheline's face. "Maybe a little. But that's only natural. She has a different father. Not that we'll ever differentiate. They're all our kids and all brothers and sisters, from Jonathan right on down to Regine."

"That must be it. She looks more like Michael." Micheline sighed. "One thing I can say about Louis. He was a bastard, but he was a good-looking bastard."

Cécile let that one pass. "I'm glad you came over," she said.

"I figured I'd better get over here before school lets out the day after tomorrow. I don't want the kids to see me this way."

Cécile agreed that was best. The kids would ask a million questions, none of which she would be prepared to answer. But Cécile felt sorry for her sister, being forced to hide from the world lest someone she knew learn her secret. "Do you leave the house at all?"

"Of course. I have to eat, don't I? I usually go out in the mornings, when I won't see anyone I know. I like going to the mall when it opens to see all the latest clothes I'll be able to buy myself once I drop this load."

Cécile covered up Regine, and she and Micheline left the master bedroom, where the crib was set up, Cécile pausing to adjust the monitor that would allow her to hear Regine's cries from downstairs. "Speaking of dropping that load, Michie, I have to ask you something," she said as they descended the carpeted stairs.

"What's that?"

"Forgive me for being so blunt, but I have to know. You *are* going to go through with handing the baby over to Norell and Vic when it's born, aren't you? I mean, you aren't going to renege on the deal you made with Vic?"

Micheline sighed wearily. "You know, Cécile, I'm getting awfully tired of you accusing me of things I'm not even thinking about."

"I'm sorry, Michie. But Vic told Norell about the arrangements, and she's both excited about being a mother and terrified that the 'anonymous' birth mother will change her mind."

"I can't help it if she's worried, Cécile. I have problems of my own, like coming up with an excuse about why I can't see Mama and Papa while they're here. And speaking of that, I find it strange that they're making a trip to Jacksonville now. They've been up here, what, twice in all the years you've lived here? I guess you just couldn't resist inviting them, could you, just to put me on the spot."

"That's not true, Michie! Mama and Papa didn't come before because of all the friction I was having with Louis. They didn't come after I married Michael because we had nowhere for them to stay. You know they'd never get a room in a hotel. They've never stayed in a hotel room in their entire lives. But they're very anxious to see Regine, and the new house as well. I knew you wouldn't be coming to Christmas dinner because you don't want Michael or the kids to know you're pregnant. I figured you'd probably tell Mama and Papa that you were spending the holiday with Errol."

Micheline exhaled loudly. "All right. Maybe I was being too sensitive. I'm sorry. It must be my condition," she muttered. She lowered herself into an easy chair in the living room.

"How's it going with Errol, anyway?"

Micheline brightened. "Good. We talk on my cell phone every day. As far as he's concerned, I'm taking care of my great aunt, who was taken ill at her home in Spring Valley, New York."

Cécile recognized the name of the suburban town that had been home to Yvonne Broussard, their father's aunt, with whom Micheline had stayed when she took a job in New York after college. Great Aunt Yvonne died three years ago, shortly after Micheline returned to South Florida. Yvonne had been a sweet woman who had no children of her own during her long marriage to a husband whose death left her alone in the world. She'd been eager to open her home to her recent college graduate niece, the only one of her Americanized grandnieces and -nephews who could speak to her in her native French. Cécile felt Micheline had done a gross disservice to their aunt's memory by making her part of a scheme to fool a boyfriend. "So you've resurrected Aunt Yvonne from the dead for your own selfish purposes," she said, her voice ringing with disapproval.

"I'm sure she won't mind. After all, I was her favorite."

Micheline's flip attitude didn't surprise Cécile. She recognized it as a dig at her because Yvonne had left part of her life insurance to Micheline but nothing to Cécile or their brothers. She decided to try another tack to ruffle her sister. "That sounds awfully lame, Michie. He actually believed that?"

But Micheline, unflappable as ever, only smiled. "Yes, he did. My great aunt and I have always been very close."

"I guess you had plenty of opportunity to work your concerns about Dear Old Auntie into the conversation before she suddenly took ill."

Micheline flashed a sunny smile. "Of course."

Micheline thought about the conversation on her way home. Cécile had hit the nail dead on—she'd begun talking about her devotion to Great Aunt Yvonne with Errol the moment she learned her pregnancy had passed the first trimester, wanting to provide an out for herself once her condition became visible. Errol had been startled by her abrupt departure, which occurred as he attended a dentists' conference in Orlando the week after Thanksgiving. He said he understood that she couldn't get away, but he offered to fly up to see her. Micheline had been hard pressed to come up with a plausible reason why that wouldn't work, particularly over the Christmas and New Year's holidays, when they really should be together. She insisted that being caretaker to an eighty-eight-year-old stroke victim kept her going twenty-four hours a day. "I see all kinds of problems. There are no hotels around here, and my aunt lives in a one-bedroom apartment. Besides, she never became fluent in English. I speak to her in French. I miss you terribly, Errol, but trying to spend time with you would present a logistical nightmare. I'd rather just look forward to seeing you when I come back." She'd said this to him just yesterday.

"But you've already been gone for weeks. Christmas is less than a week away. When will you be back, Michie?"

"I'm not sure. But my aunt was always there for me, Errol. I lived with her rent free when I took my first job after college. If it weren't for her I couldn't have afforded the experience of working in New York. I never had a problem getting a job because prospective employers see that I once worked for a New York law firm."

"Michie, I hate the idea of your being alone with a sick old woman over the holidays, even if it is someone dear to you."

"I promise that next year I'll be with you, dear."

"And the year after that, and the year after that. I love you, Michie."

"I love you, too, Errol."

They'd ended their conversation then, and Micheline wanted to jump for joy. He'd never told her he loved her before. If she'd known that all she had to do was disappear, she would have resurrected Aunt Yvonne long ago.

She parked her Bug in the private garage she'd rented so Errol wouldn't see her car if he came around. She took special precautions not to give herself away. She never answered her home phone without checking the number first on the caller ID.

Sometimes she felt she overdid it with all her wariness, but she felt certain she'd covered all the bases. She even had a plan of action all worked out in the event something went wrong. Not that she'd ever have to use it. She'd simply been too slick.

Chapter 45

Dana, standing on a stepladder six feet above the floor, carefully reached out and adjusted the angel on top of the Christmas tree. "Is it straight now?"

Brittany cocked her head to one side. "Now it's leaning to the left."

Dana sighed in exasperation. "Well, I think it'll just have to lean. Every time I move it, it ends up going too far to the right or too far to the left."

"But Mom, if you leave it that way, the only way it'll be straight is if you lean your head to one side."

"Too bad. I'm getting down from this ladder before I fall." Dana began her descent.

"I'll do it."

"No, you won't," Dana said firmly. Because of the way Kenny died she would always be mindful of the potential for household accidents. No way would she allow Brittany to climb that ladder. "Just leave it the way it is. If you want to help, you can put the ladder back in the garage."

Brittany dutifully folded the stepladder into a flat position. "Mom, this music is awful."

"What are you talking about? It's Christmas music, sung by Johnny Mathis, one of the loveliest voices of his generation."

"I don't want to listen to some old guy sing. Can we at least put on Vanessa Williams?"

"Oh, all right. Go ahead."

Dana watched Brittany head for the garage with the stepladder. This holiday season felt much more festive than last year's. Their first Christmas without Kenny had a pallor over it, no matter how cheerful she forced herself to sound. She cried Christmas night in the privacy of her bedroom, and she suspected that Brittany did, too. She couldn't even bring herself to erect their usual eight-foot-tall tree in the family room, and instead went out and bought a tree less than half that height. She and Brittany had made a halfhearted attempt at decorating it. On New Year's Day they took it down and threw it out.

This year their boxed tree stood magnificently decorated in the family room. Dana had bought some new ornaments to diminish the sentiment of the old and familiar. The fireplace crackled with orange flame. Unlike last year, when the mercury hovered around seventy degrees, this year's chilly temperatures seemed more appropriate to the season. She and Brittany each had a glass of eggnog, the only difference being that Dana's contained a touch of bourbon.

Christmas Eve, like always, would be spent quietly at home. The only thing different would be the presence of Gil, whom Dana expected to ring the bell any minute. She'd told Brittany he might be stopping by, but hadn't wanted to make it sound too definite. At least this way Brittany would have the chance to get used to the idea of them sharing Christmas with Gil. Dana still wasn't sure if Brittany was ready to see the two of them together, but she knew she couldn't put it off much longer. Somehow the impossible had happened and she'd fallen in love. She hadn't told Gil how she felt. She wanted him to say it first.

Gil would also accompany them to dinner at Norell and Vic's home tomorrow.

Dana wished Vanessa would come around. Brittany appeared to be doing okay, but Dana knew she still missed her friend terribly, and what hurt most was knowing Brittany held her responsible, even though she knew better than to say it. Everything would be so much easier to accept if Brittany had her oldest friend at her side.

The sound of chimes filled the house. "That must be Gil," Dana said brightly. She glanced at Brittany, who had just changed the CD and was concentrating on returning Johnny Mathis to his case, and her soaring spirits crashed. Brittany hadn't even acknowledged her comment.

She tried again. "Brittany, come with me to the door."

"Why, Mom?"

"Because it'll send a nice signal to Gil that you're happy to see him."

Brittany shrugged, but before she could say anything—like that she wasn't particularly happy to see Gil—Dana impatiently gestured at her to join her.

"Who is it?" she called when she and Brittany stood arm-in-arm opposite the door.

"It's Gil."

Dana opened the door. Gil stood on the other side behind Vanessa, his hands resting on her shoulders. "Vanessa!" she exclaimed. "What a wonderful surprise! Merry Christmas, dear."

Brittany looked almost spellbound. "Hi, Vanessa."

"Hi, Brittany. Hi, Miss Dana," Vanessa replied shyly.

Dana waved them inside. "Please, come in. We're letting all the cold air get inside."

"I reminded Vanessa of what Christmas is all about," Gil remarked, rubbing his palms together. "It's the season of love and good will toward men. I told her I felt this foolishness between her and Brittany has gone on long enough."

"Oh, I agree," Dana said joyously. "How about it, girls?" Brittany still stood by her side, and Vanessa at Gil's. "Don't you feel it's time to kiss and make up?" She thought her heart would burst with happiness when the girls rushed into each other's arms and simultaneously said, "I'm sorry," before breaking into giggles.

Gil casually came to stand beside Dana, his arm reaching around her shoulder. They watched their daughters rush to talk at the same time as they walked toward the family room at the rear of the house, eager to catch up on the goings-on in their lives during their estrangement. "I'm so happy, Gil," Dana said. "You brought Brittany the best Christmas gift ever."

He planted a quick kiss on her lips. "Who says there isn't a Santa Claus?"

"How did you manage to swing it?" she asked as she fixed him an eggnog in the kitchen. The sound of laughter drifted in from the adjoining family room.

"Vanessa spent Christmas Eve with me last year, and I asked her if she wanted to do it again. We can't stay long, though. She's still reluctant to leave Irene alone for long. But do you think your friends would mind if I brought her along tomorrow? I think I might be able to coax her into going, as long as she spends the bulk of the day with Irene."

"Of course Norell won't mind. She has a pretty good number of people over for dinner every year. It's an informal setting, buffet style, because people keep arriving all afternoon, so it won't be a problem if we don't get over there until six or even later than that." Dana wished she could pick up Vanessa herself and save Gil that long trip in from the beach, only to head back that way again to go to the Bellamys', but she knew Irene would never consent to that.

Dana felt indescribably happy. Now nothing stood in the way of her being with Gil; she no longer had to cope with her conscience reminding her that her happiness came at Brittany's expense. Only one thing posed a possible spoiler.

"Gil, do you think Irene will put her foot down when she finds out you brought Vanessa over here?"

"She'll try, I'm sure. Of course, it would be a lot easier if she just didn't know. But I won't have Vanessa lie to her mother, and I'm sure Irene will ask where I took her the minute she steps in the house. She asked me where we were going when I picked her up. Irene isn't stupid. She knows that everything closes early on Christmas Eve."

"What'd you tell her?"

"That Vanessa could tell her all about it when she got home. Don't worry about it, Dana. The choice about what she wants to do is really up to Vanessa. Irene will no doubt try her manipulation tactics, but I plan to work on Vanessa on the way home to deprogram her before Irene can start in."

The merry atmosphere at the Bellamy home matched Norell, who positively glowed as she tended to her guests. "You're glowing like somebody with a secret, and I know what it is," Dana told her in a singsong tone when they had a moment alone.

"Hey. I thought you guys would never get here, but I see Brittany and her friend have made up."

"Gil brought Vanessa to the house last night. Norell, things couldn't be more perfect. We're late because Vanessa wanted to spend most of the day with her mom. Irene does tend to try to appeal to Vanessa's heartstrings by playing the all-sacrificing mother routine, but I really don't blame Vanessa for not wanting to leave her mom alone on Christmas Day."

"I'm just glad to see you guys made it."

Dana glanced over at Vic's first wife, Phyllis, and her friend Karen Weathers, who stood in a corner with the cautious expressions of people who feared they might be overheard as they gossiped about their hosts while eating their food and drinking their liquor. The first year of their marriage, Vic had asked Norell to include Karen along with his daughters in their annual Christmas open house so she wouldn't have to spend the afternoon alone, and Norell acquiesed, although grudgingly. "Don't look now, but I think Phyllis and Karen are trying to figure out why you're so happy."

Norell made a face. "Oh, them. They huddle in a corner and talk about me every year. Vic said he was going to tell Phyllis to cut it out, that it's damned rude, but I told him I didn't care. Let them whisper."

"Well, I'm with Vic on that one. It *is* damned rude."

Cécile hugged her father, for no reason other than her happiness to have him and her mother at her home. She wished her parents would come to visit them more often, and maybe now that they had more room, they would. Josie and Monet willingly gave up their bedroom and adjoining bath for their grandparents and bunked with Gaby and Eleith. All four girls, and even Jonathan and Damon, enjoyed the attentions of Claude and Catherine. Michael's parents had both passed away, and Cécile felt it important for children to have grandparents in their lives.

The kids had nearly gone overboard decorating the house for the holiday. Popcorn balls hung from every door, and mistletoe abounded. Multicolored lights outlined both the living-room mirror and the doorway to the patio. The tree, a real Norwegian Spruce, stood in a corner of the living room, full with ornaments and lights, and gifts overflowed from its base. Cécile moaned and groaned all year while she purchased Christmas gifts and stocking stuffers for the children, but seeing this bountiful scene made all her hard work worthwhile.

Only one thought dampened her spirits, the thought of her sister spending a solitary Christmas in her apartment. Micheline made it a point to call and talk to their parents and the kids, keeping up the farce of being in Crescent City with Errol's family. Cécile's heart broke for her sister as she, going along with the charade, told her to enjoy her day.

She wondered if this was God's way of punishing Micheline for all the heartache she had caused, and if so, what else did He have in mind for her?

Chapter 46

Errol placed his purchases on the counter: two bottles of Cordon Negro and a three-quarter-liter bottle of Skyy vodka. Normally he'd look forward to a New Year's Eve party at Rob and Yolanda's, but without Michie it wouldn't be any fun.

He'd been so happy just one month ago, when she came to dinner at his parents' house on Thanksgiving, along with his father's cousin and his wife. Micheline had charmed everyone and done him proud. He'd known then that he loved her. He'd never met anyone like her. She showed genuine interest in everything he did, the most mundane details of his work, even taking up golf because he enjoyed it. Other women he knew never wanted to hear about his work or the sports he enjoyed; they just wanted him to share their interests, like shopping. They also went out of their way to please him in bed. Michie didn't. She had her values and didn't care what he thought. She was a prize he'd have to be crazy to give up.

He thought about presenting her with a diamond for Christmas, but then the next week she called and said she'd had to drive up to New York right away to be with her aunt, who'd suffered a stroke. He knew how devoted Michie was to her aunt, who since her husband's death had no one to take care of her, but he missed her terribly. When she came back he'd get down on one knee and beg her to marry him.

He ran his debit card through the point-of-sale terminal and keyed in his PIN number, then replaced the card in his wallet as the system hummed approval.

The clerk packed the bottles carefully in a brown paper bag inside a plastic bag for strength. Errol hoisted the bag by its plastic handles and left the store, anxious to get away from the crowd of people buying liquor for their celebrations tonight.

As he walked toward his car he caught a flash of red out of the corner of his eye. He glanced up in time to see a tomato-red Bug just like Michie's pass by at the end of the row of vehicles. He smiled. Did he have ESP or something?

Wait a minute. The woman driving the Bug had the same light brown complexion as Michie. She wore sunglasses and a baseball cap, but the lock of hair peeking out from beneath the cap was the same blondish color as Michie's. Had she surprised him and driven back to spend New Year's with him? Or was he merely imagining things?

No, that couldn't be it. He knew what he saw. His vision had measured 20/20 at his last eye exam less than six months ago. If that wasn't Michie, then she had a twin she didn't know about.

He decided to drive over to her apartment, which was only a ten-minute drive from here. If she was back in town her car would be parked in front of her apartment. She'd probably be annoyed at him for spoiling her surprise, but she'd get over it. He had to know if that really had been her.

Errol's heart beat loud as a cannon in his chest as he rounded the corners of Micheline's apartment complex. Disappointment stabbed at him when he didn't see her car.

He steered his vehicle into a U-turn, which because of the narrow width of the parking lot had to be done in degrees. When the car faced her window he glanced up at it, just in time to see the blinds shift into a closed position. Errol braked, then jerked his car into a forward gear and slid into a parking space. Those blinds hadn't closed by themselves. Someone occupied Micheline's apartment, and he wouldn't leave here until he found out precisely what was going on.

He bounded up the stairs two at a time and knocked on her door confidently.

A voice that sounded very much like hers promptly answered. "Who is it?"

"UPS."

The door opened. Afterward, Errol wasn't sure who gasped the loudest, Micheline at seeing him, or him at seeing her expanded belly.

"You said you were the UPS man," she said accusingly.

"You must have been expecting something, like a crib." His voice rang with sarcasm.

She stepped back and waved him inside. He stepped into her apartment. "I agree that this is no conversation to have in the hall," he said.

"I don't understand, Errol. What made you come over here?"

"I thought I saw you a few minutes ago over at the strip mall on Southside Boulevard."

"Oh. I stopped at Arby's to get some lunch."

"I thought you might have gotten back into town and planned to surprise me for New Year's. I couldn't stand waiting to hear from you, so I came over, even if it meant spoiling your surprise. As it turns out, *I'm* the one who's surprised. This isn't just a surprise. This is a beaut!"

"I couldn't bring myself to tell you. I knew you wouldn't understand."

"No, Micheline, I don't understand. You wouldn't sleep with me. You gave me that BS about how you didn't believe in premarital sex because you got burned a long time ago. Obviously you played with somebody and their matches again a couple of months ago, when you were supposed to be with me."

Her words spilled out. "Errol, I was raped."

"*What?*"

Micheline launched into the story she had prepared in case he showed up unexpectedly. "I didn't know how to tell you," she said with a sob. "It happened in the parking garage at work. I stayed late one night—" She broke off. "I can't talk about it. When the doctor confirmed I was pregnant I didn't know what to do. Before that I tried so hard to put it behind me." Tears streamed down her face. Micheline realized she cried out of frustration, cried for the weeks of solitude, the sadness of spending Christmas all alone in her pastel paradise, with only the television for company.

Errol swiftly took her in his arms. "Did they ever find the man?"

"No. My job has put me on a paid leave of absence until after the baby is born. I've decided to give it up for adoption."

He tightened his arms around her and kissed her hair. "Michie," he whispered. "Why didn't you tell me?"

"I didn't know how," she sobbed. "I figured you'd be angry with me, tell me it was my fault for not getting someone to escort me to my car."

"God knows I wish you had, but it's too late to change it now, isn't it? You didn't have to go through this alone," he said, rocking her gently. "But you're not alone anymore. I'm here, and I'll take care of you."

"Oh, Errol. You don't know how badly I wanted to confide in you. I thought you wouldn't understand."

"Come on, let's sit down." They moved a few feet to the elegant white sofa, where they sat close to each other, his arm draped around her shoulder, her right hand resting on his left thigh. "Have you really kept this from everyone?"

It only took an instant to decide to be truthful. "Only my sister knows," she said. "She had to help me explain to her kids and to my parents why I wasn't around over the holidays. You see, my parents came up to Jacksonville for Christmas and expected to see both of us. Cécile and I told them I went out of town with you." She buried her face in her hands. "All those lies! I can hardly stand myself."

"Michie, don't cry. You did what you had to do. Let's form a plan of action. The first thing you need to do is file suit against the owners of the garage for inadequate security."

"And relive the worst incident of my life? No. I won't do it."

"But Michie, they owe you. All your suffering and emotional distress is worth money."

"If I have to testify it isn't worth it, Errol. I don't care how much money is at stake. I want to put it behind me, not relive it under questioning and cross-examination."

"All you have to do is threaten them with a lawsuit. You won't have to go through with it. The moment the garage owners learn what you're planning, they'll offer you a cash settlement."

"Maybe." Micheline thought she might be able to pull that one off, if she was careful about it. She still had the money she'd gotten from her former employer in West Palm, as well as her share of Great Aunt Yvonne's insurance proceeds, most of which she'd invested for nice returns on her money. She could claim it all came from the garage owners in a settlement, and Errol would never know the difference. "I'll think about it. All I want is to feel like myself again, and I don't know if I ever will."

"Have you seen a counselor?"

"Yes," she lied. "She helped me understand that it wasn't my fault. I'm not seeing her anymore. She accomplished what she was supposed to do, and that's it. All I want to do now is get back to where I was in life. But I don't know if I can go back to that office and that garage." She waited for him to tell her she wouldn't have to ever face it again, that he would take care of her.

"I don't think you should. But you have time for that. When is the baby due?"

"Not until the middle of April."

Errol looked almost as shocked at that as he had when he saw her swollen belly. "My God, you planned to keep up this charade for another four months?"

"What else could I do, Errol?"

"And you made up that story about your great aunt."

Micheline fought back panic that began in the pit of her stomach and rose in her throat. Errol sounded so emotionless. Could he be re-thinking his statement that he would take care of her? "I really did have a Great Aunt Yvonne, Errol. And I lived with her after college while I had my first job in New York. She was real sweet to me. She died three years ago. I always felt a little guilty, because she didn't last too long after I moved back to West Palm. One day she got up, ate breakfast, and slumped over from a heart attack." She sighed. "Can't you understand that I didn't know what else to do? I was afraid to tell you the truth, but I didn't want to lose you, either. I hoped that once the baby was born I could come back and we could pick up where we left off."

"It's all right," Errol soothed. "I'm just trying to absorb it all. All this comes as a shock. I'm not angry at you, Michie. I'm sorry I reacted the way I did when I saw you."

She sniffled in response.

"But I'm going to ask you something, Michie, something I want you to think about long and hard before giving me an answer."

Her stomach went rigid. What could he be thinking? "What is it, Errol?"

"Do you really want to give up your baby?"

She stared at him, not comprehending his motives.

"Look, Michie. I can't plan for the future unless I know what kind of future it is. Like if it will include a baby that's not mine."

"You mean . . . you wouldn't mind if I kept my baby?"

"If that was really what you wanted, no. Regardless of the circumstances of conception, it's still your baby, still a part of you. And in case you're worried about what people would say, just remember that we don't have to explain anything to anyone about where the baby came from. It's no one's business but ours."

She had a flash of the disapproving faces of Mr. and Mrs. Trent. Then she had a flash of a despondent Norell, and Vic trying to comfort her . . . and Cécile screaming at her, telling her she'd brought nothing but heartbreak to her two best friends.

"Let me think about it," she said slowly. "It's an important decision. I want to be sure."

Chapter 47

From the moment Vanessa came to the door when Gil picked her up for their regular outing, Gil had the uncomfortable feeling that something troubled his daughter. When Vanessa smiled it appeared genuine, but when she wasn't smiling a distressed expression flashed across her features. She would snap out of it only after he brought it to her attention.

"Vanessa," he said for the fifth time that afternoon, "you know that if something is bothering you, you can always tell me about it."

"I know, Popi."

"You've been awfully quiet all afternoon. Didn't you like the movie?"

"It wasn't as funny as I thought it would be."

Gil thoughtfully nodded, then pretended to concentrate on the menu. He had already decided to order a bacon cheeseburger with a ton of fries smothered in ranch dressing. Cholesterol be damned. But he wished he could get Vanessa to open up. He'd have to work quickly if he wanted to get the truth out of her. It wouldn't take long to eat and drive back into town.

He'd thought that once Vanessa made up with Brittany she would welcome the opportunity to spend at least every other Saturday night at his apartment, maybe invite Brittany to come along. That hadn't happened. Vanessa remained loyal to Irene and didn't want to leave her overnight.

He looked up sharply at the sound of a sob. "Vanessa? What is it? What's wrong, honey? You know you can tell me anything." He felt frantic with frustration. They'd always been close. What could be so difficult for Vanessa to tell him?

A stab of fear pierced his gut. Surely she couldn't be—no, that was ridiculous. She wouldn't even be fourteen years old until March. More importantly, she barely left the house unless she went out with him for their weekends. No sleepovers with friends, and maybe just a quick afternoon outing here and there. No way could she be in trouble with some boy. But what else could it be?

"Vanessa," he said as patiently as he could. "Will you please tell me what's wrong? I'm really beginning to worry about you."

"Daddy, would I be a bad girl if I wanted to come live with you?"

Gil's mouth hung open. "Live with me? You want to come live with me?"

"I can't take Mama anymore." Vanessa now sobbed openly.

"Of course you can come live with me. Come on, Vanessa, calm down." He glanced around to see if anyone had noticed her emotional state. All he needed was for some well-meaning stranger to call the cops, thinking Vanessa was some young girl he'd abducted rather than his own daughter. "But it might take some time. You see, when your mother and I divorced, the judge gave her custody of you, and I only got visitation rights. To change that, I have to hire an attorney and get a court date. Then you'll have to tell the judge in your own words why you'd rather live with me."

"That sounds like it's going to take a long time."

At least she had stopped crying. "It shouldn't take that long. And you can always come to my house whenever you want. I rented a two-bedroom apartment so you would have a room of your own when you visited. But Vanessa, I have to ask. What made you change your mind? What has your mother done?"

"All she does is talk all the time about what a terrible person Miss Dana is, to destroy our family the way she did. She says that Miss Dana had her eye on you the minute her husband died, and that she schemed and schemed until she got you."

"That's not true, Vanessa. None of it is true. Dana didn't destroy our family. Your mother and I were divorced long before Dana and I became involved with each other. And Dana never said or did anything inappropriate. I made the first move and asked her out after you and I and Brittany came back from New Orleans last year. Do you remember?"

"Yes." She sniffled. "Mama also said that Miss Dana is a terrible mother, to make her daughter so unhappy when all she had to do was stop seeing you."

"Let me ask you, Vanessa. If I had stopped seeing Dana after you cut off your friendship with Brittany, would you have gone right back to being her friend?"

"I don't know," she said slowly. "I don't think so. I don't think Mama would have liked it. She probably wouldn't have let me go over there or let Brittany come to our house, either."

"So that means things wouldn't have been all right if Miss Dana stopped seeing me, doesn't it?"

"Nnnnooooo."

They paused a moment to give the waitress their orders. "Listen to me, Vanessa," Gil said after the woman left their table, "I don't want to criticize your mother to you"—he paused to consider the irony, since Irene clearly had no problem doing just that when it came to *him*—"but let me say this. She has a very controlling nature. She tried to make a puppet out of me, and when I wouldn't go along she tried to make my life miserable. You remember all the arguments we used to have before I moved out?" At Vanessa's nod he continued. "I hated to leave you, Princess, but I didn't have much choice. I knew your mother would insist on full custody of you." He didn't say that Irene's motives for this were purely to get back at him.

"But that wasn't enough," he continued. "Your mother went after Dana once she found out I was seeing her."

"What did Mama do to Miss Dana?"

Oops. He hadn't meant to say that. Vanessa didn't need to know Irene's involvement in the vandalism of Dana's mailbox and her car any more than Brittany needed to know about it. "What I meant was she tried to create trouble for Dana by getting you to cut off your friendship with Brittany. Vanessa, you have to promise me that you'll always have a life of your own, because I see her trying to control you as well. You'll only be a teenager once in your life. Have fun. Enjoy the friends you have now and don't be afraid to make new ones. Don't sit home and devote your whole life to your mother."

"But she never sees anyone or goes anywhere, except to her parents'."

"Vanessa, we all make choices in our lives. Your mother decided she didn't need anyone else but her family, you and I. No friends. No outside interests. But what she doesn't realize is that her . . . her personality is so overbearing that she drives people away from her without realizing it. In her mind she's trying to hold on to you because you're all she has left."

"Popi, I want to come live with you now. Do I really have to wait until we see the judge? That sounds like it might take weeks."

He thought for a moment. "The only way you can come stay with me would be if your mother signed a notarized statement giving consent."

"What's 'notarized'?"

"That means her signature is witnessed by a notary public. A notary is someone who swears the signature came from the actual person and wasn't forged by someone else. Custody is a very serious issue, Vanessa. I just can't take you home with me. I can be arrested and jailed for doing that."

"I wouldn't want that to happen, Popi." Vanessa tried to sound brave.

"Me neither. Tell you what. We'll talk to your mother when I bring you home. But you do realize that staying with me means you'll have to change schools."

"I don't care. I can't just stand Mama's harping about you and Miss Dana all the time."

"Vanessa, don't worry. It'll be all right."

Gil wished he felt as confident as he sounded.

Chapter 48

"Good news," Vic said as he joined Norell in the kitchen and kissed her hello.

"My favorite kind. What's up?"

"Henry told me today that the baby is going to be a girl."

Norell drew in her breath. "A girl!" She closed her eyes for a moment and pictured a closet full of pretty feminine outfits, her arms crossed tightly in front of her body. She hugged herself and breathed deeply, then opened her eyes. "Vic, would I be a terrible person if I told you that's what I hoped for?"

"No, you wouldn't. And I knew all along that would be your preference." He sniffed. "What smells so good?"

"Stuffed pork chops."

He pulled her into an embrace, playfully dipping her backward. "Do you take care of me, or what?"

"We take care of each other," she said softly. She held on to his neck as he straightened, carrying her with him. "Seriously, Vic, I can't tell you how happy I am. I can't wait for the birth."

"I'll bet you're counting the days to the due date."

"Fifteen days to go. Cécile brings little Regine with her to our partners' meetings, and I always hold her and think that in just a few weeks I'll be holding my own baby. Vic, you don't think I'm too old to be a mom, do you?"

"Don't be silly, Norell. You're only thirty-eight."

"Some women are grandmothers by the time they're my age."

Vic chuckled. "If anybody is going to be mistaken for a grandparent, it'll be me. So don't worry."

"We'll probably have to get a larger house," she said as she poured wine into two glasses. "Between my office and the girls' room, the baby won't have a place of her own to sleep."

"She'll stay in the room with us the first few months anyway. Norell, I think you might have allowed yourself to forget that we're not out of the woods yet. You must remember that the mother can still change her mind."

"It's so much nicer not to think about it."

"You *have* to consider it, Norell."

"Vic, why are you so suspicious? You almost talk as if you know the birth mother."

"Of course I don't know her. But these things do happen. A woman can swear up and down that she's going to give up her baby for adoption, but all it takes is holding it for one second, and then suddenly she wants to keep it, no matter how much hardship it means."

Dana had pretty much said the same thing, but Norell couldn't bear to think about that. She'd never been a parent, never gotten to hold a baby of her own and feel that bond form. But she'd love this baby like her own, even if they didn't share any DNA. "Isn't it a good sign that in all this time she hasn't said a word about changing her mind, and now she's even sending messages through Henry about the baby's sex? She doesn't sound like someone about to change her mind to me."

"The baby is due in two weeks, Norell. You can't tell me she didn't know she was having a girl long before now. That makes me wonder about her motives for telling us this late in the game."

Norell looked at him strangely. He sounded so cold, like he harbored an intense dislike for the birth mother. The only way that could be was if he had a personal acquaintance with the woman.

Their eyes met, hers full of questions, and Vic's expression immediately softened. "I mean, I wonder if she plans to try something funny, like hold out for more money or something."

"I've seen movies where that's happened on Lifetime TV, but the scams usually involve well-off white people."

"We're not white, Norell, but we ain't exactly poor, either, and I'm sure the mother has figured that out." He shrugged. "Maybe it doesn't mean anything, but it's important to remember that it's not a done deal, even after we take the baby home."

"And besides, if she's young she probably could never afford to pay you back for all you've put out," Norell pointed out. "Even if she is a scam artist, I'm sure making restitution would severely cut into her profits. It's got to add up to a lot of money that you've spent, Vic."

"It probably comes to less than what we would have paid for that procedure Doctor Patel wanted to do."

She wondered why he didn't simply name a figure. Surely he knew how much he paid the mother every month. Instead he sounded like he deliberately wanted to keep her in the dark. Then there was that venom he had displayed a minute ago for the birth mother. Something didn't add up. . . .

She forced herself to sound cheerful. "Well, I should be getting a fairly decent amount from the CDN profits in June. I'll give it back to you."

"Don't worry about it, Norell. Come on, let's sit down and eat."

As Norell cleaned the kitchen after dinner she thought about Cécile and her new baby. Much better to concentrate on that than wonder about any secret meaning behind Vic's cryptic remarks. When she finished she went upstairs to the office and dialed Cécile's number. "I just found out my baby is going to be a girl," she announced joyfully.

"I can picture you with a little girl, Norell. My goodness, she'll probably be the best-dressed female in Jacksonville. Have you and Vic chosen a name yet?"

"I'm going to start writing some down later to run by him. The only thing I've ruled out is -eeka/-eesha."

"I don't get it."

"I don't want any names that end with 'eeka' or 'eesha.' When my child finishes college and goes looking for a job, no one will know she's black until she shows up for the interview."

Cécile laughed. "And what if she wants to go to Florida A&M or Bethune-Cookman? Would you discourage it because a degree from a black college might tip off prospective employers?"

"Of course not. I just don't want to give my child a name that pegs her as black. She can go to any college she wants. But this is what I was thinking, Cécile. My daughter"—she paused to savor how wonderful those two words felt rolling off her tongue—"will only be four months younger than Regine. They'll start school at the same time, although of course with us at the beach and you in San Jose it won't be the same school." She took a deep breath. "Cécile, I know I've behaved horribly for a long time. I can't tell you how sorry I am about the things I did and said. But we're going to have daughters the same age. Wouldn't it be nice if they play together when they're old enough? They might become best friends. And our friendship will be stronger, as well."

"Uh . . . yeah, sure! It'll be a little while before they're ready to play with anything other than their own feet, though."

Norell laughed. "I'm looking forward to every minute, believe me."

Cécile hung up the phone with a shaking hand. Damn it, why couldn't Micheline have had a boy? That way they would play together as toddlers and even as grade schoolers, but no one would expect them to be best friends as they got older. Unless, God forbid, as adults they fell in love and wanted to get married, unaware they were first cousins with a shared bloodline. What a disaster *that* would be.

She sighed. Maybe it was a blessing that Micheline would have a girl after all, or else she wouldn't have a peaceful day for the next twenty years, wondering if love lurked around every corner for her and Norell's children. She would deal with it, even if the baby looked like her side of the family.

She wished she had an out, but she didn't know what to do. She hadn't even shared the news of Micheline's baby with Michael, much less its paternity. She hated keeping something so important from her husband, but it was just too disturbing. Besides, the fewer people who knew, the better. Relationships would be forever fractured if anyone should make a slip.

Cécile felt like crying until her tear ducts ran dry. Everything she hoped for in her life had come true—a happy second marriage, healthy children, a new house—but because of Micheline's indiscretion, nothing would ever be the same. She would have to learn to function with a twenty-pound weight tied to her neck.

Two days later Cécile brought Regine to visit Micheline while the kids were in school. Despite all the heartache her sister had caused her and her friends, Cécile still tried to get over to see her at least twice a week. She didn't know how Micheline could stand living such an isolated life, and she suspected that her sister looked forward to her visits. She was Micheline's only link to the world, other than impersonal contact with store and restaurant clerks.

"How's the mom-to-be?" Cécile asked, patting Micheline's rounded belly, a belly that appeared much smaller than her own had been this close to her due date.

"Oh, I'm hanging in there." Micheline pursed her lips at Regine. "Hello, little niece of mine."

Regine simply stared at her, then reached out, delighted to have a new face to explore. Micheline went along, closing her eyes to protect them from the baby's tiny probing fingers and covering her gold hoop earrings with her hands.

"You're certainly in a good mood today," Cécile said as she pulled Regine away. "That's enough groping, Regine."

"Less than two weeks to go, and then I can have my life back. Damn right I'm happy."

They sat at the dinette—since Regine's birth, Cécile had stayed away from Micheline's fabric-covered sofa and side chairs, fearing the baby might spit up on them and leave a permanent stain. "And what kind of life will it be, Michie?" Cécile asked. "Have you learned anything from this experience?"

Micheline had deliberately kept Errol's return to her life from Cécile, certain that sooner or later Cécile would start in with a lecture that bordered on smug superiority. It might have taken almost four months, but she knew it would come. Time to come clean. "A great life. Errol wants to marry me."

"Errol! I would have thought he'd have found someone new after all this time away from you." Cécile saw no need for little niceties. If their situations were reversed, Micheline wouldn't bother to consider her feelings, and she wasn't going to, either.

The telephone rang before Micheline could answer. Cécile listened, playing with Regine, as her sister spoke on the kitchen extension. It surprised her that Micheline answered the phone without checking her caller ID first. It would be awfully difficult to convince someone she was out of town when she answered her home phone. "Hi, sweetheart. Everything okay? Good. Is it okay if I call you back? Cécile is here."

Cécile frowned at the sound of her name. She didn't know any of her sister's friends, nor did she think Micheline kept in contact with anyone during her period of lying low. Who could she be speaking with, much less calling "sweetheart"?

"I see you're talking with someone who knows who I am," she remarked when Micheline hung up.

"It's just Errol."

"Errol! What's going on, Michie? I thought you were hiding from him."

"He found me out. On New Year's Eve, actually."

"New Year's! That was three and a half months ago." Cécile's brow wrinkled. "Why didn't you tell me?"

"Because I'm still trying to decide what to do."

"Do about what? He obviously knows you're pregnant. I won't even ask what lie you told him, but it must have been a really good one if he still bothers with you."

"He loves me, Cécile. And I love him. We're getting married after the baby is born. All I have to do is say the word, and it'll be the three of us instead of the two of us."

Cécile took a moment to digest this information. "You mean . . . you might keep the baby?"

"Errol promises me he'll love it as his own, and I believe him."

"Micheline, you can't do that! Norell and Vic are expecting to get the baby. And what about all the money Vic has put out to support you all these months?"

"It'll all be taken care of, if I do decide to keep the baby. Like I said, I haven't decided."

"Michie, you don't love that baby any more than you love Errol. You just want to give my friends and me a lot of grief. I'll never understand why you hate us so much. You can have other babies with Errol. Why are you even considering holding on to this one?"

"Because I never had a baby before, Cécile. I don't know how I'll react in the delivery room when they say, 'It's a girl!' I might ask if she's formed all right and then go about my business without even looking at her, but I might want to hold her. And if I do, I might not want to let go."

Cécile's hands felt moist with sweat on the steering wheel of her minivan. She couldn't believe her sister. What kind of monster could string along a couple desperate for a child, knowing all along that she might withdraw at the last minute, depending on how she felt?

One thing was for sure. She couldn't face Norell until after the baby was born and they all learned what would come next. No way could she look Norell in the eye and share her excitement while privy to the knowledge that she might have to deal with a disappointment so crushing it would haunt the rest of her life.

All was dependent upon Micheline and her whims.

Chapter 49

"Dana, you don't know how much I appreciate your calling me every day," Norell said into the phone.

"I'm so excited. I don't think I was this jumpy when I got close to my due date with Brittany."

"Have you talked to Cécile?"

"Yes. She's still under the weather, but she's hanging in there."

"Did she say if she'll be at the partners' meeting?"

"She said she didn't know. She's afraid she'll pass on whatever bug she has to you, which can get complicated if the baby comes."

"That's sweet. I'll call her later."

"So how's Vic handling the suspense?"

"He's trying to hide it, but he's just as anxious as I am. Not just for the baby, but to see what happens with the mother." Again Norell experienced that queasy feeling that Vic knew more than he admitted to. It had haunted her ever since that day last week when he told her the baby was a girl. And again, she pushed it away.

"Norell, I can't tell you how happy I am for you two. For a while there I was awfully worried. I think your problems were worse than you let on."

"It did get pretty hairy for a while there last summer," Norell admitted.

"But you hung in there, and now look what's happened in just eight or nine months. Better days are coming for you, Norell."

"Yes. I just pray everything will work out."

"Think positive."

* * *

When Norell took a break to have lunch, she pondered the sharp turn her life had taken since last summer, when she and Vic barely talked to each other or touched each other. Less than a year ago she wondered if her marriage would survive, and now she and Vic were better than ever.

This wasn't the first time her life had changed direction because of Vic. He'd entered her life after her mother died and brightened her world. He hadn't abandoned her when infertility darkened her outlook again. Instead he got his lawyer to look for a woman with an unwanted pregnancy, just so her dream could come true. Vic really loved her. Look at how much money he'd spent. Not that she knew exactly how much it came to, but it had to be substantial.

She frowned. She wished Vic had shared more information with her about the birth mother. She couldn't help thinking his vagueness was deliberate.

As she poured iced tea into a tall cooler filled with ice cubes, she thought about Dana's comment about everything turning around in her marriage in the space of eight or nine months, and the thought hit her like a heavyweight champion's fist.

The baby she waited for so anxiously right now had been conceived at the same time as her lowest moments with Vic, just before their marriage turned around, largely because he stopped complaining about her work schedule.

That, paired with his remarks of last week, made her more suspicious than ever. Exactly how had Vic managed to connect with this birth mother?

She broached the subject as she served him breakfast the next morning. "Vic, tell me all about how you arranged for us to get the baby."

"There's not much to tell," he said.

Somehow she'd known he would say that.

"I put out some feelers through Henry about black babies being given up for adoption. He contacted his colleagues, and we got a bite. I didn't tell you as soon as the arrangements were made in case the woman changed her mind. You looked so down when Cécile had her little girl, I decided you needed to know."

"So Henry found her for you. Is she local? Did you meet her?"

"Yes. I interviewed her. She seemed like an all-right kid, if maybe on the self-involved side."

"Didn't it cost a whole lot?"

"I had to pay Henry's fees, plus I paid her living expenses from the time she was about four and a half months along. She didn't want the people she works with to know her business, so she took a leave of absence."

"So she works. Somehow I thought she was a college student."

"I never said that. I just said she's young. I also gave her a reasonable allowance and paid her health insurance premiums. But I'm pretty sure I told you that already." He smiled at her. "Why the sudden interest? You getting nervous at this any-moment stage?"

Norell took a deep breath, but her eyes never left his face. "It just occurred to me that nine months ago, when the baby was conceived, things weren't going too well between us. We hardly ever had sex. I thought that maybe you went out and got some woman pregnant and were trying to pawn off your own baby as belonging to some poor, unfortunate stranger." She saw the guilt flash in his eyes, gone in an instant, but it told her what she had feared in her heart of hearts for the last week. "My God!" she whispered. "You did it, didn't you?"

"I didn't want to tell you—"

She slammed her palm on the table. "I'll just bet you didn't! How dare you, Vic." She rose from the table and headed toward the front door.

He followed her, catching up with her quickly and turning her around. "Norell, listen. I made a terrible mistake. I knew that right away. There wasn't any love involved. It was one woman, one night. All she represented was release of all the frustration I felt for being so low on your list of priorities. But the condom broke, and she got pregnant."

She glared at his hand, which was still fastened around her forearm, before lifting her face to him. "And you expect me to raise your illegitimate brat just so you can keep her close to you."

"Norell, that's not it at all. I never wanted any more children in the first place. You know that. I enjoyed having all of you all to myself. There's a lot involved in raising children. Infants need a tremendous amount of care, and as they grow they still need nurturing. I'd already been through it. I only agreed to start another family because it was so important to you. When the mother came to me—"

"So she came to you."

"Yes. I made the suggestion that she let you and me adopt the baby, and I got Henry involved to draw up the contracts and explain them to her. I wanted an intermediary so I wouldn't have to deal with her directly. I just felt awful when she told me she didn't learn she was pregnant until after it was too late to abort, and then it occurred to me that maybe I had a blessing instead of a curse. I thought that if I could get the mother to cooperate, you and I could adopt the baby."

"What a marvelous stroke of luck," she said sarcastically.

"Listen, Norell. I know this woman's type. She would have aborted without giving it a second thought if she'd known in time, and I never would have known about it. But because it was too late for that, you and I will have a child."

"*You* will have a child, Vic. I have nothing."

He reached out for her other hand. "Norell," he said in that soft tone she knew so well, "do you really hate me so much that you would be willing to forego the opportunity to attain the one thing you want more than anything, to be a mother? You might not ever get another chance. You know that most black women keep their babies, even if they're very young teenagers and not really women yet. Or the babies are raised by family members, but they stay within the family network."

She lowered her head. It hurt, but Vic was right. Black infants available for adoption had to be a rarity. But how could she still feel the same about the baby she waited to hold and love, knowing it had been conceived by her husband from a one-night stand he'd had with some nameless, faceless woman? She faced the prospect of being reminded of Vic making love to another woman every time she set eyes on the baby. It might even look just like him.

"Norell?" he prompted.

She raised her head. "I don't want to talk to you right now, Vic. Excuse me."

She got up, walked into their bedroom, and stood by the crib they'd bought just yesterday in anticipation of bringing the baby home, resting her palms lightly on its edges. Plastic-bagged packages of baby supplies and clothing filled the inside. The receipts all remained in the bags. They'd been too superstitious to unpack until they actually had possession of the baby. Still, it didn't take much imagination to picture a sleeping infant lying in the crib, her chest moving up and down as she slept.

Sadness washed over Norell like a shower spray. These last weeks she'd spent a lot of time imagining all the wonderful things she and her little girl would do together in the future: Have matching mother/daughter outfits, bake Christmas cookies, paint Easter eggs. And that was just the beginning. Now, because of Vic, it might not ever come true.

She felt betrayed, and not only by him. How could Fate do this to her? Having been promised a baby and then finding out it came to be because of her husband's infidelity was just as cruel as offering a destitute person ten thousand dollars and then snatching it back at the very last minute.

Vic had entered the room and stood close behind her. "Are you all right?" he asked.

She stared at the window straight ahead. "No, Vic, I'm not. My heart is broken. You slept with another woman. You treated me the same way you treated Phyllis. I guess once a cheater, always a cheater."

"That's not fair, Norell. Do you think I would have even told you about my affairs if I had any intention of repeating that behavior? When you and I met, Phyllis and I were divorced. I opened up to you, confided in you about my past. It's low for you to use that against me."

"I can do any damn thing I want, Vic. And right now I don't want to talk to you. I don't want to look at you. I wish you'd just go on to work and leave me alone." She choked on her last words and raised her hands to wipe angry tears from her eyes.

The ringing telephone broke into the tension. Vic crossed the room to pick up the bedside extension. "Hello," he said briskly.

"Vic, it's Henry. Micheline just called me from the hospital. Her labor has started. They're admitting her."

Chapter 50

Micheline panted breathlessly. She'd never known such pain in her life. Her lower body felt like it was on fire. My God, her body would probably never be the same. Surely her vagina had stretched beyond its limits. Would she ever be able to enjoy sex again after passing a six-pound infant through that narrow opening?

"Here she is, Ms. Mehu," the nurse said, handing her the baby, who had now been cleaned of all those membranes that had covered her when she came out.

She noticed Errol stiffen behind her. He knew this would be the moment of truth, and she sensed he hoped she would decide against keeping the baby.

The child certainly didn't look like much, Micheline thought. For one thing, she was all head. Her eyes were shut, and her nose seemed to dominate her face. And why was she so pale? Micheline could see veins through her skin, which looked almost translucent.

She decided the baby would get cuter once she got a little older. After all, she'd thought baby Regine wasn't particularly cute at first, but she'd improved a lot in four months, even if she still looked more like Michael than Cécile.

"Well?" Errol pressed.

Micheline looked at him and shook her head. When she had her baby with Errol—whom she felt positive would be a boy—she would feel something a lot different, a lot more positive. "Thank you," she said to the nurse, holding out the bundled baby for her to take back.

* * *

Norell stood in front of the nursery window, staring at the baby. The pink nametag bore the name 'Bellamy.' From where she stood, the baby's features appeared muted. At this point she couldn't tell if it looked like Vic.

Vic wouldn't even tell her the name of the hospital where the baby had been born before today. This infuriated her, for she knew he had all the details and deliberately withheld the information. No doubt he feared she would seek out the birth mother in her room and make a scene. Now she didn't even bother acting on her curiosity. She knew Vic waited until after the birth mother had been discharged to tell her the baby's location.

Now the time had come to discharge the baby, but she still had a decision to make, or at least she had to inform Vic about what she decided. She wanted this child, even with her being the result of her husband's affair. How could she blame an innocent infant for the sins of her father?

Besides, could she honestly say that she had been blameless in the deterioration of her marriage? Hadn't she played a role in driving Vic into the arms of that other woman?

Maybe. But that didn't mean she could forgive him just like that, or forget about it, either. This would hurt for a long time. But she felt reasonably certain that she could separate her anger at Vic from the love she felt for the baby.

"Norell, you all right?" Vic asked, coming to stand beside her.

"Yes, I'm fine. But I have a question for you."

"What's that?"

She turned to face him, wanting to see his reaction, and spoke in a near whisper. "If you and I already had a child and were happy, would you still have wanted to bring this baby home to me?"

"If you and I had a child and were happy, I wouldn't have slept with another woman, so there would be no other child," he said bluntly.

"Indulge me, Vic."

"All right. Hypothetically, the answer is no. I would have encouraged her to give up the baby for adoption. I probably would have gotten Henry involved in the screening process of prospective parents, to do everything I could to make sure she went to a good home. But I wouldn't have felt a need to have the baby be a permanent part of my life."

She sighed. "So this is why you've put so much emphasis on the possibility of the mother changing her mind, because you knew her."

"I didn't spend enough time with her to know her, but a change of heart can happen with any birth mother, Norell. This woman is the center of her own universe. She does what's convenient for herself without any regard for anyone else." He paused to look at the infant on the other side of the glass. "But her loss can be our gain, if you want it."

"What if I don't want it? Will you be content to come home with me and let your child go into the foster-care system?"

Vic took a deep breath. He'd tried to do the right thing, to make the most out of an unhappy situation. He'd been as open as he could with Norell once she guessed the truth, while keeping the identity of his newest daughter's mother anonymous. He knew he could never tell her the whole truth. They still had a chance for a happy ending, but Norell would never forgive him if she knew he'd slept with Cécile's sister.

He'd tried his best to be as honest as he could in quite difficult circumstances. He couldn't lie to her now.

"I don't think I could give her up," he said. "It would be different if I hadn't seen her, but I have. She looks so vulnerable, so peaceful in that bassinet. Handing her over to carefully screened adoptive parents who will love and cherish her is one thing. Letting her go into foster care, where she might be mistreated or neglected, is something else. I'd hoped you would want to keep her, to bring her up as ours. I know it's a lot to ask of you, Norell, but I believe you have it in you to love this little girl without letting her be a reminder of how much I've hurt you."

He sighed. "I guess this is it," he said solemnly. "This is where we find out what's to become of us."

Their eyes met and held. "All right, Vic," she said. "Let's bring our daughter home and give her a name."

Chapter 51

Micheline enjoyed the oohs and aahs as she walked, on the arm of her father, toward the specially built platform in the Trents' backyard. They were even louder than the ones given for her nieces, Josie, Gaby, Eleith, plus little Monet Rivers, who served as her flower girls and looked beautiful in their yellow-and-white dresses.

It amazed her that Juanita Trent had managed to put together such a lovely wedding in such a short period of time. When Micheline came home from the hospital, Errol asked her to pick a date. She chose one six weeks out from the date of her baby's birth, when she had a green light to resume sex. She smiled as she thought about it. They were going to have some honeymoon. She imagined that after waiting so long they'd spend the whole time in bed and wouldn't even get to the beach in Aruba. They'd have to pay the hotel staff extra to bring them food and water to keep from starving or dehydrating. She just hoped it would be worth the wait. Holding out had largely been responsible for her becoming Mrs. Errol Trent. That, and the crisis they'd gone through together.

She would never forget how kind and attentive Errol had been to her, especially in the closing days of her miserable pregnancy. He'd practically waited on her hand and foot. He held her hand in the delivery room, and still he was willing to raise the baby as his if she decided to keep it.

Her father bent to kiss her cheek and then handed her over to Errol, who looked delicious in his tux with a white jacket. The minister—Micheline's mother expressed heartbreak that they didn't marry in the Church, but the Trents were Baptist—addressed the gathering, and in a few minutes it was all over, and she and Errol shared their first chaste kiss as husband and wife, to the cheers of their guests.

Cécile and Yolanda, her two honor attendants, appeared behind her, adjusting her short veil and slipping her a satin bridal purse for the checks she would be presented with on the receiving line.

The warm June sun beat down on Micheline's bare shoulders as she stood at her new husband's side to receive the good wishes of their guests, most of whom she was meeting for the first time. She'd worked hard to lose her baby weight and fit into this strapless white tea-length dress with appliqué and cinched waist, and she knew she would make a favorable impression on all who saw her.

She first spotted the man when he stood about fifteen people back in the line. In his mid-thirties, maybe a little older, he stood head and shoulders above the other guests. She estimated his height at about six-four. With smooth dark skin and a shaved head, even the way his jaw moved as he chewed gum, he reminded her of Michael Jordan.

She found it hard to concentrate on the other guests Errol introduced her to.

"So I suppose you'll be having an Errol Junior before too long," a silver-haired lady whose name went right over Micheline's head remarked, her gaze lingering on Micheline's slim midsection.

"Not for a few years yet, Mrs. Miller," Errol replied. He turned his head to wink privately at Micheline. They had expected people to suspect a secret behind their hastily planned wedding, but it came as a surprise that someone actually came out and asked. Apparently Mrs. Miller felt that her advanced age entitled her to make rude comments. Micheline didn't regret it when she moved on.

At last the man she'd been staring at stood opposite her. "Michie, this is Ivan Valentine," Errol said. "Our parents are good friends, and we were at UF about the same time, or at least one year. I started as a freshman the year he was a senior. "

"You make a stunning bride, Mrs. Trent," Ivan said with a little nod of his head, while his companion, a nondescript petite woman, murmured good wishes, her arm possessively linked through Ivan's. Micheline noticed the woman's bare ring finger. Ivan introduced his date to them, an introduction Micheline practically ignored.

"Did you study dentistry, too?" she asked Ivan.

"Heck, no. Four years of college was enough for me. I went into accounting."

Her smile slowly faded. That seemed like such a boring profession for such an exciting-looking man.

"Ivan's on his way to becoming a corporate CFO," Errol said. "He left a position as director of accounting in Raleigh to become the corporate controller of a big manufacturer based in Orlando."

Micheline brightened. That sounded promising.

Ivan's next words disappointed her. "You guys be sure to give us a call when you're down our way. And I hope you'll plan to attend our wedding next spring."

"Nice meeting you," his fiancée said. "And I wish you every happiness."

Micheline watched as they moved on to greet her parents. Ivan Valentine might be taken, but after being in his company, suddenly Errol didn't seem like that much of a catch anymore. He'd probably be working at the same dental practice twenty years from now, while Ivan would change jobs, going to exciting cities like San Diego and Chicago, moving up the corporate ladder each time. That plain Jane at his side would get to live a glamorous life. And, judging by the sex appeal that radiated from Ivan's pores like blood from a shallow scratch, they probably tore up the sheets at night.

She forced a smile as she shook yet another guest's hand. She'd made it. After just one year she was now Mrs. Errol Trent.

But would she really be happy? Or would she spend the rest of her life looking over her shoulder like she just had at Ivan, always wondering if she was looking at a better catch than Errol, someone she would never be able to have?

The smile remained plastered on her face as she tried to cope with the uncomfortable hunch that she was destined to live the latter scenario.

Chapter 52

The baby awoke crying at six A.M. after sleeping for five hours. A groggy Norell staggered to the bassinet and lifted the screaming infant, carrying her quickly to the living room so Vic could get back to sleep. It looked like she wouldn't be getting a whole lot of sleep the next few months. At least she had the benefit of working at home and setting her own hours. New mothers who had to return to work in an office didn't have the luxury of sleeping in or taking a nap after lunch because they'd been up during the night and then early in the morning with a newborn. She would manage just fine.

After careful consideration, she and Vic named their daughter Brianna. Norell liked the effect of a double initial, like Cécile's daughter, Regine Rivers. Little Brianna had changed quite a bit in the seven weeks since her birth. Features began to emerge from her lumpy face: Expressive eyes, a button nose, a dainty mouth. Little Brianna Bellamy had the potential to be a real beauty.

"Just fourteen thousand dollars?" Cécile said in disappointment. "How are we ever going to get rich making profits like that?"

All three partners attended the meeting at Dana's.

"It's not all bad, Cécile," Dana said. "Remember, we've been paid every week as independent contractors for all the work we've done the last year. When you add that up we've made considerably more than fourteen grand, especially you, because you've been transcribing full time since you had Regine."

"And you have to consider that our profits are divided into

three," Norell added. "That means CDN had a net profit of about forty-two thousand. And that's less than a full year. We cut off the fiscal year March thirty-first, remember?"

"Well, if that's the case, why did we have to wait until June to get our money?" Cécile asked crankily.

"Because we had to give new profits a chance to pile up, or else we wouldn't have any operating capital," Dana explained patiently.

"Just think how many mortgage payments you can make with fourteen grand, Cécile," Norell pointed out.

"Eight thousand is our original investment, so that only leaves a profit of six."

Dana tried again. "But next year it'll be sure to be higher, and since you've gotten your original investment back it'll all be profit. The hospital account wants to give us more work, if we can get the staff to do it. So relax, Cécile. Better days are coming for you, and for all of us."

"I guess I was just overly optimistic." Cécile bounced Regine on her knee. "I guess our ship hasn't come in just yet, Regine."

"She gets cuter every time I see her, Cécile," Dana remarked as she watched the smiling, nearly six-month-old baby. "You know, looking at the two of you with your babies, I really feel left out."

"How's everything going with Gil and his daughter?" Norell asked.

"He and Irene had a real showdown when Vanessa told her she wanted to live with Gil. Irene screamed that I'm behind it all, that I'm so evil. I believe the woman is a mental case. It's not normal to carry paranoia so far."

"So have they gone to court yet?"

Dana nodded. "Last week. The judge ordered that Gil get custody, and that Irene have a psychiatric evaluation."

"I'm happy for him," Cécile said.

"The best thing is that Vanessa is happy. She's had it awfully rough, living with Irene these past months as she's become more and more unglued. Gil hoped Irene would consent to giving him temporary custody until their court date because Vanessa was so unhappy, but she wouldn't go for it."

They all looked at Brianna, who suddenly woke up from her nap and squealed. "I've never seen you happier, Norell," Dana said. "She's a real cutie pie."

"I've never been happier." Her gaze went from Brianna to Cécile, who sat nearby. "Funny I never noticed it before," she said. "Brianna looks more like you than Regine does, Cécile."

"She does, doesn't she?" Dana said in agreement.

Cécile just shrugged. "Just one of those things, I guess." She hoped she didn't look as guilty as she felt. It would always be like this, whenever she had an opportunity to see her niece who would have to remain a secret.

She wondered if it would ever get any easier.

Norell found it amusing that her baby looked like Cécile. If there was one person she knew would never betray her, it was Cécile, the most honorable person she knew.

"There's something I wanted us to talk about this morning," she said. "I think it's time that CDN hired its first employee. My hands are full taking care of Brianna. I'd like us to consider hiring a part-time person to help me with the administrative work, like payroll and billing. I don't want to neglect my husband ever again."

"That's probably a good idea," Dana said. "It shouldn't cost us a whole lot."

"Cécile, maybe your sister would be interested," Norell said. "Didn't you say she gave up her job to stay at home since she got married? Maybe she's bored and wouldn't mind doing something part time."

Dana wrinkled her nose at the mention of Micheline, but of course Norell didn't know about their unpleasant history. Cécile had honored her wish not to tell what she knew. She held her breath, waiting for Cécile to say Micheline had no interest in working for CDN. She could count on Cécile.

"Oh, I don't think she'd be interested," Cécile said lightly. She's much too busy keeping house and experimenting with cooking. But I do agree that it would take some of the administrative load off of you and Dana. We can always put an ad in the paper."

"Okay," Norell said. "That's what I'll do."

Dana breathed a sigh of relief.

So did Cécile.

Chapter 53

On the first Saturday morning after the second anniversary of Kenny's death, Dana awoke cloaked in Gil's arms. She frowned, then blinked as she recognized the furnishings of Gil's bedroom. It all came back to her. Brittany and Vanessa slept in Vanessa's room across the hall.

She'd been apprehensive about flaunting her relationship with Gil in front of their children, but she allowed herself to be convinced when faced with the realization that their chances for intimacy would be few and far between because of their dual responsibilities as custodial parents. Last night she stayed overnight at Gil's for the first time. The girls didn't even know she was still here. She would have to have a long talk with Brittany, who was almost fourteen now. Maybe she could understand that at that age, her time for romance and all it involved still lay in the future, while at forty, Dana's opportunities for love and happiness had become more scarce.

She still had plenty to look forward to. She and Gil loved each other. He told her how he felt during the difficult times trying to wrestle custody of Vanessa away from Irene, and she'd been happy to tell him the feeling was mutual.

Gil shifted in his sleep. "Don't leave," he mumbled sleepily.

"I'm not leaving. I think I'll mix up some pancake batter. It'll help calm my nerves about how the girls will react when they realize I spent the night with you."

"Dana, it's not a big deal. Vanessa has a pretty good idea of how much you mean to me. She can see the difference between the way you and I interact and all the tension between her mother and me before the divorce. And she knows the facts of life. So does Brittany, I'm sure."

"Brittany has accepted you because she knows Kenny is gone forever. But Irene is still very much in the picture. Vanessa might perceive me as trying to take over."

"I think she'll welcome a little feminine influence in her life, now that she's a teenager and interested in boys. Irene can't have unsupervised visitation with Vanessa until it's determined that her medication is controlling her paranoid state. And I know that Vanessa has abandoned any ideas she had about a reconciliation between us."

"I wonder if Irene will ever see the truth as it really is and just let bygones be bygones."

"Sounds a little familiar, doesn't it?"

Dana frowned. "What do you mean, Gil?"

But he didn't reply, and a moment later his soft breathing alternated with the louder whirring of the ceiling fan above them. He had fallen back asleep.

Dana shrugged. She pushed the cover back and swung her legs over the side of the bed.

She had several stacks of pancakes made and being kept warm in the oven, and bacon frying. The unmistakable scent served to rouse the girls. "Hi, Mom," Brittany said as she emerged from upstairs in her pajamas, which looked like a shorts set.

"Hi, Miss Dana," Vanessa echoed. "Is any bacon ready yet?"

"No, but the pancakes are."

"I smell bacon!" Gil said definitively as he appeared, bare chested and wearing checkered drawstring cotton pants. Dana realized she was the only one in street clothes, having put on the same capri pants and shirt she'd worn the night before. She felt strangely overdressed.

"It's almost ready," she said.

"How'd everybody sleep?" Gil asked.

"Good, Popi. How did *you* sleep?" Vanessa giggled.

"Mom, does this mean you two are getting married?" Brittany asked between gasps of laughter.

Dana looked up from the bacon she just flipped. "Does *what* mean we're getting married?"

"Didn't you spend the night?"

"Does it bother either of you that she did?" Gil asked, his voice low with caution. Dana held her breath.

"No. But after we went to bed, Vanessa and I talked. We said how nice it would be if we got to be real sisters," Brittany said as Vanessa nodded agreement.

Dana let out the breath she'd been holding. "Girls, right now the two of us are very happy spending time together. But no one is saying anything about getting married. So let's just enjoy ourselves and have fun, okay?" She lifted the bacon onto a bed of paper towels. "Let's eat."

She dropped the girls off at the multiplex that afternoon, and then headed home to do her housework and perhaps a little work for CDN. As she dusted and vacuumed she thought of Irene. How pathetic that anyone could harbor such an unforgiving attitude. Irene would probably still feel that she had plotted to steal Gil from her twenty years from now.

For Vanessa's sake, Dana hoped that Irene could conquer her demons. Irene's condition remained the one blemish on an existence that had become as peaceful as it was happy. She and Gil loved each other and had the blessing of both their daughters. CDN continued to thrive in its second year. Between the income from her job, from CDN, and from the room above the garage, she could afford to indulge herself every now and then. Money might not ever be plentiful, and she worked sixty hours a week, but at least she didn't have to worry about how she would keep a roof over her head and Brittany's.

Her friends were doing well, too. The blended Belarge-Rivers family had comfortably settled into their new house, united by the birth of a baby all of them could claim a blood relation to. They would never be cramped again. Cécile, disenchanted with her failed tubal ligation and determined that the much-loved Regine would be her last child, had a powerful birth control device implanted into her arm. And Norell was thrilled with her new daughter. She and Vic had plenty of opportunities to go out for time alone, for they had eager babysitters in the form of Amber and Jessica, who adored their baby sister. Those better days she had predicted had come true for all of them.

When the house looked and smelled fresh, Dana relaxed on the family room sofa with a magazine. Brittany would be calling at any moment to say she was ready to come home.

Dana caught sight of her address book on the lower shelf of the coffee table. Suddenly she remembered what Gil said this morning. He asked her if Irene's attitude sounded familiar. Now she knew what he meant.

Surely she had been angry and unforgiving long enough.

She reached for her personal address book and turned to the "B" page. She stared at the name at the top of the page for a long time, then leaned over toward the end table and lifted the cordless receiver.

A male voice answered.

"Hello, Daddy," she said uncertainly. "This is Dana. I think we need to talk. . . ."

NOTHING BUT TROUBLE

BETTYE GRIFFIN

ABOUT THIS GUIDE

The suggested questions are intended to enhance
your group's reading of this book.

DISCUSSION QUESTIONS

1. Dana lost her mother and sister due to accidental death, and her father to grief. Barely twenty years later she loses her husband, also to accidental death. Do you feel she has had more than her fair share of tragedy? Any ideas on why some people suffer more than others?

2. Cécile had quite a full plate, between work, her large family, and her business. Do you think the concept of "having it all" is realistic? How do you think Cécile managed this?

3. Do you feel, as Cécile does, that every new baby, no matter what the circumstances, is a blessing? Why or why not?

4. Some people would say that Norell lived the good life with a handsome, successful husband, a beautiful home, and financial security. But she desperately wanted a child of her own. Do you feel it was wrong of her to still want a child, even after being told it was a medical improbability?

5. Micheline, the daughter of poor but good-hearted parents who barely managed to clothe and feed her, was jealous of anyone who possessed the things she wanted out of life. She enjoyed seeing people cope with obstacles and hardship that prevented them from attaining the happiness she wanted for herself. Do you have any ideas on how she got to be this way?

6. Do you think Vic was wrong to go out in search of a one-night stand because he felt Norell wasn't paying him enough attention? Do you feel Norell really did neglect him? Why or why not?

7. Dana had misgivings about dating Gil because she had contact with Gil's ex-wife, Irene, albeit impersonal contact. Do you feel Dana was right or wrong to begin a romantic relationship with Gil?

8. Do you feel that Micheline will be happy being married to Errol, now that she has acquired the successful husband she wanted?

9. If you were in Norell's shoes, so desperately wanting to be a mother but learning that Vic had actually fathered the baby he brought home to her, could you forgive him? Or would you walk out on both him and the baby?

10. Do you think you could turn over an infant you bore to a stranger, even if you had every reason to believe the child would be loved and well cared for and would not want for anything?

11. And, finally, something to think about privately: If your spouse died tomorrow, would you be able to get by financially?